THE FEAST OF FOOLS

THE FEAST
OF
FOOLS

John David Morley

St. Martin's Press
New York

Library of Congress Cataloging-in-Publication Data

Morley, John David
The feast of fools / John David Morley.
p.   cm.
ISBN 0-312-11786-8
I. Title.
PR6063.07446F4   1995
823'.914—dc20   94-36701   CIP

First published in Great Britain by Abacus

First U.S. Edition: January 1995
10 9 8 7 6 5 4 3 2 1

For Poo, Poppy, Bonnet,
Snippo, Eeps & Co.

Contents

Contents

Players In The Feast Of Fools

Constanze, *mother of*

Martha, *elder sister of*

Stefanie, *elder sister of*

Donata ('Dotty')

Gottfried ('Bapa'),
uncle of Constanze's second husband

Hieronymus, *Martha's husband*

Brum, *Stefanie's husband*

Harald, *Hieronymus' cousin and lodger*

Maximilian, *Stefanie's lover*

Candice, *Maximilian's lover*

Johannes ('Johnny') Ploog,
Columnist on the Evening Herald

Lucas Sliep,
Photographer on the Evening Herald

THE FEAST
OF
FOOLS

PERSEPHONE

The Lady Vanishes

HIERONYMUS KORNRUMPF'S DREAM

Marvellous to relate, observes the antiquarian bookseller Hieronymus in his sleep, at the autumn equinox on the twenty-third of September (two million four hundred and forty-seven thousand and forty days since the beginning of time as reckoned by the Renaissance chronologist Scaliger), the sun passes from Virgo to the first point of Libra, casting a shadow registered by the sundials in the courtyard of the Residenz as one forty-six post meridian. At the same moment Brum and Stefanie are pronounced man and wife in a registry office in Munich.

In the dream of Hieronymus the bride is naked as she bends over to sign her name. In fact she's wearing a red dress with a puffy hem that was fashionable seven years before. Stefanie might be looking out of a painting by Ingres. She is a grey-green-eyed odalisque with a peach-fleshed, perfectly oval face and a composure that is not scrutable. There's no place in this painting for the man at her side. Shock-haired, restless, erupting energy at odds with the stocky frame in which it's confined, Brum looks as if he's been made up on the spur of the moment. He wears a top-hat, jeans, gobs of paint of irregular size spattered across his shirt-front; gobs of sorrel paint, intended for the hind-leg of a dray-horse on a mural, which escaped the artist's brush and have accompanied him to his wedding instead. None of the articles the groom is wearing was laid out for him by the bride that morning, none of the time he promised her kept, time which she has treasured in the superstitious scheme of her heart. The wedding was supposed to have been an anniversary, seven years to the day and the hour when she and Brum first met. But Brum arrives in his working clothes one hour late. While Brum is sprinting through the streets of Munich the earth moves thousands of miles through space, a thousand impulses move through Stefanie's heart, and in the order of both Brum arrives at a place no longer the place for which he set out.

The wedding guests arrive by taxi for a reception. Hieronymus in his dream sees them hover above the pavement and ascend by levitation to an upper window, obliging the ladies to hold down their skirts, but this impression is attributable to an erection the dreamer is having simultaneously with the images rising out of his sleep. In fact the guests have to climb the stairs to the third floor, where their hostess Gisela is visible through the open door to her apartment, holding a bowl of curds as she brushes Brum's cheek with her lips and whispers into his ear. Cooling his overwrought member in the curds she conveniently holds for this purpose in her lap, Hieronymus frames the bride and her mother in the doorway and takes their photograph as they are crossing the threshold.

Constanze figures in this picture as the lady with the chignon, carrying a balance on which pumpkin and pomegranate seeds are weighed in equal parts. Hieronymus identifies her with Demeter, in Greek mythology the goddess of all things that grow. The scales she carries signify the division of the year at the equinox, when the sun leaves the northern hemisphere and travels south across the equator. Stefanie is not looking at her mother. In the name Stefanie the antiquarian bookseller hears echoes of Demeter's daughter's name, Persephone. When Persephone went out of her mother's house and was stolen by the god of the underworld, the year died, her mother mourned, the winter came.

With a sense of foreboding Hieronymus looks up to find his fortieth summer gone, Gisela, her lap and the bowl of curds, Constanze, the bride and groom and all their guests evaporated in an instant. Plates abandoned in mid-air, smudged with traces of the wedding feast, course through the deserted apartment like planets hurtling in space. He hurries downstairs, and pausing outside the salmon-pink building, wonders which way to go.

The evening is warm, the sky cloudless. A waiter threads a chain through stacks of chairs on the pavement terrace of a restaurant, and hobbles them with a padlock. Through the door of the restaurant where Brum and his cronies are drinking at the bar, spools of laughter unreel and scatter in the shade of the chestnut trees. Fifty yards down the road Constanze is boarding a tram. Stefanie stands with a picnic basket under the trees bordering the English Garden and waves goodbye. By the time the tram passes she has disappeared, swallowed up in the greenery of the park.

Brum comes cock-a-hoop out of the bar for the tryst he has promised his bride, but when he reaches the stream and crosses the bridge into the English Garden there is no sign of Stefanie. The light is beginning to fade.

Crossing the same bridge long before Brum comes out of the bar, Stefanie feels an always downstream urge of water tug at her heart as she walks down an avenue of green darker than in her memory of the day when she and Brum first came this way seven years ago. She remembers the cleaners' tag attached to the belt-loop of Brum's trousers, and how she longed to take it off, if only she dared, and could think of nothing else all the way from Gisela's to the far end of the park, where at last she did, keeping it in the locket she has worn as a talisman ever since. As Brum and his party are climbing the path on the south side of the knoll leading up to the pavilion where they had arranged to meet, the bride has long since given up waiting for the groom and gone down on the other side in the direction of the Chinese Tower.

The sun of the mellow *gerstmonath*, the barley month at summer's end, rises exactly in the east and sets behind the city spires exactly in the west. Hieronymus sees himself asleep in a granary on a mountain of grain that subsides as it is shifted down a chute, dreaming of ripeness achieved and a prospect of the city from the pavilion on a knoll in the English Garden. Brum's footsteps echo in and out of the columns as he walks round the pavilion in search of Stefanie. Gisela shakes a tambourine, the wedding guests cheer the groom. Rumbling scree of cloud slides into the sky, topples the city spires and draws a lid over the evening. People strewn across the park like leaves begin to scatter.

Brum's party hurries on through the twilight. A breeze brings snatches of horse-dung, freshly-mown grass, and a lily-of-the-valley perfume betraying the bride has come this way to the cabin in the allotments by the river. The door of the cabin, overgrown with honeysuckle and vine, stands ajar. On the table inside which is laid for two a burning candle stands watch over the leftovers of the wedding feast the bride has brought in her basket.

From the fringe of a clearing by the Isar River Hieronymus looks up between the clouds and sees the capsized stars of the Plough tumbling down towards the horizon. The patter of raindrops falling on leaves merges with the rustling of Astrid, the antiquarian bookseller's assistant, brushing through the thickets in a low-cut evening dress. Standing behind Astrid, he can reach conveniently into her bodice and squeeze her breasts as they follow the action in the clearing through the fringe of the dreamer's eyelashes.

A rider enters the clearing on a sorrel horse. On the far side of the clearing Stefanie picks an autumn crocus and arranges it in a bouquet of wild flowers. She hears the bunched flurry of hooves, looks up. The stallion rises at the first jump and soars, discarding sound, an arc outstretched in mid-air, lands between jumps in bursts of sound and leaps into airy soundlessness, spanning the clearing in a fluid ripple of what seems to be a single motion.

She feels the heat of the stallion approaching her through the rain, smells sweat, brass, lathered horseflesh, bold odours that cannot be expunged, quickening an obscure desire in her by the force of their own clarity. She feels the uselessness of the flowers already withering in her hand, the candle lit on the supper table, the old taffeta dress she has patched and put on for her wedding, the childish icons of her love and the pilgrimage her love has made through all this waste of day that ends in a clearing in the rain. Sooner than she had thought possible the horse is there and she has touched him, stroking his muzzle, neck and flanks as far as the stirruped boot of the rider who asks the unimaginable question – words not spoken, audible only to herself. Without surprise she takes the extended hand that has freed the stirrup for her to mount and draws her up as effortlessly as if all her previous life had prepared her for the answer.

The wind stood up with a thunderclap, blew out the candle and slammed the cabin door shut. Snatches of voices and flickering storm-lamps swarmed out from the allotments by the river and scattered through the gusty dark. Bowled on by the storm, Brum searched the park from end to end. There was no sign of the bride. During the storm on the night of her wedding, falling coincidentally at the equinox, she vanished from the English Garden without trace. Rumours were that she had crossed the river – the sound of a horse's hooves resounding from the wooden bridge, shapes splashed indistinctly in the night, fording the

Isar upstream from the weir, may after all have been no
more than a roll of thunder or the smack of cloudburst on
the river – but only Hieronymus, rising to the climax of his
dream, could have seen the silky web snake out through the
dark, the soaring trajectory of white sperm like a liquid arch
on which horse and riders cleared the river with a bound
and disappeared on the far side.

Evening Herald

HARALD HEMSING

I am here, I am me.

Good morning, me. How are you?

By my reckoning of uterine and post-natal time, ten thousand Haraldian days since my inception, I am still waiting in the bone-house, wrapped in renewable scarf-skin to prevent molecules of me from leaking into otherness (where I would cease to be), waiting in particular this morning for the *Evening Herald* photographer, Lucas Sliep.

Stationary, I continue to move measurably in and out of myself. Nails on toes and fingers enlarge me daily by nought point one millimetres, hairs on head and face by more. In the time it takes the moon to orbit the earth, epidermal cells journey outward from the basal skin layer where they are born to the surface where they die. At this border between me and other, I flake, slough, discard dead tissue of myself. Particles of dust that may be me floating in a sunbeam where my hand writes. Not only me.

Bona fide professorial tissue, tissue of student body, flaking in great numbers as people beaver back and forth across Geschwister-Scholl Square, dusting off in corridors while queuing to register for Michaelmas term. And Lucas Sliep, fifteen minutes late, whom I now identify arriving in his cream Isabella with the red stripes, flakes onto genuine leather upholstery recently overhauled at great expense. This man believes he photographs a ghost who lives in his apartment. Rangy, enviably tall, in cowboy boots he walks from the hip with just a ripple over flexed knee-caps. What makes him so sexy? Sleepiness of eyelid? Shimmer of green dye in his hair? Study his technique, Harald. Suspend me and enter narrative with direct speech, deploying Sliep mode.

'Doobeedoobee-doo, Hemsing.'

'Doobeedoobee-doo, Sliep.'

'What's the shot?'

'Matriculation. Students queue to register.'

'Wrap in five.'

Sliep comes and goes in speech, mostly goes. Skulking in his jargon, sortie here and there to ambush sense, Sliep is a lone operator of language, on his own and unintelligible. He takes pictures instead. Camera in hand, rippling with Lone-Ranger stride, he lopes into Ludwig-Max, smelly old building, tatty light, where's the glamour, do it with a girl outside, he thinks. Ranges out, sees the blonde about to get off, behind her a stack of bicycles, fountain, more façade of university across the street, piece of cake, doobeedobee-do, snap! Your head's falling off, snap! What? Thank you, snap snap snap snap! Here's my card, Lucas Sliep, just call and leave your name and number after the bleep if you want a print, agency will be in touch. Wrap in five, that was it.

'What's this agency deal?'

'Sliep Unlimited. Cover job. Hand on cock. Keep in touch.'

'And do they?'

'Yep.'

Meanwhile, the Car. Vintage Isabella, stripped, boosted with Porsche engine from dump, ergonomic bucket seats, digital audio tape and laser sound reproduction systems hand-crafted into dashboard. Wham! fade off *The Edge of Heaven*, Sliep cuts into inside lane and coasts through green light, thumb hooked over steering wheel, does a racing change with his little finger at the turning into Brienner Street, Bad Manners blast off from underseat woofers with *What The Papers Say*.

Ka   duh   duh da boo   pé   ka   duh duh   da!

Sliep hums and taps the rhythm on the wheel. Marvellous driver, ergonomically relaxed, drives entirely on soundtrack, real road unwinds for him on video simulator. Live by play instinct. Be like me. Enjoy, admire Car. Agency will be in touch.

'See you.'

Sliep burns rubber from pole position and snatches light at corner of Paul-Heyse Street, trumpeting salute on six-pronged klaxon.

Harald of the *Herald*. The porter knows his face, nods. Morning, Mr Hemsing. Later the porter will recall the young man as courteous, withdrawn, industrious, with unassertive mouse-brown hair and features not especially memorable except for that jut of jaw in which (even then) he recognized the makings of a future editor-in-chief. Later the porter will stand, come out of his box and put a finger to his cap as Hemsing roars through the yard in a BMW, ripping the morning open with an edge of urgency and importance. Now he remains sitting, continues to slice radish and dismember a grilled chicken. Harald walks, pigeons roost under the eaves, in warm shadow the yard sleeps.

Obedient at his beck, the lift descends, opens doors, awaits his entrance and further instructions. In a decade, or at most two, a terse depression of the button will command a destination on the third floor, a suite containing rosewood furniture, three telephones, golfing and equestrian trophies, a Davidoff thermidor. Now, the lift declines further instructions. Doors have opened but do not close. Out of order again. Harald climbs the stairs to the fourth floor.

In the telex office, leaching news from the jabberwocky world, Hartmann wades entranced through litter, tears off strips of paper, pauses to scan another crop of sheets and reaches absent-mindedly for the mug of coffee dry-docked in RELIGION. Harald sees him reticulated through the viewfinder of a grid of pigeon-holes that separates his office from the corridor and arranges its occupant in topical squares. ECONOMY is stencilled over Hartmann's brow, SPORT enshrines his elbow, his belly is a diptych incorporating ARTS and LAW. Harald clears ARTS and helps himself to Hartmann's neck for a stack of items under LOCAL.

Touch Piontek for some reviewing of books, ballet etc. to ease the overdraft next month. Press releases advising Bob Dylan in concert, Roncalli Circus opening, Scandinavian Operatic Art Productions on tour in November. Harald riffles telex sheets, lays his pretext on a desk and asks if Piontek is in.

Not in. Detained by weekend injury, probably back tomorrow.

Serious?

Ludicrous. Dropped a mantelpiece on his toe.

Piontek with soft heart and squashed toe, an easy touch, dented by requests, threats, mantelpieces, the Philistine policy of the Editor. Firm on the integrity of his page, however.

Enter now an L-shaped room. L is for Local, Learn. In their final term, prior to the diploma examination, students are given practical experience in a local media institution. Stand by Nellie at her perch and record her profile, hoard of bosom resting firm on the integrity of her appointments' ledger. Harald peers round the corner of the secretary, a hand placed adventitiously on her desk, broaching the day's subjects with a friendly greeting. What has she got under her cashmere?

Yawning, Nellie fractionally recedes from the ledger,

exposing the first half of the morning encoded in her scrawl. *9.30: Sliep/Hemsing at Ludwig-Maximilian; Boysen at Town –* howl? hell? – *Hall. 10.00: Ploog at Brewers Hall, interview with* – ordure? ardour? architect? – *artist; Jelinek & Sliep at clinic, interview with moth. 10.30: Breul at Murmur of Technology, interview with tractor; ???, live brigands jollity.* Between ten-thirty and eleven Hemsing's hand spans half an hour, fingering the ledger page at cleavage of cashmere, interview with Nellie's breasts as she reaches for the telephone. Does she notice this?

'This evening? Nothing special.'

Divorcee keeps options open, appointments warm. Laughter. Surreptitiously hand under hen, tickle her fancy, steal her eggs. Amazing the way they let you do this. Fire Brigade Jubilee at ten-thirty still tepid, bra-cup and body-heat encroaching fiercely around eleven, nipple flush on the noon meridian and – what's this? – *Hemsing.* Hemsing what? Burrow into the warmth of her day, *Hemsing/Sliep at North—* Read on, afternoon must be around her navel. Nellie laughs, soft, ample, he feels her wag. Enough. Jack up these wagging obtrusions with the back of the hand and plainly see what she's got under. *12.00: Hemsing/Sliep at North Cemetery, funeral, interview with corpses.*

All right in there? Snug fit? I'm telling you there's been a traffic milkshake. A what? A titanic mildew. Ah, now, have to ask Nellie about that once she's off the phone. Signed your death warrant in her big black book.

Proceed through Local Media Centre, from Nellie at the knee downwards to the heel of the boot-shaped room, bearing in mind the insights derived from Schlindwein's basic seminar on communication training. A sharp eye left and right for significant cognitive factors, behavioural modalities both verbal and non-verbal, influence factors on journalistic reporting that are frequently overlooked. Describe atmosphere, conditions of work *etcetera* in catalyst where news is being generated.

Conditions at 10.16 sluggish to torpid, news generation minimal due to absence of staff.

Ancillary news-gathering measures elsewhere?

Various: Boysen and Breul at Town Hall and Museum of Technology respectively, Jelinek at clinic, Ploog possibly at Brewers Hall, Kurtz and Süskind probably in canteen, Kramer and Wischnewski definitely in photo lab playing golf.

Atmosphere?

Pleasant. Excellent lighting both natural and artificial, comfortable chairs drawn up in attitudes of rest at T-shaped desks with generous elbow room and computer terminals at present switched off.

Local colour?

Plant life is represented by a broad-leafed tropical species trained up the shaft of an upended broomstick tied to the ceiling. This, and the car-theft prevention clamp that has been misappropriated as a device to incapacitate Anneliese Jelinek's chair, suggest the drollery and playful vein associated with Boy Boysen's reporting on municipal government. Non-verbal modalities of desks supply behavioural indices in the absence of their owners.

Specify.

Neat, methodical, tundra, the desk of Breul, as is its occupant. Contrast the southern hemisphere of the desk he shares with Margot Süskind. Here nail-varnish, horoscopes, chocolate biscuits, doodlings of spiral whirlwinds, the wayward improvisation of the fashion correspondent and writer of human interest; there, hexagonal pencils lying at attention in sharp rows, digital clock, railway timetable, stick-man hanging from gallows at bottom corner of blank pad, the anxious order of the science correspondent and unchallenged expert on boring items. Surprising how characterless the desk of Boy Boysen, in-house comedian and anarchist. A humour that secretes things in drawers. Latent schizophrenia here?

'Morning, Hemsing. Doris was about to kick off. Come and be linesman.'

Threesome in boot of room becomes foursome. Vocabulary of Conrad Sartorius betrays influence of Local Editor's former career as sports commentator. Long blonde Deputy Doris Humperdinck at his side, kicking off in chequered blue-and-white jacket that ends at thigh where slit in black leather skirt begins. Felix the layoutman opposite, hands folded on empty graph paper, waiting to keep the score.

'Oktoberfest half-time statistics, weakened by wet weekend. Visitors in first week three-point-six million, beer consumption two-point-two million litres, decline on previous year. Hooliganism, theft of beer mugs and consumption of non-alcoholic beer on the increase, however.'

'However?'

'Well, it's a discrepancy.'

'Sober thieves steal better. What about the quintuplets?'

'Slight improvement of respiratory functions, condition otherwise still critical.'

'Any new developments?'

'Cardinal writes letter of congratulation to parents. Usual issue of contraception, unusual offer of financial aid from ecclesiastical exchequer in search for new accommodation. Administrative row about inadequate hospital facilities to deal with multiple births. I thought we could poll gynaecologists for views on hormone treatment. Anneliese's interview with mother, too, of course.'

'Open centre with that. Column left on hormones, column right on cardinal, contraception, cash. Half a page. What are we running at, Felix?'

'Two and a half, three.'

'Beer festival. No mileage out of those statistics. Free advertising for the brewers, same every year. As unavoidable as Christmas. Think anyone reads it, Hemsing?'

'Three-point-six million people?'

'All right. Dress it up a bit. Candy-floss and King Kong, litre of beer, ham roll. Box with costs of outing for family of four. Anything else looming on the horizon while I'm here?'

'Previews of Fashion Week starting Monday, but that can wait. Director of Spanish Culture Institute keeps calling about an interview he says he was promised, and the Editor wants someone from Local to represent the paper at savings' banks' dinner on Friday, question mark.'

'Send Breul to Spain, Boysen to bankers. Doris, I must fly.'

Exit Sartorius by toe of boot, enter Kramer and Wischnewski at knee, the latter bearing a photographic print, which he lays on Humperdinck's desk.

'Verdict in plumber business due tomorrow.'

'What plumber?'

'Upstanding family father, regular church-goer and active supporter of Catholic welfare organisation, been mucking around with his monkey-wrench in his daughters' drains. Incest and sexual abuse of minors.'

'Suzanne?'

'Madam.'

'Check if the unemployment figures for the third quarter are available. And I think we'll run the Care anniversary after all. What's this girl doing on my desk?'

'One of Sliep's. He said you'd know.'

'Ah yes. Thank you, Flip. Mr Hemsing? Students are back in town, twenty lines or so. Press release from Wella Hair Studios on styles this winter, which I'd like you to write up. And edit down police report on drowned pensioner to News in Brief item, would you? Johnny's done an obituary about a local Schwabing character, Liselotte Pfaffel, but won't have time to go to the funeral for the last paragraph. Here's his copy. I thought you could go instead. How many mourners, who sent wreaths. They'll be arranged before-hand around the coffin on a bier in the hall opposite the chapel. Lucas will be there. Tell him that's the picture

Johnny wants – interior with flowers, OK?'

Observe dialogic communication behaviour, interaction of Humperdinck and Hemsing. Continued use of Mister after four weeks in the newsroom suggests formally correct relationship without personal underpinnings. Easier with Sartorius, but he is losing his grip, the facts escape him, adhere like iron filings to his deputy's magnetic fingertips. Won't be long now. One foot forward, already on the advance, hand on hip bunching cloth of coat, other hand sparring, jabs a sheaf of tasks at subordinate solar plexus. Write up, edit down, commands with afterthought in parenthesis, would you?

And Hemsing?

On the balls of his feet, obsequious to please, rising to the opportunity of a career. Graduate journalists staffing unemployment figures for the third quarter next year, robbing banks the year after in partnership with Sartorius, for interior with flowers read interview with corpses before you know where you are. Hemsing needs a job in the spring. Right now he needs a desk.

'Suzanne, may I?'

'Kurtz is out. Help yourself.'

Suzanne May, help yourself. Funny girl. Funny name. Falls apart in the middle, pulls you up short just when you're expecting. Suzanne may, may not, depending on her mood. Tightest jeans in town, fingernails gnawed to the quick. Notice the way she put that 'Madam' on Humperdinck, very arch. Lack of fluid in her name, she needs another syllable. Maya, Maeterlinck. Better, more lubricity. Key in code, edit pensioner down to News in Brief item. *Love of animals proved to be the downfall* – oops, an inadvertent pun – downfal downfa downf down dow do d undoing *of a seventy-eight year old pensioner. While feeding gulls from Kennedy Bridge she fell into the river and—*

'Who put that thing on my chair?'

Anneliese Jelinek is back. Boysen cackles. Motherly but

hefty type, she takes a swing at him with her handbag, misses, scores direct hit instead on frankfurters, roll, mustard which Kramer has just brought to the attention of Boysen/ Kramer municipal affairs' desk. Health and Welfare correspondent in newsroom clash with Town Hall lobbyists over seizure of civic purse in junket reimbursement issue. Deputy Doris Humperdinck is already flashing flesh from slit leather skirt as she strides to quell mid-morning commotion with the whip of a smile, that thinnest of her glacial smiles she wears disturbingly under a frown when putting the freeze on Boy Boysen.

Silence now in the Local newsroom, where telephones seldom ring, people seldom come in and out, talk is down to News in Brief, and Hemsing hears only a slithering among dry rocks, the slithering reptilian sound of words scuttling on the interface of computer keys and processed into texts that glow luminous-green from midnight screens, encoding cardinals and quintuplets at Anneliese's even touch, Suzanne's end of season at city's open-air baths, the hopscotch of Breul's two fingers as they elaborate in painful columns a murmur of technology.

Harald switches off the reflection of his face where pensioner drowned by the bridge of his nose, and in the photograph at his elbow a girl without a name comes forward to give evidence in his memory. Listening beyond the newsroom he hears present and remembered sounds slowly swimming into focus, and the chink and jingle announcing the arrival of a dapper swagman treading sprightly in the corridor outside the newsroom. Enter here and now, leaking indiscretions in his wake (as Harald on his way out to Liselotte Pfaffel's funeral recalls the name he had forgotten of a face he has remembered), enter an artful dodger, conman and exuberant dandy in the guise of the *Evening Herald*'s roving columnist/reporter.

Enter the questionable Johnny Ploog.

Talk of the Town

As ever the first Thursday of the month lured art lovers to opening nights in galleries all over town. At the Catacomb in Oettingen Street artist-owner **Gisela Last** in rainproof Gore-Tex pyjama suit hobnobbed with Guatemalan consul **Alfonso Ponce**, glamour girl **Ilona van Loo** (no relation to the rival establishment in Maximilian Street, where currently a de Kooning retrospective is showing), divided the honours this time out between two attentive escorts, textile industrialist **Carlo Morganti** and former welterweight champion **Bruno Drews**. Morganti, wearing a purple Borsalino and white leather suit, spearheaded an influx of trendsetters who have arrived in town for the Fashion Week.

Until the end of this month the Catacomb is showing a series of twenty-three paintings by local matador **Brum**, brought together under the whimsical title 'Mismade Girl'. The Catacomb is a small gallery, and it was only with the departure of the majority of the two hundred guests when the Chablis ran out that the pictures exhibited could be seen at all.

The Mismade Girl series anatomizes the female nude,

which is dismembered bit by bit and finally disposed of altogether. The woman holding her severed hand who stares out of a blue interior at the beginning has receded at the end to mere fingertips, hovering over the keys of a grand piano that critics argue to be herself. In the interim, truncated, with pins in her shoulders and a measuring tape around a headless neck, she represents a tailor's bust or appears fragmentarily connected in a shattered boudoir mirror, facing a stool on which no one sits. Dismantled but still entirely present she figures piecemeal on shelves, arranged among the conventional objects of a dreamlike still life. An arm reclines beside an ink-well, a foot rises on tip-toe by a bowl of fruit, a breast peers through a telescope, severed ears stand in a toast-rack. Thereafter she begins to disappear.

Hands pack a knee-joint wrapped in tissue paper in a box, surrounded by other boxes, cartons, trunks, that are already packed and closed. A smile levitates in a candle flame, illuminating buttocks garnished with parsley and served on a platter at a table where a pair of crossed legs sit. The disembodied smile lingers as the most haunting image in the sombre blue and green interiors where the face of the woman gazing out over scenes of demolition from which her body is gradually being excised is never other than sorrowful.

This is a new Brum, striking a personal note one had not heard before in his gigantic Action canvases or controversial Chaos Objects (subsidised at public expense), such as the uprooting by crane of telephone kiosks, complete with talking occupant, and their immersion in wet concrete at random points throughout the city, which so scandalized local taxpayers at last year's Arts Festival. Brum critic **Katja Storm**, reviewing in the *Morning Mail*, dismissed the thirty-five year old artist's latest work as plagiarism, 'Magritte misappropriated'. Brum exhibitor Gisela Last conjectured that inspiration and title for the Mismade Girl collection derived rather from a magicians' congress where the artist

had witnessed a boxed woman sawn into four interchange-
able parts.

By all accounts magic has a lot to answer for here. A
more apt title for Brum's ghoulish oeuvre might be 'The
Lady Vanishes'. And thereby hangs a tale.

There is no doubt as to the identity of the beautiful
woman with the green eyes and celebrated cascades of
auburn hair who has been ventilated in these paintings. It
was to see her in the flesh that so many people queued for
elbow space at the vernissage in the impossibly overcrowded
Catacomb. Neither the artist himself nor his girlfriend, former model and frequent *Beauty* cover girl **Stefanie**, since
last week Brum's wife, was present for the opening of his
exhibition. With good reason. Brum is embarrassed, his wife
has disappeared, only the *corpus delicti* was there to give evidence of an affair that has become the talk of the town. The
question mark hovering like the bodiless hands at the keys of
the grand piano over the final pictures in the Mismade Girl
series is not, What does the artist mean? but, Where has he
hidden the body?

Brum's bride disappeared on the night of her wedding from
a clearing in the English Garden. Piquantly it has been
rumoured that she eloped with an unknown man on horseback who happened to come riding by. A modern-dress
production of the story of Persephone and Pluto? One has
only to try to imagine such a scene to realise its absurdity.
An apparently more plausible theory put out by backbiter
Humbert Finck, a friend of the artist's, explained the disappearance of the original of Mismade Girl as merely a
prestigious hoax to raise the value of bad paintings with
good advance publicity. More serious consideration has
been given to a widespread opinion that the lady did not
elope but was abducted. Inquiries at police HQ in Ett Street
established that no reports of wives missing had been
received in the last week – which raised, among cynics, the

issue of how long a person can remain unreportedly missing before the police take independent action. A court ruling in a recent case of law-enforcement negligence specified that reasonable doubts must be acted on after a reasonable lapse of time. On Thursday evening, more than a week after Brum's wife had disappeared, those conditions had surely been fulfilled, and the likelihood of official intervention in the Brum affair seemed imminent.

Yesterday the following entry appeared under the Services Available column in the advertising pages of the *Evening Herald:*

> Brum. Since nothing has been said between the two of us for so long that might not just as well have been printed in a newspaper, whatever needs to be said for as long as I am away can equally well be said here. Steffi.

If society sometimes chooses to identify itself by making a unanimous noise, then the noise that could be registered when the advertising pages of the *Herald* began to do the coffee-table rounds was pitched between a chuckle and a snigger. Brum's philandering is as celebrated as the chastity of his wife is notorious; or it may be the other way round, according to the point of view. While the view of many self-proclaimed Brum admirers, such as *Mail* columnist **Mimi Popper,** that their hero is more philandered against than philandering can commonly be heard wherever two or three society hostesses are gathered together in his name, it is likewise no secret that husbands between Nymphenburg and Bogenhausen are now rubbing their hands with malicious satisfaction.

Names registered in the visitors' book will not be bandied here, but among men of conservative dress and catholic inclination who are frequently in the public eye there are many who have now felt themselves moved to visit an exhibition for the first time in their lives. They will be leaving it, by all accounts, with the secret ambition of changing horses late in life and embarking, for example, on a career as a professional jockey. This season will see an increased participation at auctions of thoroughbred horses, brisk sales can be expected in riding accoutrements such as breeches, boots and whips. Equestrian sports are in. The phantom rider in the English Garden has set a precedent by elevating himself into the saddle of incorrigible male fantasy.

In recent weeks Stefanie has been sighted at the opera, at fashion shows and at smart weddings on the arm of as many escorts as the social occasions she has attended. At a charity gala in the Sheraton Hotel it was fast-food entrepreneur **Armin Übler** who wagged his tail for a sniff of her favours, while talkshow host **Harry Sackewitz**, inserting leading questions into his partner's cleavage at the Rotary Club Ball the previous week, apparently had the same interests at heart that preoccupied playboy **Siggi Sachs** in a private box at the opera house throughout an unprecedentedly long performance of *Parsifal*. But while it is easy to envisage Siggi sitting in the opera tampering with other men's wives, is he sober long enough to remain sitting on a horse? Can a corpulent talkshow host or the creator of Beef'n'Onion Brunch be imagined bride-snatching at full gallop? Can they even ride?

Meanwhile sales of the *Herald* soared in anticipation of Brum's answer, printed in the Friday late edition:

> Steffi. Miss you, please come home. Procyon pining, off his food. I can't find my driving licence. Where is the rent money for Mrs Mackensen, and the key to the Copper Lodge? Heartbroken. Brum.

With this response Brum may have misjudged the mood of an estranged wife. Pining and off his food is not Brum but his dog. Rent money and Mrs Mackensen override remorse. Tenderness finds expression as a solicitous inquiry into the whereabouts of a driving licence. On the evidence of his first attempt at negotiation one can already look forward to an inventory of Brum's domestic arrangements reaching well into the autumn and maybe beyond, with useful tips such as what drawers to look in for his winter underwear. Soul-searching, not the pursuit of laundry, will be the stuff required to effect a reconciliation with a rampant wife.

For the next few weeks Brum will indeed be searching his soul, but for the brewers' benefit rather than his wife's. The city's Big Six have acquired the lease to the disused Riemerschmid liquor factory on Prater island (after alternative plans for the development of the site as a contemporary arts pantechnicon were rejected by the council's shareholding majority) to jointly operate, as stipulated by municipal charter, 'commercial premises for the pursuit of beer and traditional folk entertainments'. In the imaginatively renamed Brewers Hall, gutted and now wholly renovated to facilitate the cultivation of beer by as many as fifteen hundred enthusiasts, the brewers have commissioned Brum to execute a mural commemorating their product and its influence on the native character of the city. The monumental work will cover an area of some three hundred and sixty square yards, and is to be ready for the formal inauguration of the building on 20 November as part of the festive programme celebrating the quincentenary of the Pure Beer Edict of 1487.

Assisted by two apprentices of the Church Painters' Guild under the supervision of the Passau fresco master **Jonas Heidenreich**, Brum set to work on this mammoth task at the beginning of September. Since then he has only emerged to get married, and after the disappearance of his wife he has not been sighted outside Brewers Hall at all. The telephone at his studio apartment in Zenetti Street rings unanswered, Mrs Mackensen is still waiting for this month's rent; behind the pretext of work Brum has gone into hiding from malicious gossip and the increasing erosion of his private life. After a fracas on Praterwehr Bridge, involving two advocates of the rejected pantechnicon plan who denounced Brum as a traitor and pygmy and were thrown by the artist into the river (giving us a foretaste of traditional folk entertainments the municipal charter did not envisage), the four painters have barricaded themselves inside Brewers Hall, a guard has been posted to repel further intruders, and the site of Brum's emerging masterpiece currently resembles a garrison under siege.

It is a triptych across three walls, the first of which is already complete. Beginning on the short north-east wall of the rectangle with the Aumeister, Kleinhesseloher Lake and the Chinese Tower in a foreshortened perspective of the English Garden, the mural follows the course of the Isar upstream along the thirty yards of the long east wall – where familiar motifs from the old city such as the Cathedral of Our Lady, the Viktualienmarkt and Brewers Hall itself have already been outlined – and encompasses the Salvator Thomas premises under the chestnut trees of the Nockherberg on the final wall to the south.

In the former liquor factory Brum is creating a vision of perpetual summer. Even by the mawkish light that fumbles through the small windows, bright resonance of colour rebounds from the one completed wall and warms the empty space. Under arc lights mounted on the scaffolding it explodes in coruscations almost palpable as heat. On the left bank of the Isar the Hilton Hotel has been demolished, hops have supplanted inedible greenery on the site of the Tucher Park and, upstream from the Aumeister, red roofs lie marooned in a wash of gold and unfamiliar barley fields border the river all the way to the Chinese Tower with a ribbon of corn-yellow light. The ingredients of the brewers' product, distributed across this bucolic landscape, are summarised in barrels that are being unloaded from a cart drawn by a sorrel dray outside the beer garden at the Klein-hesseloher Lake.

Here we encounter the first of the blockish peasant figures who people Brum's mural, painted in a naive, rudimentary style that is only apparently ingenuous. On closer inspection their faces betray grotesque resemblances. The driver of the dray-cart with muddy features and a hand cradling the cod-piece of his *lederhosen* bears an unmistakable likeness to Christian Socialist Alderman **Alfred Huber**, while the Brewers' Association chairman **Gustav Demmler** cele-brates a wholly plausible impersonation as a gross-bellied barrel-handler straight out of Breughel. And there are many more to come.

In the advertising pages of the *Evening Herald* Brum found answers to his questions, and in return a question to which his wife required an answer before she would come home:

What is the thing that is closest to my heart?

Immured in imagination made visible, Brum paces uneasily in the huge hall like a man who has uncorked a capricious djin. Images confined in the dark room of his mind have escaped onto a screen, looking back at their creator from an irretrievable reality. A three-foot counterfeit of the artist has been introduced at the top of the wall in a clearing south of the Aumeister – a painter at an easel, sketching the same landscape that unfurls across the three walls. Only from the scaffolding is the figure disguised under quaint boater and preposterous beard identifiable as Brum. The heavily whiskered artist, the period costume and picnic hamper suggest a parody of a famous Impressionist scene, but the indispensable lady is neither naked nor the subject of much attention. She stands a little way behind the artist in a pastel ochre taffeta gown with balloon sleeves that is drawn over a bustle, holding a sheaf of corn, her face turned anxiously in the direction of a mower who rests in the shade and watches her, leaning on his scythe. The painter paints, the mower waits, the woman stands between. A horse foreseen at the mower's side in Brum's original draft has been metamorphosed into a hayrick 'for reasons of composition'.

The prescience of an uneasy conscience? In his painting, at least, the artist seems to have anticipated events. *Cherchez la femme!* Perhaps it is in his painting that Brum will find their resolution.

Michaelmas

MARTHA KORNRUMPF

Summer time ended and the clocks were put back an hour on the night Liselotte Pfaffel died. Between matins and terce, respectively one hour later that morning, Father Anton admitted himself with his own key to Liselotte's apartment in the Red Cross home for old people, Christoph Street, to discuss floral arrangements in St Anna's. The caretaker of the home had adjusted all the clocks in his charge the previous evening. The Verger of St Anna's, arriving with a spanner for mass on Sunday morning, retarded the chimes of the church clock four hours after the appointed time. Civil clocks under public administration recorded two o'clock punctually at three; ecclesiastical clocks ran in and out of time with a leeway as wide as a week on either side of Michaelmas. At twelve noon as measured by the sundials in the Brunnenhof of the Residenz, the glockenspiel in the tower of the Town Hall regurgitated the hour already digested in its mechanism, releasing on their daily round a procession of dancers, gleemen, veiled ladies and jousting knights shortly after the clock above had struck eleven. Liselotte Pfaffel died in her own time. Father Anton

found the old lady stretched out in a final flower arrangement, sprawling among upended pots of zinnias, dahlias,
gladioli and autumn asters on the balcony of the apartment
overlooking the courtyard where two fountains splashed.

Consciousness suspended, curled up in Martha's mind,
resumed with the child curled up in Martha's womb the
instant she awoke on the morning of Liselotte's funeral.
Wriggling her toes, quick and awake, Martha remembered
the dead woman with her second thought, blushed at her
selfishness, and reached as routine had taught her for the
calendar of saints' and name-days lying on the bedside table.

Tuesday 29 September. Michaelmas, after Michael: who-
is-like-God? Warrior-leader of the celestial hosts against the
forces of darkness; keeper of the keys of heaven; represented
in Christian iconography with sword and scale for weighing
the souls of the dead entrusted to his guidance, replacing in
this function his pagan predecessor Odin. Patron of the
Catholic church, of businessmen and makers of scales, of
poor souls, of the dying, of cemeteries. Clear Michaelmas,
clear autumn; a hard winter follows on a great fall of acorns.

A moment's thought for Michael. Martha imagined him
with his scale, weighing Liselotte Pfaffel's soul at a counter
in a celestial clearing house that resembled the parcel Post
Office in Arnulf Street. How much did a soul weigh? Was
weight worth? Lightness rather, like down, graded in transparent cylinders: the higher the loft the higher the price.
Down from the breast of the Siberian white goose could
achieve so much higher a loft for the same weight. Michael,
a kindly man in a flannel jacket, smiles behind the counter of
Betten Rid. A counterpane for a cradle, in pink cashmere
with silk fringe. Such things her heart coveted. Michael's day
but also Gabriel's, messenger of the Annunciation, coming
in a cloud to Mary with a lily in his hand on Lady Day. But
not to Liselotte, childless and no man to speak of. Selling
flowers in all weathers at the corner of Ludwig and Schelling
Streets for as long as Martha could remember. She sighed,

lifted the marker and turned the page. Theresia tomorrow, Sophie and Hieronymus.

For the first time this morning she glances at her husband. Puckered at forty, the face already encrusted with a jaundiced sediment of middle age, Hieronymus peers into his sleep with the same expression of ironic scrutiny he wore as a philology student. Egg snared in one eyebrow, jaw dropped, occasionally from the open mouth an astonished whistle, exhaling cold ash aroma of last night's cigar. What did he pore over in his night-long sleep? Scattered leaves, folios, facsimiles, codicils to missing instruments, between nightly vellum covers the litter of his dreams collects under an indecipherable title. Can he read it without his glasses?

His child too, of course; faithless, but nonetheless his name-day. Acknowledge it with his fancy, brain, liver or lung of calf, a special dinner. Man and wife as different as their tastes in food: nothing he liked better than a plate of steaming lung, nothing she liked less. Soups for her, asparagus, lentil, the humble leek. Iron in carrots to build bone and character, fish for the intelligence. The sack of cattle feed she had hidden in the cellar, an emergency supply in a biscuit tin under the sink: why this craving? Every morning the past month, sometimes twice, three times a day it drew her down to the cellar where she stood in the guilty dark, cramming handfuls of grain, coarse feed to fatten livestock, greedily into her mouth.

What would Hieronymus say?

She remembered walking with him down Kaulbach Street one rainy afternoon, the smudged kiss of his awkwardness in the alley under the library windows, a prospect opening up when they turned into Ludwig Street and Hieronymus proposed marriage as if showing her something he had found unexpectedly in his pocket.

'A dozen of the white roses,' he said to Liselotte, counting the small change.

The florist had been standing on that corner all his life, had seemed neither old nor young, as ineradicable as the street itself. Thereafter white roses at each anniversary, gradually drooping with habit, weathered from year to year Liselotte shrank, gone seamlessly one Monday morning, a successor already in her place.

Martha at the bathroom mirror, admiring a fullness praiseworthy now, washing also the backs of her arms as once instructed by Sister Inmaculata, reaching for cherubim with trumpets in the stucco-chased heaven of a Jugendstil apartment, wriggling to receive downwards over her head and shoulders the waistless indigo frock, the wearable colour closest to the sombre requirements of a funeral mass. Her maternity wardrobe has not catered for death.

Martha wheelborne down Schelling Street, with a rear tyre listing under the handicap she is carrying and Hieronymus has forgotten to pump into account, spinning in a wide arc through an amber light at the junction of Ludwig Street, her heart exuberant, wind-snug front billowing indigo wake – Martha magnificently aloft in six-lane Michaelmas morning traffic.

Weaving between shadow and light, gooseflesh on her arms and spurts of warming sunshine, contact of her body with pedal, seat and handlebar, Martha is perfectly in time, sharpness of absolute present experienced on a bicycle in motion, her past invested in a future she unthinkingly carries in her on her way to the church of St Anna's.

A poplar and a chestnut tree endow the entrance with shade and peace. Pause here to cool the heart of still-wheeling sensations, from their fullness sift, itself desiring, that absence of desire whose name is grace.

Sentences from St Anna's convent school just down the road come back to her twenty-five years later. Deportment before, during and after devotions in His house. The woman in a hat but without a shawl, black straps mourning bare white shoulders, is improperly dressed. Before leaving for her stepfather's funeral his widow walked up and down the hall with a hand-mirror, lips pursed, surveying her appearance back and front.

Martha, step forward and lead the class.

The desire that would be absent on the threshold of St Anna's is always summoned in Martha by the thrill of incense hanging in a dark interior. Moisten fingertips with consecrated water, bob at the knee and make the sign of the cross. Coolness, clarity of heart bruised by indefinite longing, murmur of voices lingering in sibilated resonance. Occupy a pew towards the rear in the almost deserted church.

Behind her Martha hears flagstones softly slapped, leathery creak of sandals as Father Anton approaches. Resist the temptation to look down and glimpse the Franciscan's scudding feet, the suspension of hairy toes that flex and cushion his rolling gait, the heels splayed at an obtuse angle anticipating his broad-handed benedictions. Audible above sandal-slapping, as Father Anton draws level, his rustling sleeves and the swish of the hem of his gown, *slap shuffle rustle swish*, briefly the percussion of his habit is orchestrated in Martha's ear before he passes out of sound and into her line of vision. Mocca-robed immensity of flesh trussed up with a cream-coloured cord, tassles nodding at his girth, the friar surges down the aisle, shoulders absorbing his plunging body and the head above them motionless, as if artfully balanced on a plate. How he does that, Martha wonders, and about that heretical cockscomb, an undisciplined tuft of hair roosting on the crown of his head, which always arouses in her the feeling that she would like to reach out and smooth it down.

Martha opens the votive card with the picture of the Virgin mounted on a sickle moon. Between the covers Liselotte lies embalmed in permanent wave, polka-dot dress and string of pearls, looking up out of a monochrome study. Facing her across the fold, a valediction printed beneath a crucifix – *In loving memory of our dear aunt/LISELOTTE PFAFFEL/20.iii.1920 – 27.ix.1987* – and the imprint of the Mourning Press at the foot of the page. Lord have mercy on us, Christ have mercy on us, Lord have mercy on us. Let us pray.

Fanned out the starched veils of the two nuns kneeling in front of Martha. What are the sins whose confession Father Anton has prompted, to which they ritually acquiesce? The sins of nuns, monograms embroidered in petit-point on a handkerchief, illegible, so fine the stitch. Brides of Christ with gray habits, black shoes and socks, hems of tunics hoisted in attitudes of prayer, perpetrating a glimpse of ankle.

'And the napkin that was about his head, not lying with the linen clothes, but wrapped together in a place by itself.'

Martha has forgotten this verse from the lesson according to St John, but sees the image as if remembering it. Christ the contortionist in a sepulchral act on Easter morning, evacuated from his winding sheet without disturbing it. Peter denies, Mary mistakes, Thomas doubts. Reach hither thy hand, and thrust it into my side. Martha feels a twinge in her kidneys, the congregation stands.

Hand in a wound, hand in her womb, at half past two to the hospital, queasiness in her stomach, Father Anton is celebrating the Eucharist. This is the body and the blood, spurting from the side where the hand is thrust, welling between gloved fingers as the butcher scoops from a slab in a shop window shuddering membrane of lung for her husband's name-day dinner.

Aloft in Father Anton's hands she sees the consecrated Host, hears it plop into his mouth and crackle, magnified by the microphone, as if he were crunching bones. A wash of sickness swills her bowels, expletive gas escapes her lips with a sour odour, a muffled burp. Elevated in the chancel, far, far above her, impeccable the celebrant raises the chalice, drinks, impresses the taste of divinity lingering at the corners of his mouth on a napkin, and looks out over his congregation with a gesture of broad-handed benediction. *Come vnto mee all ye that labour and are heauie laden.* Martha, come.

While Father Anton at the chancel rail lays communion wafers on suppliant tongues, shutters bark up over doors and windows of business premises along St Anna's Street, and Martha in the shrubbery behind the church disgorges grain husks swimming in bouillabaisse into a clump of rhododendron.

The Harvest Moon

HARALD HEMSING

Thanksgiving therefore, who would have known if Martha hadn't reminded us? When she laid her head on one side in the lamplight a halo became visible. 'You see, we need the room for the baby,' she said, 'd'you think you can find some-where else by Christmas?' She broke the news gingerly, knowing it would hurt. In the silence that follows breakage of news she smoothed her dress down over her burly belly, dusting it off as if removing the splinters. 'On Sunday the family is going fruit-picking in Nymphenburg,' she added, 'wouldn't you like to join us?'

Tenure of the rooms in which we live as precarious as the lives they shelter, tenants we remain briefly in both. Grandma spent forty years in a rented apartment in Giesing, half of them with me, before she filled a vacancy in the old people's home. 'The family will rally round,' she said, 'you'll see, your cousin Hieronymus will take you in.' And already four years have passed in another room at the top of the house overlooking a courtyard off Türken Street.

My cousin the antiquarian bookseller with his clocks,

barometers, almanacs, ephemeris and hundred-year calendar, tide tables and astrological charts, bound newspaper volumes in which each morning he reads the news his grandfather read seventy years ago. Hieronymus Kornrumpf & Son, the same name on the same site in the third generation, the past preserved in airtight rooms beyond the surprise of any sound from the street, only the slow erosion of clocks marking a time that had ceased to exist in a household run to a standstill, as if it were a museum and Hieronymus its curator.

But not in this room, not in this life. Cousin Harald, in his four-year tenancy, cultivated the trivial and pursued the ephemeral, knowing in spite of Hieronymus that these are our only claims to permanence, and recorded his findings in the Book of Himself. Consider the hours, the days spent in this room, imagining myself to be the vase on the window ledge, the chair sheltering cautiously under the desk, to be the sulphur head of an exploding match, the shattered lead ripped out of the pencil broken on the floor. Now in the autumn, at the remembering time of the year, remember myself, pieced together laboriously in those silent weeks one summer when Hieronymus and Martha went away, lying still on my bed, counting my pulse, listening to the proof of my heart knocking in the empty house, counting the breaths that went in and out, measuring the speed of my fingernails, marginal loss of weight after bath, recording, when I fasted, the miraculous smell of water for the first time ever. And close to transparency I discovered how even the most commonplace things, coins in a saucer or the shape of a cloud, could jibe unexpectedly and hurt my heart when momentarily they lost their otherness, because when my time lay open and uncrowded the few things standing up on its bare horizon seemed so much larger and more urgent.

As I walked out in the evening the bark of a dog and light odours of jasmine from a tea shop in Amalien Street distracted my sense from the cogitations of the day, and to my closed eyes, relinquishing forms of visible things, came images of a stunned noon in a country where I have never been. That fondness for hospitals which Martha calls morbid is the familiarity of nostalgia. Now in the autumn, at the remembering time of year, remember the smell of a carbolic disinfectant soaked in tropical heat as if that heat were a sponge whose only purpose was to absorb and embalm the smell of disinfectant. Grandma admits the possibility of disinfectant but not of tropical heat, because in the three years between my birth and their death my parents were never in a tropical country to her knowledge, not in any other country at all. But whether from the past or its counterfeit in my memory, carbolic preserved in tropical heat is all that has survived, the smell of disinfectant is the sum of my beginnings, beyond the frizzled outline of Grandma's hair I see no shapes looking down over the rim at me. Natural, then, building on the only beginnings I have, to continue with smells, the dry cheese odour mingled with cooking, brooms and bicycle tyres brought down the corridor and stored in the cellar, and all the gradual odours of the neighbourhood outside, the cold, lost, poignant odour of sand in the deserted winter playground, of gasoline and grime by the American barracks – the discovery that if I shut my eyes I found a world I had lost out of the corner of my eye and could imagine under my eyelids much better in any case. 'Humour the child,' said Grandma, in old age herself receding from fact and her imagination becoming supple again as a child's, when Mrs Berger brought down her wagging finger from upstairs, 'if he wants to pretend to be blind.' She endorsed the principle with the birthday gift of a small white cane and a dotted yellow armband she had made herself, 'So that you don't fall under a bus,' and off I went into a childhood of sounds and smells and an instinctive evasion of unexpected obstacles, attributable to a gradually sensitised skin, a porous receptivity with which I still monitor present whereabouts and remember the past as an essence distilled from fugitive experience along the perfumed corridors of time, where the smell of carbolic disinfectant converges at last with the vanishing point.

Yesterday, today, at this end of the corridor the smell of lawn and apples and a lighter scent of sunlit air. Indian summer still, unbroken these past five weeks, but when I went to the window I saw in the shadow of the courtyard below the year's first morning chill, on the roofs of the houses backing off Barer Street, fluid, shimmering columns that I could not place. And turning back in the Book of Himself to October of the previous year and the year before that I found this observation had already been described twice, as transparent ribbons or jets of liquid fog, and how it came to be accounted for: somewhere along the street a stove must have been lit or the central heating turned on; the columns on the roof were shadows of smoke from a chimney. Shadows of smoke – what more elusive than that?

Martha got off the tram at Renata Street to fetch her mother and Gottfried. Hieronymus and I, with the picnic baskets under linen covers hanging out over the sides like bibs, went on to Roman Square, where the billing over the *Herald* news-stand read PLUMBER GETS FIVE YEARS FOR ABUSE OF DAUGHTERS. Hieronymus searched his pockets for coins, astonished as he is every time to find none there, I put the seventy pfennigs into the box and he helped himself to a copy of the plumber's case, stowing it in his pocket as if smuggling contraband. I could see it burning a hole there all the way to the Copper Lodge. I heard Procyon bark, and a moment later Brum looked out of the front door—

'Will Stefanie be coming too?'

—like a squall out of nowhere, with that intensity of Brum's gusty moments, subsiding as suddenly as it had arisen. Coming? No one even knows where she is. And behind just this edge of question, evidence of a concern that would not be concealed: a hundred and fifty cubic feet of red cedar and Tasmanian oak, a kilogram carton of stainless steel staples, and a mobile compressor, shuddering and panting in the middle of the floor between two unwitting accessories of Brum's shadowy conscience whom I had not seen before, a tall, thin, cadaverous man with a face as white as marble and a bluff, boyish figure in dungarees – co-opted, if necessary coerced, it was plain, for the Opening of the Neglected House.

The Copper Lodge, a former hunting lodge on the leisurely perimeters of the palace grounds, souvenir of the second of five wives of Christoph, swashbuckling old painter who talked on and on in retirement in Kaulbach Street: his legacy in turn to his protégé Brum. Inside, unchanged since two years ago when cash or enthusiasm or something ran out, an empty shell, a silver fuselage of billowing walls, bulging out of the latticed woodwork like slack gut, here and there streaked yellow where the foil has torn over a layer of insulation a foot deep. Visitors to Brum's studio in Zenetti Street have been sitting on those piles of oak and cedar panels since the Chaos Objects paid for them and improvised them as benches in the living-room. 'My walls,' yelled Steffi twelve months later, 'when are you going to stop sitting on my walls and finish the Copper Lodge?' But that was just it. What Steffi took on as the Copper Lodge, Brum thought of rather as the Copper Ship, liked it unfinished, that glittering shell of silver fuselage, reluctant to timber over what he considered a work of art. The names that each of them gave to Christoph's legacy, souvenir of a second wife, also named what divided them: the restlessness and vagrancy of the urban seafarer Brum who ideally would have liked his house to move with him because standstill for even a moment would mean the death of imagination; and her craving for rooted permanence in that inheritance of a ruined marriage, not in some interjacent silver fuselage but in a repaired, completed and settled home, which she took to be the literal meaning of Copper Lodge. And here now was Brum, two weeks after she had disappeared, with those benches on which he'd been sitting for the past couple of years already sawn to length and standing upright mortise by tenon, marrying into an appearance of wall with a *thock thock thock* as the compressor hissed and the bluff boy in blue dungarees punched them into place with a staple-gun.

'This is what she meant.'

'What?'

Hiss! Harumph! Hiss! Hiss!

'The answer to her question. The house, of course. I've given Mrs Mackensen notice. I'm moving in by the end of the year—'

Thock thock thock thock!

Just then Martha arrived with Constanze and Bapa, and suddenly there were eight of us standing in the little house and that three-legged mongrel terrier somersaulting in a sunbeam, snapping at flies. Stood there and listened to sounds of life again in the neglected house and smiled in celebration almost. Not a word about Stefanie from anyone but Bapa all weekend – thought all right, but unspoken, almost in celebration, almost as if she were already there.

Only Bapa, brought along not quite on a leash but close enough (a piece of string around his neck and a ticket with his name and address on it in case he wandered off and forgot who he was), only old man Gottfried looked out of celebration. 'Where's Steffi,' he grumbled, poking around in the shrubs as if he would find her there, and every time Constanze answering patiently: 'She'll be back in a while, Bapa.' Still an astonishingly vigorous old fellow, and he must now be nearer ninety than eighty, still with the old irrepressible urge to take his clothes off and ventilate, he calls it, in standard uniform of no shirt, shorts and sandals; and may be no wonder with that rug of hair pinned to the lobes of his ears and hanging down to his navel, a marvel of hairiness apparently surprised by the advent of a hairless civilisation and a convention that requires bodies to be covered with clothes. Props as usual, not a step out of the house in recent years, Constanze said, unless accompanied by his emergency rations, *viz.* two tins of Fanta and a couple of hot dogs in a plastic bag. This time he brought along equipment to make himself useful, garden shears, a wire brush and a tin of something that looked like whitewash but turned out to be lime or calcium or whatever it is that is supposed to be nutritious for geriatric trees. 'Old trees need pruning,' he announced as he went into the garden, 'cut out the dead wood to restore their vitality and make them abundant,' which sounded like a familiar theme in disguise. Brum's trees around the Copper Lodge probably hadn't been pruned since they were planted, and when Gottfried advanced on them with his shears I had the sympathetic impression that they actually *recoiled*. Snipping away, the old fellow harangued the trees and everything else in the garden, including ourselves, and when he suddenly proclaimed, 'The Pope is my son, so why should I disown him?' establishing himself on the highroad of his lunacy, I knew that beyond the gentle pursuit of fruit picking we could anticipate an interesting weekend.

Since Martha's pregnancy Bapa's attitude towards her had changed. Looking at Martha, he had always seen not Martha but the shade of her vanished father standing at her shoulder, host of the illegitimate child on Constanze's body, the GI passing through with candyfloss grin and unkept promises swallowed by America – the promises entirely, the grin fading on the photograph Constanze has kept for thirty years in a drawer – and behind her again, supplanting fading shade of her father, the images of the nuns at the convent of St Anna's into whose hands Martha was delivered when Constanze went out to sew shirts to earn a living. For him, unruly, heretical old man, not a religion the nuns instilled in Martha but a barren catechism of evil, superimposed on her father's wayward genes which already, unfairly, he found at fault when Martha was seven, and Gottfried showed up one day with his nephew, parked the Cadillac and unhooked the trailer containing all his worldly possessions (except an uninhabitable heap of stone in Cividale del Friuli) at the kerb outside Constanze's house. Under the nephew's name Constanze acquired a stepfather for her first child, a father for two children more – and an enduring animosity between Martha and this grandfather who was none, stuck with him in Little Monten Castle, Monten Street, where she was left a widow by the second husband, whose withdrawal from life had been as premature as the departure of the first. What could Gottfried have so disliked in a seven-year-old child? The smell of religion even then, rancid with smugness, elevated beyond mere childlikeness to an irreproachable and quite unnatural piety. And when later the old man began to grow wild (with his obsessions of children and unrequited love, almost, indeed, hedging bafflement behind accusations levelled at the Daughter of the Other Man who is as Cold as her Father, turning into a kind of suburban King Lear), in his writhing eyes she became the serpent hissing into Constanze's ear: *Have him put away, mother, for his own peace of mind and ours.* Charity inspired not by love but merely as an atonement for the feelings that are not there, he told her cruelly when Martha started to work for Care; and so it went on, the theme of her long barren marriage, until one day he stopped looking over Martha's shoulder at the grinning spectre who was less her problem than his, and saw her filling out, very ample with child.

Thock thock!

'Eh? The sound of housebuilding is the sound of peace—'

As if the war had just ended last week, and a moment later, in pursuit of some whim that had got entangled in his head, he sat down under the half-pruned tree to consult a railway timetable he fished out of his bag.

'Maybe she'll come on the train from Odessa.'

Standing in the upper branches of a pear tree on the ten thousand and fourth Haraldian day, I secured myself a commanding view of events distributed very broadly across time and space, disregarding the confined, most uncomfortable radius of my present actions as I continued to pick fruit. Daydreaming, in effect, among a murmur of insects, the pendulous, heavy-bottomed pears lolling on the palm of my hand like scrotum, inclined less to pick them than to abide by the decision of their own inherent ripeness, until, actually, just agitating a little their smooth round bottoms as a reminder of due gravity (Hieronymus, half into the tree on a ladder, resumed his reading of the plumber's daughters and waited for me to pass the pears down) they emitted a kind of brittle groan and discharged themselves into my keeping as if they had died, I followed Gottfried from his railway siding in Odessa to matters in hand among the blackberry bushes Martha was cropping, bent over and accordingly visible, from the rear, only as foreshortened withers and rump on which the old man laid his hands in firm blessing, admonishing, gently, *Careful, Martha, careful you don't squash our child* (Hieronymus in the pear tree coughed), *my little heifer,* or some such nonsense – and beyond this display of affection among the blackberry bushes a speck of white on the cinder path between the road and the Copper Lodge that gradually acquired the contours of a young woman in tennis gear, whom I had seen and not seen standing in front of a fountain, not recognised at any rate until she swam into focus in a photograph snapped by my *Evening Herald* colleague Lucas Sliep, so startling that I now lost my balance, grabbed for support the pear whose bottom I was tickling and—

'Harald!'

(The three women saw Harald fall and shrieked in the same instant Dotty came through the gate.)

Curious, one mushroom, two stalks. Looking up, as might a wood-louse lunching at the bole of a tree, up and up those savoury and extraordinarily long white stalks at the gills arranged like pleats on the underside of the mushroom cap, I realised almost at once of course that the stalks were legs and I was looking up Dotty's tennis skirt. Momentarily I must have been unconscious, but finding myself in a favourable position at the centre of everybody's attention I continued admiring Dotty's legs through my eyelashes for a little longer before deciding officially to come to. 'Steady now,' (Gottfried) and, 'Are you sure you're all right?' (Martha – might she now reconsider turning me out of the house?), while Constanze, practical as she is, said that as I had fallen out of the tree we all might as well take a break for lunch.

Stunned, *smitten*, on my ten thousand and fourth day after falling out of a pear tree on the same auspicious day that Brum undertook the Opening of the Neglected House, whether causally or coincidentally I also fell in love. During lunch this feeling, still embryonic plasma, spread sluggishly at first as a dazed sense of wellbeing, attributable (I thought) to the sunshine, lower now on the horizon with a flared brilliance through the thinning trees that gave us all a squint, or to mild ham on wholemeal bread and my favourite raspberry-flavoured yoghurt, or perhaps just to the odds and ends of family talk that drew us into a circle. Brum's house and the provisional heating that must be installed before the first frost, Constanze's condiments and preserves and whether to cook the fruit outdoors or at little Monten Castle, Martha harping on again about the miraculous tears seen welling from the eyes of an old iron statue of Christ at the grave where the flower-seller had been buried last week (and which turned out to be ooze from a wild honeycomb in the hollow inside), but this nothing beside Dotty's burst of fame with her picture actually *published* in the newspaper; bringing us, via the quadruplets born yesterday in no more than a breathing space after the quintuplets, back in a circle to Gottfried's home strait: the proliferation of children in general and Martha's in particular, a subject the old man appropriated with booming relish (while Hieronymus sat aside on a tree-stump reading the newspaper); his fertile imagination taking paternal responsibility not only for the Pope and Martha's half-dozen but also for Otto von Habsburg, and enlarging, in magnificent parenthesis, on his philoprogenitive mission by airship to the North Pole for the purpose of fathering a colony in the most underpopulated region of the world. 'Now then, Bapa, isn't it time you went back to scrubbing your trees,' intervened Constanze, when the old man began describing the gymnastic equipment he had taken along to keep fit on board, and meanwhile the plasma was curdling fast at the sight of the terrier's little flame-like tongue licking from toe to ankle along the skin to a smooth white tussock of knee – goodness! – in earnest now the length of Dotty's reclining leg, must have smelled a rat, snout nudging the quarry under frilly hem with excited whimpers—

'Procyon, stop *doing* that!'

Overnight, in the aftermath of a warm shower of rain, a tribe of mushrooms had pitched their tents on Brum's lawn, wigwams drooping in solemn clusters, probably risen from the grave of a tree for a pow-wow at end of Indian summer. The warmest Thanksgiving in living memory, forecast Radio Xanadu in the news at seven. By ten o'clock the stunned slow-motion Sunday streets had already taken on their resemblance to an empty swimming-pool in midsummer. Buttercups blazed with an overflow of yellow light lapping in the saucers they had suddenly put out, even the forsythia seemed to anticipate a glint. Grounded today on Constanze's orders, I supervised instead the ladder on which Dotty stood in a turquoise swimsuit, head and shoulders wedged in a grudging damson tree. 'Go away, wasp! Come on, you stingy old tree!' Verbs and worlds, Dotty's abbreviated to the use of the imperative – 'No I am *not* eating them all!' – and indignant denials, despite my still almost-empty bucket and the tell-tale purple smears on her thighs where now and then she wiped her fingers. In the dilemma of a hiatus between nine and teen, still with the intenseness of a child whose wishes are simple and self-evident, already with a woman's devious reserves, herself this inbetween her body too expressed – long, long, taller than Harald, her height advertised in those long legs that seemed perfect until ambushed by knobbly hip-bones still gauche and girlishly vulnerable, and the same thing again, above a maturely indented waist with ledge of hip already broad enough to balance a sizeable eraser on, in a gaunt encounter of shoulder-blades like stunted wings—

'How many have we got?'

'Eight.'

'*Eight*?'

—or cornflakes afloat in milk, brittle, *scrawny*, the years just hadn't yet filled her out. Imagine her with the progression of the years going the way her sisters went, a full-blown woman like Stefanie and, a rung or two up the ladder, smoothly casked like sister Martha, or further up again (time beckoned) to the tubby apotheosis of her mother Constanze.

'Harald? Where are you? What are you *doing*?'

Dotty had now climbed into the tree and I followed her up the ladder. Squatting in the tree, she passed damsons down between the legs that Procyon had licked, and began chirping away, all legginess and folded angles, hopping from one subject to other like a restive bird. *Thock thock* at longer intervals now from the Copper Lodge, and sometimes in a sudden shower the dull boom of falling apples when Gottfried shook the trees, a clang of lids on Constanze's pots – these sounds underlay the feel of the fruit transmitted from the tips of Dotty's fingers, sounds rising lazily with the heat off Brum's garden. Stroked the fruit feel and saw her skin, fruit stains on her thighs. *Thock! Thud! Plop!* Damsons overripe with burst skins piled up in the bucket, crush and spill of steaming blackberries Constanze filtered through white linen, the stain crept out to the edge and a dark liquid ran into the bowl when Martha wrung the linen out. From the apple trees, which yesterday the old man had pruned, now the rasp of a wire brush as he scrubbed the branches; from the old man himself, sitting aloft in the rigging of the trees, not a word today, sinisterly silent, no sound up there beyond the wind whistling in the rigging of an airship audible in his imagination, bearing him and his hoard of seed on a voyage into a white country. Meanwhile Brum came out and flopped down in the shade, complaining of a splitting headache. Constanze came over with more blackberry linen, cooled in the brook behind the house, and said, 'You must have banged your head. Poor Brum! I can see the swelling,' and everybody crowded round to look.

On the wallpapering table that almost spanned the lawn the pot on the gas cooker chortled all day and shook its lid. Constanze put the year in jars. Muttering in the background, brush in one hand, timetable in the other, Bapa chalked his trees. Already by early afternoon the brilliance of the air began to blur, the light crumbled at the edges. Aureole behind the trees, fluted sunlight in shafts of gold slanting across the lawn, drenched beams creating spaces in ground-mist enclosing whitely at half past four. Along the wallpapering table that almost spanned the lawn Constanze arranged twenty-four jars. Preserves, syrups, jellies, jams. Martha hooded them with frilly white caps. Hieronymus wrote out labels in Gothic script. Damsons, pears, apples, blackberries and the meagre crop from a quince tree. One quince, said Constanze. *19*, wrote Hieronymus, QUINCE 87. *Procyon Preserve*, wrote Dotty on an adhesive label which she stuck on the mongrel's snout, but Procyon ate it and barked for more. 'Tomorrow,' remarked the antiquarian, 'is the four hundred and fifth anniversary—' 'Two damson jams,' his wife interrupted, and Hieronymus wrote out two damson labels as the shorn tree looked on. 'Anniversary,' continued Hieronymus as the women marshalled the jars in platoons, 'of time that didn't exist,' but this remark submerged in a sudden haste to clear the lawn and carry the jars indoors before darkness fell.

The silver fuselage had now acquired a wall, running the length of the house. A light bulb hanging from a cross-beam under the roof, swinging gently to and fro, sent a giant shadow lurching from port to starboard, as if the Copper Ship were already afloat and rolling in a strong swell. Coruscating insulation foil, at odds with panneled wall plunged in shadow, gave the room a lopsided look, which Brum somehow seemed to share. With cocked head he stood under the light, two slanting shadows ran back and forth across his brow like windscreen-wipers. The carpenter and the cadaverous Jonas, fresco master from Passau (as pale, said Martha, as a resurrected Christ), wheeled the compressor out of the house while Constanze swept the floor and Martha and I stowed ballast along the walls, twenty-four jars that would hold, she said, for years at least – and the rocking-horse house was already still when Brum at last turned out the light.

Knee-deep through the ground-mist scudding along the cinder path like white water, a resurrected Christ with a mobile compressor seemed to float for an instant before turning the corner out of sight. Behind him in Indian file, Constanze, Bapa, Dotty floated one by one and vanished.

'An anniversary of time that didn't exist?'

'On the fifth of October 1582, when the Julian was super-seded by the Gregorian calendar, and by papal dispensation the fifth became the fifteenth . . .'

Hieronymus floated too, and vanished. The caulked branches of the pruned fruit trees, stumps of fingers help up behind us in sad mutilated salute, glimmered by the light of the soaring harvest moon.

The Cold Dew
and the White Nights

HARALD'S DREAM

But what was Conrad Sartorius doing outside a tobacconist's in Klenze Street in padded hose, sleeveless sayon
over white doublet and a starched ruff made of fifteen ells of
muslin half a foot wide? 'Have a cigar,' he said, as we crossed
the road and entered the same building with one accord.
From the interior of a gloomy hallway hung with cobwebs a
woman advanced, tittering behind the back of her hand.
'Height of fashion,' the Local Editor said, 'must keep up
with the times.' And gallantly he took her arm. Nellie was
wearing a bell-shaped farthingale, a high bodice ending in a
point at the waist, lined with stiff canvas and edged with wire
that lengthened the waist and imposed a severe geometrical
form on the bust, compressing the breasts until they almost
disappeared. She inserted her hand into the Sartorial cod-
piece and took out a key, with which I unlocked the lift.
'This is confidential, you know?' and he looked at me knowingly. 'Third floor, eh, Hemsing?'
    We must have ascended several thousand feet. Sartorius
gave me instructions to reconnoitre, and I set off down a

wide corridor that gradually became narrower and darker. Signs on easels standing at intervals along the corridor gave notice of forthcoming events, increasingly illegible the further I went. I took the eraser out of my hip pocket and rubbed away the dark that had accumulated on a brass plate, until I could make out the inscription

A. Koepenick
Astrological Consultancy Trismegistos Ltd.

'Here,' I called as they came forward, my Editor in enviable high leather boots and Nellie with a slight swing of her skirt as if gliding on castors.

I found myself in a long, coffin-shaped place; in fact a gallery, with stairs leading down into a much larger room where many people had gathered. 'Put on your cigar,' Sartorius advised me, 'all the members of Kalends do.' So I lit up, and Nellie arranged my smouldering weed in the buttonhole of my lapel. 'The Chairman,' Sartorius said. At a lectern overlooking the lower room leaned a man wearing a black academic gown, mumbling to himself and making calculations on a chart. In shelves on the wall beside him stood the Pope, the Lord Mayor, Ptolemy, Ebertin and other important reference persons whom he took out and consulted whenever his calculations required. Hieronymus walked up and down this narrow space with a harassed look. He broke off and went abruptly to the lectern.

'Mr Chairman . . .'

'Just a minute.'

'You have had too many. As Timekeeper and Treasurer of the Society I must point out that we have been overspending at the rate of eleven minutes a year.'

Trismegistos sneered. 'What year do you measure by? Tropical, sidereal or anomalistic?'

'At present, with all respect, such differences are immaterial. We face the more urgent problem of auditing ten unaccountable days. I declare this extraordinary plenary session of the Kalends to be open!'

Hieronymus seized the Chairman's gavel and hit the lectern smartly. I admired my cousin's uncharacteristic vigour and privately thought he would have cut a rather fine figure in barrel breeches and nether hose, had the codpiece not been so embarrasingly prominent.

Trismegistos now embarked on a long-winded discussion, bristling with arcana that were quite unintelligible. I had the unpleasant feeling that as I would shortly be examined in this subject I ought to be taking notes, but of quite what remained unclear. After some time, which we were already running ahead of by eleven minutes a year, the sight of my still empty slate induced a surge of such panic that I scribbled *Quite what?*, realising as I did so that I had merely forgotten to moisten the tip of my instrument. The gibbous moon would be full in Aries on the seventh, Trismegistos said, entailing lunar eclipse, spring tides, the inspection of rivers and increased susceptibility of the female sex, notably among kindergarten helpers and in particular with respect to the reproductive organs, body liquids in general but milk secretion especially, sperm production incidentally and retentive functions of memory speculatively, Ebertin passim. Meanwhile the earth went about its business, or a distance of approximately eleven million miles during the ten days in question. Such was the framework, Trismegistos concluded, and now somebody must fill it.

'My cousin and quondam tenant,' said Hieronymus without a moment's hesitation, 'Harald Hemsing. He fell out of a pear tree. This absence of time is all his fault. I propose he should be held accountable for it.'

The motion was carried instantly and unanimously.

Very cross with Hieronymus, and wondering how to get even with him, I hurried out into the corridor in the hope of gleaning some information from Hartmann. The telex minder was busy as usual, tearing triple-layer tissue off rolls of toilet paper and filing the sheets in various compartments, oblivious of the fact that on all of them nothing but the word KALDEWEI was printed. For the sake of appearances I nonetheless carried two or three of these sheets downstairs to the office of the Editor-in-Chief, where Verhülsdonk, Piontek, Sartorius and others had assembled for the morning conference. They all sat at the oval table with glum faces and empty hands. 'There is no news, Hemsing,' said the Editor-in-Chief, 'on account of this absence of time.' I showed them the telex sheets. Verhülsdonk observed that KALDEWEI was the name of a maker of sanitation utilities. Piontek countered that it might equally well refer to the scurrilous play by Botho Strauss, and a lively debate ensued over this point until the Editor-in-Chief intervened. Whether sanitation utility or scurrilous play, KALDEWEI did not amount to news. 'You know what you can do with these,' he said contemptuously, making a coarse gesture. 'We have columns to fill, a newspaper to produce. It is up to you to create news, Hemsing. How do you propose to do it?' I was edging round the table to catch a glimpse over Nellie's shoulder of her indispensable appointments' ledger, but the severe bodice in which she sat eliminated her bosom entirely, and under her sheer front the ledger lay open with blank pages on which nothing was written.

I hurried up Bayer Street to the main station, where I interviewed the stationmaster on the measures that were being taken to repatriate the six million visitors still stranded in town at the end of the beer festival. 'What are you doing here, Harald?' someone called. I looked round and saw Bapa, shirtless, plastic bag in hand, a timetable under his arm. He told me we must find Stefanie and the answer to her question. Some time this week she would be coming on a train from the east.

We set off down a long platform, seven times in quick succession the moon rose and set, peering in at us with broad shining face while trains whistled and came and went without Stefanie, and I knew the search was hopeless. For reasons of delicacy I did not tell the old man that Constanze had asked me to keep an eye on him until the moon began to wane. But the moon did not wane, and after we had been walking down the platform for several days and nights it broadened out into a tree-lined avenue that I recognised as Arnulf Street. I warned the old man there was a chill in the air these October nights, he would catch his death of cold if he didn't put his shirt on. 'Pooh pooh!' he snorted, taking great gulps of moonlight, and strode off exhilarated into the white night, light-footed despite the dark through which I followed him, sprung on a broad-moonbeamed road strewn with splinters of shadow, and out across a moon-flooded plain until we arrived at Little Monten Castle.

From the well of the stairs I looked up and saw Constanze's troubled face. 'Have you got him?' Riddled with moonlight, the hand he held out for me to lead him upstairs was palsied and phosphorescent. I told her to call a doctor. The old man's luminous skull was transparent, through it I could see the maggots in his brain. 'The doctor's already here,' Constanze said, 'to deal with the plumbing and the tides.' Behind the kitchen door the nurse Marina sat in a rocking-chair, knitting a sock. I asked her why she was in Constanze's kitchen and not on stage at the Kammerspiele for the opening scene of *Uncle Vanya*. 'It's for the baby,' she said calmly. 'Don't worry with women, don't worry, with women it's a perfectly natural thing.' 'But Trismegistos is not a doctor,' I protested, 'he's a charlatan, a quack astronomer.' The lecture was already in progress, however, and I sat down in the front row, craning my neck to get a better view of Dotty, who stood on the kitchen table with her nightdress held up and blood running down her legs.

'Particles of liquid on the moon-facing hemisphere,'

Trismegistos whispered, indicating Dotty's pudendum with his skimpy, lecherous baton, 'experience a stronger gravitational pull and are accelerated towards the moon, flowing into a bulge in the ocean. Preliminary symptoms associated with protuberances, soreness of the breasts, pelvic discomfort, the bulging sea of the body flush and flecked with spume. Earthlings, we marvel at the secret correspondences of micro and macrocosm. At an angle of twenty-three degrees and twenty-seven minutes the human heart rests on the axis of the body, the same angle that obtains between the terrestrial equator and the plane of the Earth's orbit. Spring tides at new and full moon, the periodic discharge of secretions and disintegrating mucous membrane – here, and here – in cycles ruled by the phases of the moon, linking menstruation, proliferation and secretion. Ovulation occurs at the midpoint of the cycle, or medium coeli, the astrological midheaven— You had a question, Mr Hemsing?'

How had I never noticed these figures before? I stood alone outside the Just Dance Factory in Amalien Street, looking up at two oxidised figures on the columns flanking the back entrance to the university. On one of the columns stood a woman pulling a towel over her shoulder as if she had just stepped out of a bath, on the other a man with a spear or a trident and a curious hat, apparently trampling on a lizard. Wasn't the woman wearing something round her neck, which she didn't take off even when she had a bath? An endless stream of people flowed into the university between these pillars without once looking up. Among the members of the Faculty of Social Sciences hurrying down from Schelling Street I caught sight of Professors Schlindwein and Eckstein, with the smug, knowing faces examiners wear. 'You'll be late, Hemsing,' Schlindwein called across the road. 'Late,' I retorted cunningly, 'late for what?' 'Ho ho,' chuckled Eckstein, 'do you think I'm telling? The questions remain in a sealed envelope that may not be

opened outside the examination room. We'll be interested to
see how you acquit yourself, Hemsing!'

Recalling that I was now to be subject to *viva voce* exam-
ination by several faculties simultaneously in the
Auditorium Maximum, I began to review likely topics, witnesses, alibis where necessary. The presence of Eckstein,
Schlindwein and others could be a blind, concocting an
appearance of the oral examination for the Diploma in
Journalism while a very different court of inquiry substi-
tuted proceedings for which I was wholly unprepared. Had
I removed the ignition keys from the counter of the
Playoutdri Pool Bar in Schelling Street without the owner's
consent? Had the subsequent joyride in a stolen vehicle led
to a collision with a stationary vehicle which I had failed to
report? And had the owner of the original vehicle proposed
a settlement out of court, to which by force of circum-
stance I had made myself an accessory? Realising the
fantastic legal ramifications of the issue, I became aware of
an acute sensation, as if my testicles were being squeezed,
and I hurried into the building to relieve myself in the toilet. But the toilet was full, and already the steward was
pacing up and down the marble floor outside the auditorium, shooting his cuffs to check his watch, and calling
testily, 'Mr Hemsing, please! Mr Hemsing for the collo-
quium at nine o'clock!'

The raked auditorium I now entered drew up sharply like
a gasp, too late I realised I would have to answer to the
Faculty of Theoretical Physics for the absence of time into
which Hieronymus had misled me. I began in an under-
tone without preliminaries, broaching my lecture in casual
asides, patently remarks not made altogether in earnest, to
the people who had overflowed onto the podium.

Time was not a continuum, I said, it should be com-
pared rather with a magician's rope trick, at one moment
creating the illusion of a closed loop, at the next a single
length of rope, at the next three parallel strands, and so on,

all depending on the sleight of hand behind the illusion as which it could be presented. The rope could be cut and then spliced, and the knot shaken out and apparently be restored to its original length, and still be shorter by ten days, and the rope before and after could be given arbitrary lengths such as Julian or Gregorian, none of which made the slightest difference, for all were equally valid illusions. 'The coefficient,' heckled a voice from the middle, 'please let us have the coefficient for the time inversion factor represented in your example by the soluble knot.' 'The knot can equally be regarded as a shortcut,' I said, sidestepping the coefficient into further analogy, 'as recently illustrated in a learned journal by the case of time moles. The mole burrows under the time curvature, sensibly arriving at the point opposite by a shorter path than if it had travelled around the circumference; a summarising activity comparable with the condensed reporting of news-in-brief items. How long was the event of a pensioner falling from a bridge through the tropical, sidereal and anomalistic year respectively? And the same event, from the reader's point of view, as the subject of a news-in-brief item or of a leading article on page three? Or of a novel by Robert Musil?' 'Throw him out,' interrupted the voice in the middle that had demanded the coefficient. I hurried on regardless, for time was running short and the fifteenth day would soon be breaking, accounting as best I could for the interim disposition of the universe, from the elliptical course of the planets to Dotty's menses, incorporating a congress on rate responsive cardiac pacing and a concert on the Arabian lute for good measure, endeavouring to explain how all these events hung together, neither more nor less significant than the next, if only one knew how – 'The formula,' called voices from the auditorium, 'the formula!' – beyond their mere coexistence, which imposed the burden of an answer encompassing all things in the illumination of an instant, an insupportable burden, bedclothes, suffocating,

toilet, unless I soon, winding up, before I go under, spirally
to some conclusion—

'Stefanie's locket!' I exclaimed, brilliantly the light mush-
roomed and sank at once into darkness

The Antiquarian Bookseller's A–Z

HIERONYMUS KORNRUMPF

Anadromous, the spawning salmon ascends the river. Upturned, to receive the stream of water from the urn of Aquarius, the glittering mouth of the Southern Fish, swimming close to the horizon through an expanse that once was thought of as a celestial sea. Aquatic creatures, real or imaginary, Delphinus and Aigokeros, the horned goat-fish, and Al Rescha, the cord of Pisces, tethering the two fishes under the tutelage of Poseidon. In the void, before the alphabet spawned the word, what fish ascended what stream first? Self-fertilizing hermaphrodite salmon, a golden fish in an inverted bowl, Eridanus, Stream of Ocean, River of Heaven. Made up of?

Beest. Evolutionary division of labour, male and female, urn of water bearer, mouth of fish. White luminosity of nebulae configured flocculently as primordial milk, squirting on parturition from Hera's breasts and floating thereafter as frozen crystals, suspended in galactic etymology.

'Mr Kornrumpf?'

'Astrid?'

'*Gaussian Random Processes?*'

'Ibragimov and Rozanov? Yes. Top shelf, I think.'

Callipygian, the female assistant impeccably employed at Kornrumpf & Son these past two years, stands on a ladder in a black dress. Astrid stretches, locates random processes and descends the ladder, rustling. Has she always rustled? Abstinence refines the senses. Since Martha began to brood in the solitude of her chastity, a rustling of Astrid either unheard or unnoticed before has become audible as the sound of suppressed desire. Spatial refinements, too: in collusion with desire the premises seem to have shrunk. Where space browsed quietly in the aisles between the shelves of books, Astrid's body now encroaches. Squeezing encounters two, three times this morning. Buttocks broached on the way to Astrophysics, brushing of breasts on the way back, groping in impressionable areas under Biology and Bletonism. Sound out her currents, wellspring and soft complaisant flow, on the spoor of pungent moistures swim into her bay. Why not, if she were willing? Weighed this question at lunchtime, organ lolling in hand over the horizon of the toilet seat. Arguments against: elder man, employer, married status. Arguments for: ditto, on naughty account of piquancy. Modest personal attractions admittedly, but the same goes for Astrid. Dowdy girls like her in cohorts at the state library, hunchbacked librarians with dimly illumined faces encouraging a glance downwards to where they have been more generously endowed.

'Shall I turn the sign round on the door?'

'Is it already six o'clock?'

'Five past. Is there anything else you'd like me to do?'

Hieronymus considers. Whisk her into the little room at the back and initiate her into the mysteries of the walnut cabinet. Premature. Already her mackintosh is rustling.

'Thank you, Astrid. See you tomorrow.'

Duplicity. Is not conscience a pair of breeches, which, though a cover for lewdness as well as nastiness, are easily slipped down for the service of both? Diary memorandum,

October the twenty-second. Two months to go. Prepare in earnest an alphabet with suitable quotations to teach the precocious philological infant his letters. New moon on Thursday. Observatory, weather permitting. Aziz, six-thirty. Auction of Egger antiquarian collection on Saturday, curiosities for bibliophiles, by invitation only. Spry old provost. Choked on a fish-bone during dinner with a whore. Urgently make appointment with urologist. Blood in stool quite frequently these past two weeks. Scorpion influence imminent? Amenities, fresh sand etc. for Siegfried. Where is that cat by the way?

'Siegfried? Siggi Siggi Siggi!'

Eurystomatous yawn, vastly distensible jaws stretched in silent growl, proud stalker of the night aroused from his nap among medieval love poetry titles, a ginger tomcat whisks his tail.

And hark! In the dark at the casement window a hand is tapping *rat-a-tat-tat*. Hieronymus lifts his head and peers over a pool of anglepoise light, picks up his keys, his way cautiously through the gloom of the shop. Against the glow of Türken Street a silhouette with a beaky nose, hatted, bearded and heavily coated, outlines a gentleman of Oriental provenance at the door, breathing steamily onto his knuckles. He bares his teeth in greeting, whiteness flashing through his beard, breathes now onto the glass where his finger writes a sigil in reverse:

VƧOꟼ

Hieronymus opens the door a crack.

'Business hours from nine to six. Private viewing by appointment.'

'VSOP.'

'Kindly indicate your interests.'

'Very special old pictures.'

'And your name?'

'Aziz.'

Fomalhaut, royal star of Persia, transliteration of Arabic
fum al hut, mouth of the fish, a gold-capped smile flashing
out of his beard. Oil in hair and ten ringed fingers, swum
into Kornrumpf's ken from the glittering Levant. Sherbet in
beard, a scent of cinnamon under his hat, carried from some
courtyard in Damascus where fountains plash. Greedily
with a gleam: 'And the merchandise?' 'This way.' Kornrumpf advances, followed by client and a glissade of sound,
rippling over the shelves where the tomcat stalks the shadow
of the hat jigging along under the ceiling. Hat and shadow
vanish into stock room, the cat leaps.

Gravigrade Hieronymus steps up to the walnut cabinet,
unlocks it, takes out a linen-covered folder from the bottom
drawer and lays it on the table.

'A bibliophilic treasure of exceptional rarity, dating from
the middle of the eighteenth century. Unattributable, but
conjectured to be the work of an Indian master either established in Persia or subject to Persian influences on the
peripheries of the Silk Road. Facetiously purporting to be
didactic, but without doubt intended for sensual gratification. Would you care to, ahm, examine the patient, and with
a magnifying glass – please! – if you are short-sighted like
myself. You will find the detail most rewarding.'

Houri with perfectly symmetrical bosoms, black-eyed
gazelles of paradise behind yashmak gaze out of curtained
faces from the windows of a caravanserai at the encounter of
a merchant prince with the virgin who is a water-seller in the
market place. While Mr Aziz grunts and pores, Hieronymus
waits, hands decorously clasped, his nostrils buzzing with
the scent of cinnamon his hatted client has interpolated into
the bazaar. Scenes in the bath-house and the bedchamber
show attendant houri in diaphanous drawers, assisting at
the Unclothing, the Naming of Parts, the Initiation and
Consummation in the Four Cardinal Positions.

'How much, the merchandise?'

Thirty thousand dollars, Mr Aziz, in cash on the table. Solvency of customer? Not in doubt. Liquidity, the universal stream of money, pouring from the urns of Arabia. Cash flow from sleeves, pockets and inside of hat, miraculous, a magician sneezing bank notes. An oasis greens on the empty table. He tucks the folder under his arm, Hieronymus locks the money in the safe, turns out the lights and escorts his client in darkness to the street door.

Inspissated night, curdled with conspiracy. The smells of cinnamon and sweated hat-band money enshroud them on the doorstep of Kornrumpf & Son. Further VSOP deliveries expected? Not of that vintage, hardly, but one never knows, one never knows. At all events, keep in touch. Via the Armenian agent, *poste restante* in Zurich? Better, more discreet. Incidentally, may one inquire where merchandise was purchased? Trade secrets, Mr Aziz, trade secrets – withheld even from my wife. Ha ha! Briefly laughter gleams and is already slipping away into the night. Hieronymus turns his steps up Schelling Street in the direction of the Playoutdri Pool Bar.

Jamboree with the boys, dear Jekyll, by way of celebration to be paid for by your colleague Hyde. Not that the boys shall know – who knows him, after all, with secrets even from his wife, the antiquarian bookseller always in the same old coat and rumour has it straitened circumstances? Between the Copress Publishing premises to the left and the corner building opposite, with the onion dome it wears for a hat, interfulgent stars shine down on Kornrumpf ascending Schelling Street accompanied by a cat treading daintily, as if offended, bearing his plume of tail erect like a banner of independence.

Kornrumpf holds the door ajar until cat will be pleased to enter. Not at first. Skirting prelude, ask-me-nicely ritual. The brisk trot, strokes of paws as regular as a roll of drumsticks, the final spurt of speed, punctuated by a full stop just inside the threshold, tail thrashing.

'Evening, Ronnie.'

'Evening, Marcel.'

Ligneous moustaches, the drooping trophies of a bartender with a mournful Proustian air, waxed and polished like a piece of the mahogany counter grafted into the middle of his face, surface slowly to salute Hieronymus from behind a splayed fan of cards. Ticklish sensation this greeting always gives of being tossed in tender parts, inguinal, not disagreeable. Notwithstanding the vulgar abbreviation of his regulars' names, appropriating them to suit his taste, notwithstanding even his gross whiskery facewear, fetishism or disguise, perhaps deep down a tacit sympathy with the proclivities of this man? A lonely gentleness. Soon Marcel will interrupt his game of cards, reach for the pump handle and draw a Pils with fond encircling fingers, put a saucer down behind the counter, Siegfried's favourite, a dash of egg-nog diluted in Guinness.

Miasmal flow, triggered off like a light beam, releasing into the room a cold dour stench of effluvia from the open door of the urinal, envelops Hieronymus as he steps down into the pit of the Playoutdri Pool Bar. Three pool tables stand in the pit under awnings of light awash with blue smoke. In the surrounding semi-darkness red and green strobes of Triomint Jacky Jackpot, Exerizer and Choplifter wink on and off from Playfair automat booths. Chink, chime, the smooth low hum of electric generators, smacking cannon of balls and a drizzle of voices muttering over the regulars' table in the recess beyond, garbled odours and sounds rebound from the walls and mingle in the thick, muffled air.

'Isn't that Kornrumpf?'

'Hello, Bertie.'

'Can't see a damn thing in here without my sunglasses. How's trade?'

'Oh, can't complain. Always patchy during vacation. Pick up again when term starts.'

'Have one on me in the meantime. Pils?'

'Thank you.'

'Marcel, bring him another.'

Nematoid second-hand bookseller, thirty thousand dollars salted away between worm-eaten covers, shelves himself in slot between companion volumes. Bertie, known as Butcher. Hefty history of processed meat products. Florid style in heavy type. Side-sewn double-breasted jacket. Feel the squeeze there. Ferenc the Hungarian, pocket manual of invisible assets in import-export flow. Previous anthology of miscellaneous convictions running into fifth edition. Hand-stitched casing-in, natty leather trimming. Eyes in the backs of their heads. Lucky it's dark in here. ILLEGAL TRAFFIC IN PORNOGRAPHY and TAX EVASION written in headlines all over Kornrumpf's face.

'What's this we hear about your scrumptious sister-in-law?'

'What do you hear?'

'Her shacking up with an undertaker.'

'That's a new one on me.'

'Word gets around, you know.'

'I know.'

'Have any problems, just give me a call. See you around, Hieronymus.'

'See you around, Bertie.'

Obscurely in the deeper shadow of the recess the drizzle of voices resumes. Kornrumpf sinks the first Pils, sips the second. Curious. A conversation about sewage. Subterranean enterprises in vaulted tunnels as much as four yards high, total length of over two thousand kilometres. Goodness. More shit mileage than urban motorway.

Putrescence? Gas masks required for maintenance work? Stuff and nonsense. Marvels of modern hygiene. Salubrious air, perhaps a tang, fairly described as invigorating. Orphic descent of the soul these days by numbered manholes at strategic points, convenient access down slip-proof rungs in polyester protective suits. Well well, the year is on the downward turn once more. Cheers. Kornrumpf eavesdrops, ruminates, cranes his imagination and swills the beer in his glass, glimpsing in the dark brown brew a maelstrom of household slops, hurtling down a tunnel through everlasting night. With an undertaker? At the downward turn of the year Stefanie and Liselotte Pfaffel hand in hand with the warden of the Eighth House, brides of Osiris and Pluto, descending via numbered manholes at strategic points in North Cemetery to the domain of never never. The Eighth or Occult House: of death but also afterlife, karma and regeneration. Merely a heautomorphic conceit of our living imagination, otherwise unable? No more karma than a cow has as processed meat products. Bertie Butcher, alias Osiris?

Quandary, apt, word of obscure etymology, mystery in a word, in life. Quandaries of life, QED. Draw a line between Astrid and Martha, forming the hypotenuse of a triangle, subtending Kornrumpf at a right angle that can simultaneously be obtuse. Quadrature of the circle, ineluctable pursuit of the insoluble. An answer to the riddle, the duality of the pun, gratifying as paradigms of immortality achieved somehow? Against the odds the billiard ball comes back. No bounce. Just top-spin. Seawash of applause in surrounding darkness. Hieronymus squints into the awning of light, sees his cousin Harald disentangle himself from a back-handed cushion shot and disappear into the toilet the moment Marcel whistles.

Retrograde motion in anticipation of malignant aspects?

Enter stage right a few seconds later a jingling figure in jackboots, whipcord breeches and leather jacket. Saunters through clicks, sticks, standing smoke, in and out of awning light, chalks index finger sinisterly, turning slowly to reveal a skull and cross-bones in silver studs across his back. At the blue felt table in the centre stands Lucas Sliep, alone, oddly, with the look on his face of someone who's just snookered himself.

Kornrumpf sizes up the state of play, stands, advances into limelight like a reluctant ghost, takes up cue in aid of fugitive cousin and strikes the ball with a resounding incursion, pocketing three colours simultaneously. Good? Room for another in Lucas' mouth, wide open in astonishment. Meanwhile Czernack replaces chalk, jogs on, checks out Exerizer, Choplifter booths, snoops around in dark corners and fades away again, faintly jingling.

'Well I never. See if you can do that again.'

'It wouldn't help. It would help if Harald stayed away from here or paid Czernack that money he owes him for the car.'

Solicit Harald therefore when he sneaks back from the toilet. Speak kind but firm words to him in your capacity as senior cousin. Orphan, penniless, prodigal, he is nonetheless your kin. Two Pils on an empty stomach are enough to elicit in Kornrumpf warm, turbid sensations that sentimentally embrace the universe and all its creatures, fermented to a state of exuberance by the thought of thirty thousand dollars. Harald? Coming. Marcel spies. Czernak's gone, the coast is clear. A draught from the door Marcel holds open already seems to usher in to the dingy premises of the Playoutdri Pool Bar an unexpected late-night guest: a marvellous scent of starlight.

Transit of three terrestrial bodies – Kornrumpf, cousin and cat – intersects traffic in transverse paths, at the junctions of Arcis and Barer Streets respectively, on their south-east passage down Schelling Street towards the Twelfth or Terminal House. Attaining the lowest point of the ecliptic at the entrance to home ground in Türken Street, Kornrumpf is momentarily aware of gravitational forces urging him closer to the floor, spinning sensations that accompany him on the ascendant through four stories in anti-clockwise spirals. And beyond, folding down the hatch that opens onto a rooftop observatory, the Jacob's ladder he now unfastens leads up sheer into the glittering heavens.

Umbral eclipse of the new moon decks diamond collars and strings of pearls, configurations of sheen and starlight brighter by the darkness of the night's velvet horizon. Glowworms and phosphorescent golden bees, fireflies, oil-lamps and candle flames, lights, light-birds, butterflies and daisies brimming among the meadows of the night, speckled with the star dust of a celestial river, the veil of a bride who conceived out of the womb of darkness a progeny of stars.

Via Lactea, Milky Way, River of the Divine Lady, nourishing the extravagant mythologies that inhabit the night sky. At her eastern breast the twins of Gemini, Castor and Pollux. Taurus, Auriga, Capella and Perseus to the north. Below Taurus and the Pleiades is Orion, the hunter, shouldering his way up over the horizon. And in the zenith, high above Aquarius, the Dolphin and the horned denizens of the celestial sea, the brilliant stars of Pegasus emblazoned in a square, the court of the Pole Star and all its circumpolar luminaries, Cepheus, King of Ethiopia and his queen Cassiopeia, enthroned between the Pole Star and the galaxy of Andromeda.

Watchers of the heavens, Aldebaran, Antares, Fomalhaut and Regulus, the four royal stars of Persia, marking the four quarters of the heavens. Above the distant brawl of city traffic and a tintinnabulation in the rigging of television aerials a light wind rises, ascending higher and higher on an interstellar diapason that seems to stroke from the stars a paradigm of universal sound—

Xylophonic, sound combed from the keys of a starway ascending faintly into sleep.

'Harald?'

'Hm?'

'I must be dreaming. Isn't that the grocer's daughter undressing in a window overlooking Adalbert Street? Bring the telescope down to the steeple of St Mark's and follow left through an arc of forty-five degrees.'

'Hang on. I'm caught here in the most wonderful cluster

of branching stars. What can it be? A constellation in the shape of a gigantic tree.'

Yggdrasil, Odin's horse, the name the Norsemen gave to the heavenly tree binding root, bole and branch of all the universe; while the ancient Egyptians, standing sideways and pointing upwards in the profile of a frieze, envisaged there the arched body of a slumbering goddess.

Will Martha already be asleep?

His watch bleeps, shows eleven o'clock in luminous digits.

Zodiacal changing of the guard. The sun enters Scorpio at one minute past.

Cusps

DOTTY

'It's Art Deco. A giveaway at the price.'

'Golly!'

'The figure's made of alabaster. The base must be obsidian.'

'So it is!'

Dotty looks at the lamp in Alexander's hands, wondering who Art Deco is. Gingerly she fingers the base that looks like ordinary bottle-glass and thinks, *obsidian*, for the first time in my life the feel of obsidian. Rub it and maybe a djin will appear.

'D'you think it works?'

'Works? It's an *objet d'art*, Donata, possibly even an original Lalique.'

'Oh!'

'The craftsmanship, the grace. Just feel the texture of the figure.'

Dotty has a twinge of embarrassment, how silly, shakes it off and strokes the smooth alabaster belly. The woman with the absurdly muscular thighs and breasts stands for Dotty's inspection in the palm of Alexander's hand. Art Deco is her name, at the end of her outstretched arms she holds two inverted flower heads with sockets for electric bulbs inside. Hideous!

Nonchalantly Alexander hands the owner of the stall five notes of fifty as if he were passing him a tip. The money he shuffles out of the wad of bills in a silver clasp looks freshly laundered and pressed. Around it there still lingers the scent of Eau d'Hermes, presented yesterday to invited guests at the boutique in Maximilian Street. He folds the raincoat over his arm, Dotty glimpses a flame of scarlet lining with the Armani label facing out. The brogues, the bow-tie, the silk shirt in the palest lavender. How elegant Alexander is!

Dotty loves the Auerdult. At the ragged end of the year the autumn jumble market seethes, sprawling across the Square of Our Lady's Grace. The year is a magic hour-glass, how quickly the grains run out, releasing already the sweet warm smell of the first hot chestnuts, pumpkins, pine wreaths for All Souls and early Christmas decorations, the new year stands the hour-glass on its head and time is full again, flowing endlessly. How round and snug the year is, with useful compartments showing where to find what, in October the time for falling leaves and the hoarse-voiced man selling potato-peelers, always here in the same place, but unexpected things too, a surprise, a treasure, even if only a horrid old lamp. And sure enough, browsing between books and blue-and-white earthenware, she finds her own: a stork's nest on a three-legged chair.

Stork! Brooding, the beaky bird no higher than her little finger stands solemnly on stilt-like legs, pondering two quacky offspring. She taps the beak. Plastic. But so lifelike, storky! What will Alexander think of this? She grips her coin, glances round furtively and sees him with his nose still in a book.

'And can you put it in a box or something?'

They wander through the market. In the raucous aisles between the stalls Dotty goes adrift on an oncoming crowd and takes Alexander's arm. A chill wind tugs in snatches across the square, awnings thump, from the chestnut trees the leaves come spiralling down. Burnt yellow, ochre, strangely the colours of the loveliest season celebrate a dying. Her eyes move up and up the tall brick church and see a steeple tie a dark knot in a blue sky. A shiver passes through her body. She draws her collar up.

'Borrow my coat? I wouldn't mind some coffee. It's not far to my place.'

Dotty crosses the road. Under the trees there the grey pavement turns to gold, muting the bright tap of her heels. She scuffs her feet and kicks the leaves up with her toes. Beneath a maple tree the fallen leaves cast a deep red shadow. The road is a river, dotted with the shadows of clouds, islands of differently coloured sounds. On the far side Alexander walks with the lamp lady reclining over his shoulder, leaning into his stride, as if he were carrying her up a mountain,

'Where d'you think all the leaves go?'

'The municipality sweeps them up.'

'It must be tons.'

'It is. Thousands.'

Trees are running out on her side, will soon resume on his. Only pavements count. Briefly Dotty changes sounds, crossing back with a bright tap of heels. All the way from the Au to Haidhausen on a carpet of leaves!

Alexander is so busy carting Art Deco up his mountain that he doesn't notice until they stop at traffic-lights and wait to cross Rosenheimer Street.

'What have you got in that paper bag?'

'Nothing. Just a present for my sister.'

'Is she the one who calls you Dotty?'

'They all call me that.'

'Why?'

'Because of my skinny elbows. Or because I'm scatter-brained and fidget a lot. I don't remember exactly.'

'I prefer Donata. Donata rings.'

Dotty ponders this. They walk across Weissenburger Square. She thinks of things that ring. Telephones and church bells. Cash registers. Alarm clocks. Does she want to be on this list?

The roads lead off from the square like the spokes of a wheel, they continue down the one that goes to another square whose name for some reason she can never remember. Something French. There must be a colony of them in Haidhausen. Orleans, Belfort. Faculty of Romance Languages, how grand it sounds, the poetry of the troubadours, in two weeks her very first lecture. Alexander lives in an apartment off Bordeaux Square.

'And so Max is giving a party tonight. Are you listening?'

'What?'

'D'you know Max?'

'Look! The fountain. They've turned it off and boarded it up.'

'The summer's over.'

Summer over, boarded up! Compartments for everything. Even a splash can be put in a box. Dotty feels a pang. Passing through the archway to the yard behind the house, she hears the echo of her footsteps and imagines what it's like to be bald. Alex has no echo, he must have rubber soles. He takes a key out of his pocket and pushes open the door. Key for a door upstairs, then. Why now, already? She steps on a date, eighteen-ninety-something, set in gold mosaic on a tiled floor. How dark in these old houses! Musically the banister rises, an unwinding scroll on wrought-iron clefs, up and up the staircase spirals.

'I mustn't stay too long.'

Dotty begins to climb the stairs. Alexander follows, creak by squeak.

'I thought we were going out this evening.'

'I told you, Grandpa's ill. Somebody has to be in the house to look after him.'

'Is that your job?'

'Mother's going out.'

Well, not quite a lie, and only to have an alibi. Just in case. How slyly he made that suggestion about having coffee. Not far to his place, my foot. A whacking half-hour walk. And how eagerly officious with that bright little key – *Hrdlick! Hrdlack!* – the lock springs back, the door flies open, already Dotty stands inside.

'Shall I take your coat?'

The scent of Eau d'Hermes, enveloping an obscure invitation to some kind of acquiescence, pricks her nostrils again as she feels Alexander's touch lightly on her collar. The coat slips from her shoulders. How cool the lining over her knuckles, hollow the sound of her sleeves somehow as she empties them of her arms. She feels poured out, a delicate balance, perfectly flush with the rim of the glass. A funny feeling, imagine, liquid with nothing to hold you together and still not falling apart. She folds her arms and clasps herself, which Alex naturally misunderstands.

'I can put a fire on if you're cold.'

'Where's the loo?'

The who? The loo. Silly rhyming game she used to play with Steffi. Turn right and through the bedroom. In the mirror she sees herself still smiling. Is this Donata smiling? More solemn, ringing, wistful at least, she imagines her in winter with cropped hair, a boa nestling round her neck. If in doubt with a man (so practical Mother's advice), spend five minutes in the loo and think it out. Is he clean in his personal habits? Roger & Gallet sandalwood soap, hairless basin, immaculate. What else would you expect from Alexander? At the very latest by the age of nineteen, Annette said, any self-respecting girl already ought to have. Should Dotty tell him she was a virgin beforehand? Would she see the difference afterwards? Some decisions can't be taken. Some decisions have to fall. Dotty flushes the toilet and goes into the living-room.

Under the window a gas fire hisses, bubbling, gurgling, the sound of coffee percolating in the kitchen where she hears Alex.

'Cream? Sugar?'

'Mmmm.'

Bending over the fire, she looks out of the window. Warmth steals up her legs. Beyond the roofs the sky is darkening. In the courtyard stands a tree.

'Donata?'

Coffee aroma. Cups and saucers chink.

'We don't have to go out. I mean, we could stay here.'

The tree is balding, downwards from the crown. She sees the tunnel under the arch leading out to the street. Noiselessly on rubber soles that have no echo, soundlessly beyond the window pane the falling leaves eddy, summer is over, inaudible the muffled splash, these are things that have to be. Alex stands behind her. He runs a finger down her arm. A single drop, no more, purses and wells over the brim. Dotty can't take her eyes off the tree. Not yet. Soon.

Soon she will have to turn.

THE KING
OF THE RAIN
COUNTRY

A POMEGRANATE

STEFANIE

A dream of snakes and spiders on the anniversary of Father's death. Snakes lay coiled around the cradle. The spiders had spun their webs across the opening of the hood. The cradle stood on the platform of a deserted railway station. No trains will pass through here, never. Come on. Papa? I followed him down the stairs, but he had already gone. The pity of it, I said, someone has abandoned their child – and awoke with ash on my tongue.

Unbearable wound of light. Days, weeks. Lay with my face to the wall in the dark. I am a snail that has lost its house. The shell torn off. Lay in the dark and bled and bled.

Dear Brum,
   Remember the first birthday cake I made for you? So happy! Tell me about it, you said. All morning we lay in bed and I told you about a marzipan cake with a ground floor and a gallery, just like the studio in Zenetti Street, adding rooms for guests, a courtyard with a fountain, a tower with a stork's nest made of sugar, and all the other

*things we would do given a couple of hundred eggs to turn
it into the sort of place we thought we wanted to live in. At
which you suddenly turned to me like a cliff and said you
didn't like marzipan. I cried, how I cried, you remorseful
and we made it up, the memory of it has slipped away,
lost in the wake of—*

Happy days with Brum, a stray, a mongrel, half wild when I
met him, doggy shaggy head of hair like a burning bush, tus-
socks of light golden hair on the backs of his hands, when I
licked the hair it turned dark. I licked him all over and dried
his skin with my hair. Always have something in reserve,
said Ma, don't give yourself quite, a man respects that and
it keeps him coming back for more, how can he see you if
you lose yourself in him altogether? But the blood rushed in
my ears when I saw him again after an absence of just a few
hours, I thought of him first when I woke up in the mornings and last thing before I fell asleep, the same even after
months, after years, still.

*You liked me licking you. You went your own way, kept
your own times, there were other women, I tasted them on
your skin. You came back to me and I licked them off.
Gisela was a smell of mint, others came and went, but
long after the two of you had broken up as lovers and I
moved in I would still find echoes of her on your skin. I
wanted to tame Brum. I wanted to lick you into shape.*

The chaos, the squalor of that place. Martha came in a blue
dress, and together we scrubbed it out. Brum didn't even
have a bank account then. Money lying around under carpets and on ledges, in tins, drawers, shoes. Brum threw
nothing away. Papers, catalogues, posters standing around
in stacks. The ones he needed he folded over coat-hangers
and hung them with his shirts in the cupboard. The weeks
of his life that must have been wasted looking for things.

That's why, I said, not for its own sake but because it saves time, spacing him out from A to Z in orderly files where I could keep an eye on him. No more than a dim awareness of himself. Urgent vitality now. Life spilled and rushed out of him and spread like a stain wherever it happened to fall. Child Brum. Not so much a personality as the raw material for one. No morals or sense of values but eddies of pure impulse, got up in the middle of the night to paint the ceiling.

Remember? You painted the map of the world on my body when I complained you'd been neglecting me. When we went to bed the first night I'd already got Australia on my bum and slept the night on blotting paper. You made up stories about the countries you were painting, and we laughed and laughed. The polar circle around my neck. Europe in the greens and browns of a contours map on my left boob, with the nipple painted brown to mark the elevation of the Alps. Asia centred on the Himalayas to the right, at that height pinkish rather then brown, so you left it as it was; with the Mediterranean splashed across my hip, and Africa wrapped around a thigh. In the mirror I watched North America spread across my back, Cape Horn ticklish in the hollow of my knee, the continent growing upwards with the Andes along the inside of my thigh, Peru bulging with the buttock crease and rounding off into the Caribbean, the fragile Central American isthmus spanning my back. Promised you the world, didn't I, you said, and soaking the brush in warm water you drew it slowly through the Panama Canal, and at once I came.

Last night I dreamed my body was being painted, stroked with a brush, only it wasn't, it felt more like a hand. I lay on the edge of waking, but couldn't quite come to.

Fine, fiddly things – Brum was very good with his hands.

The tiny screws in my wristwatch. The toys he made of
matchsticks. Threading a needle. And his hand with women,
too. Good at doing things with his hands. Coupled hands
and imagination and painted wonderful patterns on my
body. Things he could never do with his prick, uncontrol-
lable, that was the trouble, just chucked it at the wall and
the stuff ran down. Never mind. Never *mind*. The joke
about the standing joke and how it fell flat. Brum minded,
but there was nothing he could do, the life spilled and
rushed out of him there again, too.

He had his freedom. He always had his freedom to come
back to me. And he expected me to have mine whether I
wanted it or not. Friends of Brum were often dropping in,
for a viewing, they said, of the work in progress. Usually that
was me. Christoph had his hand under the table on my knee
the minute he sat down. He had a hunting lodge in
Nymphenburg. He was always dropping hints about this
property. The sort of place I think Stefanie would like, he
said between squeezes, why don't we drive out and take a
look at this some time? Brum talked and talked, ignored or
didn't notice my distress signals. Why did I stand for that?
Why did I let that lecherous old sod? Because he was also
wise and very good company, and it was not so much him
taking liberties that I minded as Brum not taking the slightest notice. So Christoph and I went out to see the Copper
Lodge, which he duly left us when he died, and Brum asked
no questions about that either.

And others, others. I felt I was on loan, free booty for all-
comers.

Brum was too sure of himself. He was sure of me. I used
to tell myself jealousy wasn't in his nature until I realised it
was lack of care. Oscar certainly gave him reason to be jealous. The trouble was that I didn't love him. The only reason
I moved in with Oscar was to provoke a response from
Brum. But Brum knew that too. He did nothing. He knew
that as much as a need for him was the need in me to be

loyal at all. Perhaps it hurt Brum, but he wouldn't show it. When I limped home after two weeks he froze me out. He was so cold. Like a marble column. There was no way I could get at him. I shouted at him. Don't you care when I go off with other men? You must do as you please, he said, I don't own you. But I wanted to belong to him. Didn't he see he was making me do these things against my own nature? It made me so desperate, the way he stood there cold and scornful and saying nothing, that I tore up one of his pictures and threw the pieces on the floor. That dented him. That was a picture of me in pieces on the floor.

In a dream I saw myself lying in a coffin in one of the empty rooms at Little Monten Castle. But someone came in and opened the lid and began playing scales up and down my body, and I realised I was a grand piano.

When Maximilian looked in this morning I asked him to open the curtains for the first time.

You began to need me because of my dreams. I couldn't sing or paint. I had no accomplishments of that kind. I could dream. Remember? I fell asleep in a chair while looking at that picture you'd left unfinished, and in my dream I saw it complete. All it needed was a patch of blue for the band master's cap and the outline of a circle round the figures in the middle – you hadn't realised the figures were supposed to be standing in a circus ring. Circus ring – of course! You got very excited, tried it out at once and found it was right. So you took out more pictures you'd left unfinished and I completed them in my sleep when I dozed in the afternoons. It worked with good pictures. With good pictures it worked because they had to be. They were there before you thought of them. I just needed to look into my sleep to see if the picture was there. It was there if it was true and it had to be. You came to realise that if a picture wasn't there it wasn't anywhere, because it wasn't true, and you would throw it away. You

thought it a miracle I could see pictures like that in my
sleep, but to me it seemed natural, awake or asleep I was
always transparent, absorbing all the shapes and colours of
your being, I carried your sound in me as a shell carries
the sound of the sea. I was always more in love with you
than you with me. Or maybe as a woman I just loved you
differently, and the imbalance of my love for you and
yours for me was no more than that inequality which is in
the nature of love.

In my fourth month I lost the child. If I made little of it,
Brum made less. Distractions, he thought it was I needed,
distractions. The days hurried on and never stopped for
anything. What a wonderful couple, such a full and active
life! What a character Brum is! How she sparkles! I began to
dream those dreams of an abandoned child, naturally the
child I'd lost, I thought, and sank under all those distractions that anaesthetized the days. House guests stayed for
months, parties in Zenetti Street seemed to go on all summer. And Brum? I lost sight of him. He hid behind guests
and distractions. I saw less and less of him, even when we
were alone. As a partner for me he wasn't there at all. I was
a partner for him in pictures. In my dreams I cared for an
abandoned child. My dream is my life, I said, don't you see
that the abandoned child is me? Brum had nothing to say.
He brought home two singing birds in cages, as a wedding
present, he told me, as though we'd been planning to get
married all along. He put the cages one on top of the other
and whistled and painted while the two birds sang. The
birds sang only when they couldn't see each other.

Max saw the light under my door and came in late. I'd
still not touched the bowl of fruit he brought me yesterday.
He asked if there was anything else I'd like. I said I'd like
him to read to me. Max has a beautiful voice, baritone with
flecks of light. He fetched a book and read aloud a poem
that began *Je suis comme le roi d'un pays pluvieux*. Rain

touched the windows softly, softly the words swam, bright
shoals in dark water through which I sank.

*For weeks you sat at the round table with your elbows on
the drawn-thread cloth I'd embroidered with our names
and the date of the wedding, and never noticed it. You
brushed the crumbs off, and I thought surely you must
notice it now, it's my name you're brushing with your
fingertips.*

There was a marker in the book. When I took it in my hands
the book fell open at the page where I must have fallen
asleep. I felt as if I had lifted a stone and saw the words flat-
tened underneath. In daylight they lay inert on the page
and had no sound. Across the landing I heard laughter,
water running. The dress I had worn to my wedding hung in
a polythene bag behind the door. Max must have had it
cleaned. Fruit lay piled in a bowl, grapes, peaches, a pomegranate, so perfect they looked artificial.

How could a drawn-thread tablecloth give me such a pain
in my heart? Brum didn't notice it. He leaned on it with his
elbows. He ate his meals off it, and brushed the crumbs
away with his hand. He didn't see our embroidered names
or the date of the wedding linking them. I couldn't believe it.
It wasn't just a tablecloth Brum didn't notice. It was me that
Brum overlooked.

For about a year he painted pictures I was unable to find
in my sleep. Then I told him twenty-three dreams in which
I saw myself gradually disintegrating. Brum looked over my
shoulder and saw the dreams. He knew my body by heart.
He looked away and saw the pictures out of the corner of his
eye, and painted them, one for each dream.

Max tells me that downstairs the house looks quite different, but upstairs it's all staid and old-fashioned, the
rooms furnished with heavy cloths in dark red and maroon;
on the landing a stove with ornamental tiles, a baldachin

over his bed with stars embroidered on blue silk, niches where the shadows stand like sentries all day long, high ceilings and deep carpeted floors as silent as lawns. The same rich, jaded solemnity of the king of the rain country in the poem he read surrounds Max himself. Clearly he identifies with this figure. Downstairs is quite different, he said, as we made our way up to the top of the house. Tiny furniture in still rooms, an entire childhood preserved under dust covers. Max is a collector of things. He put his hand on the rocking-horse and set it in motion. But for the horse, I thought—

We heard it plunging back and forth, back and forth, as we went downstairs.

The fruit is the size of a large orange. It has the burnt colours of autumn, ochre, yellow and red, and the feel of smooth leather. Max cut it open. It was divided into chambers, containing a reddish membrane and pulp. Seeds lay embedded in the pulp.

Around my chair Brum arranged three cardboard walls, like a screen. It was the design for the mural commissioned by the brewers. It felt as if my chair had been drawn up in front of a fire, the colours were so warm. Barley fields border the river with a ribbon of corn-yellow light. That part was fine. In the glow of the landscape I began to feel drowsy, and turning the corner in pursuit of the river I fell asleep. But beyond the corner the river vanished. Instantly the screen went blank. I saw whiteness. I saw a winter landscape. The river had frozen. Where the weir used to be I now saw cascades of ice, hanging in mid-air. Snow was falling, turning the river into a white road. Roads, bridges, buildings, the whole city disappeared under one of the deepest snows that had ever fallen. When I woke I told Brum that when he turned the corner and began painting the wall to the east he would have to change his design, because I'd seen winter there in my sleep. Brum wouldn't or couldn't change his design. He looked over my shoulder and saw what I saw, but he pretended it wasn't there. Brum wanted to see only summer.

But for the horse, I thought, I might never have gone. Yet long before Brum came late for the wedding and I walked in the clearing in the English Garden, I'd seen it in the images of my sleep, the sorrel horse Brum painted into his design. It was there because it was true. I'd known beforehand that it had to be. Mourning has its season as all things have. When the *missa solemnis* was over I heard the needle turn and turn in grooves run dry of music like my heart and I knew its mourning season had ended too.

The acid taste left an unexpected edge of sweetness on my tongue. The moist, sticky seeds of the pomegranate spilled over the edge of the spoon between my breasts and slid down my belly, cool, sweet the relief when I realised I didn't much care if I never saw Brum again.

The Rape of the Lock

STEFANIE

Flibbertigibbet, poltergeist, leprechaun – the house was haunted by shades of laughter. A gleeful goblin laughed with a splashing sound in the bathroom, swooped flightily up and down the stairs and rummaged in the attic, rocking the horse. Came and went, sometimes disappeared for days. And there it was again! Tinkling like a wind-chime under the eaves, booming in the hall downstairs. No child, only an adult child, could laugh like that. Sometimes it lay in wait on the landing and poured custard gustily under the door. With creaking wing-beats, like some great bird gathering flight, it cut across the soundtrack of Maximilian's sonorous voice and took off, honking, to a room upstairs. It broke crockery, grazed figures of eight on thin ice, spun coins with bright eddying echoes across floors, hiccoughed and blew horns mournfully in flues. Irresistible, I had to smile myself, smiling I opened the door.

I met Candice in the mirror. She watched me come into the mirror where she was painting her eyebrows and said, 'Darling, I wish I could be as beautiful as you, but what do *you* wish, you know that I can arrange *anything*?' 'I think I'd like to have my hair cut,' I said, and burst into tears. Candice turned out of the mirror and drew my head down on to her shoulder, rather comically, Candy being such a tiny person; and there, in a sense, my head has remained ever since.

I didn't have anything else to wear, so I put my wedding dress back on. As we got into the taxi, and Candice told the driver to take us to Vidal Sassoon's, I realised I hadn't got any money either.

It was raining, a cold wind blew down Pienzenauer Street and most of the leaves had already fallen. Summer had gone away without me long ago. I felt quite sorry for myself. When we crossed the bridge a lump rose in my throat. I felt as if I'd been in hospital and the whole world had passed me by. I felt as if I'd *died*, and it was my ghost crossing the river back into town. 'Of *course* you do, sweetie pie,' Candice said, squeezing my hand. A shower of acorns drummed on the roof as we waited at a set of traffic-lights. 'That's the sound of a heavy winter coming,' the driver said, rather oddly. He peered round the edge of the windshield as if he could already see the winter there on his roof.

I hadn't had my hair cut for seven years, of course. A little man called Harvey with a sleek moustache solemnly combed it out, creating so much static that the hairs stood up and began to writhe. With horror I saw myself in the mirror surrounded by my hair, my face white and small in the middle of a writhing bush. People gathered in the mirror and watched my hair subside, all of them with solemn faces, like mourners standing around a grave. 'Oh for goodness sake,' I snapped, 'just cut it off!' 'Madam,' said Harvey, 'we cannot. To cut off such hair is sacrilege.' So he handed me the scissors and I cut it off myself. Candice held her palms open like a prayer book and read a hair funeral service.

But I felt good and clean. I could feel the air shaping the back of my head and tingling nicely at the nape of my neck. We decided on a pyramid – short back and sides with peak on top, which Harvey permed, curls in the middle arranged to fall down the sides with a splash. Violent purple, the splash bounced out of a colour called Jet Dynamic on Harvey's sample chart, a metallic silver-grey, which Harvey used to tone the rest of my hair. Distinguished, he thought. Candy said I was in permanent take-off. I was just happy to be different. They laid the corpse of my braided hair with an orchid entwined gratis in a box under a cellophane cover – tropical flowers had been delivered fresh to Sassoon's from Singapore that morning

I walked with Candice down Ludwig Street, carrying my hair under my arm, a tingling sensation at the nape of my neck where hair had been, and thought: *You're free!* Nobody would recognise me. I hardly recognised myself. I imagined myself calling at Little Monten Castle to ask if I was there, and Mother with a worried face telling me I wasn't, and me commiserating with her for a bit until I could no longer bear it and put my arms around her and told her I was me. Steffi! It was as if I'd become invisible. Candice called from the far side of the road, running in and out of the traffic I joined her at the corner of Brienner Street. He doesn't yet know it, said Candice, but we're meeting an admirer of yours for lunch at Café Luitpold.

From a table at the window I watched a cab pull up outside Beringer & Koettgen. Max got out and crossed the street, coolly handsome in a dark suit. He glanced into the window and looked hard at me. Not that I was afraid he would recognise me, but my heart did a somersault. Sharp look! Not recognition, but barbed with something else that saw me. I felt like a fish with a hook in my mouth. But Max came in and strolled over to where Candy was sitting without giving me a second glance. So I lit a cigarette and began looking Max up and down, as Candice had said I should, acting very cool. From behind the menu Max sneaked back for another look, as I knew he would, and must have been foxed to find I'd got to him first. He looked away. Candice

nudged him and said something I didn't catch. After a while
Max got up and came over to where I was sitting. I guessed
he was about to come up with the corniest line, and that
Max would find this embarrassing, because he genuinely
wanted to find out. So when he came in on cue with
Haven't-I-seen-you-somewhere-before? both Candice and I
doubled up. I joined her and Max at their table. For a
moment Max was piqued he'd been fooled like that, but he
took it in his stride. Candice kept on prodding him.
'Different with that hair,' she sniped, 'but still gorgeous,
don't you think, Max, I mean wouldn't you say just *stunning*?' 'I think I would, said Max, showing little white teeth
at the corner of his mouth. While Candy was needling him
like this my eye was caught by the picture of a man standing
at a quarter to twelve on the minute-hand of a clock. I picked
up the newspaper someone had left on the chair, and read:
ASCENT OF SOUTH FACE OF TOWN HALL – Man Falls and
Breaks Clock. 'Oh dear, look, she's reading the paper,'
Candice went on, 'you must have bored her, Max, can't you
be more entertaining? Tell Steffi a bit about your work, you
know, *confidentially*. An anecdote with a corpse or two. You
know women find that sort of thing irresistible.' 'What sort
of thing?' I asked, 'What does Max do?' 'But darling, just
look at his beautifully manicured hands, you can see right off
that he does things with his hands. He's a *manual* worker –
aren't you, Max? I mean, you have tools and things, don't
you, King?' Candice purred, and the leprechaun surfaced in
a cartwheel of laughter. Max prodded the filet on toast with
his fork and said, 'OK, Candy, now that's enough, if you
start misbehaving in here I'll leave at once.' Candice clucked.
'Oh come on, King, don't be so stuffy, of course you want
Steffi to admire your best points, you're mad about her, who
blames you, she *is* stunning, and it *is* your best point. So why
not here in Café Luitpold, hmm? With that handsome waiter
hovering in the background. And all these nice people in *felt
hats* having their lunch. Just imagine if someone sees. The

shock. The outrage. The *disgust* on the general manager's face. Eh, Kingy?' Candice ran her hand along Max's thigh and I saw the scar at the corner of his mouth turn white. Max cut off a corner of toast and pushed it around his plate, his fork trembling. 'Darling,' said Candice in a silky voice, 'would you turn *that* way please and hold the newspaper spread out, giving us *complete* coverage of some terribly wicked event? King is so coy about showing his dick – you've not seen it yet? – it's true, you know, men with large pricks are easier to handle because they're so much more forthcoming. Really, men are as shy as the size of their dicks and King is so shy you sometimes wonder if he's *there*, but once you know how to draw him out you'll find his personality acquires a quite different dimension, won't it, Max—' 'Candy, for Chrissake!' 'Relax, King! Concentrate on that filet on toast. Darling he has a *bauble*, a real little treasure with a delicious blue *pallor* – read, darling, just read!' I saw Candice unfasten his zip and put her hand in his fly. Max groaned. A squat, bulbous dome, white with a blueish sheen but otherwise rather like a fireman's helmet, lolled in Maximilian's lap and absurdly began to sprout. I felt so embarrassed I must have blushed to the roots of my Jet Dynamic hair, and said in a small dry voice that yesterday at noon passers-by stared in fascination at the clock on the tower of the Town Hall a man climbed over the balustrade and let himself down on a rope a cry of horror went up the man had slipped and his life now hung by a thread literally the thin red rope from which he dangled was his only hope between life and otherwise certain death. 'Quick, darling, look!' A comic bald bird twitched and jumped on the finger perch Candice held out to coax him into doing his little stunts. I didn't see the waiter come. All I saw was Candice squinting at a menu that had suddenly materialised in Max's lap and looking up with fluttering eyelashes as she said, 'Just coffee for me and the lady, perhaps something *gooey* for the gentleman. Do you have caramel custard?'

'Yes Max, I know it was naughty and I deserve to be smacked,' Candice said, as he propelled her out into Brienner Street, 'and I know it's a busy time for you, but poor Steffi hasn't got any clothes, the least you can do if you're going to be paying for them is to come and help us choose.' 'No,' said Max, hailing a taxi. Candice shrugged. All right then, please yourself. But as Max was climbing into the cab she called over her shoulder, 'Haven't you got an account at Krines?'

Max told the driver to wait. 'Krines? What for?' 'What for,' mimicked Candice, one hand on the cab door, the other in her blouse. 'If you want *dessous*,' she said huskily, leaning inside the cab, thrilly frillies, briefs but also roomy bloomers, Max, *knickers*, brassieres to enlace the shudder of burgher bosoms – remember, King? – girdles, garters and suspender belts bristling with buckles, straps – well, Max, where would you go?' 'Krines,' said Max. We all got into the cab.

And? What happened? Candy leaned across and said, 'Darling, I'm dying to know about that man?' 'He was saved by the minute-hand,' I said, skimming the article in the *Evening Herald*, 'broke the clock and the glockenspiel too, it says it'll cost millions to repair.' Candice laid her arm on Max's shoulder and scratched his neck. 'Hear that, Kingy? A *minute* hand was interposed in the naughty nick of time and—'

'Speaking of which,' interrupted Max, looking at his watch, 'a quarter of an hour is all I have, Candice. I've got a sales conference at two.'

Max spent an hour and a half at Krines. If one liked that sort of thing, as Max obviously did, Krines was *the* place for ladies' underwear. Krines, as it happened, once used my outline for a catalogue when I got started on my career by modelling *dessous*. The advertising agency handling the Krines account wanted what they called a *wistful bust* to convey the genteel-conservative image one associates with

Krines. I've filled out a bit since then. I could no longer do a wistful bust now. Dotty could do it now, not me.

'Darling I'm leaving you in very capable hands,' said Candice as we were entering the courtyard, 'Byee!' And unexpectedly she slipped away.

For me the sense of belonging in a place is a mosaic of secret landmarks, familiar places in little nooks that are always reassuringly there – places like Krines. Nothing ever changed. Even the staff had preserved a – well, a sort of *krininess*. The friendly but discreet way they treated Max, as if he and they had secrets – pure krininess. Max obviously knew his way around. He was the sort of male customer they liked to cluck over – middle-aged, clucking, kriney women, strings of imitation pearls at V-shaped cashmere necks, grey in grey with quiet skirts. Actually, Max handled lingerie more like a salesman than a customer. Some men are funny about ladies underwear, a bit furtive, the way men can be when they wait for you outside the women's loo. Not Max. Stretchwear this and softwash that and fingers inserted to test clasticity, and those little grey bods nodding and clucking behind the counter and smoothing things out as they listened to his pitch, as if Max was there to sell them their own stuff. Of course I liked nice underwear, that feeling of zippy snugness nice underwear can give you, but all that really mattered was being comfy. It wasn't anything like as *complicated* as Max was trying to make out. He kept on coming over to the cubicle with *piles* of stuff. I decided I'd have to put a stop to it. 'Psst, Max,' I said. His face popped through the curtains. I had on a silk chemise, very flamboyant and rather ridiculous, with butterflies and red dragons embroidered in forbidden stitch. Max's mouth fell open. 'Max,' I said, 'it's very sweet of you, but you know, I really don't need all this stuff, I mean, I hardly ever even wear a *bra*.' 'Never?' Max frowned. He slipped into the cubicle, and putting his hands under my elbows stood behind me in the mirror. Then he asked me something strange: '*Not even when you're dead? Wouldn't you wear one to your funeral?'* I thought, *Least of all then.* I raised my arms and he drew the chemise with the dragons over my head. 'Well, wouldn't you?' I thought least of all then, but this time I wasn't so sure, on account of the way Max grazed my elbows with his thumbs and pressed them till I could feel the bone. The pointy, brittle feeling there came up like a rash all over my body, at my knees and shoulders and the tips of my breasts a funny-bone feeling of being vulnerable and exposed. 'Imagine you were dead,' Max whispered, giving me a cold flush, and the tips of me clotted and I felt fragile and terribly naked. 'Are you cold?' He put his hands under my breasts and squeezed. Closing my eyes I heard the ladies rustling outside at the counter, the image of myself flared and extinguished behind my eyelids. 'Black or white or, you know,' said Max, while I thought of doves, 'when Mary Queen of Scots was beheaded she caused a sensation with her scarlet undergarments.' And feeling myself spilling warmly into his hands I opened my eyes. 'This one's pretty,' I said. I slipped the fabric with lace borders as light as a breath over my arms and Max hooked me behind. 'White is festive, don't you think?'

Max left for his sales conference and Candice whirled me off to do some more shopping. 'You need things, you're staying, darling, aren't you?' I didn't know what to say, so I said nothing. Slyly she asked how things had gone at Krines. I told her Max was good at choosing lingerie, clearly he had a lot of experience with these things. Candice sniffed. She kept on wanting to buy me things. 'It's Max's money,' she said, 'don't worry, he's rich.' We went into stores along Theatiner Street to buy shoes, blouses, skirts, slacks, and the more we bought the less it seemed to matter, and the harder I found it to stop. We must have spent thousands at Dietl's alone. But Candice still wasn't through. She thought I needed some party dresses, something more lavish. So she took me to this couturier in an alley behind Maximilian

Street, where I chose two fabulous fabrics in white and gold and was measured for evening gowns and a formal dress in plain black satin with bare shoulders, slashed at the thigh.

When we got into the cab I felt exhilarated like I always did after buying clothes, a warm excitement, as if I was taking new friends home. But I knew I wasn't going home. Light was beginning to fade down Maximilian Street. The lamps came on and lit up bits of rain in warm yellow windows. The dense, wet, hurrying street jostled and shone. But I didn't feel I was part of that jostle and shine. I felt I was outside, looking in. My new clothes were behind glass in bright shop windows, I'd bought them but I still didn't own them, they weren't mine at all, somehow I'd lost the pleasure. It didn't use to be like that. Something in me has changed. All of a sudden I felt empty and brittle. 'Wait,' I said to the driver as we were crossing Kennedy Bridge, just wait a second—' I took that old taffeta dress and the orchid box with my hair and dropped over the rail into the river, not even a splash, I glimpsed them bob on the water and float swiftly, silently downstream.

The King of
the Rain Country

MAXIMILIAN HOLLMANN

He was the king of the rain country. He collected art and
antiques, curios, children's furniture and cased butterflies,
pressed flowers, fossils and ladies' underwear; the imprisoned scent of life in things, anything, he collected things in
which the soul had been preserved by the embalming fluid
of art. Such things came naturally to him, to the heir of the
family firm they had been transmitted genetically: in a manner of speaking he had death in his veins.

At the age of thirteen or fourteen, in the fourth generation
of Hollmann Mourning Services, Maximilian went to school
with his father and by the time he was twenty had laid out
five thousand corpses in their coffins. At night classes he
continued his other schooling, becoming the first Hollmann
to matriculate at a university. He acquired a general knowledge of economic principles and their special application to
the monopolies that interested him, incidentally advancing
his funereal career and consolidating his taste for it by having himself incorporated as a brother of the Black Lodge.
On behalf of the lodge he wore silk under chainmail at his
throat, padded epaulettes, gauntlets, a gory horsehair apron

to protect his genitals, fought suits against rival lodges and was cut at the corner of the eye while splitting his opponent's head open at the temple and releasing a fountain of blood in which the two men embraced to pledge undying friendship. They drank deep in candle-lit cellars, sang songs and thunderously rumbled glasses with other young men wearing midnight uniforms with silver braid and buttons, intoxicated by the flow from some obscure, archaic source that only the imagination of youth could tap, or from which those romantic ideals of loyalty could spring. By small quantities of shortening light their eyes shone, ah, so much more brightly against a background of always even darkness, on cheeks still smooth and still held out for swords to cut the memory would gleam when the scar had faded, everything laid in the lap of the great leveller, their cult of tradition or its rejection by others, tribute or defiance, fear, fearlessness or caution, temporizing resignation that still secreted hope, it did not matter, the stock of evergreen wreaths the Hollmanns laid in during October as superstitious valedictions on the feasts of All Saints and All Souls, bought fresh or recycled at discount as shop-soiled surplus now decked with candles to be lit, one by one, on the four Advent Sundays in a growing choir of light that would blaze from Christmas trees to ignite the sun at the winter solstice, bounce off a beacon at Candlemas to entreat the still vacillating planet in the ashen month of lustrations and illuminate the threshold of the spring equinox – the obscure, archaic source was death and everything that lived was an invocation of immortality.

Mourning Services had traditionally catered for the dying trade in private houses. Half the year, the Hollmanns said, in half the world is ours. They kept statistics after a fashion, counted the toll of the dead, watching the seasons and the stars and sudden fluctuations of barometric pressure – and it was true, groaning began in October, dying was done in a groaning rush whose parabola could be traced on a keening graph, rising steeply to infinity in the winter months and ebbing again in March. When the principal location of death shifted to the hospitals and the cavernous university clinics, traditional patterns of dying shifted too. Death was institutionalised, influenced by insurance premiums, the welfare state, the intervention of subsidised municipal establishments that squeezed the share of the private market. Maximilian no longer saw the next of kin, let alone their dead. He bargained on the telephone with the bulk suppliers, hospitals, morgues and life insurance companies, cutting costs to establish Hollmann Mourning Services in the mass death market.

Warehouses, timber yards and all production facilities were moved to the city outskirts, plots of land purchased speculatively with prior knowledge of urban development projects, branch offices quartered cosily alongside supermarkets and launderettes in suburban shopping malls. Anticipating the superannuation of congested inner-city churchyards and the rise in funeral costs resulting from land scarcity, Hollmann Mourning Services promoted attractive cremation packages at the reasonable rates made possible by accommodating urns vertically in numbered niches in mourning walls. Available either for lease or outright purchase – when paid for in instalments prior to urn occupancy they could be acquired at a spectacular saving – wall niches had the advantage over traditional graveyard interment that they entailed no additional upkeep. Hollmanns had undertaken the incineration of a certain Tillmann, a Protestant from Kiefersfelden, at the first municipal crematorium in the East Cemetery seventy-five years previously, but among Catholics the practice remained an inflammable subject until the Second Vatican Council absolved disposal by fire of unwanted doctrinal contamination. The superstition lingering on from a Christian aesthetic that found cremation distasteful was finally undermined by the more readily perceived fact of overcrowding. In twenty-four municipal cemeteries the earth had been hollowed out for more than a quarter of a million burial places. A thousand more were required each month. At two main sites of inhumation, the North and the East cemeteries, virgin burial land was now exhausted, rendering further turnover possible only by recycling occupancy of graves whose seven-year leases had expired and not been subsequently renewed. In the first year of the grave reallotment programme agreed on by an ecumenical council made up of members of the church, a municipal Graves Commission and the Association of Undertakers under the chairmanship of the director of Hollmann Mourning Services, the recycling of final resting places was implemented in no less than four thousand, three hundred and fifty-seven cases where the lease renewal option had been waived. 'A lack of piety? The ultimate interment of family tradition?' inquired an article in the *Evening Herald* under the tasteless headline DETERIORATING RELATIONS? when these figures were made public, concluding that 'the question must unfortunately be answered in the affirmative'. And shortly afterwards, when the National Health Board announced welfare cuts, including hitherto subsidised funerals, the *Morning Mail* more sonorously tolled the knell of the Christian graveyard culture in a vision of familiar marble and wooden edifices being replaced by the plastic crosses and cardboard coffins that were already in use in America.

Despite the many objective arguments in favour of a shift from atavistic inhumation to cremation and vertical storage – unsatisfactory hygiene, capital lying fallow in dwindling urban land resources – a pilot project Hollmann Mourning Services sought to initiate at this time led to outrage and protest. It advocated the indooring of terminal rest facilities in memorial malls on the analogy of closed shopping arcades: memorial malls would be used exclusively by subscribers whose coded grief cards could access the deceased with the same convenience they took for granted in any of the other services that might feature on an ordinary shopping list. Death, in short, must be modernised, and this began with the *semantic infrastructure*. A germ-proof terminology, as connotationally free of taboo and contagious superstition as was the memorial mall itself in comparison with morbid graveyard procedure, would be a prerequisite to changing underlying attitudes. *Encouchement,* a term first broached here as an alternative to burial, became the most famous euphemism on a list already betraying the hand-writing of the self-styled *encoucheur* whose visionary innovations would not however be implemented until a much later date. In a century designed as a mausoleum for a dynasty of grand exterminators, the undertaking business might be thought to have come of age. And yet the intro-duction of contemporary style into thousand-year-old ritual that still dug holes in the earth and consigned dead bodies to the unwholesome process of putrefaction was rejected on grounds of poor taste. Maximilian had underestimated the hypocrasies surrounding death, mechanisms of self-deception with a moral gratification whose motordrive was as powerful as any vanity. His blueprint for the memorial mall with coded grief cards, videograves and refrigerated booths accordingly went back into the drawer from which it had prematurely been resurrected. The modernisation of death was shelved.

Mourning Services diversified instead into business areas employing related technologies. Everything wasted, decom-posed, died. The faster the turnover of a product, the more urgent seemed to become the demand for a permanence factor as a coda to its natural life cycle. A new conglomerate, incorporated under the trade name Hollmann Storage Enterprises, grew up around the original nucleus of a refrig-erated meats syndicate and flourished like moss in a dank market niche. From obscure origins as a fly-by-night, trans-border operator, buying cheaply on East European markets and transporting venison, residual cadaver waste for soups

and broth bases, innards and assorted low-grade meats for
sausages in refrigerated juggernauts thundering west down
the empty highways of the night, the new venture devel-
oped sophisticated techniques of surface, secondary and
'deep-core' chill to conserve at varying temperatures for
varying spans of life more delicate commodities such as perfume essences, chemical solutions, blood, sperm, and a
broadening range of animal and human tissues for the even-
tual transpiration of knowledge in the medical and
pharmaceutical industries. Hollmann Storage redeployed
the know-how acquired by Mourning Services over three-
quarters of a century to offer market threshold services such
as packaging at one end which subsidised follow-up activi-
ties such as dismantling at the other; non-corrosive,
synthetic or weakly radioactive materials employed in the
former fuelled a parasite industry in the latter: Maximilian
perceived a harmony, a self-sufficient balance. With
computer-aided tooling, the analogy occurred to him,
cradles could profitably be turned out by the same lathes
and presses that otherwise manufactured coffins.

With Hollmann Storage Enterprises established alongside Linde and Hoechst-Frost as one of the big three in the
product-conservation industry, Maximilian at fifty found
himself absorbed once more by ancestral preoccupations. A
kind of mental technology transfer not unnaturally took
place when he reassumed active managerial control of the
Hollmann undertaking business. For here, too, the permanence factor as a coda to perishable life cycles suggested
possibilities of market leverage that had not as yet been
exploited. There were more people to die, but they were taking longer to do so and with signs of increasing reluctance.
The immortality of the soul as a religious conceit, a meta-
physical chest-expander stretched too far and too often for
the past few thousand years, no longer had much elasticity.
Old age now masqueraded with perfect dentures, only
somewhat grizzled and preferably tanned, as a serviceable

paradigm of longevity arrested at an indeterminate stage of middle youth. Extrapolating new vanities accommodated by new artifice – running, indeed, his own impeccably manicured hands over his well-preserved body in a sympathetic gesture of having put his finger on the problem – Maximilian could envisage a growing clientele that would find death more attractive given assurances of a qualified permanence of the body rather than some imponderable immortality of an unimaginable soul.

In the *Book of Hours*, a Hollmann heirloom he still treasured that had schooled his fancy as a child, immortality and the afterlife were portrayed in flower-bordered illustrations, inset with a broad white margin, which hung on the pages of the book like pictures on a wall. In this wall or maybe some other, there and not there, a wall that existed in a comparison, was a little door very easily overlooked but which gave access, once one found it, to the inner pages of the book, unfolding on a wary journey to a country behind his eyelids. Always there was a crossing, space or water, a chasm, a river, a threshold into a room that seemed to have no limits. In a Buddhist depiction travellers tobogganed helter-skelter down steeply banked petals into the corona of a flower. In mystic iconography pilgrims toiled blindfold through a maze of letters, hewn blocks as high as houses, quarried from the Lord's Prayer and strewn across a plain on the site of the everlasting city. An orthodox Christian view of the arrival in Paradise showed Peter scrutinising a queue of petitioners. Some were led off to the right to be bathed, anointed, robed and served a light refreshment. Others had their goods and chattels confiscated and were led off to the left to be thrown summarily over a cliff.

It was a view that terrified Max. Bald, sheer, sudden, stark – he rejected the Christian view through the keyhole of judgement and retribution. His instincts were pagan, sensual, softly graded as the monochrome illustrations of Graeco-Roman imagination in which streams were forded and oceans sailed, the crossing not that sharp hiatus of a sudden intake of breath but a gradual diffusion of light from transparency to opacity. Between different states of reality ran indeterminate borders, a hypnagogic no-man's-land where waking shadow slowly darkened into sleep, submerged life flowing on through porous inbetween to re-emerge like water strained through gravel. Pluto's kingdom was physical. The men and women who disembarked from the skiff and stood naked on the bank with fresh, expectant faces had died when they were young, their bodies unmarked by the ruins of age or the moral pillage of shame, bodies of athletes who had passed over unscathed and displayed their nakedness triumphantly.

The first nakedness that Max saw was in these pictures of the brazen dead. His curiosity was aroused as much by the men as the women. From the pages of the *Book of Hours* they moved into apartments, the makeshift dying rooms in hospitals, vaults in morgues for collection and interment between forty-eight and seventy-two hours after embarkation. He washed the naked dead with a sponge and delivered them in their best clothes. The earth was a womb, receiving the dead like seed to be hoarded in dark places; and after some mysterious gestation it began to sprout, the crop, the offspring, the dream of resurrection. Therefore the grave: a sealed secret, undertaking a promise of fertility. White, mute, prostrate, the corpses of his teens were the subjects on which he first elaborated erotic fancies. Images of the icy dead would later underlie his warmer embraces of the living, sometimes men, more often women. It seemed as if he had undertaken, with an impartial sensuality that was incapable of love, to bring them back to life. It seemed his doom to take measure of everything he saw in light by the shadow it cast. He could sit outside at a pavement café, adrift on the thoughtless illusion of an undying series of summer days, and freeze the surrounding sounds and colours with the involuntary realisation that all these people were future clients. He carried in his eye a yardstick measuring one metre seventy, the ideal stature for a pall-bearer, by which he infallibly judged a person's height to within one centimetre. In tall, sloping letters he noted funerals in his appointments book, drafted obituaries and engraved on marbled paper letters of lapidary condolence on occasions of bereavement, so many that in time he was unable to write longhand unless to pen a valediction. He followed the bond and the currency markets, the national budget and bank lending rates. Contrary to popular belief, the market mattered. The effects of boom and recession were passed on to the consumer, whose terminal decision to spend or save was duly reflected in his order books. To words like memory, peace or rest, to rectangles and receptacles for any purpose or of any shape, the smell of earth in spring and summer, burnt cooking, ovens, smokestacks, the skinny elbows of children or the bare feet of anyone, even to the announcements of departures at airports and railway stations – to all he responded with a rash of irrepressible associations. What did he do for a living? There could be no representation of the soul other than in imagery, in resurrection or metempsychosis as still physically appreciable presence. Elemental life, carbon atoms conniving to elicit perfume in a flower or stimuli in a crustacean, crossed and recrossed the narrow threshold of photosynthesis in interminable cycles of life. For him it was trapped in a diamond prism, always reduced to the same patterns. He collected art and antiques, curios, children's furniture and cased butterflies, pressed flowers, fossils and ladies' underwear, the imprisoned scent of life in things, anything; he collected things in which the soul had been preserved by the embalming fluid of art.

Maximilian was the king of the rain country, Candice by turns court jester, bedfellow, pander, never his queen. From an apartment in Ismaninger Street she ran an agency for Extraordinary Arrangements and described herself as 'The Total Work of Art'. Naturally Max was intrigued. He saw her ad in the services available column and called her up to ask if she could arrange him someone willing to make love in a coffin. Candice came herself, he installed her in a room furnished with toys and chaste white quilts for the swan-like teenage girl who had once been impersonated by his mother, Candice came and went. Desultorily on rainy afternoons boys arranged by Candice would sit in there with smooth thighs gleaming out of short trousers, virginal girls perch on the edge of the bed, licking ice-cream cones and budding precocious suggestions in novice adult underwear while Max crouched in the cupboard, scrutinising them through the keyhole. The Total Work of Art ran her hands through his midnight hair and ruffled the sad hauteur enshrined by laurels of now silver curls around his temples, mocking his seriousness, taking his money with one hand while she plied his funereal tastes with the other, dilated nonetheless (as so many women were) by the extraordinarily long white fingers of his sheet-winding hands, already singed by a sexual glow like an open wound on the surface of his skin, inflamed as if he had put a torch to a bush sometimes when he just touched her. Max needed Candice, her extravagance and quirkiness, bold surmises and provocatively shocking taste, the good humour that outshone his melancholy and the laughter that rampaged through his house. She brought life, she keyed up his slack appetites to some kind of expectancy. Compliant, susceptible to a degree, she still retained an independence untouchable by Max in the Ismaninger Street apartment where at intervals she disappeared to resume her own life. Surrounded by potatoes, large, round, real potatoes dusting off in sacks and rust-coloured alabaster potatoes ornamentally arranged instead of flowers, she swung in the moulded foam-rubber chair shaped like an outsize ear suspended from the ceiling, entangling her telephone in hanging drapes and swathes of tulle, criss-crossing the room as if a spider had spun a fantastic web, while she hatched her long-distance plots and made extraordinary arrangements for clients who might want to appear on the cover of a magazine or get married on top of a pyramid; an agile, gnome-like leprechaun, herself extraordinarily arranged in the wizardry of a double helix a Lebanese camel driver had interlaced through the eyes of a hunchbacked Parisian seamstress, whose shoulder-blades even when she lay supine never simultaneously touched the ground, to engineer at a fortuitous stroke one of the ugliest women Max had ever seen. She lived by her wits, enlarging artificially the natural deficiencies that most mattered to a woman, meeting them head on by the cultivation of a bizarre style and personality that made them seem deliberate. She teased Max with notions of getting an edge on his market by making death sexier. The Total Work of Art thought *encouchements* could be made more appealing by incorporating elements of fashion in still dowdy concepts of wrapping, more snappy and more commercial by shifting the venue to brighter surroundings with fun facilities under some such trade name as Deathneyland. He took her at her word. Dcathneyland was registered as a small-scale intermediate company, the third in the Hollmann triangle with Mourning Services and Storage Enterprises established at the base, with the aim of introducing the more far-sighted clients of the former to the deep-core refrigeration technology of the latter: a happy fusion of interests that the ambitious conservationist Maximilian had dreamed of all his life. When the commercial uses of holography began to be exploited on the market it was Candice who at once visualised its application to three-dimensional permanence of nearest, dearest deceased in living-rooms across the country, had subsequently sought out an agreeable subject willing to cooperate against a floral background on a pilot study completed only a few months before her unexpected death, coincidentally attending a retrospective viewing at a studio in Freimann on the evening Max walked through the door with a young woman wearing a bedraggled taffeta dress, chilled to the bone and soaked to the skin and still of a miraculous beauty.

There could be no representation of the soul other than in imagery. Walking down the avenue behind the house, he picked up a stick and threw it in a high arc over the river. 'A bird,' she said, watching it soar and plummet. The stick sank and reared back up out of the water, bobbed once or twice, found its level and merged with the stream out of sight. 'Fish,' she said, and turning some corner of thought she wondered why men wanted to throw things into water. Fresh her imagination and her imagery, guileless questions – sometimes Maximilian felt as if he was being observed by a child. She nudged his loss of the freshness of things he felt in himself. In the rain they walked to the weir and back.

His sleep was brittle, patchily frozen, a local anaesthetic. There were dream places where he fell through, waking with a jolt. Recently he had begun to dream he was his own client. He wandered through the house, emptying ash-trays. From a certain point onwards, on some untraceable map of his life, the sound of birdsong at daybreak, bright stabs of sound coming through the dark to celebrate light, filled him with unspeakable dread. He knelt in the warm wedge of light that opened with the door of the refrigerator, scanning the contents as if he would find there an answer, consoled although he never did. Having finished reading to Stefanie, he watched her for a while from the rim of what also felt like a warm wedge of light when she lay asleep, and thought to himself that at fifty he was a man who got up in the middle of the night to look in the refrigerator for an answer to which he did not even have a question, and no one with whom he could have shared that thought either.

'That's why.'

'Why what?'

'That's why he opened the refrigerator to look for an answer, because the question he didn't have was really the somebody he didn't have to share that thought with either.'

Stefanie leaned on her elbow and opened her eyes.

She looked at Max, but he had the impression he was not in focus, not even inside her eyes. He asked her if she was awake. She got up, and when he asked her what she was doing she did not reply either. She opened the door and went out. He followed her down the landing into the laundry closet under the staircase. Half a dozen of his shirts hung there on a rail. She slipped a shirt off the hanger, switched on the iron and began to press the collar. Max told her not to bother, the woman who did his laundry would deal with it in the morning. She acted as if he wasn't there. She pressed all six shirts, switched off the iron, went back to the room and lay down again, apparently still in her sleep. This first occurred one night not long after she had arrived at the house in Pienzenauer Street.

Two or three times something happened that induced in her this waking state of sleep. Sleepless himself in the empty hours before dawn, he eavesdropped on her sleep, talking softly to draw out the question that would magically rouse her to an answer. Unexpectedly then, as he sat and watched a spider spinning itself down from the ceiling to the maroon velvet curtains, she propped herself up on her elbow and announced in French, 'Ni son peuple meurant en face du balcon.' Max started. It was the line he had been trying to recall from Baudelaire's poem. Again she got up and went to the closet. This time she found no shirts there. He watched her fret and cry in her sleep, return to bed and shut her eyes. Max felt pity for her. He felt a pain in his heart, a thawing, tearing sensation, as if something caught there had been dislodged. For some time after she did not wake up any more. Max drifted back into his old habits, roaming the house, emptying ash-trays and peering absently into the refrigerator. But for several nights she began waking up again and then he understood the pattern. Not to things he said but to certain things he thought, the thoughts that hung in his mind long and intensely enough, did she seem able to respond, receiving them by some faculty she possessed in her sleep.

Max did not throw any stones in this water. He kept it to himself. Lightly she breathed in her sleep, he drew the curtains open and watched the moonlight shining on her arms. Laying his shadow across her mind, he slipped his moorings and stole out, drifting with the currents of her mind that could register a slight displacement of their surface where they received the shadow of the thought he cast. By moonlight Max imagined her embalmed on ice. He imagined her as the queen of the rain country; mottled her sleep, sowing things he imagined into the lining of her sleep, under cover of which she received his brood of thoughts and surfaced with a shoal of answers issuing from her mouth. She was a medium. He dabbled in her body, eliciting its answers, sighs, moistures, the secretions of her dreams. *I'll make you all mine*, thought Max, overestimating his power, and she awoke at once to disagree. He followed her into the closet under the stairs, where a thought crossed his mind to assume in hers a wholly unexpected shape. The shirts that hung in the closet belonged to Max, but she was not ironing them for him. She was ironing them for Brum.

When Stefanie had her hair cut she seemed to have surrendered something. A surface brightness had appeared in its place that fascinated his dinner guests. He glanced up at her across the silver, porcelain and glass to the end of the table where she sat, bright and chattering and flawlessly surfaced in a white dress, as if she were the living extension of these brightly polished things. Max parleyed with bankers and flirted in soft, funereal ways that excited their wives, laughed carelessly when the directors of companies who brought him their trade got drunk and exuberantly smashed his glasses, secretly despising them, their greed, their boorish manners and the stupidity of their lives, while with the other half of his attention he listened behind her brittle sentences for her other, submerged sounds, and realised with pleasurable surprise that they were accomplices in deceit. He watched her play these social charades, so deftly that it seemed natural to her, with a polished brightness in whose reflection men preened themselves, winking at images of their own vanity. For these masquerades in Pienzenauer Street, Czernak was disinterred from the basement and transformed into a butler, sinister, morose as in everything though he did it nonetheless, bound to Maximilian by hooks of steel ever since that timely trans-border evacuation when Czernak had impersonated a side of refrigerated meat, leaving him with the scars of a permanent chill on his hands and feet and an imperishable debt of gratitude to his benefactor. With a shudder Stefanie had looked down into the garden and seen him with a riding crop, teasing the dogs to rage until they properly savaged his padded arm and were rewarded with the bloody entrails that hung from a tree in a bucket. Maximilian liked to watch her when Czernak leaned over to pour the wine and his shadow trespassed across her face. Czernak frightened women, the fear remained even when he sought to detain her at the foot of the steps with his inscrutable interest in histories of South Africa, or wound a napkin more tightly round the bottleneck and silently refilled her glass. The versatile major domo was also keeper of the dogs, Max knew his sudden tigerish leanings and kept him on a tight leash. By instinct Stefanie knew them too – Max saw the shadow on her face – and there were many evenings, memorials and minor saints days in the busy month prior to the twin feasts of All Saints and All Souls when the master of the house was out and she preferred to draw up her knees inside the comfort of Candice's hanging ear. The women's talk hatched out there, Stefanie's part at least, was reported back to Max. He took a voyeur's pleasure in the disenchantments of people's marriages, a sybarite's single-minded interest in the ruthless, always temporary possession of disenchanted wives. These too, altogether compulsively, his private life a wilderness grassed over by professional encroachments, he laid out like so many corpses, buried in the maw of an unappeasable appetite.

A heart-shaped, silver-plated locket dangled from her neck. The locket began to irritate him.

Reaching into a drawer, Max found an invitation he would otherwise have forgotten, to a private viewing at Cartier's premises in Brienner Street. Arriving there from his office after a detour to the Catacomb in Oettingen Street, he found Stefanie and Candice already waiting, deep in collusion with a tiara of Cartier's gem-like guests who were admiring four or five million dollars arranged around the faun-like face of Danae, flown in from Paris for that purpose and contrived, with the help of cunning reflections, as an image only visible in an illuminated mirror. Max was taken with this subtle presentation and thought in passing, carelessly rifling velvet drawers with his sleek fingers, that jewellery might be shown to exquisite effect against the stark ambience of a dead woman.

At a reception in the Imperial Chamber of the Residenz to celebrate Tiffany's hundred and fiftieth anniversary, the king of the rain country in a grey suit with a white carnation strolled at large among eight hundred guests, artists and industrialists, politicians and princes, many of them graveside acquaintances whose families had been undertaken by Hollmanns for three generations. He observed the flight of rooms receding through the palace interior, where a flight too of sounds receded into inaudibility, as if an inescapable narrowing as a paradigm of *memento mori* had cunningly been incorporated in architectural perspective. Looking back when someone called, but this time not for him, he took in at a glance, with the chandeliers and tapestries and the broad sweep of floor already passed, the flash of his extinguished youth, trapped in a diamond prism, but this time not for him, this time for her, the light body colours of white opal, yellow, orange and red, petrified in fire opal and coruscating when they caught the light, or maybe darker still. Across the road at Tiffany's in Perusa Street a smooth man laid out on white satin a snake-like string of stones, smoothly-rounded surfaces not facetted but finished *en cabochon* to elaborate a reluctant gleam. Lustreless, opaquely mottled grey-black-blue and somehow blunt, the stones lay strung together in a necklace of black opal. 'Oh no,' she said, not so much to the necklace as to an emanation of cold and beautiful menace. Max said nothing, a ventriloquist in the background, for apparently it was the jeweller's advocate who said, 'May I, Madam?' his hands already at the nape of her neck to unclasp the heart-shaped locket. 'It's a talisman,' she murmured, 'I'd rather you didn't take it off. Although I suppose of course, I mean just to try the other on.' Her voice trailed off. Frozen in astonishment for the few seconds of what seemed a refusal, the assistant reactivated his fingers, unhooked the trinket and put it apologetically on Tiffany's counter.

To Max's irritation Candice returned unexpectedly on the Thursday evening from an extraordinary arrangement involving Moorish boys in Casablanca, slipping into Hollmann's box at the Gärtnerplatz theatre a couple of minutes after the bicentenary performance of Don Giovanni had begun. Stefanie smiled and pressed her hand. Candice appraised the cut of her black satin dress, slit Chinese-style at the thigh, shoulders bare, bust lifted and compressed, and the dark collar above. The two women whispered. Max watched her lean forward, a hand raised to her throat, whispering to Candice and fingering the necklace of black opal while Don Giovanni killed the Commendatore. Dawn broke, on the set of seventeenth-century Sevilla the lights rose and Max breathed the smell of stage dust and felt the richness of the music unravel to a point of burningly simple desire surrounding the blueish vein in the crook of her arm. *Madamina, il catalogo è questo delle belle che amò il padron mio:* in the seventeenth century a Spanish chambermaid with a brace of white breasts pursed as she leaned out of a window to pour slops into the street; in the eighteenth a courtesan reclining in Prague, smoking a cheroot, a mole on her cheek and a cat between her legs; in a wing-mirror at traffic-lights only yesterday in Prinzregenten Street a girl rising from the seat of her bicycle: forms of women remembered or imagined in a rich instant, brief, at once and entire, were reassembled in the curve of neck and shoulders and the loveliness of these white arms. He smelled the stage in intermittent draughts of powder, cloying perfume, sweat and dust leaking from the wings, and felt again that thawing, tearing sensation as if something caught in his heart had been dislodged at last, as if all longings had been summarised here in an object of desire beyond which there would be no other longing, no words beyond Giovanni's *è confusa la mia testa, non so più quel ch'io mi faccia,* which he murmured in accompaniment – and looking down into the pit at the rows of faces raked in darkness he felt dizzy, got up and opened the door to the cool air of the corridors while applause began to ripple behind him. In the interval Stefanie poised her glass on the edge of a circle of his acquaintances, gilded patrons of the Friends of Opera Society in Bogenhausen, coolly sumptuous with her Gioconda face. Something had gone out of it, Max saw there an absence. A bell rang a second time.

Candice did not return after the interval. Max sat on the sofa in the shadowy recess of the box as the lights came up on a stage street. *Lasciar le donne?* He put his finger on the blueish vein in the crook of her arm and brushed her neck with his lips. A screen descended from the flies, the street evaporated in darkness, shadow deepened in the nook of the white breasts that rose and sank beside him. A woman began singing at a window, other voices crossed and intermingled, opening the back of her dress he encountered a memory of Krines, luminous welt in darkness, a strap taut across her skin. He leaned forward and breathed her skin, traced her shoulder-blades with his tongue, the warm clasp with his teeth, a corner tearing the inside of his lip and mingling a taste of blood with the perfume of her skin. Undid the clasp and put his hands into her body. Eyes closed, in the images there of what his fingers felt he envisaged the flesh of her hips, flanks, breasts as smoothly spanned as the inside of a tent, her nipples spread and frosted, erect with a hard ache between his fingertips. Disarranged in her dress, the exposure of her a white sheet of scar from the nape of her neck to the small of her back, breathing faster with flared nostrils, lips parted in a face where the Gioconda's glaze was ruffled, desire rose sheer off her skin like a broad warm breeze. In the slits of her dress, tailored for what other purpose, he inserted his hands, stroked her knees and palmed her thighs while she sat bolt upright and stared ahead, black satin riding up her legs and bunched at the waist, hands staunched in her lap where Max ran his thumbs in the grooves of her groin, through the warm damp fabric his fingers sought out her sex – *in quali eccessi*! – slipped down her panties and prised open her cunt. She lay an arm round his shoulder and half-twisted herself onto his lap, her body askew, soft slumberous weight of woman, a thigh sprawled across his knee, a breast riding clear of her bodice and unburdened against his cheek. He grazed the nipple with his teeth and eased his fingers inside her, leaching a viscous flow between her legs. In brief darkness she caught her breath. With moist fingers he leached her crotch, she shuddered, seep of her in warm effusions flushed the insides of her thighs, a diffuse blueish sheen clarifying as slowly crescent light illuminated a cemetery. *Che bella notte! è piu chiara del giorno,* the recitative of Giovanni and Leporello warmed by the moisture of her tongue in his ear where she whispered something indistinctly. She drew back her head and smiled, a gaze came off her face that surrounded him like a slow warm breeze. Timely her hand, *per la mano essa allora mi prende,* his cock stood in her hand like a candle. She came astride his lap and slid down on him, images overlapped, an equestrian statue and the rhythm of her riding, rising, sliding on a greased maypole, white faces strained in the auditorium to catch secrets muttered in dark rooms, the swing of her full breasts and the necklace at her throat, flow, river, flow of a river slowly rising, what other woman had he ever loved, by what comparable music surrounded, gaze that came off her, feel that came off her softly like a slow warm breeze, beyond her the Commendatore advancing, a blasted voice issuing thunderously from a ruined face. Max felt the charge as a numb flash detonating deep inside her. While the audience applauded she rearranged herself leisurely, emerging on his arm immaculate in her fur coat and chatting with someone outside the theatre. The following morning Brum's exhibition at the Catacomb closed after a month, and twenty-three paintings, paid for in cash by a purchaser who wished to remain anonymous, were delivered as instructed to an address in Pienzenauer Street.

All Souls

LUCAS SLIEP

So there he pook then, the man the image maker our hero Lucas Sliep. He doodle in the foyer of the Sheraton Hotel on a Saturday night, yawning in dudgeon and feeling dravid, if not to say downright skaulked. Humperdinck say she have fixed it with manager for pics to be nailed in Miss Blomquist's suite. Ho ho. Hedda Blomquist, the prima donna? None other. The glutton jemmy with the quadruple voice. Hedda Blomquist here? In all her overweening fleshliness, trailing sixteen suitcases, indeedle. Mr Eklund, being the tour manager for the Scandinavian Operatic Art Productions, say ten minutes to powder the Blomquist nose and skiff her wear for atomic pics. Ho ho. Half an hour. An hour. Sliep called up. Eklund come down, pour gravy in person, smoothspeak and sundry PR burble in magnum technicolor handouts. And only, if the truth be told, because an abject groveller in the fanasy garble of Wagner horrorshow, particularly as rendered by the cyclonic Blomquist vocals, did hero Sliep wait two hours to slubberjohn supremo arpeggios of that famous flesh fandangled in close-up.

All this waiting while viz foyer parked within easy con. To

and fro the tireless panascenic headlights swivelled, tracking hotel slummers.

Units in all formats, the total product range.

Druids being delivered by the busload, see. Grizzles trogging on sticks and gargoyles doomed in dodo gear. Weenies, skimpering, still in short wear, and dons with jemmies moneyed out in flash wraps for the Saturday night gloat. Ho ho.

A meisje teetered by on high-heeled toots, her milkshakes churning in full swing.

Scorch!

— Doo do da duh di da doo ba ba pa —

Sliep drum his chips, tip-tap with his shovels. Electronic melody tinkle. He check his wrist. Longines show her pussy with parted shanks at eight o'clock. Lucas, lord of Saturday night? Selfsame, with luscious green curls. Power, eh. Sex. Gloat. Razzle in wallet, truncheon rodding in leggings. Video of that meisje with the quadruple milkshakes did it. Hero lit a menthol dreg and spread his muscled shanks. Feel tall, feel very very good, almost like that bimbo on atomic yacht in sexy dreg ad. Fuck Miss Blomquist. File expenses and call it grief. Change of wear in chariot. Purple shovels, silk Valentino spic. Drain a Drambuie and tune up on sonics in Cafe Megalomania. Con over likely clefts, dairymaids with long golden gloss etc etc. Scoop same and dither to unresisting swoon in disco dreamland prior to trojan shafting. Saturday night, in briefs, as usual.

Tapes of mindspeak tickered on, plotting pending gloat.

Therewithal while mindspeak tickered merrily in gloat mode, hero hefted adidas and headed townwise through revolving door.

— Oops! Beg pardon.

Incoming unit nibly squashed as hero shouldered out. Jiffily he conned him sideways spinning squashily through glass: a whisky don with glutton chassis, a champion porker at risk of mincemeat when rashly processed through revolving doors.

Caution, feckless doughnut!

Better broadwise, fatso!

Sliep snickered in silent hoot. Ho ho. What a comedian. And instantly his mindspeak blew a fuse. Not a micron more on ticker tape, mindspeak dodo, all screens blank. Our hero stalled, yea verily, as if he had been unplugged.

Comedian? Fatso?

That seemed to bleep a memory node indeedle. Rapid retrieval reviewed a billion bits before he had time to blink and spewed out Porker verified okay positive, Porker on-line loud and clear. Stage name? Unscrunchably. Bit before though, something Porker.

Fetch!

Trip tip pet spat spit pep pop sop strap prat Porket, piglet Porker. Name yes, not of fish or swine, name of unit with piggish something before the Porker, curly, quirky, pigtailish.

Hair mode or rear-end mnemonic?

Ticker ticker tapes on full retrieval system while Sliep retraced his steps conningly and mindspeak whir whir backwards through revolving door a tic, a matter of mere nanoseconds.

Where now was something Porker?

Fatly with fatman tread he splodge, shovels splayed to starch his balance. And once felicitously in motion, he take off like a mechanical toy. Waftily on Persian pile his gurdy little trotters twinkled altogethe with alacrity. Swear to dog. Chassis sped over foyer floor as smoothly as a hovercraft.

Sliep hasten after while mindspeak whir whir. Something Porker erstwhile host of freakvision horrorgiggle-nd-joke show. Remember? Ouite a telebrity in his prime time, what, five or six orbits ago, his first name rhymed with teat.

Teat porker.

Disgusting, lugubrious smudge of milkshake blubbering on male Blomquist. Scabby indeed. Now what in boodle was that name?

Nimbly with twinkling fatman trotters he patter-potter

down the stairs.

— Piet Porker! Hey, Piet!

Why now did Lucas hover, mindspeak in two modes? Mode One read abort and proceed at once to Cafe Megalomania, Drambuie, sonics, honeysuckle, total wallow and tyro gloat. Mode Two read Piet Porker, verified okay positive on line loud and clear but not compatible, viz.

CARDINAL EXECUTION ERROR

Something untoward here. Somthing quadruply hairstand, even beyond mindspeak. It lurk. It have menace. Intrepid notwithstanding cellarwise hero descended. Very droll. Saturday night in otherwise churning fullswirl Sheraton and down here not a slummer, not a single unit in sight. Empty corridors. Faintly the noseprick of floor polish. Snickily a door snik shut. Seemingly on dreamline and cold flow of weird dream that goosed his flesh in actuality Sliep coasted along corridors to all intents and purposes on automatic pilot. Conference rooms, he conned, and beyond the Mandarin and the Willow Rooms another door without a name, just a poop specknibly hero had overlooked but for the shimmy placard on which

Hollmann 75th Anniversary Celebrations
Please come in

was blackly finelined in tombstone letters.

Sliep comply. He do.

Thereupon he seemed to topple into a megadrome the size of night. He look around for truant wall, obfuscably he find none, and as his gleamer got accustomed to the scurvily thrifty wattage hero video black drapes that give the drome this swart appearance of aircraft hangar makeshift night. Gloom decor, moreover, streamers shredded like horses' tails, wire scorpions and papier-mâché crabs, Montogolfier ballooons with baskets containing incense and dusky artificial flowers hung dreadnought from the ceiling. Ace of spades! More in keeping with atomic horrorshow than snappy celebration binge.

Fluorescent bands wafted longwise down the drome, white tablecloths, soaking up the spare wattage and levitating out of swart like magic marker lines. White spics, too, veeshaped under sacs and casings, here and there white toots of jemmies squirrelling across the floor in luminous flashes, swarmed as if in glow-worm clusters eerily around the drome.

What a video. No poop show, by no means. Haemorrhage gala with a megattendance of at least a thousand units.

Where in all this weird bevy was Piet Porker? Or was the question doodled on a corner of temporarily erased mindspeak not so much WHERE as HOW?

But now a don with draffish quelt, gimbling a snip too smugly, got up on stage and begin to gabber. Somewhere a wattage technician perk up at last in all this gloom and put a spot on the don, revealing presto alderman Strunk from the municipal board of public works. Overhead halogens suddenly sparked on and ping! ping! ping! one by one the aisle chandeliers showered gleam. Wheee! Cascades of instant snow frozen in the night ceiling. Rapture units raved. Benignly Strunk gimbled, smugly he raisc a fin. Ho ho. Doughnut Strunk presume the units rave raptured for him. Error. In point of fact the gala scoff had just been wheeled in. Dispensing serfs began to ladle gruel from steaming cauldrons, meisje twinkled in and out between the tables while units smarge and raved. Conning them over, one earphone plugged into Strunkspeak droning on and on about the wattage problems, Sliep now wit himself surrounded by selfsame congregation of druids he have video being funnelled by the busload into the lobby of the Sheraton Hotel while he sat awaiting the Blomquist pleasure.

Cheapo gruel, very, dumplings and beans, but how greedy these druids were — eh? — as if this was the ultimo scoff.

They slobber, drool and smatch and clamour with greedy
druid cries for more. For all the smatch and slobber din
throughout the drome a unit could hardly audio Strunkspeak
Stagewise Sliep sidled therefore between the aisles of
scoffroar, the old smatch-smatch of masticating druid jaws
and dinning glockenspiel of spoons to catch an alderman
word or two, in passing con the guests for clues as to the
wherewithal of this doom anniversary hero have stumbled
into by cardinal execution error. Seemingly on dreamline
and cold flow of weird dream he schlenz through smatching
uproar, scanning table cards inscribed indeedle with jaunty
names like Morning Dew, Mount Pleasant, Friends of Peace
and Floral Grave Services where seated ah yes surprise surprise a pulk smattering of telebrities cheek by jowl with
actors, opera singers and local heavies, consul Kiep and
count Castiglione in cahoots with Bertie Butcher and con-
sortium of refrigerated meats, syndicate bosses who ran the
slaughterhouse quarter, plus a deep spread of sinister dons in
spivvy dinner casings and moreover members of unidentifiable enterprises whose general drift, however, was piling up
in Strunk's glibspeak despite the smatching uproar as plain
as plain could be. The clans had gathered to honour the
Hollmann dynasty for seventy-five years in undertaking matter on behalf of the municipality, of grave interest to one and
all: seventy-five years in exemplary service of croak.

Nobody say croak, though, what with all those druids
parked in the drome in their glamour wear and having themselves an atomic gala time. Strunk don't say so, glibspeaking
in his capacity as inspector of public works etc etc. Nor did
the don who now come on stage to cash in a parchment and
scabby medal Strunk drape on him in honour of quadruple
services he have rendered.

This don was pope, king of cats. Spic with ruffles and
patent zak shovels. Scenic headgear and pulpit voice, as tall
and slim as six o'clock. Total projection, in short.

— Friends,

he boom, and audio out after one dirge syllable that spook the drome. He wait. The don have presence. Unscrunchably he know how. Units left off their puddings pretty smartly. Even the druid hubbub was overruled by this premier organ. And sonorously into this dead silence don Hollmann drove a wedge of voice, a piledriver.

— Croak is among us,

he singsong hymnally,

—Yea verily, even here and now in this happy drome!

This was a spine tickler, a real threat to the old underjaggers, coming just after the scoff, some of the druids burped and had a quick guilty video round. The don laid on this croak stuff with a trowel, all wrapped up in pulpit jargon and delivered basso profundo — creepy, to tell the truth. And then he changed gear, gabbing offhandish about pricks and stings and quandary things and how they could all be taken care of by having quadruple

I N S U R A N C E !!

This was the commercial bit.

The don tuned up into baritone for the wisecracks, began to sound quite jolly. Just give old croak a pook in the snoot was what it boiled down to. Frankly hero had to shake his head, in admiration his luscious locks, at the don's cyclonic salesmanship. Not that he printed out croak by name, but croak it was, as ever among us, only this time round don make him sound like everbuddy's pal, a chummy old codger with a totally overran horrorscope. For which he had proof.

Scorch!

Turkeygobble and druid clamour up and down the drome.

Hero too extend earflaps and audio in, hero too have vested interest. The Hollmann cat snap his chopsticks and in nanoseconds the wattage drain. And on stage — ?

Indeedle. On stage the Evergreens twang a few sonics. Pope awash in purple light goes into routine emcee gab,

lazen chintz, frenzen druids assembled here (he bray), pree-
zenting at last etc etc. and in a twinkle hero did not con from
where, this jemmy number Voice Beyond stood parked
beside the don on stage.

Swear to dog, the static crackled in that drome. Dons
slavered and licked their chops slap-slop only the sound as
saliva plonked wetly in the aisles where the druids drooled.
Trifle overbodied for mental magic number? Perhaps. As
mental as marinated peaches, ho ho. Hero craned, one and
all craned to get a lick of this gloat jemmy. Pope snap her
gleamers shut, puts his voice in bottom gear and gab like a
talking tomb and in two tics he have her tranced out in a
state of total zonk.

Now what?

Pope gear down again to doomspeak and the Evergreens
pad back in Da duh da duh, da du da da da duh da da
doooo-diddally-da duh with the theme sonic of the Pink
Panther spookily on base instrument. The king of cats with
purple spic in spooklight prowl up and down and begin to
dirge about absent friends and ineffable being beyond hoary
croak and how the Voice have access on account of being
plugged in to a medial switchboard that would relay mes-
sages, and in short: were there any questions from the floor
of the hynodrome?

Yer!

A fluorescent gargoyle waddled in to purple looking pretty
zonked herself, shedding in addition a dram or two of grief.
The don chinned her up with a suave intro and after a general snivel launched snappily into the act. Who is it we want
then, dear? Hipp, Conrad, former tax collector, resident with
his spouse Amelia at 64 Teng Street, whose arrears these pas
four years collected, in default of life, in a shady marble vault
under cypresses hard by the wall of the East Cemetery etc
etc. — in short Hipp make a sensational vocal appearance in
the mouth of the Voice Beyond who yes indeed surprise surprise is none other than Brum's jemmy. Old Hipp don need

asking twice. The voice retched and gargled a bit when the tax collect trod on her adenoids, but out he came he did, in dribs and drabs from the corner of her mouth like synthesized gob magnified through woofers, a sort of throat-clearing overlaid by a yucky sound of custard spooling at ultra-low speed. Formerly of 64 Teng Street, Hipp must have been a morning smoke even in arrears and speeded up, the custard centrifugally in place, he came over heavily catarrhal. But where was he beyond croak? What, above all, was it *like*?

Thin on the ground and not all that much to it anyway on account of it not being there. It? Well—trogs, veebies, you know. Plurps. A companionable quark or two, skeeting furlishly drauwise, otherwise not at all. There was something garbled about photosynthesis and the looming shadow of a snail's horn when clean in midspeak Conrad Hipp went off the air.

Wheeee! In the drome the units smarge and rave. Yea verily, Amelia quaver, unscrunchably it was spouse's voice that croakspeak from Beyond, buff on medium if matt on message—and as druid jemmies are wont she boohoo trojan buckets of grief. At pelting spank the Voice then do a drowned meisje, a kid with a cleft palate and a truck driver from Giesing who took off a bridge and drive himself straight into croak. A cyclonic act, totally unreal. Hero not a fool, though. He flick his headlights, scanning drome and stage wings for short-wave transmitters, concealed mikes, back-up gear for hollow numbers, and none at all he con. The act was quadruple, pristine. Not that the Voice deliver much on croak. It's *how* the Voice deliver that grab the units, give dons one and all pause for gravy gloat. In chinky wear the jemmy chassis squirm and shudder purple, milkshakes swell, straining vocals groan—and out rumbled a truck driver in bottom don gear. Transvocal switchboard! Total freak show!

This pope was stereo. He have the druids flabberdrabbled. He have to cool it. He do. Creamily with popish soothe he coded in the pulpit mode and crooned a prayer. Croonily with fins folded prayerwise he dirge for absent friends — yea, yea, absent friends, prayerwise the druids too warbled in the drome while hero glimmed a dreg. Friends less absent than you think. Pope cut the croon and pressed a button. Behind him fluorescent curtains opened. Yonkers! The Evergreens, all ten of them, stood weirdly on a balcony serenading a floodlit gargoyle in polka-dot wear — hero dropp his dreg. Hero have video this gargoyle in the polka-dot wear corpsed out in her casket as croak as croak can be when he do interior with flowers a month ago at selfsame druid's funeral.

Liselotte Pfaffel, none other.

Hero drop his dreg and hairstand, paraplegic slubberjohnnd. Swear to dog the druid jemmy walked and talked and tend her weeds clip-clop with audio shears and bouquet of yellow stinkers in her fin, walked in fact with atomic nonchalance through the corner of a double bass and the tenor saxophonist's knee. Lucas foreconned, in brief, what pope now began to speak.

— Fear not,

he gimbled, for mighty dread had seized the druids' minds. No, this was not Liselotte Pfaffel risen from croak but nibly an image of same, reconstructed with coherent light, viz. continuous-wave and pulsed laser beams, illuminating a photographic plate etc etc. and giving you the whole message 3-D, namely: a hologram. The don rant on in this continuous-wave vein and gradually the druids get the message three-dee, it hit them smack between the twinklers. Hollmann have conquered croak. He bring all druids tidings of continuous-wave joy, either by leasing for home use or on subscription to the holothek.

Liselotte P. do him a quadruple ad. She chit and chat and auld a bit of lang syne and the druids streamed with grief, even hero had a snivel. Swear to dog those yellow stinkers stank, they seemed so 3-D real. After some more waddle and cuddle she reach the tether of her hologram and toss the stinkers out, the laser beams switched off and Liselotte P, disintegrated short and sharp, polka-dot wear, see-through concrete balcony, the whole caboodle, stinkers snuffed in mid-flight and a meisje tripped on stage in toga wear, bearing more of yellow same for real as consolation hand-outs to flabberdrabbled druids, the Evergreens skifflewashed a slinky playbach sonic, crooning in veteran mode Croak, Where is Thy Sting-a-ling-a-ling? — while gouty grizzles and gargoyles eager to frisk their ancient toots began to dither glacially on the dance floor.

Lucas logged his longines now narrow-clefted on eleven. What next? Exit surely, the gloat was over. But thirst and throatmost he crave a dreg and a drambuie. And at some such juncture — lounging, namely, at the bar quaffing a treble splat and tonic with Johnny Seb in skifflewash tiptoeing up and down the old arpeggios while dreamily the druids dithered, hero too groped dreamily for bowl of golden crunchies beside him on the counter — he slot his fin unwittingly in a creamy bowl of cleavage, palpably jemmy's milkshakes.

— Oops! Beg pardon!

The jemmy mirthed, sounding off a quadrophonic honk. She seemed a jolly sort of mutton, totally mirthed hero have mistake her milkshakes for bowl of golden crunchies. He video indeedly as oddly a jemmy as he have ever conned: a dwarf disguised as a clothes' stand, her ultragear hang round her chassis in multi-coloured strips, too long, in short, and nibly spatched. Gimbling, she paw him with her compatible, come-on gleamer. Lucas sniff here a snuff with gravy slot. Dredge me, her headlights seem to twinkle, oil me, her chassis clamour, barcharming in glamourous wattage and at short notice they do a dither. Candice is the meisje's label. While shuffling to Evergreen croon and skiffle crotch by crotch she tinker slyly with his bells and truncheon, it swell, clack and dong. Scorch! Already the jemmy have her fin inside his leggings and Lucas say, in as many words, as he edge her off the dither floor, his hovel, though humble, have capacious horizontal amenity to garnish trojan shafting.

Away, away, come away with me!

Away from knell of druids, old bones whispering in eerie drome!

Away on the stroke of midnight while still unshattered the neveragain glass slipper of dancing youth — !

The druids plead with outstretched hands. Seemingly on dreamline and cold flow of weird dream Sliep dislodged their importunities, their burrs and greedy tackle, treacle of reluctance, a smear of druid envy he feel starchly under foot, seemingly astride a nightmare hero horrorwade, treacle-footed the bride stumbled, escaped —

For Piet Porker, surely — ?

(Whom, fatly with fatman tread, shovels splayed to starch his balance surely hero had seen splodge, whir and take off felicitously like a mechanical toy)

Surely Piet — ?

And then the Fog.

But first by still ample starlight the detour to Ismaninger Street. Quick, quicker oooh hurry she tattled, succulent, keening onamenolescently ho ho, not even up to her apartment, not even as far as that, at the first turning on the stairs he strobe her snatch and pick her purse one-two, one-two, prod the bauble agape on the banister. Everywhere awash, plump and chortling jemmy with quadrophonic honk, telltale spillage in her mouth, gravy in her shanks and warm wet inundations, viscous ooze, funfair body flooded, meadows flooded and floating maidenhair, from lusty jemmy glands all her ample skin awash, gleegirl, jolly mutton! Ho! Oh! In the well of the stairs her gurglings, awash with mirth, mirthful and conspiratorial the truncheon wipe on sleeve. Briefly in her hand she held hero's pulsing snail, ebbing with his shrinking horn, retreating on his slime. With no small satisfaction she pocketed hero's cock and hoddled with a smile, her crotch purring, on genuine leather upholstery of his chariot as Lucas gunned the Isabella with torrid blast into the small-hour silence of thickening city fog. Disperse, felonious wraith! Fuck off! Sliep power beamed halogens, flurried salvo on klaxon, they advance through white, whiter, whitest murk, arriving at the twelve-storey tenement in Guardii Street it must've been after one o'clock. Here and there a whiter blur — windows still alight? — in the jigsaw puzzle of the night, Lucas probe cautiously Candice tetter, clop-clip the hard-edged echoes fly up tinnily from under shovel, toot, bouncing up and down the twelve storeys of the white-enshrouded stair well where high, high above a startled jackdaw wheels and caws. Spooky! The jemmy shiver and brack, a bit timorously, if hero believe in spook. Hero larf. Believe in spook, ho ho! Come hither juicy jemmy, into my laser trip-beam parlour. Video the automotordrive spontaneous image-generation apparatus. Eye of camera waiting. Day and night surveillance. Lucas supersleuth, archspoekenkieker! Believe in? Spook *live* in this apartment. Documented moreover, composite computerised images, synthesised from thousands of exposures. Hero zock her the family album; Sliep and cohabitant spook, simulated in photo-doc. Candice snigger. All she video is a smear. Pages of apartment wall defaced by blob, Lucas pointing, looks like spilt milk. Spook indeed. Hee hee. Milky smear, transparent ruse. She spiflicate his spook. Hero stretched out on his canopy and crashed. Remember? (Remember nothing. Remember waking zoned in darkness when popp-arra-pa-pop-pop-pop-pht! the laser trip-beam spark a synchronised flash and if that wasn't a spook his name was Piet Porker, which was a point, because at about this time five, six orbits ago Piet croaked while having his picture taken, poleaxed, a heart attack, keeled right over into the pig's knuckles at a telebrity binge in the Hundskugel, Hotter Street, at the very moment Lucas Sliep, on an assignment for the *Evening Herald*, released the shutter —).

Journal of the Great Fog

PLOOG'S DREAM

Ploog dreamed he was driving back to Munich on the Salzburg autobahn when the police stopped him for a breathalyser test. They told him to leave his car and walk the rest of the way. But instead of arriving at Ramersdorf, where the motorway ended, he found himself in Schwabing on the old salt road from Salzburg that approaches Munich via the North Cemetery.

The Local Editor of the *Evening Herald*, Conrad Sartorius, was waiting for him there. Ploog should consider, Sartorius said, an appropriate turn of phrase to link the motorway with the former salt road for the convenience of the many dead readers who wished to come back to the city for the feast of All Souls, but had difficulty finding their way. With a seasonal readership that was largely dead, Ploog would have to adapt his style, the Editor was implying, or he would lose his job.

Ploog was anxious to waste no time and set about this task immediately. The salt road led directly into the cemetery, but the gate was locked, and Ploog did not possess a key. Fortunately, at this juncture, some acquaintances came by. The actor Hans Gugglhör happened to be on his way home from a performance of *Brandner Kaspar*, in which he played the part of the Bone Gleaner, or Death. Gugglhör was accompanied by one of his colleagues from the play, the archangel St Peter, who lived in a house overlooking the cemetery and was able to furnish Ploog with a key. Ploog asked the actor if he would mind accompanying him, as he did not care for walking through graveyards alone at night and would feel infinitely more at ease if escorted by St Peter; to which the gentleman laughingly agreed. But it was on their way through the cemetery that they witnessed a very strange occurrence. They saw a tombstone levitating at an appreciable height above the ground and laid out, like a table in readiness for some ghostly feast, with horned cutlery and pewter ware, all of which was illuminated by the light of the votive candles that were burning there with a perfectly steady flame.

Ploog took leave of his companion and returned to his lodgings at 3 Lederer Street. As he turned down Reichenbach Street, shortly before midnight, and looked back in the direction of the river, Ploog saw broad bales of mist rolling down towards him from the heights of Bogenhausen, and felt encumbered by a sudden unease; an unease that mounted as he set off in the opposite direction, only to find himself overtaken by fingering swirls of that fog he thought to have put safely behind him. The night was still, and yet the mist seemed to be hurried on by a great wind, accompanied by a hissing, as of some gaseous emission, although he was cognisant that the production of sound could not be accounted for by any of the innate properties of fog. Yonder he heard the bells of Old Peter as they chimed midnight, ushering in the first hour of All Saints; and recalling the belief of the ancient pagans that the Feast of the Dead commenced on this day, he was seized with a dreadful fright. But arriving at the column of Our Lady in the square by the Town Hall, and taking comfort from this sentinel of the true faith, Ploog put aside his fears as being the progeny of mere superstition.

On awakening the following morning, Ploog looked out of the window and thought at first that some scaffolding had been put up around the building and hung with white sheets such as are employed for the restoration of old buildings; till he ascertained it was no sheet, but fog. And putting his arm out, he found that he quickly lost sight of the tips of his fingers, so thick was the fog.

Ploog threw on his clothes and hurried downstairs, sensible there would be a great commotion in the *Herald* offices on account of the fog, and enough work for a dozen men to do. But at the house of Beck, the milliner, on the corner of Diener Street, thinking to enter the underground and to attain by this means of conveyance the main station, whence it would be but a short walk to the premises of the *Herald*, he found a concourse of people milling at the entrance, unable to move either up or down; so great was the press. A bystander told him that on account of the fog the underground was closed, and all traffic above the ground had also ceased. The people were witless, for they had to travel to their employment, and could not.

Ploog forced his way through the press with no little exertion, instructing the guard at the gate that he was here in the office of the *Herald*, and would bring a piece on the fog in his journal; and demanded admittance, that he might do his business. So the guard opened the gate and admitted him, and descended with him to the tunnel, where instead of an inky darkness he saw only an impenetrable whiteness; for the fog had gained access even here.

Whereupon Ploog struck out on foot in the direction of Karl's Gate; and having once broken his shin on a flowerpot, proceeded thereafter with the utmost caution. For on his way he saw nothing, neither the shops he knew to be on either side of him, nor the great landmarks of the cathedral of Our Lady and St Michael's church, nor even Karl's Gate through which he passed, drawing in his head, though he knew the arch to be a full twenty feet above him. And recalling his boast in the days before the fog, that he knew the town so well he could pass through it blindfold, he was ashamed at such idle folly.

Thus far it had taken him a full hour to come a distance that otherwise he covered in ten minutes, and in this way, almost faint from his work, he reached the premises of the *Herald* in Paul-Heyse Street; a building ordinarily with a very dismal prospect he found much improved by the fog. Not so his own hands, which were blackened and quite sore from their encounters with the masonry of the city's walls; for he had made his way as much by the intelligent inquiry of his hands as by the mechanic propulsion of his feet.

Striking the glass of the porter's kennel, he heard from within a joyful baying, as of a dog surprised by his master's arrival home; and put his ear to the grille to receive whatever intelligence its invisible occupant had to impart. The poor man had been marooned in his box since the last watch of the night before, and had exhausted his provisions entirely; and still there was no relief, though it was three hours past the appointed time. And he beseeched Ploog to bring him a quart of beer and a plate of cakes. Ploog assured him he would presently. But meanwhile what news? The porter told him that throughout the night there had been such comings and goings as he had never witnessed before; men and women, quaintly attired in antique costumes, as if they had been at carnival, but which he knew to be impossible, for it was not yet the opening of carnival season by some ten days. And shortly before the inundation of the fog two gentleman had come, who had once been employed in the offices of the *Herald*, but he had not seen them for many years; and yet they were familiar with him as if they had taken their leave only yesterday, and brought him a liver pastry from Dallmayr to eat, remembering his fondness for savoury meat pies. These gentlemen were Julius P—— & Conrad M——, the porter said, and had been Editors on the *Herald* when Ploog was apprenticed there in his youth. They told him they had made shift in other countries, and later, parting company, had spent a long time in foreign countries, and now at the last they were come home.

At this Ploog uttered an exclamation, and was considerably perplexed, knowing what the porter said to be true, saving in one item: since ten years these former colleagues had been dead, poor Julius of a fever in Mocambique, Conrad of a fall from a mule in the mountains of Peru; but which the porter in the horizons of his kennel could scarcely know. And pressing his face to the grille with some urgency, he thought to solicit the porter for that token of their visit which must have put the matter beyond doubt; namely, the liver pastry they had brought him from Dallmayr. But the foolish man said he had ate it, and peevishly entreated Ploog once more to furnish him with a breakfast.

A curse on your cakes and ale, thought Ploog vexatiously. And marvelling at the greedy dullness of this fellow who had eaten the evidence of his meeting with a ghost, he opened the door and went quickly in.

In the newsroom he discovered a cabal of his colleagues, half a dozen or more, in the main these being Foreign Affairs, Arts, Sports, Home Politics and Economy, who were drawn into a circle around a pot, very busy with molasses, rum, lemon and hot water, in short, with making a punch; and showing no inclination to be engaged with any other work.

'Ho whoa!' exclaimed Ploog, in the rough manner of a man directing a horse, which the Editor used when coming suddenly upon his staff, but to his chagrin their complacence was not ruffled. Ploog asked if the Editor was yet in. 'He is in,' replied Arts, trimming lemon peel with a pair of nail-scissors, adding with a smirk: 'and this work is authorized by him in consideration of the drubbing administered us in coming here through the fog.' Approaching, Ploog saw indeed that all their hands were besmirched like his from handling of walls; and what he had taken at first to be steam from the pot was nothing other than vapour from their clothes, where the fog had lodged and now sought to escape. Whereupon, contemplating his own person, he found fog smoking wispily at elbow and knee and issuing from his cuffs in stertorous blasts, like plumes of steam from a ship's funnels.

'Pfui!' protested Arts, observing the density of these emanations; while Economy, having calculated the quantities of fog Ploog still had about his person, requested him sharply to remove himself to another part of the room till he had completed his drying out.

Otherwise there were but two men in the entire building, *viz*. P. Breul and the student Harald, at Ploog's own Local Desk; and these two assiduously at work, scanning piles of news items sent in by the commercial agents on subscription and by the municipal offices gratis. Ploog was astonished at the foolhardiness of the young man in coming the great distance from Schwabing through the fog, which Ploog reasoned to be on account of his desire to impress the Editor with his keenness; so immoderate was his ambition to encumber himself with that profession which Ploog would have gladly laid down.

'Ho whoa!'

Surprised in the midst of this guilty reflection, Ploog turned round with a start, assailed by the malicious chuckling of his colleagues. For meanwhile the Editor had entered the room with his magnificent, time-saving stride, and stopped a little way behind him; still bearing, on the lobes of his ears and at the corners of his eyes, soapy vestiges of the *extempore* shaving he had done without a mirror at the basin in the privy. Now he stood and surveyed the spectacle of Ploog, leaking steam from the perforations of every fibre, with the satisfaction of a man who feels the fresh smoothness of his cheeks; and knowing, in addition, that he was

quite dry and clean of the fog himself, having slept on a
divan in his office that night. 'The fog evidently fuels your
appetite for work,' the Editor said, taking advantage of this
dryness even in his speech, 'for I never saw you here at this
early hour in such a *combustible* state;' which was a poor
enough sally and must have dropped at once into the obliv-
ion it deserved had obsequious laughter not sustained its
leaden flight.

After more such pleasantries the Editor took his seat at
the head of the round table, with Home Politics and Foreign
Affairs on either side, and the others according to their rank;
the lowest of these being Sport, who faced his chief across
the celestial plane, being aligned with him on the same
meridian. And at once the Editor broached the conference
with a leading question: whether to continue, or discon-
tinue the production of the newspaper under these present
circumstances of the fog.

This question elicited from his staff all kinds of response
excepting an answer. Avoiding his chief's gaze, Sport peered
under his armpit, as if expecting sagacity to extrude there,
Arts ran his finger tunefully around the rim of his glass, and
Economy began taking copious notes; a sham industry from
which Home Politics and Foreign Affairs were precluded by
the proximity of their interrogator, who must have fastened
at once on whatever nonsense they had written on their
sheets. But this waiting was a mere game to accommodate
their chief and his fondness for the rhetorical question;
knowing he disliked the interjections of others in the proportion he relished the sound of his own voice. And sure
enough, having allowed that measure of silence sufficient to
establish his superiority, the Editor opened to them the
answer, counting it off on his fingers point by point (which
Ploog noted):

item: there was no news but fog. Dispense, therefore, with
foreign affairs in their entirety, the great lack of fog in the
rest of the world being as pertinent to their own circum-

stances as to a drowning man the intelligence that others are not drowning on dry land;

item: ergo, local news became the main, and the paper must be refashioned as a Fog Special;

item: yet even in the atrophied state of a mere broadsheet or bulletin, the production of a newspaper made little sense without also some means of distribution. For this purpose they might resort to the remedy of hiring students as vendors to carry the sheets from house to house, if students, and houses, could be found;

item: commonsense, and all the axioms of economy, advised against production of the *Herald* under these circumstances; they would produce it nonetheless, because this morning the *Mail* had already gone to press with a contemptible brochure, designed as a fog fold-out, for orientation about the city.

'Here here!'

The approbation of the conference was signalled by a rapping of knuckles on the table and a stamping of feet on the ground; Breul came forward with the agents' reports for their inspection; the Editor lit a cigar, and they proceeded forthwith to the day's business.

But of the day's business, and the business of several days thereafter, Ploog would learn very little, for a conspiracy of reasons that has yet to be unravelled.

The very first report that now came on the table concerned the disappearance of Bustelli's sixteen original figures of the commedia dell'arte from the royal porcelain manufacture at Nymphenburg. How to determine the precise nature of the untoward happenings? This task was assigned to Johannes Ploog; with a coverage of such events attendant on his journey as might be fit for inclusion in a miscellaneous *Chronicle of the Fog.*

J. Ploog baulked. To undertake a journey to Nymphenburg in this weather was folly, he said; and besides, he had already given his word to be present at two social occasions that morning, a reception for the Compagnie Ris et Danceries from Paris with their *Bal à la Cour de Louis XIV* at Gasteig, and a competition of cocktail shakers at the Crest Hotel, which must be given precedence. Arts maliciously inserted that Ris et Danceries had cancelled; and the Editor subjoined sarcastically that if a man felt able to travel to applaud the gyrations of cocktail shakers in the east, why should he not travel the same distance for the edification of observing the potter's wheel rotating gently in the west?

To this Ploog had no good answer.

Over this matter they might have remained at odds had the student Harald not stepped forward and offered to accompany Ploog as his guide. He knew the road to Nymphenburg pretty well, he ventured, having passed that way many times. The Editor at once climbed on to the back of this offer to establish himself in the saddle of the argument, assenting to free Harald and give him to Ploog

The young man laid out on the floor a row of articles he had brought with him that morning, *viz.* a walking stick, a torch, a compass, a map, a length of rope, a pair of firm shoes, a firework, a thermos, biscuits, chalk, and more of this kind; and checking them against an inventory, stowed them in a sack, which he slung over his shoulder. Observing with astonishment the ritual of these preparations, Ploog asked him where he had learned such thoroughness, and was told he had learned it in the army. But Ploog inclined to ascribe it rather to a family trait of pedantry the young man evidently shared with his cousin, the bookseller Hieronymus; for Ploog, too, had served in the light infantry, yet saw the necessity of no more provision for a walk across town than his pigskin gloves and gabardine coat.

Thus they set out, turning left into Paul-Heyse Street, crossing Bayer Street and continuing straight down the gentle slope that led into the tunnel. Harald went ahead, employing his stick as blind men do to obtain intelligence of the road in front; a faculty in which he possessed such marvellous dexterity that Ploog soon fell behind, and was forced to call out to him for fear he would lose him. His voice echoed in the tunnel and rebounded boomingly from the walls, startling them both greatly; but after their first fright they were so delighted, and comforted by this magnified perception of themselves, being mutually invisible each to the other, that they continued to holler and thunder throughout the remainder of the tunnel, as if they had been children discovering the game of echoes for the first time.

Emerging from the tunnel and turning left into Arnulf Street, Ploog again fell behind, and they were obliged to consider a more efficacious means of consolidating their progress. Ploog suggested the expedient of holding hands. His young friend judiciously reasoned that to proceed other than in single file would double the surface area of their exposition and thus, likewise, the risk of collision with hazards in the fog. Ploog had to concede the logic of this argument, and asked him what he advised. This, said Harald; and after some moments of absence in the fog he came back and found Ploog and put in his hands the end of a rope, which he had fashioned into the noose of a halter, to lead his companion by.

With Ploog in tow by means of this device they now proceeded at a wonderful rate, leaving the Post Office administration building behind them, and crossing the road when they had come about level with the Augustiner premises, which Harald could place exactly by the sound of his stick rattling along the fence of the brewer's garden; being the only piece of fence on this side of Arnulf Street, he said, from here to Thunder Mountain Bridge. No longer able to contain his grudging admiration for the ingenuity and dispatch of his young friend, Ploog inquired of him how he had come into the possession of such nice knowledge of what must be the dullest street in town; and how he was able, moreover, to find his way through fog with such facility.

Harald answered that, as to the first, he had run errands up and down Arnulf Street in earlier years, as a jobber for the many departments of the postal administration located there; and as to the second, it had long been a spleen of his, which he could not well account for, to walk with his eyes shut on his perambulations through the town, thus acquiring a degree of dexterity at navigation by feeling instinct rather than by sight. Upon this, Ploog fell silent, musing that the idiosyncrasies of that family were even greater than he had hitherto supposed, but that it ill became him to deride as lunatic a conduct which fog had turned to such excellent account, and of which he himself enjoyed a main benefit.

At this moment the sound of human voices crept faintly into his ears, and with joyful relief (being a man of a gregarious nature) he knew that no longer were they entirely alone in the Great Fog.

'Hallooo!'
he called. And after a while answer came gutturally to them out of the fog:

'Är hlöchlør!'
or to that effect; in a tongue with which neither of them was familiar. Harald conjectured that it might be the language of Turks; while Ploog, extrapolating his meagre knowledge of ancient sagas he had acquired in the opera from programme notes, inclined to the view that they were here dealing with Norsemen.

'Hallooo!'
he trumpeted again; and Harald set off, his stick sliding whackily along the slats of the fence with the screech of a distempered xylophone.

But this time there was no response to Ploog's salute. He adjoined Harald to leave off that jiggery-pokery with his stick, for strangers in a fog must be frightened into silence by such a horrid din. So they stopped and listened; and still hearing nothing, Ploog thought to encourage their trust with sounds approximating to that language he had briefly heard;

which he found he could most easily resemble by a rapid evacuation of phlegm from his throat. This device met with immediate success, eliciting from the fog an excited colloquy, heavy with that same catarrhal infection, and quite unintelligible.

Courteously Ploog greeted the strangers, telling them his name, and that of his companion, and inquiring how they came to be abroad in the fog; then asking them, if they understood his language, whether he could help them in any way. The strangers answered fluently:

their names were Olaf and Eric, carriers from Scandinavia,

who had left their country on Thor's day at the first quarter moon, and come a great distance inland from the coast, bound south with articles of freight;

swords, spears, helmets and horns for drinking mead, costumes for a score of warriors and their ladies, contraptions to effect thunder and lightning, and a great deal besides;

these being the properties of a company that would arrive presently to give a cycle of plays in the city, and which they were to bring to the depot in Arnulf Street, in accordance with their letters of conveyance;

but on reaching the yards at a late hour on Sun's day they found the place empty, and no sign of the agent who had contracted to underwrite the freight;

then this Fog had descended;

since when they had neither seen nor heard another human being, walking up and down for fear of losing their way, until they had given up all hope: but now, at the last, it seemed they were saved.

This narrative they declaimed in a sort of liturgical plainsong, taking it in turns to chant alternate verses, which they did with that native skill of a people born to the legacy of a great oral tradition, albeit in a nasal keening, monotonous and rather lacking emotion. Likewise, when Harald furnished them with biscuits and coffee, which they acquitted with crunchings and a whole diapason of neighings, it was difficult to find in this register any indications of heartfelt pleasure. But ever mindful of his obligation to strangers in his native city, Ploog offered to accompany them and find accommodation, though he knew of none in Arnulf Street. Harald said the nearest lodgings must be at Red Cross Square, in the hotel of that name. Olaf, or Eric, being indistinguishable in the fog, repeated the name and exclaimed;

'Yo!'

emphatically, with more garglings and whinnies. So they set out, the ballast of the two Norsemen distributed around the middle part of Harald's rope, Ploog bringing up the rear with a great deal of chatter.

On account of the meeting with the Norsemen and the detour thereby imposed, Harald soon lost his bearings entirely, and was obliged to ask his companions to search the wall of the corner building for the sign with the name of the street they were in. This they did, hand over hand for a distance of some twenty or thirty yards, in the manner of men reading braille, but without success; till it occurred to Ploog that these signs were often affixed to the wall as high as ten or fifteen feet, which in this fog they would never be able to discover.

At this impasse, when all their progress seemed to hang by a thread, the Norsemen exclaimed and set up such a commotion that the others thought they must soon fall to blows. And indeed, they beat each other about the head, but with words, for they were knocking out an idea. Olaf was a giant man, explained Eric, a hand's breadth under seven feet, a true Norseman, and a carrier besides; so their guide should mount him and stand on his shoulders to search for the sign that was surely above them. Ploog clapped his hands, Harald seized his torch, and Olaf set him on his shoulders as if he were a child, holding him up to the wall; where Harald quickly found that precious evidence they had sought in vain, and descended to the ground amid great jubilation.

Now firmly on course down Thunder Mountain Street, they resumed their journey with appetite, snug in the prospect of present relief in the tap-rooms of the lodging house at Red Cross Square, where they arrived a little after noon. But to their mortification the place was shut. Here they fell into such despair that even the voluble Ploog ran dry.

In the silence that followed this dire discovery Harald pricked up his ears, alerted by a sound of tapping. Moving towards the origin of this sound he involuntarily echoed it with the same impact of his own enquiring stick; and tipping to this other tap, tip-tapping, parrying the precedent rhythm, a fellow tapster elaborating, parleyed in counterpoint for the length of coincidence with an unseen partner's sounds; from the left, from the right, drips of moisture, eaves of fog, from all sides concurrent tapsters, sticks divining, reiterated the tattoo, overlaid tip-tap and terraced sounds in smatters of light-percussion fugue. What was this bustle at Red Cross Square, folk travelling through fog as busily as if it were broad day?

'Ahoy!'

called Harald, slowing his pace, for the likelihood of collision with these nimble inmates of the fog seemed great; whereupon two or three of those closest to him stopped and inquired if he needed help. Not a little astonished, Harald dropped his stick, and casting around to find it, was directed by one of the voices to reach about a yard on his right side; where indeed it lay. And to his jest that he knew a cat could see very well in the night but had never yet encountered a man with such sight in fog he heard them reply: fog or no fog, it made no difference to them, being accustomed to measure the world entirely by sound, for they came from the Neuhausen home for the blind, and had never known anything by the light of their eyes.

Under the broad editorial rubric, A Chronicle of Miscellaneous Fog Items, Ploog here began to fashion a piece in his mind on unexpected good fortune brought by fog, to be illustrated by the case of the blind. He asked them to furnish him with some matter, which they did, and Ploog noted on the impromptu tablets he always carried about his person, *viz.* the cuffs of his sleeves.

The blind said the fog had brought them cause to rejoice. To those who could see it must seem as blindness; whereas to the blind, being no impediment, it was as if by proxy they had acquired sight. For now the blind could help those with sight, which in the fog was none; by fetching their keepers to the home and bringing them back to their houses; by making purchases and running errands and carrying what was necessary for survival into the besieged homes of Neuhausen. With the assistance of blind guides, shopkeepers were again venturing into town to open their stores, doctors to their hospitals, and many others whose urgent business took them abroad; which they knew with certainty of Neuhausen, for since the coming of the fog they had run to and fro on such business constantly; but not here alone; likewise their colleagues in Nymphenburg, Gern, and great parts of Schwabing, everywhere those skills that compensated their impediment were being turned to wonderful account, in Haidhausen and the Au, Ramersdorf, Giesing and Bogenhausen, the ears of the blind were giving the city its eyes. *Earsofblindgivecityeyes*, concluded Ploog on his last inch of cuff, and filed this article with its headline ready-made.

Kindly the blind inquired if they were in need of services other than news. There would be no more lodging houses in this neighbourhood, they said, but if the Norsemen could make shift with rough accommodation until the fog had passed they would be glad to offer them the hospitality of the home. This remedy was welcomed by all. With many warm assurances of the friendship between their peoples, the Norsemen took their leave of Harald and Ploog, receding into the fog until there was no more sound of them.

Having brought the Norsemen to this conclusion, these Good Samaritans could now resume that undertaking on which they had set out. Their blind companion recommended to them the smooth pavements of Nibelungen Street, which ran as straight as an arrow to Roman Square. He could bring them on their road, he said, as he had subscriptions to carry to the apothecary in Winthir Street, where Nibelungen began. Harald owned he did not know this street at all, and sought his advice on some technical matters, as mean height of kerb, stick range between kerb and wall, unexpected hazards, *viz*. refuse bins trees &c., and the number of intersections he must count from Winthir to Roman; while Ploog followed obediently on his leash and held his tongue, for all this stick lore was beyond his ken.

But once their guide had left them and they entered alone the silent fog of Nibelungen, Ploog took up a tale to divert their spirits; which had come into his mind by association with Norsemen, he said, and was reinforced by the coincidence of finding himself in a street bearing this auspicious name. And he began to tell Harald of

fish-tailed maidens with flaxen tresses and white bosoms,
who guarded a hoard of gold on the fabled river-bed of the
    Rhine;
and how it was stolen from them by Alberich, high-bassed
    Nibelung.

Having attained the first junction, and verified it to be Renata Street, Harald asked Ploog to adumbrate what sort of creature a Nibelung might be. Ploog's knowledge on this point was not precise, but he believed Nibelung to be the name of some legendary tribe. 'A family name, then,' continued Harald waggishly, 'such as Ploog?' Unhappy with this comparison, Ploog let it pass for the sake of resuming his story, which he did with Wotan

the father of the gods, awakening on a mighty mountain top,
and contemplating the castle there built for him by the giants,
Fasolt and Fafner, in exchange for Freia, goddess of eternal
  youth;

but now the giants, apprised by the fire god, Loge, of the
theft of the Rhenish gold, prosily coveted the hoard instead,
causing Wotan and his fire chief to immerse themselves at
considerable inconvenience on a journey to the bottom of
the river, where they confiscated Alberich's magic helmet
and turned him into a tortoise.

Here Harald laughed very heartily, saying this was the
most ridiculous nonsense he had ever heard; and breaking
off to log their itinerary, as they had now reached the second
intervenient road, confirmed they were still on course;
indeed, could scarcely get off it, more mythology lurking at
the next corner in the name of Nimrod Street.

From the obstinate wake of silence now following him
Harald saw he had offended Ploog, and penitently begged
him to continue. Ploog admitted that the narrative might be
of less account than the music to which it had been set; for
this Nibelungen matter he was telling was in truth the stuff
of a sublime opera in four parts; whereupon Harald suggested he omit that part dealing with the helmeted tortoise
and hum the intermediate action, till they might resume
with the white-bosom'd maidens, or some other engaging
piece of narrative. This Ploog did, evoking the themes of
Rheingold and the *Valkyries* in a panoramic tenor hum (inter-
posing *recitativo* Alberich's curse on the ring, and the
metamorphosis of Fafner into dragon-guardian of the gold-
hoard), till he had hummed his way into the third part of
the tetralogy, where Siegfried slew the dragon and discovered Brünnhilde's scorching beauty behind a wall of fire;
while Harald, anticipating imminent darkness behind an
ashen wall of fog, was beginning to wonder anxiously if
Nibelungen would ever end. As they left Rheingold Street
behind them, the clock of St Stephen's opposite struck four,

and Ploog, hoarsely sounding Siegfried's horn, ushered in
the Hall of the Gibichungen, treacherous murther, and the
twilight of the gods; and by the time Nibelungen brought
them at last to Roman Square, fog-curdling night had
fallen, Ploog's tale was out, and his voice dispersed
altogether.

It now being too late in the afternoon to proceed to the
palace of Nymphenburg, Harald proposed finding quarters
for the night and continuing their journey the next day. He
saw no other remedy than to apply to cousin Hieronymus
his mother-in-law for accommodation at her house in
Monten Street, which from Roman Square was a trifle of
ten minutes in clear weather, but in fog six times that space.
So bidding Ploog to keep up his spirits, sunk very low since
exiled from his voice, he groped his way north until he had
sounded Roman Street, where he turned east once more
into the suburban wilderness of Neuhausen. And good fortune must have been his guide, for he found Monten Street
at the first attempt.

Pulling the ancient bell-chain set into the wall of the lodge
outside Little Monten Castle, to alarm the inmates of this
unexpected visit, Harald opened the side door within the
main gateway, which shuddered and yawned greeting on its
hinges, much frightening Ploog. Inside they found candles
in glass jars laid across the courtyard floor, winking out one
by one with every step they took and extinguishing again
behind them, as if guiding them along a moving carpet of
light. In these welcome candles Harald recognised the good
housewife's forethought, open-hearted Constanze, whose
voice he already heard ahead of him, calling her youngest
daughter's name.

'Dotty? Dottily?'

And to his disappointment he was thus apprised that he
would not find her at home, which had been his true purpose in coming here; indeed, of accompanying Ploog to
Nymphenburg at all.

Constanze chattered off at once. Since the eve of All Souls, Dotty had not been home, she said, with no word either out of Haidhausen, where she had gone to amuse herself with friends. Harald did not care for this mention of Haidhausen, rank with a rival's smell so sour that even here it seemed to offend his nose. Did she know, perchance, he inquired faintly, if among those friends there was one Alexander, who lodged in that part of town? Constanze assenting, Harald fell to brooding what indoor amusements would keep fresh for two days while bawdy fog, by turns pretext, alibi and pander, kept watch outside blind windows; the mere imagining of which was so offensive that he could not yet forbear wrinkling his nose.

This did not escape the housewife. She asked them plainly if they were troubled by a pungent smell in these rooms. Harald owned there was a smell, though not yet pungent, perhaps; while Ploog whispered that by the judgement of his nose it seemed very pungent indeed. Blushing now, Constanze apologised and explained her calamity, which was that in October her father-in-law had taken to his bed in the tower room and not stirred out of it since, as Harald surely knew; but since a fortnight his enfeebled bladder had begun to leak in such profusion that she was constrained to swaddle him three times a day. Yet the worst of it was that since the coming of the fog she was unable to open the windows to air the rooms, and was obliged to live in smell.

Ploog listened to the housewife's complaint with useful attention, for this was an aspect of fog he had not yet thought to cover. Imagining the stale effect of six pairs of unwashed socks without mitigation of air in his own lodgings, he compounded the fumes that must now be accumulating in the city's bedrooms, kitchens, privies, beer houses and newspaper offices in their entirety to extrapolate a secondary or domestic fog of quite impenetrable density. *Pfui!* And with his handkerchief to his nose he inquired of the housewife if one could become so accustomed to living in smell as eventually to ignore it.

But at this moment they were interrupted by Martha, who appeared from the stairway to the tower room with a bowl of porridge in her hand. He had refused his porridge, she told Constanze, and demanded truffles, but she had changed the old man's linen, at least, and weaned his extravagant appetite with a flask of milk. She evidenced no surprise at the sight of Harald, or curiosity at the presence of a stranger, or how and why they had come here through the fog, but continued to ventilate the subjects of bowel movement and stinking bed linen as if unaware of their presence, or of there being any other topic of conversation in the world. So the two heroes, big with the adventure they were unable to deliver, waited in silence while the womenfolk unravelled the old man's matter until it was quite threadbare.

From behind Ploog, at last, came a more welcome clatter, not of Constanze's nimble tongue but of the house marshal's provident hands as they levied a regiment of plates from the garrison of her cupboards, armed them with cutlery from an arsenal of drawers, and led them out on to a plain deal table to engage with pickled herring, cheese and ham. Harald at once set to with a careless appetite Ploog envied; for that acid pervading the rooms, which he inhaled with every breath, likewise embalmed his pleasure in his victuals. More to distract himself than to amuse the company he gave then an account of their wanderings through the fog, commencing with the porter at Paul-Heyse Street who had eaten a singular pie brought him by ghosts (here Martha exclaimed), the stranded Norsemen and the light-footed blind and how he had lost his voice in Nibelungen, and concluding with the vanished porcelain at Nymphenburg that was to be the end of this goose-chase; all of which, for lack of voice, he shrouded in a strained whisper correspondent with his weird tale, drawing the colour from the ladies' cheeks as unremittingly as Harald evacuated the housewife's supper and exposed the whiteness of her unburdened plates.

Tong!

As if tolling the knell of Ploog's tale, a bell sounded a hollow chime that seemed to come from the tower room. Ploog thought this must be the importunate old fellow upstairs, summoning his truffles; but his hostess declared it was the strangest thing, at intervals these past two days a bell had rung though none was there, nor had ever been, saving in that part of the castle which had once been a chapel. And this was only one of the most curious events that had come upon them with the fog.

On the Sunday morning she and Martha had gone to her husband's grave – God save him! – to lay a wreath of evergreens and to light candles, trowel out the weeds, put bulbs in for the spring; which Constanze did, while Martha went to fetch water. And then— And then, reiterated Martha, on the way back to her stepfather's grave she had passed a man, conveying a doughnut to his mouth with one hand and carrying a jam jar in the other, which she thought he must have purloined from the side of the grave; for it resembled exactly the jar of quince her mother had left for Stefanie. And looking from the jam jar to his face she instantly recognised her step-father – *Tssschiu!* – Martha rocked back and forth – as close to her as Harald's face across this table, in the dark blue worsted suit he had worn into his coffin ten years ago. Then he had gone. 'Gone,' whispered Harald, 'how gone?' Gone transparent around the middle and disintegrated rapidly to the extremities, up from his chest and down from his knees, just stockinged ankles and boots kicking up the gravel and the hat still hovering over receding ears, thin air between heels and crown of hat, dissolved in his entirety within seconds. *Pouf!* 'And the jam jar?' interposed Ploog. 'What of that jar of quince?' Jam jar dissolved too, sniffed Martha, gone from the grave under her mother's eyes, who had apprehended nothing. 'Martha sees with her faith and not her eyes,' Constanze reasoned, admitting some doubts as to her daughter's vision, notably in the matter of the doughnut; which she thought rather to attribute to the whims and fancies of her burgeoning condition.

'Very curious,' said Ploog, when Constanze had finished, though in truth he held it to be an old wives' tale. He would gladly have stretched out there and then on the couch beside the stove, for after his exertions in the fog he was immoderately fatigued. But the women were reluctant to exchange company for the solitude of their bed-chamber and bound him to the after-dinner table with more of these hoary tales till the clock in the tower of Little Monten Castle struck eleven, when by and by they went to bed; Harald very readily to a provisional cot in Dotty's room, Ploog to his couch, where he slept soundly till the following day.

After the good housewife had furnished them with an early breakfast, they set out once again through the fog; and this was on the third day of November, the patron day of the lord of huntsmen, St Hubert, by the grace of God, who would reveal to them their quarry in Nymphenburg as surely as he had divined the crucifix in the stag's antlers, Martha said; as indeed he did, a little after nine o'clock by Ploog's profane timepiece. The fog seemed lighter now, suffused with more of day than previously it had admitted, though no less dense, and thus they made their way as if down shining corridors that led secretly through a white maze, crossing the canal beyond the weir in the gardens of Nymphenburg, till they reached at last the Marstall, in the southern roundel of the palace. But the place being shut, Harald rang the bell and Ploog set up a great commotion, to elicit from the interior some sign of life, which at length came down to them from a window in the form of a very vigorous cursing. The voice above them rumbled and grunted, like some ancient engine; and after an interval of minutes, having descended to the same level, grunted at them again to step in quickly and to keep out the confounded fog.

With bloodshot eyes and breath awash with drink, tousled like a dog emerged from the matted kennel of his sleep, the Keeper of the Marstall locked the door through which they entered, turned wordlessly, and set off down a high, gloomy hall, slippered heels scuffing the floor, the keys at his belt jingling; past traps, dog-carts, coaches, equestrian gear and travel accoutrements, horses' plumes and harness that in the wake of the Keeper's jingling keys echoed memories of all the processions gone out from those royal stables; and up flights of stairs, where the Keeper twice paused to catch his breath, into vaulted chambers lined with vitrines of faience and porcelain, one empty, where the Keeper now stopped and wagged a chiding finger, clacking his tongue.

Tse tse tse tse tse tse tse!

Exhibits gone from this case here, enquired Ploog briskly. The old man nodded. And exactly when had they been stolen? Not stolen. Just up and gone. Absconded from under lock and key. Which must have been Sunday night. Absconded, began Ploog, crossed it out and wrote: *Disappeared in circumstances unexplained.* Nothing broken? A door forced? A sash prised open? None. What articles missing? Sixteen figurines of the commedia dell'arte from Bustelli's original casts. Lucinda and Harlekin, Lalage and Mezzetino, Colombine and Scaramuz. The keeper recited sixteen names by weary rote. Price of such a figurine? Estimate of Harlekin, for example? Priceless. And copies? Copies by the chequered score, porcelain descendants of the father cast through a hundred generations. The Keeper shook his keys and sparked a shower of sound. Anything else? Yes, said Ploog. What was Keeper's judgement in this matter? Keeper had no judgement. Kept to himself. A foggy affair. *Foggy affair*, Ploog noted, and wondered what else to ask. Again the Keeper jangled his keys, reminding the two gentlemen that he was at their disposal whenever they needed to be shown the way out.

That was surely the most ******** piece of humanity he had ever met, that Keeper who was none, Ploog communicated to the fog, where they were deposited once more after a quarter of an hour. Indeed, came Harald's voice, substantiating his presence, these were very small pickings after so great an endeavour. And they repaired at once to the porcelain manufacture in the northern roundel across the way from the Marstall, in search of more matter to eke out Ploog's column.

But the master potter at the porcelain manufacture was such a garrulous fellow that Ploog soon wished himself back in the oasis of the Keeper's taciturnity; one of nature's schoolmasters, who cannot see a layman but must educate him before he lets him go, beginning at ten o'clock in China with porcelain made from petuntse, and not embarking for Europe until eleven, having quarried enough feldspathic rock to pave the highroad to Nymphenburg, Ploog reckoned, and convey them speedily to the matter in hand: when Harald, evincing more of his studious keenness, must foolishly inquire into the nature of soft-paste porcelain, spinning them off on another orbit through Florentine enamel, unglazed base and ground glass, from which they had still not returned by lunch.

An hour later their schoolmaster reappears, patting his lips with a napkin, and having digested in the interim two or three centuries besides; for he resumes in the present tense with Nymphenburg biscuit porcelain, reminding Ploog unpleasantly of the dry meal gleaned from Harald's sack while the potter has been more profitably engaged with his napkin. Biscuit porcelain, says he, because fired without a glaze, which he drew to their attention to avoid misunderstanding regarding the liability of colours to fire away at high temperatures, or dissolve, namely, as was the case with underglaze painting. And here was a great mystery. How could colours disappear from overglaze painting on porcelain fired at low temperatures? Not just colours, but entire designs on plates that went painted into the kilns and came out white. Ha? And straightaway the potter led them into a gallery resembling a greenhouse, where the culprits awaiting firing stood in racks along the walls.

Here was Scaramuz, cutting a caper with his shapely calves on a saucer shared intimately with Colombine; Corine deep in her perusal of a love letter, surprised by the tedious Anselmo on a cream jug; Lalage storming across a plate to box the ears of the masked pierrot, Mezzetino; and wasp-waisted Leda, drawing up her skirts to flee the Capitano, petrified in a never ending chase around a tea-cup – four couples, Bustelli *fecit*, confined for all eternity in porcelain intrigues illustrating a commedia dell'arte dinner service. But in that oven which otherwise ensured their immortality they were of late incinerated, extinguished inexplicably without trace, as had already happened twice this week; which the potter invited his visitors to verify for themselves when the kilns were unloaded that afternoon.

Ploog's curiosity now aroused from its lethargy, he waited with Harald at the manufacture till four o'clock. And everything came as the potter had said. A dozen overglaze floral designs and pastoral scenes emerged from the kilns unscathed; Bustelli's company alone had quit their service, leaving no imprint on that whiteness where once they had figured.

And all these things happened as set down by Johannes Ploog in his celebrated *Journal of the Great Fog*, during the week beginning on the eve of All Souls, which was believed to be the week of the dead since immemorial times. Only the author himself, discounting the evidence collated in his own writings, would have no truck with second-hand superstition that disabled reason with imagination, hoisted the dead out of their graves and embellished inanimate matter with soul.

On leaving the pottery as darkness fell, Ploog and his

young companion again saw themselves constrained to seek lodgings for the night; and nowhere more eligible for that purpose than with Master Brum, who had recently carried his household to Nymphenburg. The former hunting lodge lay a stone's-throw from the pottery in the palace grounds, but with no access to the highroad, hidden behind such a labyrinth of paths that it was difficult enough to find in daylight, and in fog as proverbially evasive as the philosopher's stone. Indeed, it is for the main part a rural area, lacking lights, pavements and the familiar conveniences of the city. Thrice they went adrift; and Ploog, by his own admission a poor countryman, having taken a ducking in a stream and become entangled in a thorn bush, refused to go any further. Yet even in this critical pass Harald knew a remedy, exploding the incendiary flare he carried in his sack; in which burst of light he saw enough to take his bearings. Thus they arrived at Master Brum's, who was not at home; whereupon Harald put his hand into the third branch of the stag's antlers above the door, and retrieved the key from its hiding-place, as Martha had surely foreseen. No sooner entered than a fire kindled in the hearth, a grog brewed, his poor colleague Ploog huddled in blankets and set shivering by the blaze, plucking his thorns, till the liquor made him merry and the ague passed. So they talked, drank, snoozed and drank again, Ploog continuing to pluck his thorns late into the night, until he was entirely smooth, and at some point levitated out of his smoothness into an interlude suspended between wake and sleep; when the sideboard in Master Brum's kitchen springs open and a pair of scissors steps out.

The prima ballerina teeters forward on her points and executes a dainty *pas seul*, flashing her long legs in a stainless performance complete with splits. Four sets of cutlery follow from the drawer, knives paired off with forked ladies in a stately quadrille, to which the dessert spoons beat time; while three horn-ware egg-spoons, a partner short, lean their shafts against the teapot and watch. Candlesticks group for a conga; whisks, ladles, ill-sorted drawer-dross cobble together a mazurka and shake out a shimmy, an upbeat corkscrew anticipates the twist. Ploog is drowsily amused and wishes to applaud but finds he cannot reach his hands, spellbound forty years and more away in a forgotten dream of childhood. Through the fringes of his eyelids he is now apprised of movement on the chess-board on the table by the fire. Pawns in facing chorus lines open the black-and-white minstrel show with a tap dance as the court looks on; which is followed by a synchronised polka, performed by knights in triple time, while bishops begin to sidle and connive, and castles exchange their sites, and kings engage their queens in a solemn square dance. *More, more,* murmurs Ploog. Whereat his pumps get up from the hearth and show a few sprightly steps to Harald's hobnailed boots, which come at last out of their corner and shuffle a homely dance well enough for country clogs. *More, more!* And he sees a stool tilt on one leg to oblige with a pirouette across the floor, a lampshade reel, salt-cellars shake, vases cavort, a bucket do a jig, and Constanze's jam jars jive on the shelf. Everything around him has begun to dance. And happy in this persuasion, lulled by the sounds of self-moving objects that Ploog has never heard before, he holds his heavy eyelids long enough ajar to witness all their motions gradually subside and withdraw again into mute thingness; with no more than a glint, just a hint of mockery, as one by one they make their bow.

The Inauguration of
Brewers Hall

Brum was there when it happened. The brewers' lawyer
and insurance agent met the artist on the site, as soon as the
weather permitted, to ensure that he had fulfilled his contract, and to get his signature to a waiver concerning any
additional claims that might have arisen during the execution of the work. The insurance agent was facing the other
way at the actual moment the culprit stumbled. Startled by
Brum's exclamation, he turned in time to see one of the dec-
orators career at speed along the planks of the scaffolding
under the ceiling and release, or more properly jettison, as
the only remaining option if he hoped to save himself, the
ten-litre canister of paint he was carrying.

The insurance agent recorded the event with the video
camera he had brought along to document the evidence for
his company's files. The trajectory of the canister and the
diffusion of its contents, already fanning out in flight and
attaining maximum dispersion on the moment of impact
with the south wall, could not have defaced the mural more
thoroughly if the accident had been scientifically planned.
The cone of white paint, spreading down from the chestnut

trees and eliminating in its deluge most of the company at
the table underneath, resembled a gigantic bird-dropping –
in other circumstances perhaps comically. The insurance
agent adroitly tracked down the wake of damage, panning
from the initial white burst still detonating in the trees down
to a severed toecap, before cutting to the artist for his reaction in close-up.

By no means dismayed. On the contrary. The artist looks
interested. Stimulated by this intervention of chance, as if it
has brought him exactly what he has been looking for and
not found, Brum continues deliberately what has begun by
accident. Only a week before its inauguration, he paints over
the south wall of the mural that was to be the jewel in the
crown of the quincentenary celebrations at the refurbished
Brewers Hall.

Mix through Brum's eyes, superimposed on images of
Stefanie's medial face and the stertorous utterances of her
visionary sleep and Brum (then) with a look of cold incom-
prehension on his face, to Brum (now), standing on
scaffolding, pouring cans of paint with gusto down white-
streaked wall. Inserts, cutaways. Lawyer, insurance agent,
shaking their fists in puny rage on distant floor. Gradual
disappearance of mural from wall, seen briefly in its entirety.
Slowly pull out from Prater Island and dissolve in wraiths of
river mist. Music over.

Meanwhile, in a cloakroom at the Old Town Hall, last-
minute adjustments to Duke Albrecht IV's beard, a dab of
powder on his chancellor's nose. A clerk appears narrowly in
a crack in the door and inquires ingratiatingly if the two
actors are ready. The chancellor hawks nervously into the
basin. Duke Albrecht IV extinguishes his cigarette.

From the state assembly room of the Old Town Hall pull
back to observe ducal progress through a flight of rooms.
The pudding-basin haircut of a councillor (more if budget
allows), waiting in the foreground in plain simarra with
ducal sleeves, sets off the magnificence of court fashion at

the close of the fifteenth century. Duke Albrecht wears a chaperon as a turban with a falling point in German foliate cut-work, the cape and pourpoint trimmed with ermine, the silk costume with slashed sleeves, parti-coloured from top to bottom, a jewelled garter on his left leg, poulaine shoes on his feet. Contrast his chancellor – ecclesiastical cap, quiet gown with housse, tabard and mantle sparely trimmed with otter – following at a respectful distance.

Diffuse light at window. A sense of cold brilliance in slant of pale November sunshine from casement. The sound of a pigeon clapping its wings as it snatches flight.

The representatives of the six breweries, in period costume, bow as the duke and the chancellor enter. The mayor and the minister of finance, in contemporary clothes, make brief speeches of welcome, flavoured with a discreet twinkle of self-parody while preserving due solemnity. In a re-enactment of the ceremony of 1487, Duke Albrecht's Pure Beer Edict, that no ingredients other than barley, malt and water shall be employed in the brewing of beer, is proclaimed by the chancellor in an abridged modern version. One by one the brewers' deputies step forward and put their seal to the document, kneeling to kiss the sovereign hand before returning to their places. At a nod from the chancellor the doors to the balcony are thrown open. Expectant roar of crowd, voices off. Low camera tracks the duke approaching from throne to balcony. Ducal tread of poulaine-shod feet, motes of dust somersaulting in the sunlight where they pass.

From observation platform on the church tower of Old Peter ZI on neo-gothic gateway of new town hall. Sedan chair emerging, rocking through crowds. Flowers, paper streamers etc., undiminished roar of crowd. As if on rising heat of roar of crowd, dolly up. Patchwork of roofs around the heart of medieval town are seen from above. Pan and rest with slivers of terrestrial horizon and sky, framing clock tower of town hall where the hour is now beginning to strike.

Cut to Brewers Hall. Ushers in period costume pacing, pausing to examine timepieces. Serving men and women bob between hall and kitchens, where we glimpse scullions toiling, vats, barrels etc., an ox turning on a spit at an open fire. Hectic activity of Brum, Heidenreich and others, rushing up and down ladders, bedaubed in smocks, with clotted hair, feverishly painting over wall.

Undiminished roar on soundtrack, boiling crowds in the gorge, it seems, of Burg Street.

The sedan chair at the head of the procession emerges with a splash of colour in the greyness of the deserted Old Court. Pan up to window of abutting bower. A lady in a conical hat, a modesty front spread across the décolleté of her bodice, leans out of the casement. Curtains of sedan chair part. The duke's face looks up. Brief dalliance of gazing damsel, duke, cut off by masonry falling into the image as the arch intervenes through which the procession passes on its way to Maximilian Street.

Procession, crowd sequences, vignettes of protagonists, condensed in images conveying the ducal progress at suitably scenic spots between Marienplatz and Prater Island.

Dense, close textured impressions from the swaying interior of the sedan convey the bustle of the arrival scene in the courtyard behind Brewers Hall. A bird's-eye view through the bare branches of the tree in the centre of the courtyard from a crane above shows the duke alighting from the sedan, surrounded by attendants in livery of red and burnt gold. From this height it is the only appreciable movement in a still haze of colour that suggests visual associations with a carpet of fallen leaves.

Muted, feathery sounds of rustle detailing this movement on the soundtrack in the open air rise by the interval of a sharp when the duke enters the building, dispersing as hollow whispering as the camera follows and the interior of Brewers Hall opens up before our eyes.

The hall is full. A great drinking is in progress, and in a

sense has been for the past five hundred years. Pan down from the roof of the hall, a wide-angle lens attributing to the scene a distension of space and time infinitely greater than what is actually visible in the scene, summarising the casual passage of centuries stacked in tiered galleries, losing identifiable persons, all sense of individuality in the blur of faces, freezing frame by frame as a slow-motion tracking down gradually seizes up, the sound descending by octaves to a no longer human babble, until there is a picture with neither motion nor sound, overlapping with the still images that are painted on the walls.

On the first and second walls the mural unfolds in iconic style a somewhat fictionalised prospect of Munich as it might have appeared on a summer day at the close of the twentieth century. On the third wall a winter scene shows a deserted, snowbound amusement garden. Silent images of more whiteness continue across the fourth, unpainted wall, with a view filling out in the frame of a window where the camera comes to rest, and something in the image moves. In the cone-shaped light of the lamps along the river bank white moths seem to flicker through the bright bars of the night as the first snowflakes fall.

ADVENT

Martha's Advent
Calendar

The calendar Hieronymus has made for me shows everything, beginning with Brum's dream on the eve of the first of
Advent.

Faintly discernible under the hundreds of superimposed
illustrations and inscriptions is the figure of a centaur in
sepia wash.

The bearded man with bow and arrow and from the waist
down the body of an animal is Sagittarius, the archer. His
lower, animal half seems to be leaping over a chasm, in fact
a gap between parted thighs: the thighs of the beautiful
androgynous being whose body is depicted in a folio of the
Très Riches Heures of the Duke of Berry as the astrological
microcosm at the hub of a revolving universe.

Hieronymus has had this detail of the archer blown up by
laser technique for the Advent calendar because the weeks
before Christmas belong, of course, to the ninth sign of the
zodiac. Unless one's been told one wouldn't know about the
cosmological background, the whole, of which this detail is
just a tiny part. Unless one's been told about it one wouldn't
recognise or even see the centaur jumping over the chasm.

What one sees is a photograph of the city.

When one looks at it again, one sees not a photograph but a map. For a while it jumps back and forth – now a map, now a photograph again – until one realises it's actually a montage of both, or what Hieronymus more technically describes as a computerised synthesis of a satellite photograph and the Falk map projection on a scale of 1:33,000. With the aid of a magnifying glass one can make out every detail. Hieronymus says it is only approximate to reality and that even if one magnified it to infinity a disparity would always remain.

The top part of the calendar shows the night sky more or less as it would be seen over the city from the observatory in Rosenheimer Street at 9.30 p.m. at the beginning of December or 7.30 p.m. at the end of it. Day by day the length of daylight between sunrise and sunset becomes less and less, until the sun reaches its furthest point south of the equator and marks time at the winter solstice.

In a footnote to the night sky it says that owing to the precession of the equinoxes, the retrograde movement of the first point of Aries at the rate of 30° every 2,160 years, the sun will not reach the constellation of Sagittarius until 18 December, or about the time zodiacal Sagittarius is succeeded by Capricorn, the horned goat-fish.

Throughout the city there are windows into days.

The windows are shuttered with tags that fold up like concertinas, containing information about their name and number, anniversaries, birthdays, church feasts, ecclesiastical traditions, folklore, superstitions and their pagan origins, horoscopes, astronomical data, a bulletin of local events in December.

Unfolding the shutters with all this information, I can open the windows chronologically and view the days one at a time.

The Advent calendar is bordered with tinsel and hung with decorations, pencil-shaving Christmas trees, trumpeting angels and paper stars, and finely sprinkled with silver dust.

Through layers of finely-sprinkled silver dust, beams of a quarter moon glimpsed emerging from a nebula of annotations surrounding 28 November, Venus ingress Capricorn, *Troilus and Cressida* at the Kammerspiele, the Schubert cycle now over at Gasteig where Candice, not yet home this evening but already on her way to Brum tomorrow, can still be heard laughing in the foyer bar an hour later, through words and images now beginning to stir: through all the layers of my Advent calendar the leaping centaur shimmers.

I open the first window and look inside——

Hieronymus Kornrumpf's Diary

To St Mark's, where Martha wanted to hear Bach cantata. Our eyes this month on Higher Things. That Which Should Be. Why and Wherefore. The Mystery of Life.

'The thick-walled, pear-shaped uterus, measuring no more than three inches when vacant, weighing only one ounce, at term becomes a thin-walled, fluid-filled cylinder a foot long, weighing in at two and a half pounds, with a capacity of four to five quarts.'

Oof!

'Thickening, softening and relaxation of the loosely folded, succulent lining of the vagina and the sodden tissues beneath it greatly increase distensibility and capacity of the vaginal cavity,' it says in the manual, while 'changes in the external genitalia are similar to those inside the vagina. The tissues become first softened, and more succulent(!), later extremely fragile, taking on a purplish-red colour.'

Is this true?

Well, she's not showing, is she. Tried to peek and tamper as she lay hugely sprawled, apparently asleep. Extraordinary stuff inside. Crêpe-like matrix of placenta from which clotted blood can be squeezed. Arborescent mass of villi. Trophoblast-lined intervillious blood lake. Lake!

Tetchy after that. It seemed fair enough to ask her for a helping hand instead. Tetchy a whole damn week. One has to show consideration. On the other helping hand there is Astrid. There is an alternative. Astrid is willing. Eased her into VSOP matters by way of litmus test. Didn't change colour, not in the least. Cocksureness. Five-finger exercise. Frankly reached in and helped herself. She is very understanding of the situation. But where is this going to lead?

Martha does her morning exercises on the floor of the living-room now. Locks the bathroom door. At dinner with the Koepenicks she looked unassailably smug. K had the same manual on his shelves, if for different purposes, lurking among what he calls his astrophysiological miscellany. Removed marker and out they popped from the section on Muscles & Ligaments:

'The breasts become larger, the aureola around the nipples becomes first *florid* or *dusky* in colour and then appreciably darker, later taking on a hue that varies with pigmentation from a deep bronze to a *brownish-black*. The veins beneath the skin over the breast become more prominent, as do the *oily* or *sebaceous* glands about the nipple. A milky fluid, colostrum, *exudes from the ducts or can be expressed from them.*'

Tremendous erection. In some discomfort sat down at table to face mushrooms stuffed with snails and shuddering in aspic. Martha, her shuddering self, plunged in a fork and ate with really quite vicious greed. For afters we had Mrs K's familiar flour arrangements, bodied out with whipped dairy products, topped with cream protuberances. Spanned between this beginning and end, by way of a middle course, the spitted corpse of a suckling pig, oily, sebaceous gravy etc. exuding from ducts, mopped up with white bread. Slurp! Martha had second helpings. K had spoken himself warm and promised to get entertaining once astride his hobby-horse of horoscopes, when the problems of (a) Martha's weight, and (b) Martha's diet intervened for attention.

Reserves and intake of iron and calcium must be enough not only for her own needs but for those of the foetus too. On an adequate diet the total blood lipids increase to a thousand milligrams during the latter part of pregnancy, the two to three grams of nitrogen derived from the metabolism of ingested protein are needed for the growth of foetus, placenta, uterus, breasts, etc. Between the third and the ninth month a gain in weight of around twenty pounds is common. Five pounds consist of stored fluid and fat. Uterus and breasts account for five more. Infant (*sic*), uterine fluid and afterbirth weigh in at a total of ten pounds.

On Marthan day 1, which she may have fiddled a bit to get the benefit of the Annunciation on 25 March, she weighed 121 pounds before breakfast. On Marthan day 237, with 33 days plus or minus still to go, she was stroking 152 – a gross increase of 31 pounds. Perhaps attributable to over-eating (second helpings of suckling pig, red cabbage, bread and dumplings), excessive weight may alternatively be caused by an abnormal retention of fluids and salts (in which case it may be the first sign of *toxaemia*). But with so many cases of hormone disturbance reported recently, isn't there an even more dreadful possibility? Quintuplets in September. Quads in October. Irremediable, non-refundable. Ruin a man's life.

As a result of these nagging interventions, missed many of K's dinner-table points. To fit the part of the fashionable astrologist he's now become, K has grown himself a little black beard. Facial hair and hair of head are streaked with silver, theatrically touched up. A louche Mephisto, badly lit in a black and white photograph. The most recent acquisition of Trismegistos Ltd is the Director General of the National Theatre – hence the complimentary tickets, box, intermission champagne etc. for final performance of

Götterdämmerung. Even a special operatic chair to cope with Martha's spread. Top-heavy, but may drop yet (or not, if oversized foetus, as seems unmistakably outlined). Resplendent, she throned. How meagre Mrs K by comparison. All joints and angles. Deckchair beside sofa. Gala occasion, everybody there. K's gossip is as ingenious and just as speculative as his horoscopes.

(Even accounting for deposit of brownish pigment common in brunettes, by the glow of the theatre sidelights an extraordinary flushed duskiness in Martha's face. Blood pressure? Should not normally increase. Any continuing rise may signal the onset of *toxaemia*.)

K's gossip is as ingenious and just as speculative as his horoscopes. Lurid story of Martha's sister screwing Don Hollmann during performance of *Giovanni*. This must have been triggered off by one of Ploog's snider columns about Hollmann Mourning Services having been stretched to accommodate eloped wives. Ploog has eye witnesses, if that is the word for the group of voyeurs assembled in the wings – stagehands and singers, notably the Commendatore, who could testify impressively from the far side of the grave. Apparently Steffi is delirious about this man. He keeps her tied up in the attic. Thrashes her. That kind of thing.

Usually a nimble talker, K got bogged down here and couldn't find a way out. Ironic how the purveyors of gossip, dwelling on their secret preferences, effectively indict themselves. Easy in fact to imagine K being cruel to Mrs K. Manacles removed from drawers of linen. Mrs K's muffled cries during long tie-in on Sunday mornings in Klenze Street. Because K himself manacled, K himself in servitude, the slave of a master idea whose will to comprise the sole and complete solution is itself of course a tyranny. At opposite ends, master and slave remain attached to the same stick.

Meanwhile Hollmann has taken Stefanie off on a world cruise or something, K said conclusively, eliciting a tear-laden sniff from Mrs K, who asked for news of Brum just as the curtain went up and Martha gave a terrific sneeze.

'As the bladder and urethra are pulled upward and distorted by the growing uterus, the stretched muscles that control urination are less efficient. The woman may lose some urine involuntarily when she *coughs, sneezes* or *laughs*.' (This is known as stress incontinence.) Poor old thing. Pår Nielsen as Siegfried, Hedda Blomquist as Brünnhilde. Between them and Wagner it was an incontinently long evening.

What, incidentally, could one say in reply to Mrs K's inquiry? That Brum grins like a dog at the end of his tether and runs about town disguised as a horned goat-fish? A severe case of psychosomatic cuckold, doubling as carnival fool in cap and bells? The flair for self-dramatisation is a shrewd business streak in Brum, of course. But when he takes to posting himself at Karlstor and complains to passers-by about the secrets his wife keeps from him in a locket she wears around her neck, the family must step in. Something Must Be Done About Brum.

November the twenty-fourth: *brevissima*, the day that ushers in the period of least light. Barometric pressure rising steadily since the dispersal of the fog but pitch-dark at seven and still an ominous, lowering sort of sky at eight.

Difficult to keep one's eyes on Higher Things when lowering one's trousers for rectal inspection in the basement practice of Dr Blavatsky, Schelling Street urologist, on a haggard November morning. Martha went in first. Haemorrhoids shape up as points in common between husband and pregnancy-estranged wife. Period of least light. Constipation and haemorrhoids, in her case, due to pressure of uterus on lower bowel and inhibition of reflex stimulus. Loss of urge to defecate, plain lazy, in fact, always was, squat for a week and not open her bowels. Stagnation of gastro-intestinal tract perhaps analagous to retention of foetus in self-inflated, self-satisfied uterus? Won't deliver. We're very

nice as we are, thank you. And Mr Kornrumpf? What about
his case?

Dr Blavatsky doesn't look up when patient enters room.
Continues writing. Napoleon at his desk. Who else but doctors have such manners? Bald, white-haired, white-coated,
brisk, sober, entirely impersonal. But then, with that profession. All day long with fingers up cunts and bums.
Hundreds, thousands, so many so long that what remaining
hair he has has in the meantime quite understandably
turned white over them. Those murky conversations. Blood
in stool? Yes. Fresh? Fresh colour? Freshish. High consumption of pastries? Not as a rule. Of doughy, flour-base
foodstuffs generally? And alcohol consumption – a rough
average? But no one can honestly answer such questions.
One doesn't count one's pastries, drinks. Answering dis-
honestly, one screws up one's eyes and peers into a middle
space slightly to one side of Dr Blavatsky's head, sees ghostly
paradigms of larders, bars, partitioned off into days and
weeks, sees with a squint – is that two there on the shelf, or
three? – and gives oneself the benefit of the doubt. A bottle
or so of Pils a day. Blavatsky doesn't think much of a bottle
or so. More concentrated carbohydrates in a glass of beer
than in just about anything a man can put into his mouth, he
snaps, opening and shutting his terrific jaws emphatically.
And then: cut it down. How does one cut down a bottle?
But with his spare hand he is already fingering the examination chamber down the corridor, waiting with its obscene
chair.

Coolish in white with severe pleats, agreeable, suggestive
of lawn tennis and lettuce sandwiches, the urological assistant is waiting. Already pounced and extracted on arrival the
remaining drizzle of urine. 'Can't you manage any more?'
Now she speaks cool, formulaic instructions for removal of
lower garments. Breathing heavily, Blavatsky gives orders
to mount chair. Eek! Look down and see a capsized beetle,
pinned on his back, thin white legs pedalling the air. Gloves

and vaseline, stretching and rubbery slapping sound of former, tactile awareness of latter. A cool smoothness. Toast being buttered. Foreplay of urological act. 'I shall not hurt you,' says Blavatsky, sounding almost tender as he brings his nose down to bear on bum. In an interesting perspective of knees his head recedes to a dome, a roc's egg clasped gingerly between the legs, and in its place, as it vanishes and a plump finger can now be felt breaching the anal entrance, a nest of dark hair bobs up around his assistant's white onlooking face. Claw-like her eyes are fastened on Kornrumpf's penis, a somnolent mole whose contours are fatly outlined under the at first quiet surface of his shirt, beginning to make involuntary leaps as a ripple of exquisite detonation is felt all the way up his arse, and already *a milky fluid irrepressibly exuding or expressed from ducts* has spread a warm wet stain across his shirt.

About the size of pigeon's eggs, concluded Blavatsky on withdrawal, and also described his encounter with a significantly enlarged prostate. Outlined dietary measures etc., but all this had become a minor issue. Was actual experience of the urologist's chair necessary to arrive at such insights? Into masochistic, exhibitionistic and homosexual linings of sexuality—? Ugh! Has the pleasure become available only in an aesthetically distasteful or morally degrading form? And under the eyes of a demure assistant in white who is somebody's teenage daughter you wouldn't like to if you were her father would you—

Is the object of desire that dark tunnel through which it is seen?

In Martha's heart of hearts – pushed up and forward as the thrust of her uterus elevates the diaphragm, swelling in symbiosis with cardiovascular and lymphatic symptoms – she is giving birth to Christ.

Seriously. Nothing else will fit that nine-month slot between the Annunciation and Christmas. It has to be a whopper. The second coming by way of a cellar in Türken

Street, an illusion nourished more easily in darkness and acquiring very sturdy legs after Martha has munched her way through the hundredweight sack of cattle feed she keeps hidden in the corner. A monster infant, a body-builder of a babe, a champ of Martha's manufacture (if not the one she had in mind) is certainly on the way. But what if Christ is quads? Or a girl? And as Koepenick pointed out in the horoscopes for children born around Christmas, when apparently this issue is in doubt: who is the father?

Martha's Confiteor

'Father Anton, I confess I have sinned.'

'In word or deed?'

'In my thoughts.'

'Tell me, Martha.'

'I've been reading my husband's diary.'

'Without his knowledge?'

'Of course. But I don't want to start there. In fact I don't think I want to talk about that at all.'

'Very well.'

'I want to talk about my happiness. A snug feeling.'

'Smug?'

'Snug. The feeling of a person who's warm, looking outside into the cold. I feel it now it's turned cold, since the first fall of snow a week ago. Funny things pop into my head when I walk to the kindergarten in the mornings. For example, I set the street to music. Schelling Street I've scored in the bass clef for wind instruments, a bassoon, two oboes and a French horn. D'you know the kindergarten in Arcis Street?'

'I don't believe I do.'

'St Mark's kindergarten, right opposite the institute for bagonalistic.'

'The what?'

'Bagonalistic, I think it's called. Each morning we start with a song, usually followed by a story. On Wednesday it was the story of St Catherine. Not an easy one. I skipped the wheel and the beheading by sword—'

'Very sensible.'

'—and concentrated instead on the house Justinian built for Catherine on Mount Sinai. The children do a drawing of the story, you know. They get totally absorbed. And when I listen to their breathing, and the hurried sounds of their imagination traced on paper, and all their warm little noises, I stand at the classroom window, looking out at the white epaulettes left by the snow on the shoulders of the stone cherub standing in the yard, and have that snug feeling inside, indescribably happy. And I know this is wrong, but I don't care, which makes it even worse.'

'So long as the reason for your happiness is not the cause of someone else's unhappiness, Martha. That's what counts.'

'Is it? The thing about happiness is how little it can be because of and how much it will always be in spite of. Walking through the underpass at Pasing Station, for instance, with my gloves on for the first time this winter, and the fur boots mother gave me last Christmas, feeling sort of tingling among all those other gloved and booted people, trailing their bubbles of condensation as if they'd all turned into fire-eaters, I look down as I come out of the exit between the pub and the gents and see this bundle of old clothes. But it's not a bundle of old clothes. It's a little man folded up inside his coat, drunk, asleep – something thrown into a corner, while men step over his leg as they go in and come out of the gents and streams of people from the exit are passing by. I feel a twinge and a dash of cold as the sight of this man jumps into me, but really it's felt as a dash of

cold because of the surrounding warmth he's jumping into.
My pity takes him inside my snugness, you see, and I watch
him sinking down into it, and gradually he disappears, leaving nothing but a pleasant feeling of emptiness. I look down
at his disappearing head and shoulders and I'm actually
relieved to see him go, because I can't cope with him in my
happiness.'

'This is distressing, Martha.'

'It distresses me, too. I think about it on the bus. I care
about it. Sometimes I forget to get off the bus at Dach Street
and have to walk back a stop. And when I get to the offices
of Ecumenical Care For the Lonely By Letter I feel such
doubts about my fitness for what I'm doing that I want to
turn back. I see Miss Pickering purse her lips, and those
extraordinarily deep-set, heavy eyelids of hers when she is
looking down at her typewriter. She has this wonderful
knack of identifying with people. Whereas my letters – what
have I got to offer by comparison?'

'Are you fishing for compliments, Martha?'

'Goodness, no. You see, I'm still thinking about the man
outside the gents at Pasing Station, and how he does those
weird little jumps into my snugness. Because when I get
down to the task at Ecumenical Care For the Lonely By
Letter, it's the other way round.'

'The other way round?'

'I feel I'm able to sort of *plunge* into those letters. Or to
put it in other words: as if I could *spread* a feeling of snugness on to the page. I feel there is so much inside me I have
to give. It's an odd thing I've noticed – usually we have
twenty to thirty letters coming in each week, but at this time
of year, always around the beginning of Advent, it's almost
double that. It's like the way people feel their amputated
limbs.'

'I beg your pardon?'

'They feel legs and arms they haven't got. It has something to do with fluctuations of barometric pressure. Around

the end of November people start missing their absent partners. Especially elderly people who live alone. The nearer to
Christmas, the worse it gets. Inside the letter-box you can
almost hear the groans. You can hear the thumps of people
landing on pavements all over town – old people, for the
most part, jumping out of windows. The letter-writers are
the ones who don't jump. Not yet. As long as they feel a
need to communicate, there's hope. I remember how
shocked I was when I began answering ECLL letters, and
Mr Dietsch said to me: "Imagine this person is standing on
a window ledge. It puts a tremendous sense of urgency into
your letters when you imagine that." Side by side with us,
apparently in our world, the unhappy might as well be living
on a different planet. The joy I feel over this coming child is
a happiness others can share because it can help to nourish
happiness in them. I just bring them inside an aura of snugness. They join me under my bell-jar. How does it look
inside? Cream wallpaper with a wave design in blue. The
centrepiece is the cradle, of course, something sensible and
a wee bit old-fashioned, from Schlichting's I dare say, that
has probably been made in Scandinavia. After spending
such a lot of money at Schlichting's one has had to say no –
not just with feelings of regret but envy, I must confess, for
those who can afford it – to that adorable pink cashmere
counterpane with the silk fringe one's had an eye on at
Betten Rid. It's not just my own I'm looking after. I've not
forgotten my obligations to World Child. World Child do a
worm cure for just two marks. I've arranged for a standing
order with my Post Office account. Ten marks a month is
really not much to us, but in the course of a year that adds
up to sixty worm cures. Sometimes I have a sneaking feeling
that charities are a penance for the fact that really, at the bottom of our hearts, we don't want our lives disturbed by
other people's misery. Perhaps the real meaning of care is
willingness to be disturbed. Which brings me back to happiness. The snug feeling of someone warm who is looking

out into the cold. The thing is, you can't be snug unless it's
cold. And I wonder if you can't be happy unless . . . D'you
see what I'm driving at, Father? I'm worried that somewhere inside happiness there has to be a deeply selfish
thought. Father? Father Anton?'

'What? Who's there? *Brrphiu* . . . What point had we
reached, Martha? World Child, was it?'

'Father!'

'I must've . . . Just for a second. Perhaps we should slowly
be . . . *Nnkyääh!* I don't mean to hurry you, Martha. But
perhaps we might slowly . . .'

Even in my imagination this is how it always ends. This is
what you say even when it's me saying it. You simply drop
off. Is love such an intrusion, such a burden for a man to
bear? When all I would like to do is to share that miraculous
lightness the thought of you— The tingle I feel in my cheeks
when I step out of the house in the mornings, feeling that
everything, however ordinary, is special because somehow I
am collecting everything for you. I understand now why
love is grace. It all becomes *for* something. You seem to be
looking into a kaleidoscope, all the pieces rush together and
make patterns. Everything sticks. I am the world's flypaper,
Father, and a brimming vessel whose yearning is still hollow.
The child is coming, and in my dream last night had come
already, and in my dream I came to your chambers in St
Anna's and laid the child at your door. I awoke to an
unspeakable thought formed with perfect clarity inside my
head. I laid the child at your door because you are the father
in me of the desire from which in me otherwise barren
because undesiring that warm March evening the child
grew. It was a Wednesday, but you won't remember that. It
was a Wednesday late in March. Friends of the Mission in
Ethiopia were waiting by the ticket machines in Pasing
Station. Mr Dietsch, Miss Pickering and I had been invited
to the outing too. Already at nine o'clock the expectant coolness of a hot day, before the heat comes, coolly the morning

is paying out slack. I stood beside you in Constanze's straw hat with the yellow ribbon and could feel your outline on my skin. I stood between my feet on the cracked paving and a sensation of such lucidity it seemed empty in my head. Before the event is the small bright hollow of expectancy in which perfect happiness lies. This moment was the prism in which I remember the anticipation of all the colours of the day, gulls dipping with painful cries, like green flames the crackle of the chestnut buds opening overhead and the picnic on the promenade of Lake Starnberg, soft haze of streaked blue where the breathless sails of yachts stood like white napkins on a table. This is a picture of my soul, a reflection in still water, agitated by a ripple when you leaned forward and touched the surface with a fingertip. Ripple still swaying in me when to the sound of traffic that seemed to come hot and impatient through the wide open window I conceived that night. When I awoke I remembered the dream, and the picture of my soul, the one overlaid the other and mingled as the confession I carried like an icon in my heart on my way to St Anna's this afternoon. I always try to think of an excuse to come early, but I can never think of one. Instead I sit right up at the front and if you looked at me more often you'd think I was half-witted the way I screw up my eyes, but when I squint like that I'm shutting the other committee members out of the corners of my eyes and imagining the two of us alone. For us who work in Christ the year begins tomorrow, in the season of Advent we prepare in our hearts for the mystery of His coming – so brief and with such simplicity your words of thanks before directing the committee's attention to the sideboard with the cheese and cold meat plates. Was it my imagination or did you include me very specially in your gaze when you laid emphasis on that magic word *us*? Would you consider it presumptuous that I think of you and me as twin tonnage, hewn of the same block, the same beefy turn of flesh? Beside you I have always felt at my ease, and when I faced you at the buffet, our bellies almost nuzzling one another like two vast creatures in mute sympathy, it was all I could do to stop myself – suddenly exuberant, figure-skating, transformed into one of Schlemmer's portly ballerinas, or even a shiny round bumper-car – from giving yours a little nudge. How I love to see you feed. How I love to see the ripples on the lardy dewlaps of your throat when you drink. Seen in the perspective of the aisles of St Anna's your volume shrinks; how right, how noble you looked at mass on Saturday evening. You must have had a shower, Father. For once your incorrigible hair was firmly plastered down in place. Briefly, but only very briefly, I glimpsed you under a shower in my imagination, concentrating as hard as I could on the soap, and during the *Agnus Dei*, sinking my fingers into a foaming fleece, I daydreamed I was washing a sheep. The lamb absorbs our sins. But sometimes the blind arrogance of priestly men irritates me, their unseeing, selfish churchiness. Can it never have crossed your mind that the confessional is the only place where we are alone? Is the notion of my squeezing once a week into that little box in order to be close to you something so stupendous that it never enters your imagination? Or His body and blood before their transubstantiation into the solitude of eternal celibacy – wasn't there a woman somewhere, and a hole in the city wall, and a flapping desert wind that raised the goose pimples on His flesh when the sun went down? I would do anything. I would reach in through the grille where otherwise I must watch your fingers pluck the fleshy lobe of the great hairy ear milked for its attention and unbutton, if that were the penance you imposed, and suck gluttonously the bald livid hermit that leered in at me from a gaping cassock, anything but the drowsy habits of rosary and *paternoster* to which your indifference condemns me. For this is how it always ends. And not for the sins I have been committing in my thoughts while confessing others but for the lack of courage of my silence, worst sin of all, I impose my own penance. The first Advent dream, which shall come true in the first quarter of the new year – and nightly, the moment the soles of my feet no longer touch the floor, I think of it, the cashmere coverlet at Betten Rid's with the matching set of baby-wear, when the world is no longer under my feet and I curl up, a dream projectile, wondering if ends ever do more than merely meet, ready for take-off, or think of a kiss reflected in the water of a lake, or of a thousand and one other things – this dream on the night of Advent I shall not claim for myself, Father, this dream shall be dreamed for Brum.

A Window on
Oettingen Street

MARTHA

Gisela sleeps on a platform an arm's length from the ceiling, leaving room for a desk under the bed. This arrangement has survived a quarter of a century since the days of the commune in the Oettingen Street apartment above the gallery, and has been shared with more men than Gisela can remember. Sometimes she sat and wrote to former lovers while their successors were sleeping overhead. Sometimes former lovers left notes on the desk while Gisela was sleeping overhead. Brum did so when he left her for Stefanie.

Martha thinks of Gisela as a crowd of people. She sees her moving and blurred on a photo, with half a dozen arms and faces. Even on her own she has always made up a commune. A gravitational field of hospitality, laziness and convenience surrounds her. Men are drawn to her for their comfort. Stepping into Gisela's field, they think they love her. One can see it in their eyes. In fact it is the reflection of the aura of love, the good-naturedness that beams off Gisela.

This is the remarkable thing about Gisela. This is all there is to it. There are no hidden motivations. She is as she seems, in the surface and the core.

In the end her men were left with nothing to do. They had nothing to work out. Even-keeled she floated under a sky without a cloud on a sea as smooth as glass. The men got bored. Bit by bit they drifted off to remain friends. Love affairs with Gisela were not resumed.

Brum sleeps in the vagrants' room with the episodic, always-turning-over tail-end of the eight or ten people who are usually accommodated between him and Gisela in her room at the other end of the corridor. Brum and miscellaneous guests sleep here on the twenty-five-year-old mattresses that have been left lying on the floor.

The Passau fresco master, Jonas Heidenreich, and his two apprentices stayed here while they were working on Brum's mural. When the work was finished the apprentices went. Brum still came and went. Jonas came and stayed, leapfrogging the giant four-poster bed in the adjacent room, where he touched base for a night with the Egyptian girl, the Syrian boy and the hermaphrodite Lebanese, to land with a crash on Gisela's platform under the ceiling, from which he has not stirred for several weeks. Brum continued to come and go with the other vagrants who since the onset of the cold weather had begun to wait for Gisela in the street. These men she charitably let in for the night had something blank, bony, shiny, backed with a dank odour of rotting canvas, which made Procyon bark and give chase in his sleep.

Jonas had nothing to lose but the rent he paid for a small whitewashed room in a town at the confluence of three rivers. He lay in Gisela's bed, mesmerised by the ceiling a yard over his head. An unending flow of images, scenes he had painted or now imagined, passed across the ceiling. He saw the mower there, and the sorrel horse, and Brum's wife. He saw her behind his eyelids when the warmth of Gisela intervened and she lowered her body on to his.

Jonas cracked the nuts that Gisela brought and made things to fit inside the shells. 'Pretty,' she said, her head on one side as she looked at the crib in his palm. For weeks he lay in bed and made things to fit in nutshells. He carved a set of a dozen pieces of furniture, which Gisela laid in egg cartons and put away.

On the ceiling he saw the confluence of three rivers and thought of his home there as only the more familiar of many possible solitudes. He could help with Gisela's stall at the Christmas market in Schwabing. She would be pleased if Jonas stayed for the winter. It was easy to find any number of reasons why he should have the thing he wanted.

'Wait until she comes back,' he said to his self-portrait on the ceiling. He visualised his head there on a plate, like John the Baptist's. Next he saw his head and face attached to the body of the mower with the scythe whom he had painted on the north-east wall of Brum's mural. Between Jonas, now, and Brum stood Brum's wife. Brum had done the face and hands, leaving to Jonas the sheaf of corn she was holding and the costume, a pastel ochre taffeta gown with balloon sleeves. Gradually this image came to dominate the ceiling.

Jonas fell in love with the portrait of a woman he had never seen. He had contributed the period costume to fit around the hands and face the man she loved had painted. Gradually this image came to dominate his life.

Between Jonas and Brum the three mimes who travelled as The Wandering Stars sleep in the four-poster bed that belonged to Gisela's great-grandmother. Gisela picked them up at the trampled edge of the grounds where the tents were coming down at the end of the summer theatre festival. As pierrots they played Roncalli's season throughout the autumn. Now the circus was moving on without The Wandering Stars, and Gisela had taken them in for the winter. Leila had an engagement as a belly-dancer at Byblos, the restaurant in Maximilian Street. Dada the Syrian was busking in the pedestrian zone. Zeo spent his afternoons in a basement room near the main station hired by a Lebanese compatriot, who took the customers' money at the door.

Martha thinks of Leila, Dada and Zeo as a trinity. She sees them symbiotically arranged in Gisela's great-grandmother's bed. She is no more able to segregate them as individuals than she would be to detach an arm or a leg and envisage it as a self-sufficient body. The Syrian boy and the Egyptian girl sleep with the Lebanese hermaphrodite in the middle. It is as if the sexes both accommodated in Zeo's body have peeled off as male and female on either side. The male and female charges are neutralised. There is a balance, a perfect harmony in this bed.

Dada's breath barks mutton and onions. At Zeo's request he sleeps facing out. Leila lies on her back with her arms behind her on the pillow. She is sleepwalking horizontally to the Nile with a pitcher on her head. Zeo sprawls in midstride between them, hurdling. A part of her hurdling body touches both sleepers, as if nightly it undergoes some mysterious process of ionization.

All these inmates of the Oettingen Street apartment have to be introduced in their sleep because of the time and location, the late period of rapid eye movement required for the window into Brum's dream. The nature of the dream affects them all. But the dream is still not forthcoming. Against a background of blurred breves of sound, early morning traffic draining in bars down Prinzregenten Street, washboard of sleepers' breathing begins to agitate, soft nasal blathering and whispered kerfuffle, syncopated whistle and snore, as if hectoring Brum to deliver, honk and poop, bleepers' wreathing, skiffle of sleepers' breathing begins to orchestrate a protest.

Anticipating Brum's dream by four or five thousand years, Leila sees her first in the antiquity of her Egyptian sleep, afloat in a skiff on the flooding waters of the Nile. The image is a flash on the retina lasting microseconds.

Jonas sees a confluence of three rivers in spate as an image projected on to the ceiling just over his head. He does not see her but he knows she must have come, because he is home, and the three roaring rivers are in spate with the snow-water that melts in the spring.

In the vagrants' room Martha recognises with a shock a sleeper's posture that seems familiar. It is the same huddle of a man who pricked the bubble of her happiness outside Pasing Station. Now the city has thrown him up in the warm bay of Gisela's apartment. He has no antecedents. Forever he loiters here and now. He is loitering in his sleep, giving whimpers of impatience. He senses there'll be a bun or a hand-out when the lady comes. He badly wants a nice dream.

Procyon yelps. He has sniffed the bun on the far side of the odour of rotting canvas. Colour-blind in reality, in his dream the dog experiences Stefanie's coming as a marvellous greening.

Even the objects in the house wait impatiently. Corks fidget in bottle-necks. The folding walnut table shifts its flaps and creaks. The tubular steel cantilever chair rises buoyantly in an attitude of tense expectation.

Hurry hurry!

With a flustered scuffle of springs, as if it had almost forgotten, the grandfather clock in the hall hurriedly girds up its mechanism and dongs the hour.

Brum brum brum——

Brum's Dream

——and the haze clearing, greening. Sense of her in the green distance. She can be heard grumbling about rows with insurance agents, the costs, the paperwork, the sheer inconvenience of rising from the dead. Then she is visible as a dot at the end of the cinder path. Hard to say at this distance whether she's coming or going. She's going. She seems to be walking on the spot. No, she's coming. The confusion arises because she's walking backwards. The sun comes out. Light gives green a reassuring sense of place. Green takes the shape of bushes, sprays of white and violet identify hawthorn and lilac blooming on the green fringes of Nymphenburg. Procyon barks and hompers colour-blind into the greening distance. Steffi's coming along the cinder path to the Copper Lodge. She comes and comes. But she comes no nearer. There is a sense of the need to go out and meet her in order for Stefanie to be able to come. Already this awareness brings her closer into focus. The edges are fuzzy. Still walking backwards, she fills out the image. The illusion of closeness is due to the telescopic lens that can pick out the date on a coin at a distance of seven kilometres.

Between the illusion of Steffi on the cinder path and the place where she actually is lies a large part of the city. Actually she is in Montgelas Street, walking down the hill to Tivoli Bridge. The illusion of closeness is due to the fact that the telescopic lens can look across vast reaches of space and thus also of time. Between the appearance of her setting foot on the cinder path and her arrival in fact at the Copper Lodge lies an interval of many months. Between them lies a long journey. Perhaps she is not coming here. Perhaps she is still going away from somewhere else. She has yet to cross the river. She is in two minds. She walks forwards backwards. She comes and goes. She goes. Perhaps she will never be coming here again. There is the pain when for a moment you have mistaken for alive a person you know is dead. The illusion of living closeness is due to the telescopic lens that has picked out the monogram of two initials, *S* and *B*, intertwined on the clasp of the locket at the nape of her neck. Sense of her in the green distance, and her spring coming again between the violet and the white along the cinder path to the Copper Lodge. If only one could see. If only she would turn. Ah my love, turn round just once. And the wish is so simple and true and free of false remorse that it goes to her heart, yes and to the thing closest to it, Brum remembers it at last, the cleaners' tab she has taken out of the locket and is fiddling with when Brum remembers and at last she turns round. What a pity you didn't say so sooner, you chump – taking his nose by no means playfully between middle and forefinger and giving it a sharp tweak. 'Ouch,' said Brum. And he woke up.

The Dredging
of Brum

Candice kept her jealousy well concealed. The practical conclusion she drew from the law forbidding a body to be in two
places at once was that if Stefanie were in Nymphenburg
with Brum she couldn't very well be with Max in
Bogenhausen. This wouldn't work, Candice reckoned, until
Brum had been properly house-trained. So she borrowed a
key to his apartment from the Greek grocer in Zenetti
Street, and let herself in.

She found the artist in bed, apparently for ever, wearing
a mackintosh and a balaclava. Tins with food in various
stages of decomposition lay on the floor around the bed. She
found the telephone wrapped in underwear in a drawer.
Clothes, kitchen utensils, pictures, the inventory of Brum's
life – the chaos was that nothing seemed to care enough to
want to belong any more.

Brum said he had lost interest in life. Things in the room
were threatening him. He was unable to go out or to see
anyone. He didn't even want to get up, and he asked
Candice to go away. Candice said they had interests in common. Slipping her shoes off, she got into bed beside Brum.

By and by, under impressions of a different texture of warmth, a mysterious alloy of sweat and perfume, a lack in the groin that had previously been felt as an emptiness, Brum's interest in life began to reassert itself.

Candice agreed, on certain conditions.

The squalor around him was the squalor inside him. Self-neglect was also self-love disappointed. At bottom there was nothing more in him than this murk of self-interest, polluted by a sheer lack of care for others. Ceasing to flow, he had naturally fallen ill of himself. He would need to be dredged, said Candice, or words to that effect. Brum was aghast.

But when he had got up and showered, removing the balaclava he had worn since November on account of a recurrent nightmare in which he was sprouting horns, and stood drying his hair at the kitchen table while Candice ruminatively weighed his fat prick in one hand and a coffee cup in the other, the thought of being dredged for a moment seemed rather nice. But then she pinched his foreskin hard and said it was no use, clearly he did not understand women, she would rather get on with the washing-up.

The dredging of Brum, said Candice, would first of all require him to show more consideration for women. There must be an end of overweening cocky assertion, self-gratifying impositions at inconvenient moments – no, he needn't bother to deny it, she had it from Stefanie personally. Brum must altogether get rid of this notion that his cock was a cudgel for the enslavement of withheld compliance; think of it rather, Candice paused, the suds running down a steaming plate, as a dowsing rod or a tuning fork, not entirely ruling out arousal by application now and then of tender punishment, but mainly to pitch a sound or divine a frequency. Woman was the oscillation latent in the stillness, the standing water that was waiting to run. The church in western Europe, crude progenitor, had never wanted to understand the artistry in such matters, and sex manuals merely described mechanisms with instructions for use;

whereas she, Candice, whose genes had been soaped in the bath-houses of Baghdad, and with all the spices of the Middle East well and truly under her belt, refined experience with a flair of musky intuition which equipped her to instruct him in pleasure.

Brum was fairly astonished at Candice's words to this effect. He forgot his first impulse to chuck her out. He even overlooked his injured vanity. He saw the absurdity lolling between his legs and hurried to put on his pants.

Self-restraint, Candice urged, as Brum crawled under the bed to clean up his litter, could equally well be expressed as equilibrium with other, whether other was a human being or an object or just a space allowed to be itself and not encroached on, like the surface of Brum's table unnecessarily pitted out of disrespect for its tableness, or the flowers that had been dead in vases for weeks, or the Guzzini lamp on which Brum hung his shirts. Smear, stains, ash, everywhere Brum's hoodlum fingerprints, not a cohabitation with the things in his apartment but their neglect or coercion, his greedy male encroachment on them, heedless spillage, the corpses of other everywhere, drowned in Brum's obliviousness, the stinking pollution of the rooms in which he lived.

Candice lectured on in this vein while she climbed ladders and took down curtains. It was pretty strong stuff. Moodily Brum scrubbed the stairs between the pit of the studio where he worked and the gallery where he and Steffi once slept, bleeding moderately when he interacted with his surroundings and contracted a splinter in silence.

Candice allowed him to share with her his bed. She allowed his hands to search her body, giving precise instructions as to where Brum could locate her orgasm to her entire satisfaction. Her moans were most frustrating. Brum hankered, but she kept him dry.

He cleaned the apartment, on his hands and knees. He submitted to the force of her personality. Yes, he ate humble pie. When Candice was satisfied she sent him downstairs to

fetch cardboard packing cases for the move to the Copper
Lodge.

'Time to get packing,' she said.

'Surely,' she said, 'when all the things of the years of one's
life with someone— How many, incidentally?'

'Seven,' said Brum.

When all the things of seven years of his life with Stefanie
passed through his hands, then surely just by handling those
things Brum could not escape a few general impressions,
perhaps draw some conclusions, as to how those years had
been. Hmm?

This was a tricky channel, and Brum foresaw some hard
dredging. Mrs Mackensen had said there was still plenty of
time for the move to the Copper Lodge, he told Candice, all
of three and a half weeks. Candice thought this a childish
attitude, not in the spirit of their agreement. Reluctantly
Brum opened the bedroom cupboard. Most of the insides
jumped out on him joyfully.

Whose stuff was in here, Candice demanded. His and
hers, said Brum. Steffi wore his clothes, queried Candice
sarcastically, giving one of her terrific snorts that made
Brum feel there was a horse behind her about to kick him.
He began to build little piles, in a fairly offhand sort of way.

Later he began to whistle. After a while he stopped
whistling. There was no disguising it. Brum had never
realised. Steffi's pile was so small. He felt the same embarrassment he had recently felt, laughing heartily in a
cemetery, when he realised it was not a dwarf's but a child's
grave he was looking at.

The bedroom cupboard was more his stuff, he explained
to Candice. Steffi had the chest of drawers, and the tin trunk
under the bed. The little oak chest was Household.

Candice said OK, so let's start with the chest of drawers.

Thirty-six pairs of Brum's socks lived in the top drawer, a
squad of his shorts drilled in the second, threatening a
reserve detachment of bikinis huddled skimpily in a corner.

In the third Brum had to disinter Steffi's underwear from beneath a layer of his, his boater smothered her blouse, two paint-stained sets of overalls put the squeeze on an aerobic outfit in between. Candice estimated drawer space allocation and kept the score. Submerging in the fourth and fifth, Steffi died by degrees. A glove made a showing here and there, a scarf or two would still surface, but come the sixth and bottom drawer she had been rubbed out altogether by an invasion of ironmongery, rocks, lumps of clay in damp towels.

Opening the drawers, Brum uttered yelps of astonishment, as if overwhelmed by these discoveries. Surprise and remorse were genuine. With some difficulty Candice resisted a softening she felt in her heart, flicking a mental switch to set in motion the dredging apparatus.

Evidently his wife had left him, she said, because in as many words he had been telling her to do so. No no, said Brum. Yes yes, said Candice. For he had taken away her room. He had leaned on her and crowded her out. Vestiges of wife had been tidied away or blocked out altogether, his sketches of her turned to the studio wall, her photo on the mantelpiece forgotten behind slices of stale toast, her golliwog stuffed behind the sofa cushions. Why was this?

In dribs and drabs her belongings went into a carton marked STEFFI. Brum said he didn't know. Frankly he hadn't thought too much about these things. Three squat, bulging cardboard boxes, taped and strapped as if to stifle some irrepressible jollity, some queer dense quality of thingness that wanted out, already stood massively behind him. He knocked out the bottom of a fourth carton and marked this one BRUM too. Through a crack that suddenly opened up as she watched the fat black letters spill out of his hand and sprawl across the side of the box, Candice saw reasons why Stefanie might have hated Brum.

Brum said listen, there was a blind side to this story too. When Steffi met him she chose a mess. She liked to tidy things. She needed to run things. She was spilling over people and things in her own way, too, running them and tidying them up. Were the things and spaces in this apartment any more allowed to be themselves or encroached on any less when she imposed on them her tidiness, and their natural fluctuation, their lack of symmetry, their inclination to chaos were made to correspond to Steffi's will and order?

Candice said Brum should sit down some time for an hour or two to observe the inclination to chaos of a mantelpiece. He should just sit down and try watching the natural fluctuations of an armchair. Brum said this could easily be shown on a twenty-four-hour or week- or month-long video significantly speeded up – the shifts of objects, the cycles of accumulation and depletion through which they lived. Candice thought his sense of humour needed brushing up. Brum told her Stefanie was a bad loser. Give and take, said Candice. They broke for lunch.

Give and take, she resumed, balance, it didn't matter of what, all that mattered was the equilibrium with the other. In the emptying apartment her voice began to sound hollow. Brum had already packed quite a lot of it in cardboard boxes, seven of his, so far, and three of hers. Equilibrium, Candice repeated pointedly, came about through the art of sharing, and sharing came about through love. Love was the common resource, the ground water, the seepage, drop by drop the smoothing of the rock, the fluid surrounding element that made fractious borders contiguous and compatible. It was not something but anything. It had no colour, shape, taste or odour itself, yet to everything it imparted their vividness. It arose naturally, but if uncultivated it melted away naturally too. It was there in detail or not at all. Candice couldn't see much detail in Brum's love for his wife. She couldn't see how he cared for her very much at all. She could see he'd been lazy about cultivation. She could see the ground water under Brum's feet sinking pretty fast.

Brum felt thoroughly dredged. Man and dog were in a

bad way. Procyon hung his ears at half-mast and went into a corner with his tail between his legs. Brum wished he could have done so too. He was troubled by a persistent sense of dirt under his fingernails and an unpleasant feeling his prick had shrunk. The man ate without his customary relish for a day or two. The dog went off his food altogether. Candice was not the first person to remark that the best thing about Brum was his dog.

Going through the papers in the little oak chest marked Household, Brum found that everything he paid for to be allowed to exist had either expired or was about to. A dinghy he had forgotten about had been forfeited three years ago. His car had officially deceased in October. According to Procyon's licence his dog had only a few weeks left in him, and from the beginning of the year would become twenty-five per cent more expensive. Brum looked at Procyon snoozing away his grief on the mangy rug beside Steffi's rocking-chair, and wondered if the old dog was worth the renewal.

The emanations from this chest, the camphor whiff of remonstrance and creeping disaster, depressed Brum so much he felt unable to cope. He locked the chest and buried it in a cardboard box, double-taped to prevent it from leaking any more damage.

The tin trunk under the bed he dreaded even more.

When Candice was out he spent a day looking through Steffi's things. There were the sensible girly things such as her swimming medals and the certificate awarded on completion of a First Aid course, her school reports and photographs – these he could manage without trouble. Then there were the memorabilia, mementos of special occasions. The horn-handled corkscrew Constanze had extraordinarily bought her on a joint visit to Copenhagen. The duck whose head screwed off, still containing traces of sherbet, which she had been intending to give her first love when she was nine but in the event had eaten herself. The prayer book for

her confirmation. The favourite party shoes she had kept
and put away in case of a daughter – these things already
caused Brum discomfort.

And then there were the keepsakes kept for nothing, pure
evidence of herself, secret footprints, fragile claims on a
place in the world. Among them was a bowl where two
white birds sat half-embedded in sand. Brum remembered
her arranging shells with their ribbed sides upwards around
the birds and saying that between this bowl and herself there
was nothing, no sense of otherness, the still life was an
image of herself, the longing and the fulfilment overlapped.
Look, she'd said, I can move the birds around and arrange
them as I like. Happiness. As simple as that.

Without their person belongings were corpses. He looked
at her dead useless things and closed the tin trunk.

Curtainless, the room seemed naked. He watched a
bright spot mushroom on the floor under the skylight,
recede and vanish.

The sun moved across the street. Gradually Brum heard
the silence.

Santa Klaus

Was he real? Anticipating her child's question a few years from now, Martha couldn't resist a sneak preview of St Nikolaus to find out what he was made of, in what sense he was *real*. Well, real in the sense that there probably *was* a Bishop of Myra a rattling long time ago when bones moved crypts, travelling from one place to another in that restless, posthumous way that seemed to be the lot of saints. At any rate, he became a legend as the friend and helper in time of need. Real in the sense that you could see his picture on stickers and Christmas wrapping paper. Real in the sense that you could *eat* him. Thousands of tons of chocolate went into the making of those Nikolaus figures in the shops. Catholics liked him dressed up as a bishop. Protestants preferred to eat him plain. But what about his impersonators? The men who brought the swag in sacks. In what sense were they real?

Opening a window on to Zenetti Street, Martha looked down and saw her lodger Harald Hemsing, pointing with gestures of helplessness at the eight-foot styrofoam figure of a naked woman on the roof of Brum's old Citroen (it was supposed to go with the first load of things Brum had been meaning to move that weekend to the Copper Lodge). Seen at ground level in profile, any likeness to Brum's wife was obliterated by the proximity of breasts looming like light-houses, thighs with high-tone muscles fraised out like lighthouse window-ledges. But seen face up from a third-storey window, Hößli's preliminary study for a monumental bronze nude bore an astonishing resemblance to Stefanie, which must have been why Brum asked his colleague to let him have it, and had remained very fond of it ever since.

Martha meanwhile began to share her child's impatience. What did all this have to do with Nikolaus? And did it *have* to be Harald who was Santa? The connection was the Santa Klaus costume in the plastic bag now lying on the seat of the car Brum had said he would lend to Harald on condition he drove out to Nymphenburg and dropped off the styrofoam figure at the Copper Lodge. Strictly speaking, Harald Hemsing had exams that afternoon. Alternatively, he could also be seen driving to the Rentasanta office in Untersendling on an errand connected with some money he owed Czernak, and despite Martha's clear preference for the first of these alternatives the second was unarguably the case. Martha didn't care for the background she watched being rapidly sketched in here: how her lodger had gone on calling Czernak's bluff until that night when the Czech had sussed him out in the men's room of the Playoutdri Pool Bar and demonstrated sinister reasons why Harald would pay half of the two thousand marks he owed him within the next ten days. Smarting, Harald called Rentasanta first thing in the morning. And yes, there were still vacancies for motorised students working suburban beats in pairs, after-noons and evenings, five hundred plus fuel allowance and tips. Coming out of the phone booth in Amalien Street, he bumped into Christopher. Topher said yes. Brum said yes. Harald called right back to confirm car, co-pilot, Rentasanta said yes, present themselves in costume for briefing in their office punctually at two o'clock. Martha was indignant. She felt cheated. At some time (she knew) she'd have to take a clear line on the issue of Santa versus impersonators; she would have preferred, however, to deal with them in a pastellish sort of way, vague and general, as a white-bearded red-coated species somehow valid in itself. The entrance hall, downstairs corridor and two rooms of Rentasanta's office in Untersendling were packed with dozens, even hundreds of just such Santa specimens, who would be chinking in and out of the premises for the next couple of days on their way to pay thousands of professional calls, but the Advent calender closed the door of the manager's office collectively in their faces. Martha found herself having to make do with two student extras in greasy costumes, not otherwise pastellish, who gave their names as Strack and Hemsing.

A small fat man swivelled in response and fingerchatted with a computer on his desk. Long-legged, a girl roamed up and down, sticking red and white flags into a map of the city on the wall behind him. Ready, Corinna? Ready, Mr Schnepp. Fingerchatting, eyes on screen, fat man ran through applicants' Santa inventory. Gown or two-piece costume in red cloth, optional white trimmings? Hood? Beard? Sack with zip or pull-to-neck, minimum capacity twenty kilos? Corinna checked each of these items with a snarl. Talk naturally unless otherwise requested, Schnepp advised, although neither of the students had opened his mouth except to give his name. Schnepp elaborated. On the whole, clients wanted a solidly traditional figure; the moralising old man from the hoary north with a voice straight from the freezer was out, however. Talk natural. Keep it clean. Don't crack jokes. Avoid political subjects. Further instructions were detailed in their itinerary. The Rentasanta manager ripped off the schedules that had been tickering out of the printer while he talked, and handed copies to each of them.

It left them no time for the detour to Nymphenburg. Their first engagements overlapped: a walkabout Santa routine in a supermarket in Perlach that began at three, a reading for the blind with a selection of Advent music in a home in Ramersdorf at four. On the motorway out to Perlach the porous styrofoam figure whistled in the wind like a sieve, making scrunching sounds on the roof that set their teeth on edge. They agreed it must go at the first possible opportunity. Harald dropped Topher off at the supermarket. On his way back to Ramersdorf it began to sleet. Topher had suggested a toss-up, but Harald had rooted for the blind.

The caretaker came out of the home and flagged the Citroën through a series of parking manoeuvres as if it were a 747 that had landed in his yard. The styrofoam statue, extraordinarily light for its size, was carried inside and stood dripping in the cloakroom among the anoraks and umbrellas. Guests were already arriving. Staff and inmates of the home escorted them into a warmly-lit room at the end of a dark corridor. Harald distinguished the in-house blind making their way alone down the corridor towards this light with quick, confident steps and an indefinable air of hope. A woman greeted him at the entrance, clasping and unclasping her hands as if she were about to pray and kept on changing her mind. Was he a student? Yes, said Harald. The woman peered thoroughly into his face, clearing it of the undergrowth of hood and false beard. That was good. Just a little reading. Pocket money. Bring joy in to seeing hearts. All the way in this nasty weather. She murmured and patted his hand. A chair and a table with a lamp stood in the middle of the room. Otherwise the room was lit only by candles. Rows of chairs rippled out into shadows that gathered at the edges. The blind sat with cocked faces. They could feel the candles. They could feel the winking stainless steel jugs and plates with biscuits under napkins on the trollies, wreathed with evergreen, that were waiting in the background. They could feel the reader in their midst. If need be they could feel the fine molecular displacements in the composition of the air that would betray him, Harald sensed uneasily, should it occur to him, for comfort's sake, to unhinge his beard or remove the hood or impair in any way the fully-equipped Santa with all his props intact whom the blind had hired for their Advent celebration.

The woman rang a bell, the room hushed. A harpist made loping motions with her arms, a zither player quivered into sound. When the music stopped, Harald took the marker out of the book on the top of the pile, and began to read. He read for an hour and a half. Between readings there were musical flourishes on the zither and the harp. He read about winter and old age, about the old men and their long wait, about the star of the nativity and the coming Christ-child and an altar picture in which the child lay curled up in his mother's womb with a cross on his back; and always his voice was competing against a background of audience sounds – shuffles and fidgeting agitations, groans, smacks of relish, snorting physical glee when the going was good, waves of restlessness, great draughty sighs and rivets of exclamation whenever on the downside. The woman rang the bell again when he had finished, announcing to terrific applause that cookies would now be served with tea and rum. Harald felt maladjusted. Everything about the blind seemed to take place at heightened audio levels. Everything in the rooms of the blind seemed to be magnified through some kind of woofers.

He left the Hößli styrofoam in the cloakroom. He had to race to pick up Topher at the supermarket and meet their next deadline at six, a double Santa bill for the opening of a new furniture store at a housing estate in Neuperlach. Topher's sack and shepherd's crook were stolen. Harald sat on a folding table and effortlessly collapsed. It was already half past eight when they reached Schwabing and eventually found a parking slot. As he got out of the car Harald realised he'd forgotten to collect the statue from the home for the blind on their way back into town.

For two days non-stop from noon to night they paid

Santa calls on institutions, business premises and private homes. In a bank their swag bags and phoney beards were viewed with misgivings, and they were asked for identification. In a zoo they made a surprise appearance, and to the even greater delight of the children were nibbled by a giraffe. Topher specialised in department stores and schools. Harald worked his way through an erratic list of kindergartens and old people's homes, up and down vast corridors of municipal institutions with presents for the inmates for which no one felt authorized to countersign. In rooms behind grey façades between Ramersdorf and Giesing, where one was deafened by the trucks thundering past, he had to raise his voice to tell his lies to shrewd, uncharmable kids whose fathers sat drinking canned beer in their underwear in front of the TV. Mothers took him on one side and spoke haltingly, apologetically, in the next room. Their children were slow eaters, yes, and they bit their fingernails, were disobedient or wet their beds, didn't they, begged, bullied, bragged, had bad table manners or disturbed the neighbours on Sunday mornings. Harald stood somewhere in a doorway telling them not to do these things, as Mr Schnepp had paid him to. He would bribe the children not to do naughty things with the presents hidden in his sack. Smaller kids, conscious-stricken, or just embarrassed at this intimate attention from a grotesque stranger, stood on the spot and performed slow writhing motions, their callisthenics of awkwardness. Older kids knew the routine and just waited to collect. With shrewd, uncharmable eyes they looked right through him and told him he wasn't real.

Unreal, detached, cobwebs draped around his heart, he sat in the black Citroen, double-parked on Saturday night in Leopold Street, smuggling pizza through strands of beard and listening to Topher laugh. No better angle, in fact, between his own self-enclosed premonitions of sadness and the efficient sounds of Topher's life, skidding off at a tangent, from which to see Dotty come walking down the street with Alex at her side, leaning into him, hell, *glued* to him, a three-legged race, so tied up she didn't even notice her sister lying in styrofoam on the car roof or Harald's face, like frozen washing, only a few yards away at the wound-down Citroen window. 'Just a sec,' he said to Topher, 'just two secs,' and he slid out of the car.

It was easy to follow them through the crowds, almost fun, if it hadn't been so cold – fucking cold in that outfit, just a bit of skirt around his legs. Warmer in Caterwaul, yes, he guessed it the moment he saw them turn off to Feilitsch Square. Dotty's choice. Certainly not his. It was so dark in there that Harald could hardly see their faces across the room. Dotty probably imagined here what she felt to be the flair of a student milieu, *viz.* smoke and stale air, bad lighting, cramped seating and slow service, the Hee Haw Pickin' Band, now in their mid-thirties, recruited like their clientele from a crop of professional students, still dodging seminars and well inside their second academic decade now. Time told here. Come and see the oldies in beard-gear with antique profiles, their dated, gentle slang, just an edge of moral superiority showing through the shabbiness. His Santa outfit was perfect in Caterwaul. In it he stood with arms, legs, face etc. as usual, but tipsy in ten minutes, after one of those maverick beers that floated what was maybe a latent tendency to diabetes – felt, at any rate, as if it had taken the lid of his head off. Still semi-darkness, purporting to be fifty square metres of room with iron pillars like old station girders along the sides and the Hee Haw Pickin' Band on a stage at one end, a bar inset in a giant picture frame at the other. Alex and Dotty sat in this picture drinking something shaped like a cocktail. When Harald stood on tiptoe he could see straws. He was standing at a round table sprouting a girder like it was some kind of sunshade, and three girls in heavy check lumberjack shirts drinking beer there and smoking brands like Gauloise, and a man with a big grin, scraps of hair, not much else, uprooted sprout of vegetable whose body must have stayed put underground, but the hair growing, extraordinarily, from one minute to the next. The man ordered Ox Blood and a Vandal Toast with Camembert, green peppers etc. from one of Caterwaul's slinky midnight waiters, lean-hipped man or woman, it didn't matter, chains, key-rings, snaggy tackle at wrist and waist, fat open purses in their hands chock-a-block with warm moist bills that smelled of leather and sex—

What was Alex doing with his hand? Walled in by all this *junk* for Christ's sake, getting a little leverage to steady himself on tiptoe for a mo— Oy! Fucking hand now on her *knee*, sitting at the framed bar as if it were already a goddamn *wedding* album! Hemmed in by all this crap, the fantastic irrelevance of all this *stuff*, Harald felt such anguish that he threw back his head and howled. Someone tugged his beard and let go, the elastic snapping back with a painful *zing!* You're rather a naughty Nikolaus, aren't you, said the lumberjack shirt to his left, personally she fancied older men and wanted to know if it was real. This was three rolled in one. Groping, Harald answered yes to cover all eventualities, of which the lopsided smile dimpling under the peak of a leather cap set rakishly over her eyes was undoubtedly one of the most charming. It was a longish story, he began. Ox Blood, twanged the waiter, Vandal Toast? Here, rasped veg, hair growing at a quite phenomenal rate. It was a long story, Harald went on, but sinking, swamped by the Hee Haw Pickin' Band and a strobe light that was turning the whole interior into something of a chequered shirt. What? A very long story how he came to be here. Harald was appalled at the banalities already creeping in. Her ear loomed to receive his communication and, unpleasantly, a smell of aniseed. What he might have wanted to say was that at least the subjective impression of being in one piece with one's surroundings (and so effortlessly that this remained unreflected, yes) was the essence of life, perhaps a secret of happiness. But this belonged unexpressed to a rueful *esprit d'escalier* under the bright lights of Leopold Street again a few minutes later. For just a tick when his attention had gone missing – almost as if they'd arranged to have his attention *kidnapped* by all those junk distractions – Alex and Dotty had sneaked out of the picture, gone.

OK now. Harald stood on the corner, looking left, looking right. The blare of other people's fun hit him cold in the face. Citroen gone too, yep, and with it the keys to Türken Street in a trouser pocket on the back seat. He crossed the road and traipsed down Georgen Street. Would Alex? Would he what? Well, *with* her, possibly at this very moment, would he? With his, Harald's, Dotty, all the bits of her?

Harald skipped and yelped. Should he call the fire brigade? Report smoke, flames, a suspicious smell of gas from the windows of a fifth-storey apartment in Sedan Street? Go and howl under same windows? But maybe Dotty wasn't there at all. Maybe she was sipping Caotina while Constanze laid patience at the kitchen table in Little Monten Castle.

Maybe.

He crossed the road without thinking and turned automatically into Türken Street. He would call. And if she was there, he would—

Hang on. Time now? One-fifteen. Too late to knock up Hieronymus and Martha, assuming they heard the bell. Old, at forty. Around forty, people did begin to get seriously *old*. Tire easily. Stiffness. Fixed habits, fixed paths, regress, retrace your own steps. Harald duly crossed back over the road and turned down Friedrich Street.

If she was there, he'd—

Well? Go on. Give her a nice surprise. Give her a treat. Give yourself one. You can afford it. You're Santa Klaus, aren't you? Harald chortled. That was a good one. Things were looking up. Chortling, he turned left into Hohenstaufen Street, minding not to step on the cracks in the pavement. If he stepped on a crack, Dotty was not at home. Continue down Hohenstaufen Street with care. If he stepped on a crack he would call the fire brigade to extinguish inadmissible flames in a five-storey building in Haidhausen.

Brum's car intervened unexpectedly at the kerb. He looked inside. On the back seat the pocket of the trousers with the keys to Türken Street, indeed. The styrofoam was off the roof. Too big for the front door. Topher must have brought her in through the window. For about two and a half seconds Harald kept his balance on a hairline ledge of plaster at the foot of the front wall of the house and managed to rap on a ground-floor window before falling back into the street.

Took a while for Topher to show. Briefly a pale round face in street lamplight at the window, his Swiss ancestry showing at the window, yellowish like a raclette cheese, before melting into the dark.

The front door clicked and gaped. Harald came up the steps. He glimpsed scudding white heels, calves, bounding buttocks as Topher retreated naked in haste.

A smell of changing-room lingered in the corridor, growing bolder as Harald went into the apartment, and ambushed him thoroughly when he closed the door.

Sporting establishment. Hanging at the entrance two pairs of boots and a skipping rope, a rowing machine lurking like a bear-trap on the floor, tennis rackets on the cloakroom shelf. Topher and sporting students sharing apartment, smell, urgent need of ventilation in unsavoury armpit of their accommodation.

Exhaling slowly, Harald lifted the phone out of the empty parrot cage at the entrance and carried it into the kitchen.

Three, two, one—

Inhaling as it began to ring and Dotty answered almost at once. He put the phone down and opened the fridge.

Harald here, feeling peckish.

'Fraid there's been an accident.

Yes. 'Fraid so. Alex.

What on earth was this stuff?

Car accident.

Peanut butter?

As you were. Not car accident.

Fall from roof of Sedan Street building while fiddling with aerial. Harald smeared a finger-full. Unidentifiable, gooey. Seemed to be some kind of meat paste. He carried the phone back into the corridor and tiptoed into the living-room.

Dotty *was* there.

An eight-foot styrofoam effigy, with ample clearance under high ceilings, stood breathing whitely in the dark, looking on as Harald pranced and hopped around in a glee-ful dance.

Santa Klaus, imagine.

With his hand on his cock as he fell asleep on the sofa in the living-room Harald imagined how he would, of course, how of course they would, if Dotty was there—

Jingle Bells

HARALD HEMSING

I am here, I am me, but more often than not a sense of displacement, of loss, as if not here, not me. A longing for other, heart swooping from high air, so clearly imagined it might have been remembered, submerged pointers to that other existence as pebble or cobweb or someone in a white suit moving through cool resonant morning down the corridors of a glass-panelled office in some South American city. What was this other life neither here nor me, perhaps in the end not imagination at all but fragmented memory, as if I had been recycled, gases and atoms and bits thrown together, composite past intuited, indecipherable—

Walked down corridors of glass-panelled office on undisclosed business, while with quick, predatory gestures Schroeder outlined the subjects that had been taken between the fifth and the eighth terms. Techniques of communication – some headings, gentlemen? Mr Blok? Thank you: the collage of reality. What contextual changes occur? Is the montage of reality in effect a *dé*montage? In which connection, Professor Freitag's seminar on mass entertainment:

are we entertaining ourselves to death? The drug in the living-room, and so on. Dr Paderewski's lecture on local journalism – a rich field. Examples? Conflict between extensivisation and intensification of local communication caused by influx of electronic media in the locality. And? Surely, Mr Hemsing, you, as our—

With quick, predatory gestures Schroeder outlined in his jargon the subjects that had been taken between the fifth and the eighth terms of the diploma course. Kidney punches to syllabus. Kill it. Skin it. Chop it up for the examination cauldron. Please to review during the Christmas recess. After Epiphany we shall be resuming not on Tuesdays, gentlemen, but Wednesdays. Schroeder's athletic eyebrows rose extraordinarily at this announcement.

Daydreaming exploration of other, the corridor in the cool building (with the smells of money and cigar and sweated linen at a guess dating from the 1920s) about to give way through swing-doors of frosted glass to a prospect of a florid grandee with hat and cane and a letter of introduction in his silk-lined pocket, at this crucial turn in other life recalled to here and me by the ironic ellipsis of Schroeder's *Surely, Mr Hemsing* – irritably Harald returned to the monochrome December morning, neon-lit in an attic room of the Faculty of Social Sciences in a rear building off Schelling Street.

You as our what?

For example, as our chronicler of eyebrows. The leverage of eyebrows as a form of salutation, a habit Schroeder shared with the members of some African tribes. Harald loitered in the classroom to savour aftermath, still twitching silence, still jostled emptiness, the brief human residue people left in rooms. At the window he watched Schroeder crossing the courtyard below, briefcase exuberantly swinging, as if it were suddenly empty, as if the dead weight of uselessness of the knowledge in Schroeder's briefcase had been jettisoned in this room.

Frosted glass door at the end of the corridor led into the secretariat. Harald swooped along the counter, breathing on the papers there until they rustled.

Candidates for the Diploma Examination in Communications Sciences this winter term would file an application form for admission, accompanied by photo and handwritten cv, not later than 15 January. Suppose he forgot to file? Failed exam? Was unable to find accommodation or to pay Czernak the money back? Or suppose these considerations that seemed so urgent now suddenly ceased to matter, and he emerged from the audience with his South American benefactor in that cool 1920s interior into sunlight sixty years later, dispensing with letter of introduction, now dated anyway, the addressee deceased, and made do instead with a modest opening in the import-export business, living unobtrusively on the border of shadow and light in a two-room apartment where the walls sweated, free of the past and all sense of displacement because at last become other—

Blok and Unschuld were waiting in any case. Alternatively, then, you as our budding local journalist, target of the Schroeder smear on account of your association with the *Evening Herald,* for which Schroeder obviously had nothing but contempt. Unschuld would drudge in the provinces, Blok eventually put on a tie and become some sort of media consultant.

'Lunch?'

'Why?'

'Why not? Don't you eat lunch, Hemsing?'

'Because it's lunchtime. I've cancelled lunch and decided to emigrate.'

'Any particular reason?'

'I can't stand the sight of your faces.'

'Oh piss off.'

The collage of reality. What contextual changes occurred when savagely, unnecessarily, his mouth slipped? Threesome knot on corner of Schelling Street, for which the pattern of all their previous lives had in some sense been a preparation, unravelled and dissolved. With a mental apology to Blok as he burrowed into the blancmange-pink building that vaguely deterred appetite, emerging in front of the students' canteen in the courtyard on the far side, Harald reflected that Tuesday lunchtime he'd probably find Dotty here.

Would-be eaters inside, looking hopefully up. Lepers in quarry. Not manna descending to them but menu, displayed on closed-circuit TV screens suspended from the ceiling for grandstand-crowd-viewing seven deep. Menu I, pork roast and dumpling, salad, yellow ticket for DM 4.50 at Staircase 2. Blue ticket, Staircase 4, mincemeat balls. But Dotty's colour preference, and perhaps her vegetarian instincts after a childhood scampered through by a much-loved guinea pig, two cats and three dogs, had more likely drawn her to a green ticket and the headline MEATLESS, lentils and corn . Harald bought a green ticket from the woman in the glass booth, took the third staircase up.

Steam, stainless steel, a booming cauldron played by man in white, sport as analogy, or orchestral percussion – probably the latter, for now the chorus came into view, strong kitchen women with moustaches, dressed in pink or white tunics and juggling plates on their apron-stage, brilliantly lit, to donging percussion accompaniment of ladle and ten-gallon tin and high-pitched shuffle of plates, choreographed for daily staging of feeding of five thousand down to the last detail, lentils and corn and the green ticket please, thank you, spiked, and still as Harald retreated down the dining hall a gonging demi-urge continued to sound his cauldron—

Send-off or summons (corn-green my lady's colours, not Persephone swallowed up in green when the year died but her sister, the lady of corn and lentil), summons to enter lists between benches and tables where ladies and sporting gentlemen of the philosophical Faculty of Language and Literature, students of romance languages, could be descried lounging, tilting in philological disputation at end of high hall.

Herald Harald, of shapely calf if short in shank, courier of the green *billet doux*, with books, brolly, World Child donation tin, his gear all higgledy at clank, cut jingle swathe through babble (his lunch tray balanced single-handed in addition), jauntily this artful joglar came clink-a-chink on tinny sound track through drone of dinning hall. Stefanie, *midons*, looked up in round-eyed surprise and dimpled at the arrival of the tin knight.

'Harald! Nobody's seen you for ages, you noddy. Where've you *been* all this time? Come and sit down here. D'you know Rebecca? Stefan, Martin, Melissa . . . Anyway. Where'd we got to?'

'By the late eleventh century a distinction had emerged between the two classes, the truly elegant poets, or troubadours, and the vulgar mountebanks, or joglars, who amused their audiences by jugglers' tricks and exhibiting performing animals.'

'Right. Next?'

'*Amors de terra lonhdana . . .*'

Sideways view *midons*, the shadows under her eyes. The amours of her troubadour, Alexander, keeping her up with his leys at night?

'Spell?'

'n-h-d . . . Aitch! . . . *Per vos totz lo cors mi dol . . .*'

'*Cors mi dol.* Doleful corpse, body, is it? What's he on about?'

'Love from a far-off land, for you all my being aches—'

Midons tossed her head and ran a hand through a falling strand of hair that Harald could imagine had been falling across her predecessors' brows for a couple of thousand years; while mountebanks in green-and-yellow striped hose, tin knights, the lower sort of joglars without even a decent pair of shoes and lacking the elegance of the troubadours though manned by the same desires, loitered hopefully at the blue velvet hour of Provençal evenings for a chance to entertain ladies-in-waiting with a trick or two, such as unbuttoning their leggings and exhibiting performing animals perhaps, to be recommended to their cold-hearted mistresses. Whereas the true attitude of the troubadour, Martin was saying as he leaned over the table, it seemed in order to engage Melissa opposite, was one of slavish devotion to a lady whose unrelenting coldness was required of her by convention. But that slavish devotion, Melissa objected, was itself artifice, a Trojan horse that the lady in her boundless sympathy – curiosity, murmured Martin – would naturally want to take between her gates, winding it on a silk cord into the perfumed citadel. Stefan took this opportunity to brief those who had missed that morning's lecture with an account of the song of Lady Biatritz, whose beauty so far outshone her contemporaries that they jealously declared war on her and laid siege to the citadel of her perfections. Taking advantage of the animated conversation, the tin knight was meanwhile laying siege to the citadel of his own ambitions at the other end of the table, where Dotty was copying Rebecca's notes, advancing the vanguard of his knee to skirmish tentatively with her leg. '*Doussa car*,' Rebecca dictated to Dotty, '*a totz aips volgutz*' – but Dotty broke down over the spelling and cribbed the translation instead. *Sweet face, with every desired quality*, read Harald, reminded bitterly of his more elegant rival, Alexander, *suffer I must, for your sake, many signs of disdain*.

'That's a comma.'

'Enough. *Lo cors mi dol*. Let's go and have some coffee.'

Wasn't it the case that the subjective impression of being in one piece with one's surroundings, so effortlessly that it remained unreflected, was the secret of happiness? Unreflected in one piece until the moment when Dotty said 'Ciao!', walking on, and Harald turned right, taking the short cut through the university hall into Amalien Street when, reflected, the piece cracked and he found himself again on bi-location, making his way up the stairs and opening the door to his room—

'What the hell's that?'

—where an enormous, horned cradle, and the rear end of Martha bent over it, trunkless legs looming vast and white under the hem of an indigo maternity dress, had a terrifically alienating effect.

'What the hell's going on in here, Martha.'

'It's the cradle for the baby.'

'I can see that.'

'From Schlichting's. I just wanted to try it out.'

She shortened as she straightened up, fingers to lips in mock silence, embarrassingly infantile in her grossness, and tiptoed over with a smile.

Martha's self-interest had become so inflated with her ballooning body that she could no longer see over the rim of herself. Harald's bad luck that today was the feast of the Virgin Mary, plus delivery from Schlichting's by two winged men in spotless overalls. This unbeatable double-billing monopolised Martha's advent calendar, obliterating everything else, including Harald and his unwantedness, subtly advertised by the cradle Martha was now parking in his room. It led to bitter accusations on both sides and a reshuffle of news-in-brief items in the late editions of 8 December,

Homeless Students On The Rise

hitting Harald with the full significance of the cold night he walked out into when later that evening he left his cousin's house forever.

False Grandee Exposed As Schroeder

Martha had called him a sponger, a hanger-on. There was some truth in this. Lack of money, the vague shambling beast that sometimes shook its chain, now pounced on him with teeth that felt a lot sharper in the cold night wind. Harald saw he must start earning a living. Suddenly his exams were urgently there: under that street lamp; round the next corner. He was wearing a duffel coat with the middle button missing, the white suit had been whisked away to the pawnbroker's, the munificent grandee in South America had unpleasantly been transformed into Schroeder, who now seized him by the ear and pulled him back down the glass-pannelled corridor, away from Schwabing, the Playoutdri Pool Bar, Caterwaul etc., that minefield of distractions through which his life had zigzagged for the past six years, very firmly in the other direction down Ludwig Street, to the vast tomb of a reading room in the state library. All right all right, I mean I have *been* here, I do *know* the way—

The phantom Schroeder frogmarched him into the building. They halted at the foot of the stone stairs, unfolding ledge by ledge like an allegorical prospect of the career it was now incumbent on him to climb. There, pronounced Schroeder in a ringing voice. The monuments in the gallery had got off their pedestals and gathered at the top of the staircase, not the conquerors in marble wigs with dates in Latin but a gauntlet of familiar faces, joglars between the first and the eighth terms in a variety of disguises which at the time he had found amusing – faces with sieves through which the years had since vanished. Harald shuddered and hurried on.

Herald Chosen For Diploma Thesis

Mornings and afternoons he hurried on thereafter, floodlit by neon in that mausoleum of a reading room where the bound issues of back numbers opened white with reluctant pages and he looked out over the heads of fellow readers at the bare trees in the courtyard beyond with a feeling hair-triggered between exuberance and sadness.

Student Accommodated In Cupboard

Nights he improvised in Brum's cupboard, a closet under the stairs with a bed that folded out, anything was possible, it was an improvising time. Objects stood in the room, tall, strapped parcels containing Brum's household. Brum was supposed to be moving them. Becoming interested in their spontaneous self-arrangement, he had begun to document them instead, photographing them, photographing himself measuring them. He made odd drawings in which the parcels seemed to be leaning forwards and listening, with handles that resembled ears. Harald woke out of his cupboard and saw them in the night, a ghostly army on the move. During the same night Brum dreamed he was in the gardens of Nymphenburg in an avenue lined with boxes, enclosing statues of his wife – so that the frost doesn't get at them, someone explained. Harald wondered about any parallels between Brum's dream and other events. What, for example, was the nature of the connection between Brum's impulse finally to move house and the first object then impulsively moved, an outsize styrofoam figure of his wife? Brum having to take out the front door and frame to squeeze her across the threshold of the Copper Lodge ten days before the winter solstice: what was the nature of such correspondences that might be at large in one's mind? In his Book of Himself Harald recorded the affinities unearthed by the juxtaposition of coincidence, dovetailing disparate needs, creating unexpected symmetries of interest, from Martha's claims for her baby and Harald's walking out of the house in Türken Street to his arrival at Little Monten Castle, where by coincidence he sat in the kitchen listening to Constanze snap thread with her teeth and to himself saying yes, yes, yes, when she asked him if he could move in for a week to help look after Bapa during her absence.

The day after Constanze left for the funeral in Friaul, Harald bumped into Conrad Sartorius coming out of a tobacconist's in Klenze Street. Have a cigar, the Local Editor said, as they crossed the road and entered the same building with one accord – triggering off in Harald the memory of a dream in which these events had already taken place. His editor had exchanged doublet and ruff for a leather jacket and polo neck, and the cobwebs from which Harald recalled Nellie emerging gave way this time to the bright interior of The Blue Ram on a Sunday morning.

Blank tables shone. The swept floor ran towards them at a tilt, giving the impression of a room marginally capsized. Motes of dust, smoke, talk, a warm emanation of human density that hung in the air almost visibly, rose from the cabal of Sunday morning regulars – Piontek once again, his foot at last out of plaster, Verhülsdonk and Johnny Ploog, the *Herald* gang now reinforced by Sartorius, who also lived locally; Koepenick and his wife, who lived over The Blue Ram and came down for their breakfast; and a few others, among them Harald's cousin, Hieronymus Kornrumpf.

It was in fact his cousin he had come to see, or rather the package that was in the bag under his chair. For the time being he sat and listened to Verhülsdonk discoursing at one end of the table on the origin of Christmas trees, Koepenick at the other on the ambiguity (strictly from the astrological point of view) of the issue of paternity in Christ's horoscope. Harald sipped a small blond beer and heard them talk without particularly listening after a while; in fact after a while the floor of The Blue Ram began to tilt a lot more and he clearly heard Candice speak. Her voice droned on and on. This was irritating, disturbing the sense of wellbeing that came over him as he felt himself rounding, taking shape as a salt cellar, heavily, heavily, it seemed of pewter, and he began to appreciate the total passivity he shared with his fellow objects. It was not incumbent on them to do anything other than sit, hang or lie in the places they were assigned; to be pot-bellied and blue like the china mustard pot to his left; or cylindrical, transparent, enviably light-headed, a toothpick holder made of plastic that was nodding off under the menu in the middle of the table; warm, snug, on a sound footing – if it were not for Candice keeping one awake by talking all night long. What was going on up there? From his closet he heard Brum groan, and then a screech. Harald's head fell forward and he woke with a start as Johnny Ploog pushed back his chair with a screech, and got up.

He left with Ploog, taking the parcel Hieronymus had brought. It contained the pair of underpants and two pairs of socks that had been in the wash the day he left, and a second-hand anthology of medieval love poetry he had asked his cousin to locate for him.

Ploog said he was going in the direction of Lederer Street. Harald said he was headed that way too. They walked in silence. Harald remembered a previous visit to Johnny's place, when his colleague had been laid up with a bout of flu. The visit had been well-intentioned, but it turned out to be an intrusion into the private life of the person Harald only knew as the buoyant columnist Johnny Ploog.

Johnny didn't have a private life, or there was no space for one in the dark little room overlooking the alley off Tal. The room was full of things, but Harald couldn't remember them. When he went away he remembered the room as empty. He couldn't understand this. Now, as they reached Gärtnerplatz, and Johnny mentioned he would be picking up his daughters to take them to the rink at the Olympic

Centre, because the second and the fourth Sundays of the
month were his, and how there was a court ruling about
this, Harald recalled two photographs he must have seen in
Johnny's room on a shelf – looked round the edge of that
dingy room, as it were, which screened off the view of so
many other places Harald had never imagined, better places,
that Johnny had lost – and felt ashamed. Probably the small
dark room off Tal, daughters on a shelf, was as much private
life as Johnny could afford. But there was no way Harald
could have said any of this.

Around the middle of the day he drove out to
Nymphenburg with Brum and helped him move more of his
stuff into the Copper Lodge. It was a clear wide afternoon,
frozen under foot, the pale blue sky above boundless, dispassionate. Ice had formed on the canal, hoar-frost cropped
and dusted with white the grass edges along the bank. The
sound of traffic receded as he walked down Notburga Street,
and turning off to Little Monten Castle he heard his footsteps bounce off the surrounding stillness. With the key
Constanze had given him he let himself in at the door in the
main gate, went round the back and entered by the side-
door she had left unlocked when she set out earlier that
morning. Bapa would be all right on his own for a couple of
hours, she'd said. Dotty had gone out for lunch and was not
back yet.

He must get used to you, Constanze had said the previous
week, as he followed her up to the tower room. A shaft of
light from the landing reached in as she opened the door,
touching the white sheet folded back over the coverlet.
Constanze continued talking without lowering her voice,
moving briskly about the room as if it contained nothing but
the furniture. For a moment Harald wondered if the old
man had been moved somewhere else. With a start he saw
the shrivelled white face that turned up to him out of the
shadow. It had changed so much that he didn't recognise it as
Gottfried's at all. Through the open door opposite the bed he

caught sight of nappies hanging on the balcony, it seemed by the yard. Constanze propped up the old man and lifted his feet over the side of the bed. Between them they supported him to the bathroom, half walking, half dragging his feet, sat him on the toilet, washed him, powdered him, changed his nappies and nightshirt and put him back to bed. Constanze had done this three times a day for the past few months.

Harald was put in the room that was used by Martha when she came home. From the door he looked down a couple of stairs across the kitchen to a passage leading to the rooms where Constanze and Dotty slept,

Where Dotty Slept

and as he perched at Martha's old school desk a new-found warmth in these words, or a warm imprint they left on sheets more readily imagined across that kitchen, interposed itself between his diploma thesis and a necessary degree of cool attention; by degrees warmed now the sheet of still unwritten white paper into an image of the nape of Dotty's neck. His attention to this could never be distracted, not by the musty odour of urine that came up off the old man's body, and Harald, holding him under the armpits, looked down as Dotty bent her head and addressed herself to his bedsores, nor by the dust storms of sweetly smelling powder that could only briefly overlay the pale, the almost-imperceptible vanilla scent of her he carried in his nostrils,

Slept

heavier in the mornings, essence, the lees of sleep, her scent curled up around her body while she slept, gathering there like the sleep dust in the corners of her eyes.

She was out the first few nights, nights he did Bapa alone.

Bapa had lost twenty pounds. So small the body in the bed, so frail and shallow that there was hardly a mound, sometimes it seemed a head was there without a body at all. In oval frames ancestral portraits hung on the walls of Gottfried's room: pale father with clipped moustache; broad, hirsute, rambling, barging his way out of the obscurity of a nineteenth-century photograph, the extravagant grandfather to whom he bore a far more striking likeness, and out of several more photographs, the restless traveller surveying prospects in Turkey, Greek islands, the Bay of Naples, while below him his bedridden grandson, eyes screwed up, more and more like a wizened mummy, lay muttering in the dark and scanned his memory for missing connections, destinations at which he would never arrive. Harald sat with a book on his knee. Sometimes he read. Sometimes his eyes travelled with the grandfather out of the oval portrait on to the silk embroidery he had brought from China. An old man sat on a dolphin, a younger man took his leave of two women, a silk road passing through a temple gate led inconclusively to a baldachin.

Amors De Terra Lonhdana

Sometimes he read, and looking up suddenly would catch the old man watching him through slits of eyes. He closed them again at once. Cunning, or shame perhaps to feel himself some kind of exhibit, peered at by strangers, shivering with bare skinflint bum, genitals, leaking jerkily over his grandniece in the bathroom— Harald glanced back over his shoulder when he heard the car pull up in the street outside, and noticed for the first time the women whose oval portraits he had been missing, and the window, and the tree beyond, and understood that Gottfried had his travelling days behind him, if he travelled with anyone it would be these women he would take his cue from,

Per Vos Totz Lo Cors Mi Dol

women in long skirts and with baskets slung over their backs, standing at the foot of a mountain.

The Siege Of Lady Biatritz

Strategically Harald was best placed in the kitchen, facing the door through which Dotty and Alex would have to come, with the digestive biscuits already on the table, three mugs, the milk just coming to the boil as he chatted away, matter-of-fact, jolly: Anyone for cocoa? After two successive nights, ambushed on his way to Dotty's room by an irrefusable offer that poured boiling milk over erotic intention, Alexander did not come up on the third evening, and on the fourth Dotty stayed at home. She could not square it with her heart to go out with Alex and come home with him to find notes from Harald in the bathroom and on her pillow, flanked by Haribo jelly babies. Notes on pillows were compromising, and their presence there annoyed her, but jelly babies were irresistible. She found them lying all over the house, on window-sills and banister posts, popped them into her mouth and thoughtfully licked her fingers. One led on to another – there was a trail of them – chair, stair, handle of door to Harald's room that stood ajar, a Santa Klaus jelly baby in the middle of the bed on a note that said: *Per vos totz lo cors mi dol.* Dotty laughed and bit off Santa's head. With colours changing across the spectrum of his feelings, an unstable vowel began to slide out of shadow into light, light-headed by degrees in Harald's doleful corpse a syllable of ache, *totz* or tits in either case *lo cors mi dol* but especially for the latter, lighter, especially mornings when the scent uncurled like warming frost on her waking body and at the kitchen window she stretched,

Because I Have Never Seen
A Body Better Shaped

her arms above her head, transparent, and her breasts stood up in the light.

Jack Frost was out and about, cock-a-hoop on cold nights, his frozen breath left splintered on window-panes in the morning, the trees stiffened, the white grass shrank, the ice locked up the canal. When Dotty walked along the avenue on leaves frozen in puddles, she remembered, to the accompaniment of popping sounds under her feet, an autumn carpet of leaves from the Auerdult to Haidhausen, walking Alexander receded, she turned to wave. Alex didn't skate. In the cold air the blurred figure at her side swung sharply into focus. 'Come on,' she said, 'beat you to the bridge.' Her blood pounded, her legs raced, braking sharply she bent panting and a spray of ice from Harald's skates spurted up into her face.

The cold lay coiled round Little Monten Castle; inside, the rooms retreated, stopped, transfixed, the house lay in a hundred-year sleep. Harald tiptoed up and down the stairs from the tower room. He looked at the prints of the Boxer Rebellion, watercolours of the Bay of Naples. 'Convenient,' muttered Bapa, when Harald gave him his drink, 'very convenient these cups with their elongated spouts.' Bapa didn't say much. He slept with the window open and in the silent mornings now his breath was white. His bed was surrounded by clocks, which Constanze wound up once a week. He had asked for all the clocks to be brought in, and all his trophies, silver cups he had inscribed and awarded himself for imaginary achievements in flying, gymnastics, big-game hunting. Beyond the open window the tree, too, was white with crystals, configurations of moisture frozen where hoar-frost settled. In his Book of Himself Harald noted the hoar-frost, the old man's white breath and the spray of chipped ice on Dotty's cheeks

Doussa Car'

under an entry for the ten-thousand-and-seventy-ninth Haraldian day, seventy-five days after sustaining concussion complicated by emotional haemorrhage on falling out of a pear tree. Words edgeways in that teeming interim had become less and less concerned with the weights and measures of Harald's body, a metabolism in solitude, more and more with the impact of hers on his, with monitoring the progress of Dotty herself. Self-absorbed, he saw and understood her self-absorption, it was hers that gradually became his. Drawing his fingers up over his groin he thought of her body already given, but still the desire in her for her body to be desired to be given all over again. This was how Dotty had sometimes stood between Alex, to whom given, and Harald, who desired. This was how she now came and stood just in the doorway of his room, book in hand, trying out on him a comparison between troubadour and *minnesänger* to be handed in before the Christmas holiday, coming forward, as she read, to take a jelly baby from the bag on the bedside table, sucking fingers between sentences, putting stickiness on pages, and finally plonking down on the bed with a terrific crash.

Monitoring the progress of Dotty in the Book of Himself, hovering between sentences, monitoring betweenness, Harald found himself unable to rest long enough at any one place in her punctuation to occasion a full stop; at best a semi-colon, half-way house from which she might go on or might equally turn back, always caught in a conditional or interrogative mood between intentions; and in the actuality of her being to which this breathlessness corresponded he was always catching her on the hop between places, too, such as the entrance to premises on Ludwig and Leopold Streets, for the most part cafés, or on the landings between the flights of stairs joining the many living levels at home in Little Monten Castle; for she was never in the kitchen, nor

in his room, nor upstairs with Bapa, but really always on her
way to one or a combination of these, and in the same way
never sitting down to meals but nibbling between them,
hamstrung between choices of pleasure, things in her
mouth, headphones in her ears, fingers in her crotch, her life
between commas, distractions that took her away and
brought her pleasurably back to herself. Too often between
places himself, Harald saw and understood this, grateful to
Dotty for gradually becoming all places to him, in a manner
of speaking, and allowing him at least that subjective impression of being in one piece with his surroundings when at last
she sat down on his bed with a terrific, a deliciously
resounding crash.

From the door he looked down a couple of stairs to the
passage leading to the room where Dotty slept; and as he sat
perched at Martha's old school desk a new-found warmth in
these words, or a warm imprint they left on sheets more
readily imagined now, interposed itself between his diploma
thesis and a necessary degree of cool attention, warmed by
degrees the half-written sheet of paper into an image of
blueish indentations on the nape of Dotty's neck. The hardly
perceptible vanilla scent of her he carried in his nostrils was
heavier in the mornings, her scent curled up around her
body while she slept, gathered like sleep dust in the corners
of her eyes. Colours changed across the spectrum of his
feelings out of shadow into light, especially mornings, when
the scent uncurled like warming frost on her waking body
and at the kitchen window she stretched, her arms above her
head, and her breasts stood up in the light.

In the cold air the blurred figure at her side swung sharply
into focus.

'Come on, I'll beat you to the bridge!'

'You've already— Hey!'

Her blood pounded, her legs raced, braking sharply she
bent panting, and a spray of ice from Harald's skates spurted
up into her face.

'Why don't we ever go out together?'

'Because of Bapa. That was why I came.'

'He'll be all right on his own for a couple of hours. We'd be back by six.'

'Having done what in the meantime?'

'I don't know. Window-shopping. Why don't we go and see some food, for instance?'

'Seafood?'

'Dallmayr's. There's the tram.'

And the sight of her white-faced, the skates slung over her shoulders still icy at Roman Square, thawing out from stop to stop, the blood roaring in her cheeks, stains spreading across breast and back and her face on fire by the time the tram lurched into Pacelli Street. See on foot, dream seafood among shoals shoulder-rubbing on Theatiner Street in late afternoon twilight, spent sun at slant, shouldering towards the winter solstice. A warm wind blew, clouds scudded, walking down Diener Street Harald heard chimes, and looking up he saw the wind-scoop on the wall above the entrance to Dallmayr's revolving at speed, thaw drip-dropping fast fast fast from the guttering under the eaves. Burble and hot air blasted from the door, garbled bauble, babble, Doppler effect of vowel-shift acquiring lightness under the vaulted ceiling of the interior and blending with the aroma of coffee, Ethiopian crown, Prodomo, Antigua Tarrazo brass-lettered in porcelain urns, ground at the counter by women in blue uniforms crossed with white aprons, chortling in percolators, aromatically the grains were released from the urns and rushed into packets at the bottom of chutes. Dotty, symbiotic among the honeys, thyme leaf, rosemary, lavender, yawning and showing white teeth against a background of loganberry, quince and apricot preserves, turned left at teas and went upstairs. Hardware department. Nothing to eat. She prodded a terracotta Santa standing watch with sack and lantern over festive tableware, and went back downstairs to favourite racks, stacks, snacky rosettes, cheese crispies and the temptation of tortelettes, cakelets at the cooky counter, boxed and labelled under the imprint *By Appointment to the Court, Alois Dallmayr, Diener St. No. 4.* By piles of Dresden fruitcake loaves laid out like corpses whitely dusted she stood wistfully, her fingers pointing at the spiced pies and pastry horns behind the glass, cinnamon stars, arrak and marzipan in chocolate coats, the incomparable Marraschkino-kirsch flanked by nougat oysters. See some food and feel hole in stomach. Hole in pocket. Short of cash and peckish, through cold eyes of stuffed pike hugging the overhead wall (briefly Harald glimpsed Schroeder), see Dotty swimming with the shoals into the marble bay of the shop, livebait wriggling her shoulders, and consider angles of approach. Orgy angle, physical attractions foremost? Her aromas, honies, juices, all her girlish condiments? Insinuation via jelly babies, harbouring carnivorous intentions? Cold eyes of stuffed pike on dainty morsel with hopping shoulders? Harald rested his hand on a marble infant astride a fish with a water-pipe coming out of its mouth and discharging into a basin, warm eyes on Dotty following her progress, intermittently blocked out by beef tournedos, goose-liver cream paste with artichoke, venison pâté garnished with peaches, snack by snack anticlockwise round the counter. Fresh at twenty, in her element of snackiness open all year long and still fresh, still decomposing deliciously towards ripeness, still edible in all parts (snot, why not?) as palatable as salmon roe on toast, with tangerine slices to offset the saltiness. Dotty in her salad days, morsels of terrine de foie gras scooped out of her ears, gobbets, niblets, spice of sleep dust in morning eyes, her fragile, crunchable collar-bone, pink morsels of chilled nipples and sheer skin, with shoulder-hopping strides she walked crisply past green salads on into a broader aisle. At some time, inescapably, the subject of meat. Scotch rib-eye, T-bone and club steak. Though lean at first, dainty and snackish, the lamb chops would gradually put on weight and qualify sheepishly as a main course. The way of florid hams and bulging, swart sausage. A gigantic shoulder of mutton past its prime. Imagine her with the progression of the years going the way her sisters went, remember, a full-blown woman like Steffi and, a rung or two up that pear-tree ladder, smoothly casked like her sister Martha. Following her down the broader aisle with a floor laid out in marbled *mettwurst* patterns, red meaty floor veined white, he heard a surge of fuller sound, fuller at the centre, booming vowels, booming clamour *boing bing* at cash register and heavy green smell of damp Loden swirling at a gusty entrance where splinters of chimes from the Christmas market,

Jingle Bells

audible in Diener Street, shattered now in the open air with the bells of St Peter's. Illuminations hung like cobwebs under the towers of the cathedral, illuminated the red roofs, copper steeples green against a black sky, the lights of the spruce tree outside the Town Hall tossed and shimmered in the wind, shimmering in the wind the mobiles of upturned glass thimbles hanging at market stalls, strings of rings enclosing stars of David, silhouettes of gilt angels, shepherds and kings shimmertinkling in lulls between donging gusts, jingling, jingling, jangle-donging in strains of snarled sounds a warm wet polyphonous wind blew across the square and around the corner and on, to Christmas.

Tropic of Capricorn

HIERONYMUS

There's a lot of argument as to who is supposed to be telling this, and what they are telling, and where, and how. By professional habit Koepenick argues for the future tense and a prediction. Ideally this would be in his apartment or on the premises of The Blue Ram downstairs. Brum says the nativity is a painting, and doesn't need any words at all. Of course the past tense, rejoins Father Anton. And incidentally, without the words of the evangelist, recording the event in question two thousand years ago, there wouldn't be any nativity for Brum and his colleagues to paint.

Hieronymus has to overrule this. As yet there is no event in question. Father Anton is jumping the gun. It is incumbent on Hieronymus, as chairman, to clarify a still diffuse state of affairs. For the sake of argument he settles for hypnagogic, between dream and non-dream, in the early hours of Tuesday 22 December. The present tense will do as well as any other to record the neuter of dreamtime, they're in it now, seems convenient, why not go on?

And all went to be taxed, every one into his own city. These are Martha's words, breaking tense, archaically chiming in with Father Anton. Does she suspect? Is this the event – a summons to Deroy Street to give an account of himself to the tax inspector? Taking stock during the last couple of days, Hieronymus has entered VSOP earnings in a separate, secret ledger, naturally they won't be declared. *To be taxed with Mary his espoused wife, being great with child. And so it was, that, while they were there, the days were accomplished that she should be delivered.* Hieronymus tosses and turns, feeling himself confined in a narrow space, perhaps a condition of tax, perhaps of being in bed.

At this there is a general outcry. The chairman is accused of hijacking the scenario and arranging it around his bed out of sheer laziness. Hearing heavy rustle, unmistakably the sound of stockinged woman crossing her legs, Hieronymus admits to convenience of bed: as a matter of fact he had Astrid in mind. He looks round to test reactions. He sees everyone nod knowingly. More than nod. Actually, they bounce. Eight or ten people, with faces in which there are still traces of outcry, sit ruminatively bouncing up and down. They bounce for a while. Probably this is because the road is up or speed bumps have been installed on this stretch, suggests Mrs Koepenick of all people, pointing out that they are in fact sitting in her husband's mobile astrological practice, a converted VW bus, which Koepenick is driving.

This is a stroke of genius. Agreement is instant and unanimous. There is the incredulous silence of bickering people suddenly robbed of their argument, stranded in instant, unanimous agreement.

Tentatively the chairman now seeks to establish other coordinates. Consulting the ephemeris on his lap, he gives Koepenick directions. The astrologer is taking all this remarkably well, considering he is in striped pyjamas in the present tense and would much prefer to be out of them, in some speculative stripeless future state. It's already eleven o'clock. For the last quarter of an hour, having reached the horned goat-fish, the tenth sign of the zodiac, the sun has been dawdling at the winter solstice at maximum declination of 23° 27′, tracing an imaginary circle along the Tropic of Capricorn. Koepenick peers up anxiously through the windscreen.

This isn't just any old astronomical map reference, says the chairman, having waited in vain for some audience reaction. This represents a fulcrum of civilisation in the northern hemisphere. With light pared down to the shortest day of the year, the sun dithering so low on the horizon that it seemed to risk vanishing altogether, the question for unenlightened ancestors had naturally been how to persuade it to come back. Hence Christmas, which the church, as always, had shoplifted from a rival heathen establishment (the religion associated with Mithra). In the Julian calendar, 25 December was reckoned to be the winter solstice, the nativity of the sun, when robed men had been accustomed to burst forth from inner shrines in Syria, Egypt, Mesopotamia etc. with ecstatic cries. The virgin has brought forth! The light is waxing!

Same with Easter, says Koepenick's neighbour from The Blue Ram, the actor Hans Gugglhör. Locally he's known as Bone Gleaner, on account of the play at the Cuvilliés Theatre where he has appeared as Death more than fifty times. Bone Gleaner says the demise of Christ on 25 March, coinciding with the vernal equinox, merely followed the precedent of the Phrygian god Attis, whose death and resurrection were mourned and rejoiced over at a spring festival of far greater antiquity.

(Still hungover from the previous night but looking as spruce as ever after a shave and a change of linen, Bone Gleaner is considered something of an expert on these matters. When he expatiates on the mysteries of birth, death, resurrection etc. and the paradigms of these in the succession of the seasons and the solar equinoxes he is heard out in respectful silence. Ironically enough, it's Bone Gleaner's birthday, and some of the guests invited for brunch at

Koepenick's house hadn't even arrived by the time the others piled into the VW bus and left, their departure precipitated by the onset of Martha's labour pains.)

The next contribution comes from Martha, as if in timely onomatopoeic response to Gugglhör's conjecture regarding the inner shrine. A gurgling levitates into an aspirated hiss, conveying a rough idea of waxing light. At the higher pitch in her scale of moans she achieves a remarkable quality of transparency. She is lying sideways in the luggage compartment, with her legs over the back seat. Mrs Koepenick is hanging on to those legs for dear life, apparently under the impression that Martha will otherwise fall out. Father Anton holds her hands and speaks words of comfort while the bus remains in orbit of Gärtnertplatz, as Koepenick and Hieronymus revolve in lengthy ellipses around the question of the quickest route to Neuhausen in the mid-morning traffic. Koepenick is in favour of turning back down Klenze Street, if only because this'll give him a chance to nip into his house and pick up some cigarettes. Hieronymus wants to take the exit that leads into Blumen Street. Arguing, for the time being they continue driving round and round the square. Martha moans, and Father Anton again intervenes between pilot and navigator to remind them of the urgency of their mission. Meanwhile it has begun to snow.

Bone Gleaner bounces back with the information that the midwinter solstice was traditionally the season of the dead. Dead kinsmen were believed to come inside the pale of human fellowship, sharing with the living in banquets held on their tombs and in rites involving yule log, evergreen, the tree of paradise. Ancient Roman festivals between Saturnalia and Kalends contributed merrymaking and the exchange of presents to the modern Christmas feast, traditions of cheerful prophylaxis, wishful magic, the flip side of a beleaguered human spirit. Funerals supplied occasions for whacky wakes, death made for some of the best jokes. It made sense to celebrate when things were at their worst.

Taking a swig from his flask, Bone Gleaner smacks his lips. Brum and the news photographer Lucas Sliep, who's in this for the human interest, investigate a hamper bootlegged under the middle seat, making noises of appreciation when they open it and find six bottles of Nymphenburg *sekt*. Martha, in the boot, hears corks pop, effervescence gushing in bottlenecks, while a woman's voice remarks in musky accents that Epiphany, in ancient Egypt, was the date of a solstice that was celebrated as the time when the waters of the Nile overflowed and fertilised the delta. In this connection there had arisen certain mystery cults, celebrating a new age born of the virgin Kore, daughter of the goddess Demeter, who was Mother Earth. And not only here. In other places in the Middle East this was a season of miraculous fountains, from which wine would flow instead of water.

Father Anton leaps at this mention of Epiphany from the unexpected quarter of a belly-dancer in Byblos. Leaps is an exaggeration – he leans forward slightly, receiving the plastic cup that Lucas has poured for him, apparently with the intention of speaking to Leila, in fact to move physically in edgeways on Hans Gugglhör, whose Bone Gleaner has been hogging too much of the stage for the friar's liking. 'For Christians,' he says, 'Epiphany commemorates three manifestations – the birth, the baptism and the first miracle of Our Lord at Cana, just that water-to-wine phenomenon Leila has identified in the Middle East. For the eastern and western churches had synchronised each other's incarnation festivals by the end of the fourth century, thus establishing the dodecahameron, the twelve-day celebration from Christmas to Epiphany.'

'i.e. from Saturnalia to Kalends,' reiterates Bone Gleaner dryly, 'twelve days and above all nights of orgiastic feasting, eh?'

'Twelve nights,' says Brum, 'that rings a bell. Aren't we talking about the original Feast of Fools?'

Hieronymus concedes they may now be getting close to the event in question. Spinning round and round a patch of green at the centre of Gärtnerplatz while the sun stalls at the Tropic of Capricorn and traces an imaginary circle, ten people drink cheap champagne in a Volkswagen bus that only after Brum's remark does the chairman recognise for what it is: a custom-built *carrus navalis*, or ship on wheels, transporting his wife (who more than any of them will be instrumental in shaping the event) to the maternity hospital at Red Cross Square. And reaching across Koepenick's lap he gives the steering wheel the decisive yank that gets them off the roundabout.

Koepenick curses. Passengers shriek. The bus skids, burning rubber and swaying perilously as it takes the corner but steadying again as it levels out in the exit lane. And already they are bowling along in the direction of Neuhausen.

Gugglhör can't resist another crack at Father Anton. 'What is the Christian story but plagiarism from start to finish,' he says, 'just one more rehash of that immemorial saga of fertility rites culminating in the death of a sacrificial king, Hanswurst or Pierrot, Don Cristobal or Arlecchino, Harlequin, Hariloking, half human, half supernatural being, king of an army of dead souls – like Christ these bogeymen were all successors of that atavistic figure with his evergreen sceptre, the Bough of Life, who ruled over midwinter rites between Epiphany and Candlemas.'

Bouncing gently, the Franciscan takes the chance to sneak in an impromptu mobile homily in Koepenick's bus. 'All these many different figures,' he says, 'surely testify to one and the same impulse of adoration, whose manifold forms are aspects precisely of its immanent universality. The pagan celebration of Sol Invictus, the unconquered sun, at the time of the winter solstice, gives way to the celebration of the nativity of the man-god because the urge to adoration is answered in him not by terror but love. What is this adoration? It is man's wonder before the mystery of creation. Bone Gleaner,' he points out slyly, 'may find himself as out of season as Scrooge at Christmas, when this mystery of creation will be given simple expression as a birth, the nativity of a messiah whose gifts to mankind will encompass his spiritual renaissance. Forasmuch as many have taken in hand to set forth in order a declaration of those things which are most surely believed among us—'

To Gugglhör's embarrassment, who feels equipped for anything but this, Father Anton whips a handy little New Testament out of the inner recesses of his cowl and begins, incredibly, to read *The Gospel According To St Luke.* The chairman feels this keenly as a blow to a situation that has been nursed out of uncertainty entirely by teamwork and has so far still managed to keep its options open. Certainty, in the form of the Franciscan's unrelenting voice, a needle stuck on the evangelist's record, reiterating the same old message message message for the past two thousand years, now closes like a dreadful vice; and in its grip, deprived of speaking parts, the other passengers relapse into resigned silence. Even Martha's moans subside to coos and gurgles in the boot, roosting pigeons. Hieronymus and Koepenick haven't even begun to explore the connotations of the solstice in the Tenth House – mid-heaven, no less, the House of the Father, Public Standing and Aspirations. Father is very much a subject on which Hieronymus desires a professional opinion from Koepenick, best gleaned from the child's horoscope, which first requires the child to be born. Thus he involuntarily finds himself caught up in the narrative of Elizabeth and Zacharias, who had no child because Elizabeth was barren and they both were well stricken in years. All this is ruefully familiar stuff. Hieronymus listens with increasing discomfort. How shall this be, seeing I know not a man? The Holy Ghost shall come upon thee, and the power of the highest shall overshadow thee. Who? What? Over my dead body. The snowfall thickens, and all went to be taxed, with Mary his espoused wife, being great with child, and the father's voice begins to fade, eroded by the sound of windscreen wipers that are becoming panicky in their insistence. Hieronymus feels himself fade, the wipers stall, windscreen clogs up, dropping off he feels them all fade one by one, until he knows there will only be Brum, left in a ship on wheels come to a standstill, stranded somewhere in a white silence—

THE HORNED
GOAT-FISH

The Twelve Nights

BRUM

The First Night: *A Star Over Haidhausen*

I wake early with a light heart. I remember this feeling from Christmas mornings when I was a kid. I get up in the dark, make coffee, light the stove. These actions are part of a conspiracy of early morning silence. I open the front door and listen out. The same silence stretches and stretches. Snow stands almost up to the eaves. From the porch I can't tell if it's still snowing. Can't even see any sky.

Drinking coffee, I sit in silence and listen to the rafters crack. Procyon lies in his basket, pretending to be asleep, but every time one cracks he pricks up his ears. I reckon there must be five or six feet of snow on the roof by now. I'd better have a look.

It takes me long enough to clear a path just the width of the shovel from the eaves to the ridge of the roof. It doesn't seem significantly higher up there. After a snowfall that has continued for three days and nights the ground has risen by six feet. Smoke climbs in steady vertical columns from buildings no longer visible. A crow flies out of a white tree.

These are the only signs of life. No sound of traffic from Verdi Street to the east. I can make out the flagpole and flag at the petrol station opposite, but the pumps, the kiosk and a whole inner city highway have all disappeared under the snow.

In the cellar I unearth cross-country skis and an old knapsack, which I pack with a few jars of preserves for Constanze and a change of clothes. Procyon knows the drill. No longer with his old enthusiasm, still as obedient as ever, he allows himself to be stowed in the knapsack with his head under the flap and his snout sticking out on my shoulder. Since Steffi's departure his spark has gone. He holds me responsible for her absence, and he does not approve of Candice. Our relations are not unfriendly, but Procyon is withholding his affection. In things like this the dog is very human.

We set out around midday. Climbing the snow bank outside the front door, I push off from an elevation that is no longer recognisable as my neighbour's garage, and coast down to Verdi Street, poling as I go. Here and there I sink in up to my ankles. The surface holds.

Reaching Verdi Street at the point where the road curves away in the direction of the Botanical Gardens, I can hear a muffled rumble in the distance. I see flashing yellow lights, and gradually, as they draw nearer, the drivers' cabs of two snow-ploughs behind what I make out to be an advancing wall of snow half a highway wide.

The bridge over the canal has been obliterated. There is a faint rise in its place. In that level white landscape it looks as if something underneath has breathed. I make tracks down the canal. White-capped, shortened by six feet, the trees on either side look stunted, absurd, like rows of cauliflower.

I find I am able to step without difficulty over the garden wall in Monten Street. If it snows a bit more, Constanze's guests will be saved the trouble of walking upstairs, able to access the apartment via the balcony on the first floor.

She and Dotty are about to sit down to lunch. Her first news is about Martha. Hieronymus has called to say that during the night his wife gave birth to twins. The mother is comfortable, the two girls healthy, what more can one ask for? Well, to see the grandchildren for herself, of course, but until the roads have been cleared there's no way for Constanze to do that. A blessing Hieronymus is stuck out at the hospital. Otherwise Martha would have been without anyone. She was just thinking of me, too, she says, stuck at the Copper Lodge without a telephone.

This is my mother-in-law's way of hinting she'd like some news of Stefanie. As a matter of fact a postcard arrived a couple of days ago. She and Hollman have been cruising in the South Pacific. She says they expect to be back early in the new year. I tell Constanze about the card. I don't tell her how this first direct message from my wife since she left me three months ago has raked up a pain that had been growing numb. What did that mean, *expected to be back*? Back where? The two of them back in Bogenhausen? What made her think I'd be interested in hearing that?

We talk about the weather. Weather is more than an old conversation piece these days. It may soon be added to the list of the four last things, if not by the Pope, whose celebration of mass in St Peter's is billed to be shared by two billion TV viewers. Snow has fallen right across Europe, in some places the greatest recorded snowfall ever. After two or three snowless, exceptionally mild winters, and the six hottest summers of the century within a decade, this freak winter seems to be another distress signal from a planet on tilt. Where's the two-billion audience for *this* Christmas message?

Constanze got up to make coffee and put out cake. Her heart wasn't in a conversation about the death of the planet when her thoughts were still so obviously with the birth of her twin granddaughters. While Dotty cleared the dishes I went to the tower room to fetch Gottfried down.

Reflections from the snow beam off the ceiling and make the room white. Frost settles on the old man's face and gives him this white shadow of a beard. Closer, I see his beard has turned white. He scowls when I come in, asks if I'm the doctor. I tell him I'm the steward. The airship has arrived at the North Pole and will shortly be making its descent. Perhaps I can be of assistance on the stairs. Bapa finds this acceptable. I pick him up and carry him downstairs, giving him our altitude at intervals. We descend three thousand feet.

Bapa is wrapped up on the sofa in the living-room. Nothing of our Christmas interests him. He huddles there as mute and unrecognising as a pygmy from central Africa. The present he gives himself is a jumbo pack of Pampers at wholesaler's discount. These are familiar, his bow and arrow, sparking a flicker in his eyes.

For Constanze he has bought useful if boring household items: a pressure cooker, an electric can-opener. From far away Bapa peers at them with hatred and distrust. Constanze, doing her pitch, shows an exaggerated appreciation for these articles she has given herself. Bapa looks at her as if she's off her head. Whatever is going on inside his, there's no way we can share it. He huddles on the sofa, peers, scowls, zones out for minutes at a stretch. Cake, tree, candles, electronically melodious Christmas cards from Hong Kong, nothing gets past his silence. Later in the afternoon I carry him back upstairs. Constanze is in tears in the kitchen. Daily heroism. She cares enough to cry, even if she is crying for herself.

I decide to leave Procyon with Dotty. I have him and Bapa very much on my mind as I pole off the wall of Little Monten Castle with enough momentum from the snow drifts piled up there to carry me down to the corner of the street. Two old codgers. Cranky, enfeebled or just different – I feel all households should have their codgers to keep them human. Consider that singles account for fifty per cent of all households in this town. Consider long-term effects of this.

Erosion of human climate comparable to the other ecological ruins we have built. But to believe in the urgency of this I would have to feel about it with some anxiety, which at the moment is impossible. The freak weather I take to be another distress signal from a planet on tilt is itself a reason for light-heartedness. I may feel anxiety about myself, my wife, my bank balance, but not about my planet, which at the moment is opening up a prospect of Nymphenburger Street utterly deserted under six feet of snow on the kind of miraculous winter afternoon one is unlikely to experience more than once a century. The sunlight may be suspiciously ultra-violet, thawing the snow-stricken trees and setting off a rushing discharge of loads from their branches, and the air may be polluted in which I watch a spray of crystals, shimmering airborne reflectors, fan slowly up and out, but these are rational structures which the sheer animal exhilaration I feel cares nothing about. A traffic light at waist level turns red, exuberantly I slide past. It feels like it's downhill all the way. As the sun sinks on the horizon the temperature drops, and on the freezing snow I make fast tracks. I slide past everything, unable to stop until I reach a great bank of snow pushed up by the bulldozers clearing Stiglmaier Square. Clattering over the road, I slalom down between the No Parking signs at the top of Brienner Street. Briefly I have the impression of looking down a billowing white sheet curving away at the edges, where the snow falls obliquely, thinly, under the eaves; a wind-inflated sheet, smooth as a convex glass cylinder, which now gives way to a view of Königsplatz with the columns of the Glyptothek drawing shadows in that stillness which remind me of the desert ruins of Baalbek.

Urban civilisation has been restored to the centre of town. Stachus swept clear of snow as far as Lehnbachplatz, clear all the way to the crest of the hill at the north end of Mars Street. Cars venture out again, performing toe-loops and pirouettes in slow motion on the ice-rink that has been made

out of Karlsplatz. Snow-changed shape of the bowls of the
fountain at Lehnbachplatz, upreachingness and flowing
plenty, still my favourite fountain. My conscience. My bank
account. My dog, toothpaste, global warming. Problems
with my. In Roman script the lack of a visual dimension to
words – contrast Seafood Princess Garden (the name of the
restaurant in the arcade at Karlstor) with ideogram of
Chinese Garden showing bird's-eye perspective of same, a
walled enclosure seen from above. Scholars went up in kites
to view their recommendations to imperial pictogram committee? Transliteration of idea into sensuous experience.
Texture of Chinese thought. I whizz through the arcade
among astonished strollers in the pedestrian zone and turn
right, heading south.

Eisenmann, Damenstift, Kreuz, old names in old and
narrow streets where the wind has collected the snow in
drifts and steep roofs pour down avalanches. Huge snow
boulders lie strewn. Negotiating an abyss, I clamber down
and up, ski level with first-floor windows, taking stock of private Christmas afternoons, already darkening interiors
illuminated television-blue, evergreen wreaths and Advent
candles, the smells of roast and other more subtle emanations through people's windows, a distension of space, until
the boredom in these rooms becomes intolerable and someone snaps a toothpick, getting up to open the window. I
reach Pestalozzi Street. It's getting dark as I enter a tunnel of
frozen trees in the old South Cemetery. Then I look out over
the Isar.

Looking downstream, I think of the barley fields bordering the river and the chestnut-tree garden on the
Nockherberg originally painted into the mural for Brewers
Hall, and I remember Stefanie's dream. Turning the corner
in pursuit of the river, I see again the images of her sleep.
Beyond the corner the river vanishes. I see whiteness. I see
a winter landscape. The river's frozen. Cascades of ice hang
in mid-air where the weir was. River, roads, bridges and

buildings have disappeared under the snow. I see the landscape she saw, and wonder why I resisted this, unable to
change my design. Always moving on to other places, the
restlessness of my desires resisting their fulfilment, insuffi-
ciently consolidated and failing to stay in place: I stand with
a feeling of unease between emptiness of time past and
shrinking time ahead, the narrowing avenues of possibilities
I know will remain unexplored for ever.

Across the river the evening star has risen luminous in a
pale sky. I remain standing for a long while, undecided what
to do. I no longer feel like making the visit to Zenetti Street
I had planned, not even just to drop off the key to my apartment and say merry Christmas to Mrs Mackensen. Looking
back downstream, my attention is caught by an extraordinary brightness that has become visible very low in the
northern sky.

The illumination appears to be over Haidhausen. Drawn
by curiosity, I backtrack down Pestalozzi Street, crossing
the Isar on a snow bank that I take to be Cornelius Bridge.
I continue east, moving up the heights of the Au, before
heading again in the direction of the light, which I now
identify over Gasteig. There's some kind of light show going
on there at the Culture Centre. I can see the light changing
shape and colour as laser beams are bundled and dispersed.
Reaching Preysing Street, I look down the road and see
them bond a star of David, coruscating in the night. The
road has not yet been cleared, but people with skis, snow-
shoes and sledges are converging from sidestreets, forming a
crowd that fills the road and soon comes to a standstill. The
queue extends for a hundred yards at least. Wisps of condensation snake out of collars and curl up under the rim of
hats. Preysing Street is asmoke with large numbers of people
waiting outside on a cold night for what seems to be some
special event. This is indeed the case.

The Second Night: *Interstellar Medium, Thermonuclear Explosion*

Custodian of Arthouse, Enno Leibowicz, is about to do his runaround with the press. We have a nodding acquaintance from the committee that approved my Chaos Objects at last year's festival. He invites me to tag along.

Leibowicz is a natural leader. Beside him there's no room for anyone else. He's so fat he fills out corridors on his own, and he's in the habit of asking people, rather cunningly, if they mind him going on ahead. So off rolls Leibowicz, talking in his loud voice about the Arthouse project development in the former sausage factory that has been purchased and converted by the municipality, about floor space, running costs, ventilation and fire precautions etc. before edging more interestingly towards the project's objectives. A representative of one of the tabloids cuts him short, however.

'Where's the hermaphrodite?'

'Could you wait just a *minute*.'

'Is it real?'

'Isn't a display of this nature offensive? Would you comment on Alderman Huber's view that it's in contravention of the by-law permitting entertainments only of a serious nature on religious feast days?'

'It is of a serious nature. It is not an entertainment.'

'Whatever, Huber calls it blasphemous and obscene.'

'Alderman Huber is in contravention of even the minimum standards of culture and intelligence.'

'May I quote you on that?'

I detach myself from the journalists and join other visitors in search of the sound-track spooling out of the hall. Events taking place on platforms on either side of the room compete for our attention. In front of the platforms tables have been set up, with visual display materials and lists of petitions laid out for our inspection, hopefully our signatures.

The pope is indicted as an accessory to incitement to world famine on account of his veto of contraception. A montage of the Adoration of the Magi by an old master shows the Virgin holding out an Ethiopian baby with hypertrophic stomach for inspection by Red Cross staff. Winged United Nation officials in flight overhead peer sympathetically down. Victims of torture and suppression by the governments of the world sign testimonies and petition for political asylum.

Some of the signatories have been brought over from the provisional refugee camp in Trojano Street and are standing on stage in a chain-gang, symbolically roped together. We see them in close-up in a video clip, talking heads subtitled and interspersed with scenes of violent death. Arthouse visitors tend to ignore these serious-faced men with dark moustaches who are physically present on the stage, preferring to watch them in the video. Placards round their necks identify them as the world's Christmas refugees, alluding to the outcasts in Bethlehem. This may be stretching the point for some visitors. They look embarrassed, a bit dissatisfied, frankly. Not much festival about this. Outside of the video no one is doing any talking. Not enough action around here.

'So obviously the idea is—'

Leibowicz is back on top, journalists tamed, nibbling their pencils as he lectures. Modernise the Christmas theme. Actualise the events in contemporary political, cultural and scientific terms. Inquiry into miraculous conception and origins of life. Dust off superstition, refurbish it with knowledge. Update virgin birth with facts of life, via the theory of spontaneous generation – origins of life in dew, decaying corpses, dirty old rags or pieces of cheese – and its refutation by Harvey, Redi, Pasteur *inter al*, proceeding to descriptions of agamogenesis, asexual reproduction by the techniques of spore formation, budding etc. etc.

Binary fission is about to take place on the stage opposite the refugees. A woman introduces the protagonist. Amoeba is the simplest of all animals, she says, a one-celled organism, or *protozoa*. She claps her hands. With astonishment we watch something, or things, covered in a sheet, stagger out from behind a curtain. Part of it tries to walk. Part of it tries to do a forward flip. Amoeba collapses, children giggle. Amoeba is *amorphous*, the woman says, as the sheet sprouts tentacles and gropes forward again in the direction of a plate labelled DOUGHNUTS. The protoplasm within the cell membrane, she continues, flows into projections known as *pseudopodia*, or false feet, which convey the rest of the cell in the direction of *food*. A hand appears and whisks the plate with the doughnuts under the sheet. The audience laughs. Amoeba eats.

When Amoeba has eaten and attained maximum growth, the woman resumes, it is time for the nucleus to *divide*. A small boy steps out of the cytoplasm on cue and begins to unzip the sheet membrane in two. Dividing cytoplasm, represented by one of two girls in polka-dot tunics, rolls out and puts her arms around nucleus, embracing him as he covers her with the other half of the sheet. Sheeted amoebae one and two, each enclosing their own nucleus and cytoplasm, reach out and shake pseudopodia in a no-hard-feelings gesture before parting to enthusiastic applause. We are told that there will now be an intermission. Refreshments will be available in the refectory during a slide show on the sex life of Christmas trees. In the kitchen area, adjacent, examples of gestation of plum pudding and Christmas cake can be viewed in flagranti in the exuberant activity of yeasts. I decide to give myself a tour of the building.

Origins of life begin with exhibition in basement. Entry here, into Arthouse, of everything required for maintenance of thermodynamic system, fossil fuels, burner, electricity, water plus backflow of liquid biological wastes. Counselling and recreation areas still under construction. Black insulating tape scars the walls. Half a ping-pong table.

Pictures of darkness hang in the passage leading out of the

boiler room. Captions in inexplicably small print, difficult to make out in this light. THERMONUCLEAR REACTIONS: *explosions in nucleus of stars, distributing the major elements throughout an interstellar medium, from which later stars would be born.* COMPOSITION OF LIFE: *half-way between the average composition of Earth and the average composition of the universe, 99% of which is made up of helium, neon, hydrogen, carbon, oxygen and nitrogen,* it says. On the wall outside the boiler room hangs a photograph of a radio telescope in a desert, dishes listening in to all of this going on. Incredible. Big Ears can hear a ditty whistled on Pluto. Caption quotes researcher as listening to a sound like the sighing of stars as they shudder in the depths of space, thermonuclear reactions, self-immolating geysers spewing out matter on a dark interstellar tide.

The basement throbs. Somewhere I've taken a wrong turning and have to retrace my steps. I emerge from semi-obscurity into light in the downstairs lounge for visitors. Leibowicz rolls through. Only two journalists are left in orbit.

'Further wall space for exhibitions of guest artists on invitation . . . currently showing children's pictures on Christmas subjects. Facilities for guests. Coffee machine. Cloakroom. Mind the step. Do excuse me going on ahead.'

The children's pictures show the nativity. In the tail of a comet, bearing extra-terrestrial life, a starlit manger glitters. Olive gloss surrounds golden hive. The honeypot of Palestine is a molten core scorching darkness. Instinctively their beginnings grope out of night, on the dark interstellar tide the Earth washed up in the solar system four or five thousand million years ago. Think about that for a while. I do so while I'm having a pee. The coffee machine is out of order. I go back upstairs to the main foyer.

'Brum!'

Here I bump into Mimi. She's rounding out a bit more, appealingly pregnant. Seed-bearer has pollinated in flowering bush. I note the glow. Sheen is standing inches off her skin.

'Theo's been awarded an Arthouse bursary. So we're moving in here for a year.'

'And the studio?'

'He's keeping it on. We're sub-letting the apartment.'

Take Mimi by the arm. Admire her health, teeth, concupiscence of fertile bush. Her body throbs, origins of life in basement, rising buoyantly on anaerobic yeasts life originated several hundred million years at least after the formation of the earth. What, really? Chatting, we promenade the foyer, looking at the fossils exhibited in glass cases. Problem with biogenesis: where did the first bacteria come from? Well, where did they? We don't know, Mimi. So? So the alternative is biopoiesis, taking us back to smelly old rags and bits of cheese and the hocus pocus of spontaneous generation of living from non-living matter.

'And Steffi? Is she back?'

'Expected back. In due course.'

Carbon, hydrogen, nitrogen etc., the building blocks of protoplasm are the same in the inanimate universe, by the way. Fossil records of life date back a mere six hundred million years. Spiral forms, helices. All organisms adapted to life in water. Blood has the salt structure of seawater. As the ultra-violet solar flux diminished, submarine creatures rose tens of metres from protective depths to ocean surface, sniffed the ozone and crawled ashore. Photo-dissociation of water vapour, photosynthesis of plants. In the absence of ozone, ultra-violet radiation would have nuked those amphibians in a couple of minutes. Think of the hole in the ozone layer. Think of me, Mimi, you and me, Enno Leibowicz and Alderman Huber all scaling over, counter-evolutionaries with fins and gills, regressing back to the sea and diving in protozoan wet-suits down down down—

Visitors keep on coming down, chromatically chatter

slides past. They must be the last. I hear silence ahead of us now. Mimi and I continue up. At the top of the stairs she pauses to get her breath. Mimi doesn't know it, but while she rests enzymes in her body are catalyzing the synthesis of a hundred molecules a second. I put my hand on her breast and feel her heart jump inside. I tell her she is very, very special. Mimi smiles. I tell her she is a very special, a highly specialised protoplasmic structure of the mammal class (has hair, four kinds of teeth, mammary glands to suckle young) that emerged a hundred million years ago and began walking tall between five and one million years back, an ambulatory collection of 10^{14} cells existing as a direct result of life having insinuated itself between the earth and the sun in a lull between thermonuclear explosions. I tell her, in effect, that she's altogether miraculous.

The Third Night: *Spanish Champagne from the Supermarket*

Mimi heaves bosomy, booming her mamilloid smoker's laugh.

'You wretch. Come and see our apartment and have a glass of champagne. Spanish, from the supermarket. But very nice.'

'Later.'

I see flashes at the end of the corridor. News photographers crouch, angle, back off an open door and hurry in pursuit of the posse of tabloid newsmen now coming right at me. A story has broken somewhere, some film star, or film star's dog, found dead in a hotel. Behind them the journalists leave ashtrays, litter, soiled oxygen, a used feeling in the air. I go down to the end of the corridor and look in through the open door.

The Fourth Night: *The Horned Goat-Fish and the Hermaphrodite*

Zeo lies asleep in a white room.

At least, his eyes are shut.

I say his. The atmosphere is not male, however. Male intrudes into the description only because of the penis I see lolling on a thigh. The atmosphere surrounding Zeo's body, with the lift at the breast and a tapered waist like a drawn breath, is one of feminine expectancy. From the waist up that is how I see her now. Her arms sprawl on the pillow, as if in submission to the incubus and the succubus alternately meddling with her in his sleep. I lean over and lick Zeo's nipples. Softly I squeeze her cock. It unwrinkles, inches out across her thigh and begins to rise. I take the pad out of my knapsack, settle it on my knee and begin to sketch rapidly. This opportunity may never come again. Five thousand million years after the formation of the earth I sit in a room in a converted sausage factory with a hermaphrodite as my model, a rare anomaly whose chromosomes are patterned XX/YY in male-female mosaicism, while the external genitalia charmingly display features of both sexes. From time to time Zeo's erection topples. With tickle and suck I shore it up. Hours pass. I fill one sketch book and begin a second. Gradually my interest in the biological phenomenon of hermaphroditism recedes behind admiration of Zeo's beauty. It unsettles a sexual ambivalence in me. As I draw pricks and tits on one body I can feel my senses flicker between a rapacious urge and a kind of supine hollowness. Energy drains out of me. I haven't had a dream for weeks. I lie down beside Zeo and shut my eyes. On the bed in the white room Hermaphroditus lies beside Aigokeros, the horned goat-fish. A Chinese scholar is already approaching and invites us to step aboard his kite to view mythical creatures cavorting below in an enclosed garden. Hang on tight, he says. I insert the hermaphrodite's nipple into my mouth, cock into the sheath of my hand. The kite soars. Instantly I begin to dream.

The Fifth Night: *Der Weihnachtstod*

I was walking down Maximilian Street on a winter night on my way to the Kammerspiele for a performance of the *Weihnachtsoratorium*, or it may have been Händel's *Messiah*, for which I had been commissioned to design the sets. It had been snowing and the road was white. I wondered why there were so few people out. It occurred to me I might have got the time wrong, and the performance had already begun. I went round to the back entrance of the theatre. In the backstage area huge sets leaned in stacks against the wall. I saw that they were my designs for Act One of the *Messiah*. Dietz, the stage manager, hurried past in a cassock. I asked him if there'd been a change of programme for St Stephen's. He said it was already the twenty-eighth, not St Stephen's but the feast of Holy Innocents, and in accordance with the programme they were playing *Weihnachtstod*, the new play by Kroetz. I opened a side door leading down into the auditorium, but found myself on stage instead. It gave me an uncomfortable feeling to be on stage without any knowledge of the play I was in. I improvised, frisking and capering around a bit. The audience laughed. Taking my cue from the audience, I went on horsing around. Apparently *Weihnachtstod* was a comedy. I noticed I was dressed as a billy-goat in a costume with tail and horns. I pranced around and shook my tail. The audience shrieked. I was hilarious. The ringmaster putting me through my paces cracked his whip and laughed so much he choked on his lines. Dietz came on stage to say them for him. Hieronymus had been held up by snow but was on his way with his wife's afterbirth. He pointed to the back of the stage. At a distance I saw what seemed to be a human wall approaching. As it emerged from darkness into light I faced a tableau vivant

made up of people packed in tiers on a slowly advancing
float. The idea of using a mobile tableau vivant struck me as
familiar. I remembered having recently admired it in
Meyerhold's brilliant Gogol production for Diaghilev in
Paris. From the auditorium the effect of a human wall bearing down on one had been overwhelming. On stage it was
terrifying. Looking up from a foreshortened angle just below
the float, I saw paunches, bosoms, double chins and the
dark cavities of laughing mouths telescoped into a
Rabelasian caricature of the *condition humaine*. People had to
bare their teeth in order to laugh; or was it the other way
round? I had an uneasy feeling that *Weihnachtstod* was not a
comedy after all. As the float approached I recognised the
people on it. They came from my painting in Brewers Hall.
They stood in tiers on the looming float and shook with
laughter. They hooted and jeered. Hieronymus walked out
in front. He held up a polythene bag containing Martha's
afterbirth. 'For your horns,' he said. 'An old household
recipe prescribes the application of a fresh afterbirth as a
poultice.' Half-heartedly I cut a caper. The audience was
stricken with laughter. The stacked tiers creaked. The float
shook. Tears ran down the spectators' faces. Tears ran down
their faces. I thought it was for me. I thought it was
applause. Tears ran down their faces and they burst into
song. The float surged past with its tableau vivant, brilliantly lit, the men and women singing. I stepped aside to
make room for their dirge. I'd got into the wrong play. I'd
got everything terribly wrong. Martha came walking out of
the east, carrying something in her arms. She laid the burden down. The twins were dead. 'Made a bit of a chump of
yourself there,' said Dietz. The music broke off and the
lights went out. 'Didn't you,' said Dietz into the silence,
'eh?'

The Sixth Night: *In a White Room*

The video camera runs all night long. Zeo gets up a couple of times to change tapes. Sleep, snores, dreams, going to the john in the middle of the night – when morning comes it's all on tape. Waking, I talk straight to camera.

'The idea is to document something creative, something in the act of becoming. As of last night I've begun to dream about a window I've been commissioned to design. A stained-glass window for a consecration hall in a cemetery. I need the dream because what's in the surface of my mind, the part I can access at will, is mostly junk. Problem is my dreamlessness. I've come to rely on Steffi, the lubricant of Steffi's dreams. Since she's gone I've not been able to work much. Actually, not at all. Ideas come into my mind, but no dreams to fertilise them. Until last night. With Zeo plugged into me, negative-positive, the dream nodes functioned. Stay with the dream function for a moment. Think about an average day. At the end of an average day of driving aimlessly around town with the car radio on, reading mostly comics at lunch and watching TV in the evening, not much more gets done at night than garbage disposal, mind clearance. My mind's becoming polluted same as everything else is. I adapt. I become trivial. My dreams have become as trivial as the input is. Not dream enrichment but erosion, blankness, what I feel as dreamlessness. Zeo tells me my chest and arms feel armour-plated, like a carapace. I'm turning into a crustacean. Today's my birthday again. Capricorn, Aigokeros, through the interstellar medium a horned goat-fish swam ashore, stinking, in need of a wash . . . [*abridged*]

'A true language to describe acts of becoming would be double-gendered, self-pollinating by the interaction of stamen and pistil. Conjugation of male and female parts of speech. Male and female helically spliced in a grammar of hermaphroditism. Steffi's dreams secrete liquids to fertilise

notional pearls in my mind. Stick with hermaphroditism.
Think about it for a mo. Has a marvellous economy. In
some plants and animals is fertile. Teems with sex. Just think
of the pollen spilling onto the stigma, growing a tube [!]
down the style and infiltrating the ovary. Wow. It makes me
tingle just to think of it. Already feel the agitation of something becoming. In a state of self-excitation, I spill onto my
own stigma. Take myself by surprise. I've been out to take a
look at the consecration hall now under construction in
Perlach and carry around with me this image of an oblong
hole in a dark interior thirty foot high, like a piece cut out of
the sky. I've been asked to submit a design for this window,
which in some way should address the theme of reconciliation. I don't look directly at oblong hole. Don't think about
it particularly. Look and think slightly to one side of it. I'm
doing this now as I document the genesis of an act of
becoming: specifically, the inception of an idea for the
design of a window. Slightly to one side I see tits and prick
on one body, male-female stained-glass mosaicism, chromosomes reconciled in hermaphroditism. My instincts
flicker between a rapacious urge and a kind of supine hollowness and I feel very clearly that reconciliation must
first spark the tensions that are to be shown in balance;
before one can show the idea of reconciliation, is what I'm
saying.'

Depressed, I played back my sleep and watched myself
dream the *Weihnachtstod* while Zeo gave me a massage. Zeo
says that if the muscles and sinews are so hard it means I
must be permanently tense: as if I have something to ward
off. Maybe I'm dreamless because I don't open up to let the
dreams in. Armour-plated, how can I be receptive? Suggests
I put my sketchbook under the mattress and sleep on it.
Apparently Stradivarius did this with his unvarnished violins, stored them for a while in his bedroom – though not
under the mattress, I guess – so that they could tune in
on the frequency of the maestro's conjugal and other

intimacies. Hence rugged, romantic strain in violins' later polished performances. Zeo on top of his job in masseur's position admitted a sneaking desire to bugger me. Promptly I found myself dipping into that mood of supine hollowness, and had I been a duck I might additionally have done interesting things with my neck. Zeo claims it would do me good to be imposed on, to receive the will, physically the brunt, of my partner's lust in an attitude of prostration, but I'm not so sure. I play hard to get. I don't mind Zeo's promiscuity in private, but its professional dimension in a basement near the main station has recently been brought to my attention. And then there's Bo. We are, after all, in Bo's bed, Zeo is Bo's pal and I am staying in the white room only while Bo is away over Christmas. In subjunctive mood I'd quite fancy being fucked by Zeo. I'm open to the idea. This stuff about not wanting to spoil Bo's pitch is crap. Now and then I rather like myself in a moral pose. I know, it's a weakness. The truth is I'm worried about AIDS.

The Seventh Night: *Can Morality Do Without Fear?*

'Brum?'

'Hello?'

'It's me.'

'Who's there?'

'Mimi.'

'Me who?'

'Mimi. Champagne later is champagne now. Theo's bringing some glasses.'

'Oh, come on in. Join us inside the video. On second thoughts . . . Zeo?'

'Hm?'

'Can you switch it off? Thanks. I was just thinking th—'

[*abridged*]

The Eighth Night: *Watch This Space*

'I am in a white room. Haven't yet seen any of the others in Arthouse, so don't know if this is standard issue or Bo's personal colour scheme, decor of Bo's soul. White, the poor man's aesthetic. Irreproachable. Avoid any decisions. Same thing with Bo's pictures. Empty shelves and horizons, antiseptic, bacteria-free. Lifeless, in fact. Bo's room just restrains itself from fussiness. He keeps things pretty much out of his pictures, but they all creep back in here. Toys, knick-knacks, souvenirs. Photos of a woman and stacks of different men. Photos are OK, but photos arranged in a semi-circle at equidistant points . . . The neatness in Bo's rooms, the ones he inhabits and the ones he puts frames around, smells to me of something like terror. Out of sight, in Bo's pictures, just around the corner, is the tailor with the scissors to cut off the little boy's thumbs. Bo has censored himself. Bo is self-excised, but even in the withdrawal this is a declaration of personality. What Bo does, I do too, of course. We try to chart ourselves. We arrange objects and look for colours, shapes, parameters, something appreciable out there in which we can make out our phantoms and attempt to recognise ourselves. What shape am I? I'm obsessed with this because I have a sneaking feeling maybe I don't have a shape, maybe, like Amoeba, I'm amorphous. What is outside of me comes into me by osmosis, my guest, ghost, becomes part of me and goes out of me again. I am constantly in flux. I can record flux. This is a genuine activity. But I can't pin down what's behind it. What it is that's in flux. Less and less am I able to do this the further I go on. I don't want shapelessness in flux. I want certainty. I'm beginning to want some kind of . . . uh . . . repose. The idea that something's not real unless it's documented is comfortable. I can make so many more marks of myself so much more easily, copies, faxes, polaroids, videos . . . Reality changes its medium, the creative principle becomes one of reproducibility. If it's not on video it doesn't exist. The difference with Stradivarius was (a) he believed in souls, also of violins, (b) he had a conjugal life. I for my part, untraceable but presumed somewhere behind flux and with no conjugal life to speak of since Steffi left, am not much of a believer in anything these days. I exercise the old symbols, I walk them out, words like soul, marks on pages once called art, without much sense of hope. I am the dreamless artist. What emotional sounds matter enough in me to soak into the grain of a violin? Towards the end of the year I stand at a window in a white room, looking out into whiteness. Empty shelves and horizons. The colour I'm looking for is not green but blue, the blue that comes in a rush at nightfall with a feeling of relief, even serenity, and disintegrates in dark, darker, the blue-black emptiness of space.'

The Ninth Night: *New Year's Eve*

Even loyal followers of the traditional New Year letter in these pages have begun to complain of feelings of déjà vu.

Not yet another gala like last year's glittering scrummage at the Bayerischer Hof where two thousand guests fought tooth and nail in tuxedos and evening gowns for trough space at a buffet a hundred yards long. Not the sight of politicians stuffing themselves at Käfer's yet again, or of film stars starving themselves, come to that, at Kay's Bistro, with a glimpse of *Soraya* in a silk kimono against a background of nouvelle cuisine, soothsayer *Rita Tusselli* sitting in a coach, the bells of San Marco and ships' horns in the Lido booming incongruously on cassette tapes.

What was needed was a radical change of venue, and the response to the *Herald's* request for suggestions has brought in some radical ones indeed.

There's no reason why one shouldn't report (as the secretary of one welfare organisation suggested) from the car park at St Jakob-Platz, where vagrants will be celebrating

New Year's Eve in circumstances of straitened jollity from 5 p.m. on; no reason other than that no one would listen. Many thanks also to the Director of the Observatory in Rosenheimer Street for his invitation to attend a private viewing of *Chi* and *H* with a free glass of champagne. We take the opportunity to pass on the information that these galaxies at a distance of more than seven thousand light years from us can be seen at their best on clear January nights.

Coming down to Earth, we must admit we were rather tempted by the Air Trade and Hilton offer of New Year's Eve in a jumbo jet for a very reasonable DM 595 per head, including personal firework, airport transfer and in-flight cocktails. But the multi-media, multi-location show at Arthouse, with its thirty-foot flexiscreen for video and live TV access to several venues simultaneously, was successfully hustled by crafty Arthouse manager **Enno Leibowicz**, and clinched it in the end.

High tech has made it possible. The aerials and electronic equipment installed at the top of the Olympic Tower beamed first test pictures into cable TV households between Christmas and New Year. They can receive two new private stations on channels 24 and 59 along with RTL+ and SAT 6 for no extra charge. HIFLI Z13 and MADSAT went on the air with their first live pictures broadcast out of Arthouse on New Year's Eve.

Technicians had already moved in on the premises of the former sausage manufacturer in Preysing Street several days before. Something very like lust gleamed in the technophile eye of Leibowicz as he watched electronic hardware worth ten million being installed. First thing to show up on the mammoth flexiscreen was the sullen off-air face of MADSAT programme host **Dieter Popp**, who is well known for never having smiled in his life except to oblige a camera. He obliges now, breaking into a thirty-foot smile. Computers reassemble him on the two dozen component units of the

flexiscreen in equally unprepossessing alternative patterns –
switching an ear to the site of his nose, a corner of the Popp
smile to the centre of his forehead, and so on.

From eleven o'clock onwards the multi-screen facility
hosts in-house videos for invited guests only. Recipients of
Arthouse bursaries contribute videos on 'Aspects of
Becoming' as part of their Alternative Christmas Work
shop. Sixteen clips, shown simultaneously, run all day long
without interruption.

It is something of a relief, then, when links are established with the live broadcast sites and the first pictures
start coming through in the course of the afternoon.
Applause greets the view of a thirty-foot watering-can in the
Botanical Gardens, even if we have been promised orchids,
and when this dissolves into a dozen different images on as
many constituent screens we all crowd round for a closer
look.

Of the twenty-four sites from which the New Year's Eve
programme will be broadcast one can already identify
Marienplatz, the Olympic Tower, the Municipal Observatory, the churches of St Mark's, St Luke's and St Anna's,
and the twenty-second floor of the Arabella Hotel, thinly
disguised as a Caribbean island.

This is why the Arthouse invite is the indisputable winner.
Why bother to do the rounds when one can check out what's
happening all over town without moving from the bar?

On drip-feed by the big screen, one can watch the cos-
sacks of A Night in St Petersburg dancing furiously in the
Penta Hotel, and at the same time be a voyeur of a Caribbean Night on an adjacent screen. Guests at the Caribbean
Night are sunning themselves at solarium temperatures in
the Arabella or swimming leisurely to the Batista tropical
drinks' island for cocktails with MADSAT newscaster
Belinda von Späth, attractively edited down at the pool-
side to the briefest possible two-piece item. Macedonians in
folk costume are dancing and making a noise with what

seem to be long-haired tambourines on the tables of the Schwabinger Bräu, while among the sedate guests seen walking by invitation only against a herbaceous background in the Botanical Gardens the moonish face of former state Minister of Culture **Alfons Bayer** is glimpsed in close-up, communing silently with Steuben's *pomeranzenbaum*. Midnight mass is now in progress at the cathedral, Mozart's *Krönungsmesse* at St Michael's, an organ recital at St Mark's, a Bach chorale at St Luke's.

The New Year's Ball at the Deutsches Theater offers a preview of the decor that will grace, or encumber, the carnival season opening on 6 January. Also a foretaste of **Poppy Eglinger's** review girls, which draws the biggest crowds. Poppy's girls at first parade demurely in knee-length skirt and intriguing head-piece, a yellow, spikey apparatus at the forehead with a huge green bow behind. Stripping down for a samba, they reveal bras made of leaves and loincloths of bananas. A tropical, if not to say sultry idiom, reminiscent of Josephine Baker, and very much in keeping with the Brazilian theme of this year's carnival.

Whether the New Year mood is one of cosmic greed, insecurity, narcissism or just jaded surfeit, Enno Leibowicz has gauged it correctly. The flexiscreen bringing to Arthouse a choice of party venues from all over town has also brought to the audience here a gratifying sense of power, a reassurance that however little they may be enjoying themselves, *at least they won't have missed anything*.

By two o'clock, however, when the 747 has landed and the Verger gone to bed, churches emptied, Macedonians drunk, the Marienplatz crowds dispersed and one by one the screens go blank, we are happy to close down transmission and bring up the lights, happy to be left to ourselves and the images of ourselves slow-dancing up there on the big screen. Surprisingly few of us are drunk. This year booze is Out. As is last year now, all 365 discarded days. Green Party members have stationed a container at the exit, and on leaving we are invited to make a symbolic gesture of depositing our used year for recycling. Time is the ideal trash, a placard says, self-dissolving second by second and leaving no trace. Some of us shudder as we fumble our way out.

The Tenth Night: *New Year Horoscopes*

In a few days the earth will pass within a hundred and forty-seven million kilometres of the sun, reaching that point on its somewhat elliptical orbit which is known as perihelion, when it is closest to the sun.

What prospects will there be of observing the planets?

Mercury can be seen in the last week of January deep in the south-west, where Venus is conspicuously prominent at present. The red planet, Mars, remains out of sight until June, but reaching opposition in September will be unusually close to us at a distance of only fifty-nine million miles. Jupiter now shines high in the southern and south-western sky. Saturn can currently be seen in the early morning among the stars of Sagittarius.

What prospects will there be of observing Brum?

There was no trace of Brum, or he could not be identified, among the galaxy at Arthouse on New Year's Eve. Odds were he might remain in hiding until illuminated by a full moon on a dark enterprise at Epiphany. But amateur astronomers at the observatory in Rosenheimer Street, directing their instruments south-east to capture the glory of the winter constellations, registered a small object that swam into their ken on the far side of the river early on new year's day. Vacillating for several hours at the south end of Klenze Street, where it remained tethered by some obscure gravitational force, this object displayed characteristics that first led observers to identify it as a white dwarf. Later calculations regarding its size, position etc. verified it to be the alpha of Canis Minor, Procyon.

Procyon, from Greek *Prokuon*, 'before the dog', is so

named because it is the star that precedes the rising of the dog star, Sirius, the alpha of Canis Major, and the asterism of Orion. Where Procyon came, the Greater Dog would follow. And sure enough, mid-morning-ish, after the loyal animal had been waiting on the pavement outside The Blue Ram for some hours, Brum was sighted, somewhat the worse for wear, on elliptical course down Klenze Street. At this prospect the alpha of Canis Minor got up and shook itself, sneezed, barked and wagged its tail. 'Oozadoggy,' slurred Brum, leaning forward and smacking his thighs, 'whezzadoggy! Oozadoggy!' The three-legged animal limped to its master. Thus the conjunction of these two bodies after long separation was effected with unmistakable signs of mutual affection.

The Blue Ram was shut. Brum punished the door for its inhospitality with a tremendous kick, inadvertently upsetting a delicate balance, or balances, in the apartment overhead, where Mrs Koepenick was in the process of transferring soft-boiled eggs from saucepan to sink, while her husband sat in the next room plotting a particularly ambiguous horoscope, and Hieronymus Kornrumpf, rushing down the landing with half-lowered trousers, was attempting to reach the lavatory before exploding with diarrhoea. Mrs K dropped the egg, Hieronymus gave a cry of anguish, Koepenick jumped up in exasperation and flung open the window. 'Pee in your ear,' Brum was understood to have said in greeting from below, but this misunderstanding was soon cleared up.

It was at this New Year lunch, hosted by the Koepenicks in Hieronymus' honour and gatecrashed by Brum, that a first report of the Christmas birth was given by the father of the twins. Mrs K served pig's head garnished with bacon, but the guest of honour, complaining of viral infections in the head and stomach, was in no position to eat pig's head. For him, then, the boiled egg, the toast and the camomile tea. Brum's recollection was of Hieronymus sitting opposite him with streaming eyes, either snivelling as he told his story or, when things became unbearable, getting up and sprinting away from it altogether.

Between tears and explosions Hieronymus reported it had been a miraculous birth worth at least a footnote to gynaecological history. The twin fruit of Martha's womb had totted up to an amazing 5 kgs, 850 grams. Katryn came shortly before ten o'clock on Christmas Eve and brought 2 kgs, 700 grams to the scales. Liselotte, who hung out in her mother's womb for an extraordinary three and a half hours more before joining her sister, weighed in at 3 kgs, 150 grams early on Christmas morning. Both girls had a florid appearance coupled with a general air of beefiness that Hieronymus attributed to the quantities of livestock feed Martha had surreptitiously been eating throughout her pregnancy. His wife had known, by her inner lights she had *known* the baby would be a boy. After Katryn's arrival she was devastated. She was speechless. Informed by the doctor that they were still waiting for another, Martha shook her head, crossed herself and closed her womb. Hieronymus was alarmed, knowing his wife's obstinacy and particularly the stubbornness of her retractive functions. But three and a half hours is a long time in labour, and during it some re-wiring of Martha's inner lights appeared to have taken place. She named the second daughter Liselotte a few minutes before she was born. She named her after the florist who had died at Michaelmas that autumn, giving Hieronymus a clue as to what must have been passing through her mind. Ten years of marriage for better or worse; ten years marked off at wedding anniversaries by the flowers Hieronymus had always bought from Liselotte; how these flowers had quickly faded in vases, ten years with them, florist faded too, put in the ground and now, in a manner of speaking, perhaps a chance to sprout, perhaps for her death a life, obstructed only by Martha's vain and selfish wish for a boy: it was Liselotte Pfaffel down there clamouring to get out, and she, Martha, was merely the vessel through which another's will would pass – in some such spirit of acquiescence in her fate as part of the mysterious balance of the universe (Martha responded to the idea of herself as sacrifice) she opened her womb and the child slipped out.

Prompted by Mrs K, who ladled encouragement whenever he faltered or fled, Hieronymus monopolised the lunch table with the raw material, so to speak, of the twins' birth. The trim and polish to this account were provided with the liqueurs after lunch. Here shone the midwife of the stars, delivering the verdict of their horoscope. Here Koepenick was ascendant.

He laid a piece of paper on the table. It showed two concentric circles marked with numbers at the circumferences, divided into segments containing pencilled codes, and intersected at the centre by two flamboyant green lines showing mid-heaven and the ascendant. *Twenty-four, twelve, eighty-seven,* Brum deciphered in a corner of the page, *at twenty-one fifty-nine.* 'Here is C1,' said Koepenick, patting the sheet of paper.

'Who?' asked Hieronymus.

'The first child, whatsisname.'

'Katryn,' prompted Mrs K.

A box of cigars appeared on the horizon of the empty table, making Katryn's fate seem a little less solitary.

'One is sensual,' said Koepenick, pretty much out of the blue. 'One is an enjoyer. Instinctively one is drawn to the arts,' by which point it was clear he could not have been referring to the cigars or liqueurs but was already launched in mid-horoscope. 'And yet,' Koepenick continued, 'one is also more cautious than C2, more sober in one's judgement than the younger sister. Reactions are often analytical. Decisions are still weaker. By nature one is inclined to pettiness. One makes no display of baroque extravagance. It depends on this.'

Koepenick made a crease with his thumbnail through a segment of the circle that was littered with annotations. Hieronymus creaked forward to look. Mrs K, coffee-pot in hand, rose on tiptoe to look. But Brum watched Koepenick run his fingers through his trim little beard and saw how he enjoyed himself in his queer, inward, beard-stroking way that somehow shut other people out.

The astrologer drew their attention to the high incidence of planets in or on the cusp of the Fifth House. The presence here of five planets including the sun reinforced the in-house preoccupation with love and the arts; and when this nucleus, as Koepenick put it, began to vibrate, one might literally be *beside oneself*. One then overstepped the limits of pleasure. One went *too far*. There was a danger of addiction here. Here one didn't take up some office occupation. Here there was a strong chance of one's winding up as a cloakroom attendant in the theatre or behind the counter in a Pils bar.

Hieronymus sat and streamed for a while. Snivel could be seen plonking on the tissue stationed under his nose. There was not a great deal to be said in reply, and Hieronymus said it in his muggy, adenoidal voice.

'Well, I mean, that nucleus had just better not begin to vibrate.'

Astrologer-magician – card-sharp: this resemblance occurred to Brum as he watched Koepenick rub the sheet of paper with his knuckles. Presto! A second sheet emerged fanwise from underneath. Here was the horoscope for the lower berth. C2 came out of hiding.

Koepenick prayerfully joined his fingertips.

'One arrives in the world at a point exactly between midheaven, at twenty degrees in Gemini, and the ascendant, at sixteen degrees Libra in the east. The moon is in Pisces, from which can be inferred that one will take up some occupation involving therapy. The Sun, Neptune, Uranus, Saturn and Mercury are in the Third House, reinforcing in-house tendencies: one's motivation in life is curiosity. One wants to know. One acquires knowledge, book-learning. One makes one's way in the world by learning to be reasonable. One *reads* a great deal.'

Considerately Koepenick paused, giving the antiquarian bookseller an opportunity to look more encouraged by these prospects. Hieronymus dripped.

'Katryn the sensualist, Liselotte the intellectual. Here is the division. But one has a lot in common. One is independent and imaginative. One tends to be introverted. One has a knack of teaching people things in a playful way. Katryn remains more attached – perhaps the mother has some ailment, and it will be Katryn's task to look after her. Katryn cares more about where she lives, and she will keep everything in her home in better shape. She is altogether vainer. She is the more companionable of the two. She has more charm. Jupiter in the Seventh House indicates the high expectations she will have of her partners. The position of Neptune in Katryn's horoscope suggests that she will have the greater resources of imagination. She will tell more fluent lies than her sister.'

Koepenick paused.

'In both horoscopes, however, the father is something of a problem figure . . . From the father's side comes a weakness, perhaps involving something he keeps secret, some kind of dishonesty, embezzlement, an evasion of some kind. Perhaps the father is illegitimate. The father's contours are very diffuse. The lack of a clear outline of the father figure is a disappointment for Liselotte in particular. One finds him not quite scrutable . . . doesn't get from him the support one expects . . . in the extreme case one might go so far as to say that *one doesn't know who the father is.*'

Koepenick took a puff at his cigar. Hieronymus sat and streamed.

The Eleventh Night: *How Much Does Koepenick Know?*

As he sits and streams in the astrologer-magician's apartment and sees him pluck these amazing slanders from thin air, Hieronymus wonders if it's all up there somewhere for the asking, perhaps available on cards in astral stores. He reviews his relationship with Koepenick for any previous slurs, putting mental question marks beside such things as Koepenick's collection of war memorabilia, his taste for Wagnerian opera and leather jackets. He even gives voice to a suspicion of anti-Semitic tendencies in Koepenick when walking down Klenze Street with his brother-in-law afterwards. Brum pooh-poohs this. Hieronymus says people are susceptible to irrational explanations because they have emotional needs that do not respond to logic. They go into a Pils bar to drink each other's health. Hieronymus regrets this the moment he catches sight of the frowzy woman with bags under her eyes who is serving behind the counter. It is surely a prophetic glimpse of week-old Katryn forty years on. Brum thinks the point about astrological predictions is less how such claims can be made than why people want to hear them, which depresses Hieronymus even more. Parting from Brum at Sendlinger Tor, he drips home by underground. He blows his nose, but inside him drip persists as nag. How much does Koepenick know? By the time he reaches the university he has finished his supply of tissues and is wondering if Koepenick might have somehow overheard his conversation with Meow when he dined at the Chinese restaurant in Hohenzollern Street on New Year's Eve. On Meow's intelligent, graphic, thoroughly scrutable face expressions of pity, alarm and paramedical curiosity contest the issue as he watches his guest snivel and drip into the chop suey. Hieronymus asks Meow if he has powders to help. Meow says his condition is beyond powder. To judge by his quantity of drip he is badly in need of a woman. The fluids are rushing to leave his body. How long since he last have sex? Hieronymus dodges Meow's perspicacity under a smokescreen of fake laughter. Secretly he is aghast. It is in fact six months since. *Does it show like that?* He looks in the mirror and blinks. His nose turns into a piece of cheese, an overripe pear, between bushy brows his penis hangs insolently from the middle of his face. Koepenick is looking over his shoulder. Hieronymus wakes unhappily from this dream and calls Astrid, but Astrid is not at home. From the father's side comes a weakness, perhaps some kind of dishonesty involving VSOP matters. Maybe this is the sun spot to which Koepenick was not so playfully alluding. Consulting Julian, Gregorian, Chinese and Jewish calendars etc. and forwarding them where appropriate to 2 January, he notes that yesterday was the Jewish feast of Circumcision and that today, on the octave of his own Liselotte's nativity, he has made an appointment for a vasectomy at the clinic of Dr Castringius. He wonders if his sperms are playing him up, out of some canny protozoan instinct for self-preservation, before they get the axe. On the underground he reads the brochure the clinic supplies its patients. The operation is quite straightforward. All it requires is a small incision in the vas deferens, the duct that passes sperm from the testes to the reproductive organs. The scrotum is locally anaesthetized, the vas deferens isolated by external examination. Clamps, incision, sever, cauterize and stitch. Bob's your uncle. Or rather, was. Caution, however. Patients will continue to emit small quantites of sperm for a couple of months afterwards. In danger of dripping onto the brochure, Hieronymus hastily reaches for his handkerchief. The hatted woman opposite is looking at him sternly. Clamp? Sever? *Cauterize?* Hieronymus has second thoughts. Should he at least have consulted Martha? At Thunder Mountain Bridge he gets out of the train and walks up and down the platform. His mind doodles on the clinic's brochure and comes up uselessly with a deferential vase. One has a knack of teaching people things in a playful way. Hieronymus pulls his mind together, lights a cigar and rehearses the arguments in favour. Already overcrowded world. 272 children born every minute. Hormone treatment and multiple birth risk, financial ruin. Risk of Martha acquiring the taste. Trouble-free sexual enjoyment in countless extramarital affairs. He finds himself standing beside a red-headed woman looking delicious on her poster. In a bikini she is advertising liqueurs. Hieronymus has flowers arranged in handy deferential vase and sent over to Caribbean pool-side with his card. Not so useless after all. She smiles availability. At the crucial moment he drips, has to get onto the train in any case. She accompanies him into the cubicle at the Castringius clinic, where a terrific hard-on embarrassingly refuses to subside. Nurse fetches male attendant who takes him in hand and shaves the operative area. Ticklish business. Same fastidious manner barbers have of holding client's nose aside when getting a blade angle on his moustache. Left to themselves for a while, his genitals lie slack and cold like plucked poultry carcase. The surgeon arrives, prods. Examination is external, anaesthetic is local, vase is deferential and vasectomy quite straightforward. It may be a rational achievement, but submitting to this goes against all his instincts. Maybe his acquiescence, derived from superior insight, at the same time signals a decline of vital energy, a degenerate kink in the evolutionary line. Hieronymus feels a snip and a yank and reflects that the Kornrumpf line has here been severed without male issue. The father's contours are very diffuse. The male issue was always Martha's problem in any case; her ambitions, not his. He doesn't care much either way. He perches on the edge of the seat with thighs well spread to accommodate his swollen scrotum. The red-head in the bikini comes round a second time with the liqueurs. What's the difference? Connections have been severed with the matter uncontested, no issue at all. Bye. Otherwise he continues to drip. Otherwise he still hankers with an obdurate, pleistocene urge to put his cock inside as

many females of the species as possible. Sterile, he will still
go on reproducing desire. Whereas his life should somehow
change. Whereas he should learn to be tangibly supportive
of the daughter with the rings under her eyes. One doesn't
know who the father is. But in the wings he now sees taking
shape an extra he has not considered for this role before,
firming up paternally, as his memory supplies the bits and
pieces and imagination glues them together, is somebody's
favourite Franciscan from St Anna's, somebody's Father
Anton. How much does Koepenick know? Thoughtful,
bow-legged, Hieronymus drips up Schelling Street into the
New Year.

The Twelfth Night: *Epiphany*

The three kings arrived by van, which Brum had hired from
Budget. Leila, Dada and Zeo, the latter wearing a pale blue
turban improvised from a blouse Brum remembered having
been worn by Steffi, stood shivering in the hall in a ragbag
collection of capes or gowns which Constanze had stitched
together at short notice. Outside there were twenty degrees
of frost. The deputation from St Mark's kindergarten came
on foot under the guidance of Father Anton. While the friar
corked faces and fixed moustaches the protocol was dis-
cussed. It was agreed that the three junior magi would go
first, carrying candles and the broomstick with the star of
David attached. Their senior colleagues would follow with
gifts. They politely declined Father Anton's offer of burnt
cork, pointing out that with their natural olive complexions
they were, after all, the genuine article from the Orient.
Teeth chattering,they tramped upstairs.

The visit came as a complete surprise to Martha. Sitting
there hugely as though self-enthroned, a baby asleep on
either arm and surrounded by admiring guests, she listened
to her former kindergarten charges sing and recite poems,
rewarding them with Chistmas cookies and donations for

World Child. The senior magi performed humorous mimes, illustrating the distances they had to travel and all the difficulties to be overcome as underpaid representatives in the adoration business; but how it was worth it in the end. Martha especially liked this bit. Finally the Zoroastrians handed over their gifts. When she saw the two tiny cribs, which Leila lifted out of their nutshells and put on the palm of her hand, Martha was so overcome she burst into tears. The twins woke up and bawled. Hieronymus snivelled over to comfort and assist. Martha clasped his hand and streamed uncontrollably, while Father Anton boomed on tiptoe in the background and made unhappy shooing gestures with his arms.

Brum blinked, recording this image for later use, perhaps as an aspect of reconciliation. Meanwhile Caspar and Melchior had slipped away unnoticed; and Balthazar, the prince of light in the blue-silk-blouse turban who only a moment ago had been right beside him, impaling prawns on cocktail sticks, had suddenly vanished too. Brum blinked again. The warm bright enclosure disappeared, He stepped forward in the dark hall downstairs and pushed open the night. A full moon bounded out of the sky and raked the threshold with screeching light. Brum looked up at the moon and cursed.

In the back of the Budget van, Zeo and Dada were changing into boiler suits. Brum started up, switching the heating full on. They cruised down Ludwig Street, turned left at von der Tan Street up Prinzregenten Street, and crossed the Isar. A silver strip of river sparkled in the moonlight. The van dawdled through the sidestreets of Bogenhausen, coming to a halt at the end of Pienzenauer Street. Brum and Leila got out. They looked up at a billiard ball of a moon banging about an empty sky. There was too much light, but they could see a bank of cloud building up in the west.

Brum killed half an hour by driving round the block. Ten minutes more, huddled at the kerb with the engine running, keeping an eye on the cloudslide across the sky. A shadow lunged into the white road. Brum drove round the corner and parked opposite the house in Pienzenauer Street. Zeo and Dada got out.

They crossed the road, hopped over the fence and climbed the tree in the garden. From a branch of the tree they gained access to a balcony. Brum heard the splinter of glass across the street. Dogs barked. The moon rose, and whiteness flared from the surrounding snow. Brum froze. He saw Czernak standing at the foot of the steps outside the house. In the moonlight he was exposed as if on a photographic negative. He stood staring into the street. The moon rose and dipped behind cloud. As Czernak turned and looked up at the house it had already melted back into shadow.

Brum started the van, drove to the end of the street, turned and coasted back, cutting the engine as they approached the house. Cautiously he and Leila got out, leaned the door to and listened for the dogs. Leila went to the fence. Brum opened the doors at the back of the van. He turned to see a coil of white flashing towards him through the dark. Leila picked up the rope. Brum found an end, climbed into the back of the van and made the rope fast. Leila whistled. Zeo and Dada came out onto the balcony, lifting something over the edge. For a moment the object hung in the night. Dada stepped back. The object dropped, rolling down the rope with a creak and a whir directly into the van, where Brum unhooked it from the pulley. One by one he removed them from the sack and stacked them in the van, counting eight pictures in all. He hung the sack on the pulley and yanked the rope. Dada on the balcony hauled the pulley back up.

While the dogs in the basement continued to bark, three lots of paintings came sliding down, followed by Dada and Zeo, whirring into the back of the van as Czernak appeared again in the garden, Leila cut loose, Brum put his foot on the gas, the moon slid out from behind the cloud and went donging around the empty sky.

Twenty-three hostages to fortune, the pictures Brum had painted of his wife and subsequently sold to her lover, were removed in this way by the painter from the purchaser-lover's house on a moonlit Epiphany evening at the end of the twelve nights.

Foolscap

HARALD

Circumspect udders laugh horizontally. Prostrate coffee sneezes under water.

Carnivorous leaves pledge termites?

Suck, when stuck, the window. Or try looking out of the pencil for a while.

Harald Hemsing tossed the pencil on to the desk. He got up in exasperation.

'Finished?'

'Just about.'

'Conference at six, remember.'

'Six remember at conference.'

'What?'

'Nothing.'

'While you're standing . . . could you put the kettle on? And pass me my cigarettes. And the ashtray.'

'And check the thermometer and tell us what the temperature is . . .'

Office women chortled circumspectly deskwise, udders laughed horizontally, four of them in a row. At the window Harald stooped to peer through a chink in the frosted-over pane of glass.

'Minus twenty-nine. Shade below minus thirty.'

Slantwise through the window he could make out the ramp-like structure on trestles sticking out a yellow tongue, encroaching glacially down Neuhauser Street.

'Instant or real?'

'Well, of course if you really want to *spoil* us—'

Whistling, Harald set up three symmetries, cup, spoon, one cube of sugar each. Finger tap. What next? Bubbles eructate in percolator. Prostrate coffee sneezes under water?

What if the Chomsky virus caught last Thursday at Dr Grundig's introduction to moderm linguistics refused to go away? Hung around for a couple of weeks. A year. Hung around all your life.

The starting point of Chomsky's enquiries, Grundig said was the grammatically irreproachable but meaningless sentence *Colourless green ideas sleep furiously.*

Harald seized his head and went back to his desk. A headline and a first paragraph looked up at him expectantly.

COURTURIER RECEIVES OVATIONS IN WHEELCHAIR

'Madame' was graciously disposed to receive guests and celebrated her by now traditional ball in the Bayerischer Hof on Saturday night. The fashion magazine had to compete with the opening of the Prinzregenten Theater, which took place simultaneously, leaving MC **Rainer Wallraff** with only one prominent political guest to greet, Minister for the Economy **Anton Jaumann**. Rival attractions notwithstanding, the ball was packed to the last seat.

'Here you are then.'

'Thanks.'

Marianne had already turned away and didn't catch the smile. He took a sip of coffee, glanced over his notes and released the margin.

A fashion show was, as usual, the centre of the evening's programme. With dresses chequered black-and-yellow and yellow-and-white, hemlines for the most part above the knee, designer **Manfred Schneider** brought a touch of spring and summer to the stage. The couturier, who had recently met with an accident, received ovations for his show sitting in a wheelchair.

Last para. Who else?
Give the bands a mention.

Max Greger and his band meanwhile brought a touch of nostalgia to the dance floor with foxtrot and tango tunes. **Sound Corporation** played in alternation with the veteran Greger, and **Milva** put in a star guest appearance. From *Carmen* to her latest hit, the Italian singer's repertoire had something to suit everyone's taste.

One more item to come. Asterisk?

Ovations plain and simple? Did they sit or stand? If standing ovations, could this be interpreted as discrimination in poor taste? Couturier receives standing ovations in wheelchair. Absurd. But always just round the corner. The anarchy of ordinary language. Meaning accrued, like barnacles. Standing, couturier receives ovations in wheelchair. To a blind person, imagining ideas of greenness in a world without colour—

Marianne caught his eye and looked away. Did she regret it?

There was no mention of his going to the Madame ball with able-bodied madam in the notice he had just written for *Foolscap*. No mention of his arm round waist of older woman. Thirty-five? Thirty-eight? Years in inches. Hands full of girthy feel. A sense of considerable enclosures.

Pasture. Sheep, cows, God's plenty grazing on her slopes. Sheet of cleavage, pendant scarab resting on off-white bosom. May I see? Plants in the living-room and a tropical aquarium, prefers Toscana for holidays and sees her ex from time to time, Marianne lives alone. No sign of madam this morning. Shutters down. Business strictly as usual in office blouse.

Harald turned on to Sunday 10 January in his notes. 'Would you like to come back to my place for a drink?'

Noon, Marienplatz, minus twenty-seven degrees. Public enthronization of monarch fools Nikolaus I and Stefanie II. Fool's reign beg. off'ly today. Too cold for c'mony to be crd out as pld. Unblowable trumpets. Only m'bers of gen. plc watched smugly from windows of Cafe am Dom. Free grog for morris d'cers, already incap'd by 11. Mayor, city key etc., usual unfunny r'der to give back on Ash Wed. Narrhalla President B. broke m'zipan crown when p. on N's hd & mended with band aid. Fucking cold. Evbdy ran back in to town hall.

Title?

The Silent Tears of Marianne S. Title of story before, of which there would be no mention in his notices for *Foolscap*. Plumpness of able-bodied madam's wrists he noticed when they danced. Unexpected springiness, and grace, and a rising air of warmth. Symmetry of madam backwards and forwards, Marianne encoded in shapely anagram. Eroticism of bare shoulders. Nothing personal. Just in the air. Her shapeliest simply available, for him and him and him, her whoever wherever dancer. Backwards and forwards the bare shoulders of madam sloped and ran ah, but out of sight. An open invitation from Marianne's unaddressed shoulders (white under ballroom lights, crème de menthe in shadow), he was her dancer and they invited him. Sleek naked shoulders he desired among crowds as impersonally as she displayed them there. She must have felt the heat of his eyes, and of his fingertips, on the coolness of her skin, but she did not say anything, her face at three-quarters all evening, not until the moment when she closed her coat and turned and looked right into him.

'Would you? Would you like to?'

Several cocktails, he couldn't remember, stayed at her place until six. Random drift of early morning hours, adrift on pleasant random muddle-headedness, a thinner and thinner transparency. What's that? Aquarium. You mean for fish? No, actually, for mice. Without any sign of a smile. He saw slow green glide and glints in dark watery shadow there, and around that aquarium in Marianne's living-room the sentence that had wriggled in his head all week slipped unhesitatingly into place. 'Colourless green ideas sleep furiously,' he began, stretching out on the carpet beside able-bodied madam with his head propped against the sofa, and couldn't stop, drew her dress down backwards and forwards over madam's bare shoulders where they sloped and ran out of sight, uncovering her spine and her breasts. Sat on the floor and spoke nonsense, licking able-bodied Marianne's crème de menthe shoulders with pleasure but not necessarily desire, while the night thinned and light crept up outside the window as Marianne sat in silence and tears ran down her face: *The Silent Tears of Marianne S.* Why? Hey, Marianne S. Hang on, I mean *why?* But Marianne didn't, wouldn't, couldn't say.

Audible in his pocket, an electronic pulse now hummed on the hour. Harald got up, tore sheet of paper from type-writer, and walked down the glass-pannelled corridor of the Carnival Organisation Committee's office.

Public relations. Wave, wave. Hello Tina, hello Horst. Apathy of Business Administration, adjacent: heads turned incuriously and sank back as he passed; stale air, smell of powder and fart, leaked from door ajar. Finance, the permed, heavy-jowelled and broad-arsed accountant looked grimly up, licked her thumb and went on counting. As he reached the corner of the corridor a mask shot up behind the glass. Theatrically Harald staggered and clutched his heart.

Roman popped out of the door, grinning.

'What ball do I represent?'

'Happy birthday, son of Dracula.'

'Uh uh.'

'No? Perfect for the part, Roman . . . Pontos Ball? Joker Club? Bal Classique? I don't know. Sir Laughalot and the Horror Nights?'

'Come on, you're not trying.'

Roman was like a little kid. This mattered to him. He'd be disappointed if Harald didn't guess.

'Give me a clue then.'

'Water.'

'Water?'

'Painter who painted water had one in his name.'

'Canaletto. Carnival in Venice.'

Roman looked relieved.

The men's room seemed to follow retroactively from this. Roman declaring a need, Harald instantly felt one too. Like sneezing, this could be contagious. Or was it infectious? Water passed manually, accordingly by contagion. The water-bearer, Aquarius. Sometimes spouts epitomised their owners. He sneaked a glance at Roman's spout and decided Roman's did. Bigger than yours. Bristled in Roman's hand, knobbly, pimpled, extrovert, prankish and unimpeded in full spate. Whereas his didn't. Didn't epitomise, hell, didn't *pee*. Come *on*. Harald screwed up his eyes in panic.

'Beelzebub! Good God.'

Horst's voice. Harald tracked him out of the corner of his eye. Flanking movement to the right. Only three urinals in here. Things were getting tight.

'What's that Beelzebub thing?'

'I was just saying to Tina.'

'What, have we got Tina in here?'

'In the corridor. On our way to the Editor's conference.'

'What were you saying to Tina?'

'Long story, Roman. Wouldn't interest you.'

'Yes it would.'

The conversation bounced over the middle urinal. Roman was like a kid. It would genuinely interest him to know about that Beelzebub thing or whatever Horst had told Tina. Not curiosity. A kid on a treasure hunt. Greed. If it's shut, open it. Check for hidden candy.

'Finished, Harald?'

Horst found Harald's *Foolscap* copy on the basin and read to the sound of running water.

'Hands off, Kempinski! Ovations in wheelchair . . . marzipan . . .'

Harald shook discreetly, completed undercarriage retraction, turned to see Roman combing his hair. Roman watched him in the mirror. Slyly,

'Well?'

'Well what?'

'Did you penetrate?'

Horst held copy in wet fingers, read and dried his hands by the blast of the Secomat on the wall. Roman combed. Harald rinsed.

'So what's she like?'

'What's who like?'

'Marianne. Don't make such a secret of it. The whole office knows.'

Greed. Grab. The candy snatch.

Horst's hands trembled as he read under the drying machine. He took them out of the hot air and pointed.

'This bit won't do, you know.'

Roman took his place at the drier. Horst followed Harald out.

'This bit about the morris dancers being incapacitated. Bad image. Can't have morris dancers falling around.'

'Well, they were.'

'The carnival sponsors won't like it.'

'OK, so they won't.'

'Not OK. Narrhalla subsidises *Foolscap*, dancers, our folk-lore heritage, lots of things besides. Pays for you and me. They want their fun to be taken seriously.'

'All right, compromise. *After downing litres of grog the morris dancers passed out*, insert *of the Town Hall* here, and continue with them *reeling in front of a small but appreciative audience who had braved the cold on the square.*'

'Litres? And do morris dancers technically reel?'

'They do when they technically drink, I'll say.'

'Listen. In two hours for Christ's sake—'

Fortunately Horst broke off at the open door of the Editor's office.

Remember six at conference? Tuesdays and Fridays Tina in first with crossed legs and neatly folded hands, Horst, himself, Finance, Business Administration, and the Chairperson of the Carnival Organisation Committee, who doubled as the Editor of its broadsheet, *Foolscap*. Harald inspected her drawn up at her enormous desk, boxed in by crates of liquor, crêpe, foil, bunting, the sacks of Russian teddy bears still. Now she was on the phone, diverting responsibility for five hundred undelivered champagne glasses.

As always the fascination of the Chairperson, the rings under her eyes, her sad face. Tragedian mistakenly given comic part? Mischievous prompter out of sight was feeding her funny lines instead. She always seemed to be listening and laughing at some joke she heard inside herself. She looked quizzically across the desk.

'Glasses delivered to wrong address. Mercers, Drapers and Haberdashers' Guild is threatening to cancel next year. Isn't that terrible?'

A grin popped up like a jack-in-a-box. 'How have ticket sales gone this week, Hans?'

'Down on last year.'

Things were mostly down with Business Administration. Everyone else laughed.

'I said down. Do let me in on the joke. If we were in this business for a living we'd have gone bankrupt long ago.'

'You're doing a great job, Hans.'

The Chairperson now looked tremendously grave. Gravity weighed heavily round the desk as Business Administration tugged the lobe of his ear and grudgingly released the strips of paper, crowded with jottings and stapled together, which he kept imprisoned in his pocket. Meanness of format of Business Administration's notes: miserly stroke cruel streak in Business Administration's nature? Stinginess in the grain ran right through a person from surface to core, from a cautious way he had of opening his wallet to arrangements for paying off his ex-wife, insurance covered plain pine coffin but no wreaths at funeral, grave insecurity, preferred cremation, he was terrified of being in debt. Over two standing beers in Donisl's draughty entrance Friday night he had shown Harald his life and death in its meagre, dust-sheeted entirety. This man was one of three full-time members on the Carnival Organisation Committee subsidised at local taxpayers' expense. *This man was a professional organiser of fun.* Figures were down on him but that wasn't his fault. The public ate, drank and fucked too much all year long. People had amused themselves to death. Stupefied with fun, couldn't take any more. The figures were down on him, grumbled Business Administration, and cuts in his budget didn't help, and while he was on the subject it'd be nice to feel he had his colleagues' support. Finance now bridled. Haughty indignation *de haut en bas*. Hair dome quivered *en haut*. Jowls shook *en bas*. People in glasshouses. Sweep outside your own door first. Finance trotted out her smelly old adages, challenging Business Administration's competence. Beaming, the Chairperson intervened. Horst reported first issue of *Foolscap* ready to go to press tonight. He passed round the cover design, featuring a peacock lady from the Carneval do Brasil with gorgeous plumes fanned out behind her. Good, said the Chairperson, with its twenty-fifth anniversary coming up Narrhalla should be pleased, Carnival in Rio had always been their favourite do. How were advance sales looking? Strong as ever, Business Administration thought. Just as well, said the Chairperson, what with the catastrophe she could see approaching in the shape of the Carnival in Venice.

The Chairperson produced one of her broadest grins, occasioning a full-frontal display of teeth. The room lit up. Three dozen original Venetian gondolas were already on their way by road and tomorrow would be crossing the Alps. It was too late to send them back. The designated aqueduct along the pedestrian zone was now under construction in any case. Snag was that gondolas didn't normally operate on ice. Thirty degrees of frost already and forecasts predicted arctic weather all the way through next week. The Chairperson grinned for all she was worth as she told them she saw TV rights worth a hundred thousand rapidly turning into frozen assets. And not only those wretched boats they were having lugged over the mountains. Behind the gondolas came a gondolier for each, the twenty-five families of the Compagnia de Calza i Antichi plus attendants, an orchestra, a theatre group and service team, numbering over a hundred and fifty people, all expenses paid for three weeks. The Chairperson beamed. It was a catastrophe. They stood to make a historic loss. On the telephone she had already mooted an emergency plan with the Grand Prior of the Compagnia, a charming gentleman by the name of Piero Zancopé. The Venetians would be dressed up as Laplanders and transported on the elevated ice rink between Karlstor and the Opera House by sleigh instead of boat. In the meantime she had spoken with Mr Shevchenko at the Soviet consulate and had been authorised to distribute at her discretion. Would anyone like a teddy bear?

＊

Caution icy surface. The pictogram was supposed to represent an ice crystal. But note the resemblance to an asterisk.
Another item to come? 'Fraid so, said Horst and Tina, just as
he was stepping into the elevator. Sex World had cancelled
ad. They were short of a dozen lines. Harald opened the
door into the street. Icy surfaces. Flat-footed, splay-heeled,
cautiously he went outside. The cold was standing there
like a board. Ouch. He had walked smack into it.

Anything. By phone. By eight. By you. Anything you like.

Collect materials on the way. Harald skirted still unassem-
bled canal, planks, scaffolding, duck-walked down
pedestrian zone. A short paragraph, inset in the wall of
Antonio Viscardi's Burghers' Hall, recalled the Italian architect's services on behalf of the Marian congregation. It was
followed, left, by a portrait of soon-to-be-canonised Father
Rupert Mayer, facing GOLDLAND and JEANS PALACE,
TRETTER (shoes) and BLUMENFELD (jewellers) in
banner headlines just across the street. Mayer, the martyr,
faced golden land. While TRETTER etc. – the remarkable
number of shoe stores along the pedestrian zone suggested
natural symbiosis of footwear there.

Harald echoed out of the Tivoli Arcade, dropping in at a
store to pick up the parcel Dotty had asked him to collect, and
continued along the Färbergraben, huffing up his shoulders
against the cold. Market place, deserted. The wind scudded.
Harald shrank inside his coat. Crossing the Viktualienmarkt,
he broke into a trot. God it was cold. Legs seemed to be getting thinner and thinner. Scuttled down Reichenbach Street
and fairly jumped into the lobby of the Vietnam Hotel.

Asterisk?

You bet. Cold item completed. Man survives icy surface,
arctic walk. Change to warmer subject.

Swing-doors opened. Out came Diep, trailing smells and
clatter of restaurant.

'Row, Harrer.'

'Hallo, Diep.'

'Coal', huh? Too coal' goin' a party, huh?'

Diep slotted coins into a cigarette machine.

'Gahr goin' a party. You goin' too, Harrer?'

'No.'

'Too coal', huh?'

He bent to pick the carton out of the chute and laughed. Glint on hair, specs, white shirt and show of teeth, briefly everything laughed

'I've brought you a teddy bear, Diep.'

'Wa'?'

'A teddy bear. Here. For your kid. Present from the Soviet consulate.'

Diep backed off in consternation.

'It's OK, Diep. Look, I've got lots of them.'

'So'yet?'

'Don't you want one for your kid?'

Diep laughed frantically.

'See you aroun', Harrer. I gotta work. Like come in ha' beer?'

'No thanks, Diep. Not now.'

'Sure, any time.'

The Vietnamese skedaddled in a flurry of elbows and swing-doors.

Odd.

Harald started up the stairs. Colourless green ideas had tentatively been exchanged. Communication had failed to take place.

He reached the top of the stairs and knocked. Scuffle inside.

'Who is it?'

'Us.'

'Harald?'

'He's the other guy.'

Door opened, Annette red-faced, standing flustered in

white party dress. Behind her the clutter of an attic room, ornaments with a smell of musk, Mexican bark painting, Japanese lantern, a globe-trotting decade taken in at a glance. Mattress in corner. A piece of mirror leaned against wall.

Dotty's reflection in this, hands at her armpits, holding up a skimp of red cloth, turning and looking back over her shoulder.

' 'Nette you must have been tiny. I can't believe it ever fitted you.'

'Ten years ago it did.'

'Ten!'

'Teaching French in Salamanca. I'm fairly ancient, Dotty.'

'Hello, Hoo. You've got a bright red nose.'

She kissed him vaguely as he passed.

Sprawling on the mattress, Harald watched Annette take a silk flower and a piece of black elastic out of the paper bag he had brought. With an effort she closed the dress at the back and hooked it up.

Dotty gasped—

(In Salamanca ten years ago she might have heard the dogs scuffling on the cobbles and the canaries singing on the balconies, passed the House of Shells and felt a pulse, that indescribable threshold hour in Spanish cities when silent afternoons began to throb, shopkeepers ran up their shutters with a rattle and, as if this were a sign, the Plaza Mayor filled instantly with clamorous evening life.)

'What?'

'You just don't listen, Hoo. With the flower or without?'

'Oh, with.'

'And the red dress? It should all have a rather Spanish look.'

'Definitely with.'

'When are they picking us up, Dotty?'

'Alex said at eight. Where are you going?'

'There's a sewing machine in the basement. Quicker to go down and fix it there.'

Annette went out.

'Come and give me a kiss, Dotty.'

'No.'

She remained perched in her underwear on a stool, hugging her knees.

'There'll be an earthquake. You'll fall off anyway. You might as well come now.'

'You don't listen, Hoo. It's because you're not properly there.'

'I was wondering where it'd all gone.'

'What had gone?'

'I was imagining Annette in Salamanca. Annette turned to you.'

'I don't want to be in Salamanca. I don't want you to imagine me there. I want you to imagine me here. I mean, you could just *be* here. You could even leave out the imagining bit.'

' 'S a disease, Dotty. People who have it can't help it, you know. Ten years ago in Salamanca – *bing*!'

'What d'you mean, bing?'

'You're off. Can't stop.'

Harald raised his legs and started pedalling in air.

'You go around pretending all the time. You're missing the real bit, Hoo.'

'What's the real bit?'

'The real bit is being there. This evening. You could have come, you know.'

'Who with?'

'Annette.'

'Thanks.'

'Well why not? Instead you get huffy and build up this Alex thing. This stupid rivalry thing.'

'I'm not huffy.'

'No, I don't think you *are*. I think you're making up this whole business with Alex. You just like imagining things. Sometimes I think you *need* Alex. For some sort of play that's going on inside your head. He's an excuse for not getting on with things you prefer to lie around imagining in any case.'

'Thanks.'

Harald stopped pedalling, flexed his knees and pointed his toes at the ceiling.

'I can prove you wrong. Dotty?'

'I'm waiting.'

'I want you to try and, hm, see things from my point of view. Come and – see things – horizontally – from Annette's triple-sprung camel-hair Slumberland mattress. Donata?'

Dotty perched on her stool and hugged her knees.

'It's impossible for anyone to be *just* here. Nothing I can do about that. The question is where do I *want* to be. Here or— somewhere else.'

Dotty gave a sniff. Harald backpedalled.

'When *you* are here, I don't want to be anywhere else. Snag is— Want to know about the snag with here?

'Hm.'

'Which one?'

'Which what?'

'Yours or mine? Your here with the three legs you're sitting on or the much comfier here I'm lying on with a, huh, a tremendously *hin*cheresting prospect of the ceiling. 'S always like that. We could pool our resources, Dotty. I mean, we could live together.'

Dotty's head moved up a few inches on her neck, as if to get a better view of this.

'Just a suggestion, Dotty. To get a perspective of here, and who's really there, and who's hanging back.'

Dotty rocked. Harald pedalled. Annette came into the silence with the red dress on a hanger.

Sisters

DOTTY

After ten minutes at the Fencing Associations' Ball Dotty hated the red dress. In the ladies' room she tried a few dance steps, watching herself unhappily in the mirror. Two girls wearing stunning evening gowns came in and began to laugh. Dotty felt they were laughing at her. She decided the silk rose looked silly, and threw it into the bin. She was cross with Annette for having talked her into it. She was cross with her mother for having so little money. She had been looking forward to seeing her sister again, and was cross with her for coming so late. She made up her mind she would punish everyone and be grumpy all evening.

Annette and Joachim had got up for the opening polonaise and not been back since. Alex was horsing around with his pals in their silly braided uniforms and caps. Their table was right on the edge of the dance-floor, and sitting there alone Dotty felt uncomfortably exposed. No one was asking her to dance. She read the wine list three times. Yet when the bald old man wearing a ridiculous striped ribbon across his chest came up and asked her with his odd little bow, that didn't suit her either. She didn't want to look as if she needed anyone's charity.

With purposeful steps she left the ballroom and scoured the corridors, pretending to be in search of someone. In the foyer she watched a tide of strange people pass back and forth. On the stairs they puffed, they were so horribly old, moved on up so slowly. She tingled with impatience just seeing them in front of her. Come on. Come *on*! Slipping past, she ran all the way to the top.

But what for?

Dotty leaned over the balcony railing and looked down into the theatre. It reminded her of an enormous blazing birthday cake. She practised being draped over the balcony in ways that might look interesting. The reflection of herself she saw in the black plastic casing round a pillar was more satisfying than the reflection in the cloakroom mirror. It softened her pointed chin and made her look older. Normally she didn't look particularly mysterious, but in the friendly pillar she did. Dotty felt a twinge of frustration that she couldn't have a pillar on permanent call.

When she next looked down she saw Max and Steffi at their table. Dotty's heart did a somersault and she ran downstairs.

Suddenly everyone else seemed to be showing up at the same time, and she had no chance of talking to Steffi alone. Something about her sister's appearance nagged her. She looked terrific in a black satin dress, and Dotty liked her hair short. Corks popped, Max handed round glasses, they all put on smiles before they drank. Steffi laughed jumpily. Phoney. This skittish hilarity. Was she on pills or something? Under the table Alex was taking her hand, but Dotty wasn't in the mood for this and took it back. Above the table Alex was being clever and amusing and she sensed it wasn't for her benefit. It was the same at all of the tables where she'd ever sat with her sister. Plonk her down anywhere and men started to show off. Even that carthorse Joachim whom Alex had harnessed for Annette was having a go, neighing for all he was worth. 'I'd like to dance,' she interrupted, getting up and walking away from the table. When she turned on the dance floor and lifted her arms she found herself already holding Max.

For once there was room and they whirled away. Dotty forgot her resolution to be irritable. A feeling of pleasure stole upwards from her feet. Max said all the right things. He complimented her on her dress and her hair (which Dotty worried was thin), and didn't mention Stefanie once. Dancing, you were right on someone's edge. You were standing on the border of their skin, and there was a sort of buzz, a threat of looming closeness. Max had it. Hoo didn't. That was just the trouble – Hoo's lack of buzz.

Dotty frowned to herself. Why did she get buzz from men she didn't care about? And why didn't she get it from men she did? Why were things so badly arranged? Dotty was getting into her irritable mood again. All this whirling around. Waltz. Silly dance. She withdrew her wrist as soon as the music stopped. Max claimed his minimum reward, giving her a peck on the forehead as they came off the dance floor. Dotty noticed the same aftershave she had sniffed on Alex.

Alex wanted a Scotch. She went with him to the bar in the foyer upstairs. Pretty, expensive girls draped everywhere, showing lots of flesh. Grudgingly she looked over their assets and felt piggy-bank by comparison. They all looked so shiny, as if they had never heard of teeth problems, thinning hair, cash shortage at the end of the month. There they were, all draped at the bar, showing flesh for the men from the fencing associations. What regular girl wouldn't? Parties, dances and bright weekends. Prospect of solid, bankable careers ahead. These things counted for more than all those dark sword rituals in secret places, which the men took so seriously. The girls had a giggle over this. All that cock-crowing oaths and sword stuff – ridiculous. They nonetheless came in droves to watch fencing practice and flashed their bare shoulders, laughing excitedly at just that edge of threat and showing their white teeth. Martina, Dolly, Franziska. This one's mine. She told Alex she wanted to dance.

Always so obliging, Alex. Solid, about as captivating as public transport. In bottom gear he jarred on the turns but improved when he picked up speed on the straight. Same aftershave as Max. Off they went.

What? Darling something or other. Inaudible when romantic. Couldn't tell his feelings in an ordinary voice. Dear Alex. Alex with the loyal, doggy eyes. And when he was aroused he reminded her of a dog getting up and barking at her on his hind legs. Panting doggy male excitement. They always wanted you to watch them do things. Panting in the attic, leather and steel and a swirl of sweat. Dotty stood up there, pressing her knees together, all the girls did, all the knees together, drawn up to that attic room by the scent of blood.

'Christ it's warm,' said Alex. Perspiring male. The toiler. The hero. Look at me – no hands! Dotty pursed her lips and blew cool air around his throat. Blueish, ice-cold Glen Miller sounds pumped out of a saxophone. Dotty felt cool, her feet extraordinarily light.

Watch me! She watched him sculling on the river. She looked down from the bridge and saw him exercise on the water. Later thought of him as rowing on her in bed. Comic. Panting male excitement with oars and swords and the skinned rabbit jumping at her between his legs.

Look – no hands! She smiled. Alex misunderstood and brought his cheek alongside in answering tenderness. Irritating male habit. Always referred causes back to themselves.

'What?'

'Nothing.'

'I thought you said something.'

'Well, I didn't.'

'Oh.'

'I didn't say anything. Nothing at all.'

The weaving blueish stream broke off, stranding them stone-cold in the middle of the dance-floor. It was two o'clock.

Max rallied the boys and girls for snacks or something back at his place. All that helping into coats. Women being popped into packages like slices of cake. Mind she doesn't crumble. Careful, Dotty – crumble here on the steps! The men fussing and self-important, ushering cake-boxes down the stairs. It was absolutely freezing outside. Everyone froze on the spot. Martina was a block of ice in two seconds. Got her, Frank? Strong men tipped Martina slice longwise into the cab.

Alex freighted Dotty in his own car. Or intended to at least. What's that, he asked. Bears, she said, just plain ordinary Russian teddy bears. He was having trouble getting the car started. The car sounded as if it wanted to clear its throat and then die as quickly as possible. Dotty was so cold she could feel her bottom shrinking back from the seat.

'Bears, plural?'

'Two or more. Wouldn't it be a better idea to take a cab, Alex?'

He wanted to know where she'd obtained the bears. Just as a matter of interest.

'One doesn't *obtain* bears,' she bickered, 'but leaving that aside: via Harald, from the Russian consulate.'

'But why two or more?'

The other one was a present for Steffi, but Dotty didn't tell him that, irritated by the way Alex was going on about it. 'Male and female,' she said instead, surprisingly that was taken to be an arrangement that worked. And incidentally, why couldn't Alex admit there wasn't the slightest chance of getting the engine to turn over, even she could hear that. Alex thought, amazingly enough, that (a) the car would start, and (b) the teddy bears were unacceptable, as they were clearly Soviet propaganda. This supplied the pretext, though it was not necessarily the reason, as Dotty afterwards told her sister, why at this point she got out of the car and slammed the door.

From the landing in Maximilian's house she looked into the room where dinner-jacketed men stood feeding at a white-cloth table, chattering and honking like so many penguins socialising on the shore. All that waggle and chatter gathered round a smell of fish – ugh. Dotty had no desire to go in. Luckily she caught her sister's eye, and Stefanie at once came out.

Dotty told her she'd squabbled with both her men on the same evening, she was fed up, and when could they have a talk? Now, said Steffi, Dotty could stay the night. She took her upstairs and showed her into a room with a high ceiling and heavy maroon velvet curtains.

'Wow. What's *this*?'

'Spare room. Max put me in here when I came.'

'More like *wheeled* you in. This place is a funeral parlour.'

Dotty flung herself on the bed.

'God. I'm dead. Have you got a cigarette?'

'There are some in the drawer.'

Dotty reached and lit up.

'Got to hand it to you, Steff. Couldn't wait to see you. Know why? God what a place. Look at those *curtains*. This is the gloom room all right.'

'You refer to the tomb?'

'The whom?'

'The room.'

The sisters laughed.

'We'll be doing that routine in our nineties. I've missed you, Steff. I couldn't wait to see you. Not just to horse around and stuff. Tonight I found out an awful thing. I found out how jealous I am of you. D'you know what was behind wanting to see you again? I wanted to see if you were beginning to lose your looks. I was secretly hoping you might have got a bit old. Well, you haven't. But you've got something else. You've gone serious. I don't know, but like – very *quiet*. Like you'd been put in the shade.'

'I have been put in the shade, Dotty. I've been unhappy.'

'Don't you think you've been overdoing it a bit?'

Dotty stubbed out the cigarette viciously.

'I mean, it's been *months*.'

'I wrote. I called. Constanze knew how I was.'

'It's not enough. And Ma's not the problem. The problem's Bapa.'

'The problem's always been Bapa.'

'Bapa's gone right off his head. You know he worried himself sick about you. I mean, he's become a total invalid case. Ma told you that. But you still wouldn't come.'

'That's emotional blackmail. I won't go for it. Of course I love Bapa. You know what I've done for him. I don't need to prove anything.'

'Bapa's dying.'

'I'm glad for him. He's an old man. Maybe Bapa's time has come. Is that so terrible? Dying's not half as bad as it's made out to be.'

'You *have* been put in the shade. You give me the creeps the way you say that.'

She lit another cigarette.

'You're beginning to read all over like an obituary. Is that what Mourning Services Inc. has been doing for you, Steff?'

'Dotty, you're detestable. What's wrong with you? Why did you bother to come? You're in an absolutely *shitty* mood.'

'What about Brum?'

'What *about* Brum.'

'Clunk.'

Dotty bashed the pillow and exhaled noisily.

'Is it a new moon or something?'

'How should I know.'

'The weather's going to change. It changes with the new moon.'

'That's just Bapa's theory.'

'I can feel it changing. I can always feel it changing in advance. Here.'

She rubbed her elbow.

'In my leg. I know, Steff. That is, I don't. I'm *sorry*, dammit.'

' 'S OK.

Steffi came over and kissed her sister's nose. She took a bottle out of the bedside cupboard and poured them two terrific shots. Dotty picked up her glass, frowning.

'Max and Alex use the same aftershave. Hoo uses none at all.'

'Is this going to be the start of one of those quiz questions?'

'I'm not sure he washes properly. He's sort of smudged. At the moment I couldn't say for sure where he lives.'

'How come?'

'Even when he's *there* I can't be sure he is. Hoo drives me crazy.' Dotty took a swig. 'He's a dreamer. I'm not allowed to be me. I have to be someone in Hoo's dream.'

'All men are dreamers. All men are like that.'

'No way out?'

'Except by never going in.'

'Pfui! But if there was *no* way out, whose dream would you prefer to be in?'

'I'd prefer someone to be in mine.'

Steffi put her arms under her head and worked out patterns on the ceiling.

'You know Brum broke in here when Max and I were away and stole those pictures of me Max had bought?'

'Stole what pictures?'

'The pictures of me that were exhibited at Catacomb.'

'You're kidding.'

'All twenty-three of them.'

'How d'you know it was Brum?'

'Because he sent an invoice.'

'He what?'

'For, quote, "Twenty-three worthless copies, which will be restored as soon as I am in possession of their original again," unquote.'

'Wow!' Dotty drew up her knees, raised her legs and began pedalling. 'Ro-*man*-tic! What did Max say?'

'Max said he'd prosecute.'

'Max is a turd.'

'They're his paintings. He paid for them.'

Steffi got up and stood at the side of the bed with her hands behind her neck. She unclasped her necklace and put it on the table.

'If Brum's stubborn he may find himself landing up in jail.'

'Oh *no*! You must make Max promise not to prosecute.'

'I don't know . . . It might be rather fun to visit Brum in jail.'

'Steffi!'

Dotty came down with a crash. Steffi leaned over and kissed her. Dotty put her hand to her sister's throat.

'So that's it.'

'That's what?'

'The locket. That's what's missing. That little silver locket. I've been racking my brains all evening. I'm so used to seeing it I find you look different without it.'

Stefanie picked up the necklace and went to the door.

'Where is it, Steffi? Did you lose it?'

'No. It's in the next room.'

'Don't you wear it anymore?'

'Let's say I'm wearing it again. G'night, Dotty dear. I'm going to bed.'

'What's the time?'

'Almost five.'

Dotty yawned.

'G'night then.'

She lay awake for about fifteen seconds more. The evening flashed past her eyes. Then the floor rose level with the bed and she was lying on a shore and a warm green wave broke over her echoing echoing echoing—

The Great Cold

BRUM

Something began to nag around the middle of the week. Maybe the nag was the aftermath of the dream I had. At a Chinese restaurant in Hohenzollern Street I was served a moist and warm mass of something that the waiter identified as afterbirth. He bounced it on a tennis racket a couple of times, to soften it up, he said, wrapped it in a napkin and stuck it on my head. I asked him how much longer we would have to go on with this poultice treatment and he said indefinitely, otherwise the horns would grow again. When I awoke I still felt the ache of a bruise in my sleep. Later the recurrent horn dream gave way to the dream of the faceless antique lady rising in the east.

The reason for this was clear. Stefanie was back in town.

Candice told me over dinner at Janus in Elizabeth Street, where we meet for our weekly review. It must have been the day after I snitched my paintings of Stefanie from the house in Bogenhausen. She was back, said Candice, and had apparently signalled willingness to negotiate.

At her apartment afterwards she put on her leathers and

stood over me, prostrate and grovelling during the Question-
naire, with the chastener ready to hand in case I had
misbehaved, but the chastener remained unused. All week
long I'd been a good, a perfectly boring boy, earning top
marks from Candice for remembering to pee sitting when I
went to the loo to avoid splashing her Italian tiles. Candice
shed a tear or two. She saw that the time had come to discharge me, admitting that recently in her role as dominatrice
my education was becoming too much her pleasure. She
gave me one of her alabaster potatoes as a parting gift, and
promised that whenever I rubbed it she would appear.

I did not see the lady in the dream, just sensed her, and
her great antiquity, and her rising somewhere in the east, out
of the corner of my eye. But she left a message. When I
woke I found words in my handwriting on a pad on
the bedside table, words I had no recollection of having
written.

burial of the queen of hearts

Car refused to start, categorically, after the onset of the
cold. I went into town from Nymphenburg by tram instead.
It's so cold at Mayer's stained-glass and mosaic workshop
that we all have to thaw out our fingers in hot water before
we can start work. The cold slid down and down and down
until it supposedly hit rock-bottom at $-38°C$, where it settled as the all-benumbing topic of the week.

Cold bulletins were first issued on radio and TV around
the middle of January. Children were exempted from school,
homeless people allowed to stay overnight in the municipal
warm rooms, measures taken to rescue other endangered
species. Popular carnival fixtures like Meet the Movies and
the Chrysanthemum Ball had record low attendances. The
state reception for the consular corps, traditionally held in
mid-January at the Residenz, was cancelled at twenty-four
hours' notice. No one went out unless they had to. Streets

emptied. Windows froze up. A silence descended on the city.

Woke to silent mornings in the Copper Lodge, reaching for pieces of paper on which traces of sleep had overflowed, as lucid and noncommital as inscriptions one might have come across among ruins.

When the temperature sank to −40°C public transport closed down altogether. For convenience I moved from Nymphenburg to Gisela's apartment in town, where I stayed with one dog and seven other human inmates Gisela allowed to sleep on her mattresses for the duration of the Great Cold.

Some mornings Antonio's old diesel engine grunted and turned over, some mornings it did not, and then we walked to Mayer's, so muffled up we looked like zombies, Antonio wearing an interesting contraption on his face, goggles with padded nose-guard stitched on so that he didn't lose anything on the way. Not all the snow had been cleared, and what there was left of it bequeathed sculptural presences kept in storage by the frost for weeks. We looked down a colonnade of stalactites hanging from the eaves all the way down Ludwig Street. Builders' plastic streamers criss-crossing the scaffolding on a building site, moist in the thaw at Christmas, had transformed the façade into a miraculous filigree of threads of ice.

Mayer has phoned from New York and given the staff a holiday from the cold, not in a charitable spirit, but to keep the heating bills down. The people from the university institute on the third floor have long since capitulated and gone home. So Antonio and I are left to ourselves in that sprawling junkyard of a building, now as bleak and silent as a morgue.

Every morning I checked the paintings of Steffi hidden in Mayer's attic. She was distributed in lots, tucked away between tracings of rose windows for the restored Cathedral of Our Lady and copies of the grisaille panel from the

Cistercian church at Altenberg. I took the pictures out and switched them around and sat looking at them in the freezing attic.

the knave of hearts, said the lady,
was brutish and snored in bed

Antonio would keep a bowl of water on a bunsen burner to warm his fingers from time to time. He is a pale-skinned, balding, nasally-drawn-out Venetian whose affinity with glass seems to be something bonded in his genes. In the cold he had to warm the wax in order to be able to knead it at all. On the floor I laid out pieces of stained glass and sorted them by number. Antonio waxed them in place, like bits of a jigsaw puzzle. Then he set the sheets of glass in frames in front of the thirty-foot composition window where we could see them against the light. On the scaffolding in front of the composition window another window began to grow, coloured glass by coloured glass, wax provisionally bonding them in place of leading – the window I had been commissioned to design for the consecration hall that was to be inaugurated at Easter.

Putting together, putting together.

Captivated by Bo, Zeo had still not returned from the Arthouse, and Gisela, short of floor-space, assigned me the vacancy in her grandmother's bed, which I shared with Dada and Leila. The mattress-room clientele had begun to harbour for Procyon an intensely interesting collection of smells from sardine through various rancid fats to a beefy pong of old leather, items of which Antonio, burrowing in for his creature comforts like the rest of us, would smuggle out of the house in the mornings. He shed them as he walked, quite unselfconsciously. On car mornings they accompanied us all the way to Mayer's.

Night for night the antique lady drew closer in my dreams, moving centrewards out of the corner of my eye. I

would lurch up, take hurried dictation by flashlight and sub-
merge again, leaving words from some-other-where stranded
on a cold white morning page.

the bloody tides on which the plumed shoals suck and swim

Rejecting any figurative solution early on, I addressed the
theme I'd been given for my window in configurations of
pure colour, gradations of colour-change so subtle that the
eye detected no boundary as it moved from one configura-
tion to another, only a friction, an oscillation of neighbour-
ing colour energies on the porous borders between forms,
life, death, osmosis between fractured instant and unimag-
inably compounded eternity—

burial by water I wish to be my last and only exequy

Midweek plumbed −45°C, a faint clunk as our submarine
hit the bottom, stirring sea-bed ooze, and then silence. Gone
those liquefied mercurial days, every day's terrifying quick-
silver pace, time or the sense of time stalled, the days arched
and arched and exploded in slow-spreading motion by a
span of light about a half-hour longer now. Gisela took food
out and sometimes came home from the English Garden
with small frozen animals she laid on the kitchen table like
bricks. A duck, hedgehogs and stray cats, animals Procyon
approached with mature restraint if not affection, thawed
out and survived, but the songbirds Gisela tried to rescue
died. The extreme cold brought the deer down from the
mountains and wolves out of the forests to the east, where
they scavenged in villages and plundered rubbish bins on the
outskirts of cities. Hospitals were treating cases of frostbite,
people died of cold in their cars. The threat of a natural disaster, from which for the time being one was safe and which
would pass in any case, also had a stimulating effect. Nature
that hung out there largely forgotten, even irrelevant, was

now baring its teeth and would nip our ankles the moment we stepped outside.

Upstairs at Mayer's we whined up on the hydraulic platform, now reaching the twenty-foot mark at the composition window. We were out of the greens and into the blues. Here and there I experimented with smalten, chips of solidly vitrified glass, to get light-resistant spots, occasional pockets of opacity. The blues would continue up through shades of semi-opacity from midnight blue and black to the point where the ceiling began to soar and (this at least was the effect I was hoping for) the roof took off, into space.

While Antonio moodily trimmed glass-cake to size with glazier's tongs (he didn't approve of these experiments), I sneaked upstairs, and took out the portraits from their safe-keeping between grisaille panel and rose window. Furtive voyeur of my wife's ruins, I saw the sorrowfulness I had painted there.

all hours, pleasures, pains   plumed shoals suck and swim
            my body's caves become coral for the ocean
            to comb and spin and scatter as grains of sand

Through finely-graded blues and greens came a glint of the afternoon sun as it touched the top corner of the window for the first time this year. The sun had orbited my head. Memories glowed up, light spread and spread through the midnight blues and blacks in front of me like stains regressing through transparency, and then snuffed out, the window invisible in darkness by the time I left.

Had I been too preoccupied with my work? Had I lacked compassion?

Warmth lit, or light warmed, and as I reached the point of maximum extension of the hydraulic bridge at Mayer's and began to move back down the composition window, suddenly the temperature began to climb. You could hear the wood crack, buildings, the objects and even the people inside them, they all seemed to have their own sounds as they emerged fragilely from stiffness, still in the low thirties, when already by comparison it began to feel warm. On bright days Gisela would come to watch, too. On bright days she and Antonio and I set up our chairs at half-past-three in the afternoon and waited for the epiphany at Mayer's.

Touching the top corner of the window, the light struck a chord. The sun warmed the blacks and the blues and they began to melt into light. A stain spread quickly from opacity through degrees of increasing transparency. I could feel it jar down my shins and the backs of my arms. Colour began to take on shape in the obscure January afternoon, turquoise and green, hanging luminously in the air. For just a few minutes in the afternoon twilight the frozen window thawed out, a blue-green waterfall shimmering on the edge of the dark.

I had a headache and couldn't sleep as we surfaced through twenty degrees in as many hours. From Mayer's windows I looked across rooftops and a tangle of television aerials at the mountains stalking much closer than they were supposed to, nobody needed to tell me the Föhn wind was blowing, because when I looked out of the attic windows the Alps had stolen a march on the city in the night and at dawn stood glittering in the suburbs. All through the day and way on into the gusty night I sat in the dark at Mayer's, surrounded by huge impending objects, cranes and tackle and block, listening to them creak as I looked for the oblong piece of dark that might be my extinguished window. Maybe, to fetch her back, I'd be like a strolling blind memory, a disembodied soul imagining the faded incarnations of itself, as whiteness recalls magnolia bloom or greenness remembers summer grass. I heard a drip every few minutes, and when I went up I found a patch of moisture on the attic floor, and I knew the winter weather had broken. The ice began to rustle over the tiles. I opened a skylight and climbed onto the roof.

The wind ransacked the city and turned it inside out. The illusion of the Föhn foreshortened so phenomenally that I seemed to be looking at mountains just beyond the rooftops across the street, and unaccountably I could hear the sound of waves smack-smacking, echoes of choppy water slopping against masonry in drowned arcades, swilling through streets and flooding highways, a muttering sound which overlaid the drone of traffic, sound of a windswept urban sea.

THE FEAST OF FOOLS

The Water Bearer

The Venetians embark at night and come by water through a dry, windstill city. The half-moon space with the fountain, on the west side of Karlstor, has been raised by ten feet and transformed into a lake. Cranes have been at work since noon, unloading the gondolas from trucks and lowering them onto the water, where a flotilla of vessels has now assembled. Musicians in the livery of the Doge appear at the top of the steps leading up from their dressing-rooms under the lake, and board the two leading barques. The following barques, each of them oared by six gondoliers, accommodate floating stages on which characters from the commedia dell'arte will perform comic intermezzi en route. Other actors arrange themselves in a series of tableaux vivants. The boats wait in readiness in the shadow of the arch. A hush descends. On the stroke of the hour there is a blast of trumpets. At intervals the gondolas shove off from the archway and emerge one by one on a bright sheet of water. Hundreds of lamps suspended from cables illuminate the aqueduct built on trestles that runs the length of the pedestrian zone from Karlstor to the Opera House. Music for strings and brass by the Venetian composers Vivaldi and Monteverdi begins to drift down the water with the leading barques, and is lost in the boom and roar that goes up from the crowd. The spectators stand in raised galleries on either side of the aqueduct, throng at the windows of the upper storeys and wave from the roofs of houses looking over the water. As the barques with the musicians and actors reach the church of St Michael's, the last gondolas in the procession of families of the Compagnia de Calza i Antichi are still setting out from Karlstor. Piero Zancopé, the Grand Prior of the Compagnia, and Mafalda, the Queen of Courtesans, travels sumptuously in a barque with a dais of green and lilac cushions on which the lady reclines. She is followed by the Doge, seated on an ornate Byzantine throne. At the cornices inside Karlstor stone faces look down from a frieze on rocking light and shadow as a plain black gondola slides swiftly out from the gloom of the arch across an empty stretch of water. In the last gondola rides Death. Death stands motionless at the prow in monk's habit and a skeleton's mask. He carries a whip and a distaff. His vessel is bare of ornament. The gondolier wears a cloak and a three-cornered hat and the *bautta*, the Venetian carnival mask. The floodlights go out. Gradually the spectators fall silent. A backwash of silence ripples from Karlstor all the way to Marienplatz. Lights are extinguished here, too. The flotilla assembles on a second raised lake that has been built over the square. Water slaps boats softly, wood rubs and creaks. The surrounding walls throw back echoes and the square is awash with the unfamiliar sounds of water in a place where water has never been before. A voice exclaims. The boats jostle and buffet one another, the slap-slapping of water scouring walls reaches the spectators' ears. A man shouts across the square. The dark seems to shimmer with the sounds of water splashing, the bright scattered shouts, igniting in one boat after another. A light shows in the middle of the lake. Shouts rebound from the walls of the square. Rows of lamps light up, outlining the shapes of gondolas in the dark, shouts bounce off the water, which comes ablaze as underwater searchlights illuminate the lake. The boats turn, prows pointing back in the direction from which they have come. Fifty, a hundred yards away there is a gleam of black lacquer on the fringe of light, and above it, like disembodied stares, the masks of Death and Death's gondolier hang luminous in the dark. The Venetians strike gongs and cymbals, hiss and shout at the gondola gleaming on the dark water. The spectators around the square are silent. Water laps the black gondola, casting gleams on lacquer where the boat rocks on a fringe of light. Death hangs his white escutcheon in the dark, a mask of never-changing expression. The Venetians clatter with crossed oars. The crowd murmurs. Death waits. He is refused admittance to the square. The ding-dong continues until Death raises the hand with the scourge, acknowledging defeat, and turns his face out of the light. The luminous escutcheon vanishes. His gondolier brings the boat round and the crowd applauds. The illuminated flotilla of the Venetians slips through the bottleneck at the entrance to Diener Street, floats out across Max-Joseph Square and arrives at the Residenz in glittering formation as fireworks mushroom in the night sky above.

Their Excellencies
the Lord Mayor and the Doge
Exchange Civilities in
the Chamber of
the Four Elements

The Master of the Revels receives the Doge and his retinue at the entrance to the palace. The Venetians are conducted through the candle-lit antiquarium. They walk without haste. Semi-obscurity in this long narrow place unravels and brightens piece by piece. Echoes chase sounds under the low vaulted ceiling and quickly fade. No one looks back. Everything moves forward and is irretrievable in the same instant. Candle flames standing motionless before the cavalcade comes in are flickering long after it has gone out.

In the Chamber of the Four Elements, where the municipality receives the Doge and his court, a celestial globe has been constructed that takes up the whole room. Their Excellencies the Lord Mayor and the Doge advance and shake hands at a spot approximating to the centre of the earth. The Mayor bids the Doge welcome in our city etc. etc., and waits for the interpreter to translate into Italian. The Doge, responding to the Mayor's greeting, clearly feels that the occasion calls for something more. The south has come to the north, he declares, bringing a touch of spring to the northern winter with its celebration of the carnival in

Venice. While the Mayor smiles his way through flowery
conceits, the Doge is looking around him with a gesture
that seems to ask: And what sort of ingenious toy is this?

Reproducing the tilt of the earth in the plane of its orbit,
the structure filling the room rests at an acute angle to the
floor, giving the impression that the room itself is lop-sided.
The walls of the chamber, forming tangents to two vast
hoops representing the ecliptic and celestial equators,
enclose a simplified model of the earth and its companion
planets within the solar system. Around the surface of the
spheres, which are strung on wires anchored to the ceiling,
a childlike imagination has painted mercurial, martial and
saturnine features expressing aspects of the planets. Some of
the brighter mid-winter constellations, the Dragon and the
Plough to the north, Orion and Capella in the Charioteer to
the south, have been projected onto the ceiling, where they
interfere with the stucco mouldings. A chandelier has disabled the Pole Star entirely.

Scenes from the
Commedia Dell'Arte

Among the Doge's retinue are members of the Zancopé family, the Grand Prior and his twin nieces, who are eighteen years and three days old. Giovanna and Francesca wear gowns of white silk over panniers, bodices of the same material, the shoulders bare. The skirt has a train which they simultaneously pick up and carry, as if co-ordinated by the same nervous system, when the party leaves the Chamber of the Four Elements and continues through the Residenz. Where Giovanna's costume begins to feel tight at the waist Francesca responds with a sympathetic ache. The girls share the same feelings of exhilaration too, sparkle of bare shoulders in their own aura of brightness, a glittering sensation they perceive briefly as flare and the frisson when it douses, almost palpable the sizzle and whoosh of a burning stick plunged in cold water as they step out into the night air and cross the courtyard of the Brunnenhof. In the Cuvilliés Theatre they encounter the same expectant brightness, magnified and thrown back at them from the rococo interior lit by thousands of candles.

A play of sorts is already in motion but the audience takes

no notice, in fact behaves as if it is part of the play itself; struts; poses; pays social calls in the stalls and lounges around the proscenium, chatting, very much caught up in itself. Disqualified by the width of their panniers from sitting, the girls stand and peer over the heads of the spectators, looking down from the balcony at the grand corso devolving on stage, with its plumage of bonnets, hats, fans, masks, extravagant collars and cuffs, the swarm of eighteenth-century costumes overflowing into the auditorium and up through crowded tiers to the royal box where the Mayor and the Doge are sitting with a party of eminent Venetians, the Nicolotti, Balestri and Zancopé families, masked *zanni* and *amorosi* engrossed in their hide-and-seek games of flirtation, the Queen of Courtesans in turquoise brocade receiving admirers in her box, and in between the spectators a gap that is left by a white mask, the cold stare of the *bautta*, falling like a shadow wherever it is cast.

Meanwhile a ragamuffin figure goes unnoticed, approaching slowly from the back of the stage. It shuffles forward, shaken by occasional spasms. The figure pays no attention to the people around. Under a flapping, shabby gown he wears a red jacket, a pair of torn trousers. On his head is a skullcap. Moustaches spray out from under a mask whose face shows an old man, the Venetian merchant Pantalone.

Reaching the proscenium he stops, tilts back his head and turns it back and forth, as if following something in flight. Surprised by intermittent spasms, his head and shoulders jump.

The stage drains.

From the twins' point of view in the balcony there is an impression of things pouring off stage. People are diving into the wings. Knots of actors still remaining on the stage, digging one another in the ribs with theatrical nudges to draw attention to Pantalone's antics, break up and drift away. Pantalone is left alone on stage.

With his head thrown back the actor stares up into the

flies. He brings his head down slowly in a looping descent, tracking something invisible in flight, the spiral narrowing until his head is spinning on the spot. His body convulses. For the first time there is an audible *plop*! The absurdly meagre quantity of sound to emerge after all his previous exertions makes the audience laugh. Pantalone has hiccoughs.

He approaches on tiptoe, stretches out a hand, is about to grab the hiccough when it erupts. The phantom sneaks up behind him unawares, leads him in circles and lures him over the edge of the stage. He treads on hiccough and it squeaks under foot. Wind is broken over an organ-pipe span of registers. He sounds it like a conch in his cupped hands. It belches from the back of the stage and soars with a shriek up to the flies.

Pantalone shuffles forward; stoops, peering. He is like some gaunt bird, an old man rummaging. Testily he fishes around, poking with his stick. A hand fumbles up the line of buttons. Slowly, as he comes forward, he is doing up the buttons of his gown, gradually he is straightening up. He has lost something, it has escaped his interest but it no longer matters because he has ceased to look for it, dismissing the illusion of the banished hiccough with a magician's glib flourish, seeming to be shedding age with every step he takes, removing skullcap and mask and hanging them on his sleeve as he emerges as a not so old, even youngish man who now stands in a spotlight under the proscenium arch.

He greets the audience and introduces himself in a rapid convolution of half a dozen languages. He is Cesare d'Arbes, actor-manager of the Medebac Commedia Dell'Arte Company. He reminds the audience that this is not the company's first visit to Munich. A commedia dell'arte *canovaccio* was commissioned from the resident composer Orlando di Lasso for the wedding of William, son of Orlando's patron the Duke of Bavaria, in the year 1568; and when the young couple, after a decade of felicity, retired

to Trausnitz Castle, they sent for players from Italy whose
faces were recorded more than four hundred years ago in
the murals on the castle walls. These murals and Orlando's
canovaccio are the earliest commedia dell'arte records to
have survived. Little has survived. The actor leans more
closely into his audience and smilingly confides: his is not a
surviving art. There is no text. There is only the *canovaccio*,
a scenario hanging on the green-room door for actors to
glean an impression of the play before stepping into it on
stage; a bare outline of stock scenes from life – pride, greed,
hypocrisy, deceit, foolishness, lust and sometimes love – that
depend on the actor's improvisation, bending coincidence to
a purpose to bring the stereotype to life. This is his art.
Briefly the actor interrupts Cesare d'Arbes to don
Pantalone's mask, bows ironically to acknowledge scattered
applause. Comic interludes of the kind the audience has
just seen belong to the commedia's repertoire of stage business known as *lazzi*. In the following scenes the audience
will be privy to many more. They will be entertained by
remarkable acrobatic agility, by fireworks and exquisite
tableaux vivants, by scenes of high seriousness and ludicrous intermezzi. They will be spectators at the bazaar of
human passions. The Medebac Company herewith humbly
presents the story of a young woman and her thwarted
lover – but already figures are coming forward to the accompaniment of faint music, and the actor-manager of the
Medebac Company, fading in upwardly shrinking light, only
has time to extend to the audience an invitation to a ball at
the Carnival in Venice before disappearing in the extinguished spotlight, and the faint strains of an antique music
heard before crescendo suddenly as other figures step into
the light.

Carnival in Venice

1

Bored at one end of a table noisy with other people's laughter, Piero looks down from the gallery over the dance-floor in search of a description. There are two thousand guests at this ball. As Grand Prior, their nominal host for the evening, he has shaken many of their hands and can sympathise with claims to individuality. Individuality long since disappeared into the blur of averages, however. As marine biologist, contemplating the analogy of a sea of faces with a scientific prejudice, he doesn't shrink from other descriptions. A sea teeming with a mass of micro-organisms, coccolithophorids, for example, or prochlorophytes, those minute photosynthesizing cells in densities of sixty million per pint that make the sea look green. But blurs of averages describe only a composite face. Mass identification is useful only for eliciting mass effects, such as green shimmer or collective sexual susurration. Doesn't convey the richness and complexity of the parts that make up the organism.

2

For example the twins. Their mother has allowed them to go on this jaunt only if Piero keeps an eye on them. He glances over his shoulder. They are still leaning against the railing at the far end of the gallery. In those symmetrical attitudes that often strike him, both girls are resting one hand on the railing, the other on their hips. Why aren't they dancing?

They are interested in the tall young man with the green hair who stands between them demonstrating a camera. He attaches a telescopic lens and lifts the camera to his eye. Focuses, points. Over there. See it? Giovanna and Francesca, symmetrically each girl raises a hand. They take it in turns to encircle the fat lens with their fingers and squint down the pointed line. In close-up, Piero scrutinises tell-tale flush on skin. Still closer in, breaking cuticle membrane, moisture from increased activity of the glands might be observed with the aid of a microscope. Piero smiles. He has no more than observer status.

Who is this observer, incidentally? What about him?

3

Less detached than he appears to be. He is missing something in the evening, a sharp edge to whet his appetite. The boredom that used to be a posture has become, through lifetime habit, Piero's natural manner. Privately he agrees with himself that he would have liked to be an actor. He looks down the table to where Cesare is sitting and imagines himself for a few seconds inside the comedian's life. The polymorphous raconteur is as usual the centre of gravity, as usual bending his listeners around him. The attraction to that life may just be a dissatisfaction with this. Or it may be something close to the core, envy of Cesare's facility for dodging in and out of existences, discarding masks to suit his convenience. The desire to be an actor might even be some regenerative urge in nature to reproduce itself, an overlap of cell division into consciousness, the ego's thirst for self-renewal. As a young man there was exhilaration, almost bewilderment, at the infinite possibilities that seemed to stretch ahead; then narrowing ambition, the brief illusion of accomplishment; then hope, still hope; no longer hope, and at last insight into the fraudulent pretensions of mortality in general – Piero sees these things but no longer has any use for them. He is standing at the edge of a hole and looking into it with no excuses. The mood passes, and he turns to his neighbour. He can be amusing, agreeable; attractive because he knows how to convey to people that he is interested in them. This is how he is seen by the wife of the Master of Revels, in whom Piero is not interested, when he turns back to her after watching his nieces, the briefest span of attention in which a pulse has nonetheless travelled the length of some kind of integrated circuit of his life. He asks her if she would like to dance. She is already getting up as Piero wipes his lips with a napkin. He looks down a foreshortened line of bottles, takes in wreckage of dinner table, crammed benches and barrage of noise, the Doge at the opposite end in conversation with the Mayor's wife. Beyond them he notices someone appear at the top of the stairs at the far end of the gallery. The figure is dressed in black in a page's costume, tights, tunic and mask, all in black. Piero takes it in at a glance as he is wiping the corners of his mouth with the napkin. He stands. He sees that the page is not a boy or a man. The figure walking towards him as Piero escorts his partner along the gallery is unmistakably that of a woman.

4

Ploog is holding his liquor well. At a distance of fifty yards he might even have been given the benefit of the doubt by his ex-wife. Sartorius is the caricature of a drunk. He is moving in zigzags along the steps, a man treading with caution on a xylophone, uncertain if the tune goes up here or down. The decision is not always his. Something near the top of the steps, perhaps the height, has alarmed him. He sways back down at increasing speed. As Johnny begins to argue with the theatre doorman, Harald Hemsing pays off the cab and turns to receive the Local Editor in his arms.

Doorman prefers clear-cut decisions, and this one is the clearest he's had all evening. Two and a half drunks, no costume, no tickets: no admittance. Not for any amount of money. In doormanese he signals zero with swimming motion of both arms.

Johnny continues to insist quietly, with a drunk's exaggerated sense of his dignity and the need to keep up appearances, while the doorman tries to keep out of range of the fog of beer in his face. It's taking a while for the message to get across. Doorman listens in disbelief. Far from paying, the smelly man seems to be telling him, he and his colleagues will be admitted with open arms, complimentary vouchers for food and drink. They are gentlemen of the press.

5

Narrhalla President Brenthrop chortles. A gigantic corrugated paper ruff detaches Brenthrop's head from the rest of him, his pink round face resembles a blancmange left shuddering on a plate. The President of the Society of Friends of Carnival is taking the lead in responding to his own jokes. Others dutifully follow. Brenthrop uses these functions to promote business interests. His guests are mostly large men with even larger wives. Blancmange heaves. Chortle does its jolly rounds. Waltzing past the tables along the edge of the ballroom floor with the wife of the Master of the Revels in his arms, Piero Zancopé has an impression of looking down through a snorkling mask at marine sponges, billowing on a gusty ocean floor. In the meantime, what has happened to the dark lady?

6

Unisize T-shirts and boaters are obligatory for guests without their own costumes. On payment of a deposit they are available at the cloakroom. The three newsmen check in their coats and jackets in exchange for gondolieri outfits. Half way out of his pullover Conrad Sartorius gets stuck, loses his balance and spins off down the foyer. Already boatered and horizontally striped, Ploog turns and sees his colleague teetering on the edge of a canal.

Stage painters from the Opera House have turned foyer, corridors and stairs into a panopticum of scenes from Venice. Palazzi shrink to be accommodated in perspective on a twelve-foot wall to the left, water and boats crowd the foreground to the right, spires and sky reach far away to the horizon. Seen with the degree of blur that Ploog brings to bear, the illusion looks a hundred per cent authentic. He walks into it, exclaiming.

The Local Editor is retrieved and costumed. Harald Hemsing's T-shirt is too large. Johnny's is too small. Conrad's is back to front. Kick to the left, kick to the right, hat in hand and linking arms they salute themselves in the mirror. They look sensational.

7

Careful though, says Johnny. They take Sartorius between them to keep him away from the water. Sure it's an illusion. Johnny's taking no chances on that either.

They cross a bridge or two, pass wharves and busy market scenes. Masked men sidle round corners. Women's heels flash on stairs. Skimming the sights of the floating city, they soon latch on to the signs pointing them upstairs to the Lido Bar.

Turning the corner they reach a piazza before it vanishes in perspective on a wall. A sign hanging from the ceiling reads: LIDO BAR. A TV crew is videotaping. Noon glare is reflected from a battery of lights. Audio backdrop on tape supplies the scene with footsteps, voices, horns, clatter of pigeons' wings taking flight. The soundtrack is unnecessary. There's plenty of real noise here already. Representatives of the media, colleagues of Johnny Ploog, extras, professional gatecrashers in the same boaters and striped shirts – there must be at least a hundred gondolieri propping up the bar, some of whom are genuine.

8

In the meantime Piero has placed her. He burrows a short-cut through the backstage kitchens and intercepts her at the Rialto. 'I've seen you before,' he says, taking her arm and walking her into scenery with a distant prospect of St Mark's, 'here at the Rialto, three years ago in the summer.' The dark lady stops and quizzes him. 'Men have always seen women before,' she replies, ironic but not unfriendly. 'Perhaps because they are always seeing the same woman. Tell me about it anyway, how it began at the Rialto that summer.' Piero looks into his memory and an image appears like a photographic negative coming up in solution.

'You were wearing a sleeveless white dress with a chequered hem,' he reproduces, 'and holding a white parasol. At first I thought you were a tourist. A photographer was taking pictures of you. Then I realised you must be a model. The photo session went on for hours.'

She frowns. 'You stood around watching all that time?'

'I was sitting at a pavement café. I had time to kill before a couple of appointments. I let them both slip. The sun went down. The photographer went on taking pictures in the dark. I would have sat there watching all night. You stopped, however, and I invited you to join me for a drink. Of course I thought you were beautiful, but it wasn't beauty that mattered. It was the aura – can I put it like that? – your charisma. When I passed you in the gallery upstairs a while ago I recognised it again at once, unmistakable, despite the outfit and the mask. But even on that occasion when I first saw you three years ago I already recognised it, you see. How was that possible?'

She thinks for a moment and says: 'Maybe the woman was the copy of a memory of someone else. But anyway. What happened?'

'What happened? You mean you don't remember?' Piero squints as if he's looking back at her through that Rialto sun. 'You only had half an hour. Nothing happened. I walked you back to your hotel. You had a plane to catch the same evening.'

They have done a circuit and now arrive back at the main ballroom, which is set in the square of St Mark's. She walks out onto the dance-floor, turns and raises her arms. Piero is no longer missing anything, doesn't even think of it as he glides through a maze of dance.

The lady says: 'I've never been to Venice in my life.'

9

The music stops. She brushes something from his shoulder – just brushes, in fact, there's nothing there.

Piero shakes his head. He's taking it in. He begins to protest.

'Don't talk about the past,' she interrupts, 'bite my lip, go on. Bite it till blood flows.'

Piero is nonplussed. The music starts. He doesn't move. He's not sure he knows the woman he's got his arm around.

10

Costume judges award the prize to three couples dressed as commedia dell'arte figurines. Corine and Anselmo, Lalage and Mezzetino, Leda and the Capitano are called on stage to receive their Weekend-in-Venice vouchers from Narrhalla President Brenthrop personally. Zeo in swan-like drag as Leda gets the biggest round of applause, rather to the irritation of the two unambiguous women, Gisela and Mimi.

The fourth couple in the Bustelli quartet have failed to show up.

Jonas, in the role of the tedious Anselmo, wins a prize as Gisela's partner, but for most of the evening he is left to watch her dance with Brum. Brum capers around and plays the fool, dressed as a harlequin in a two-sided costume, lemonade vendor in front and laundress at the back.

Jonas sits at the table in blue velvet coat, cocked hat and britches, smokes, drinks, drumming his fingers against his glass as he watches around him the swirl of a somewhere else in which he can't believe. Powder on his face covers the pallor of his skin, almost physically bleached by his jealousy of Brum. Stronger than any of the reasons that might originally have caused it, jealousy has begun to paralyse him. Jonas no longer has choices, can neither stay nor go nor set his will to anything. He feels his own envy as a lethal force, some mysterious kind of radiation. People appearing in his field of vision are exposed as if on an X-ray screen, excoriated, skeletal, not recognisable human beings. Sympathy seems to have dried up in him. He feels desiccated. Jonas is living inside a stranger with no way out, suffocating inside someone else he can't stand. Pursing his lips, he softly whistles, catches Mimi's eye at the tail-end of the joke her husband's telling and gets ready to laugh a fraction before Theo delivers the punch-line.

11

Colombine in search of Scaramuz. Prizeless fourth couple that hasn't found itself. Dotty wanders in search of Hoo. 'Look out for me,' Harald had said, 'in a straw hat and striped shirt, you can't miss me, I'll come as a gondolier.' Dark eyes track Colombine's white ankles as she approaches across the piazza. A hundred gondolieri are waiting for inspection at the Lido Bar.

12

Spontaneous generation, no one knows just how it begins, the dragon dance is spawned somewhere on the ballroom floor. Hands reach for the person in front and stick fast, forming a chain. The Capitano sticks fast to Leda, Leda to Mezzetino, Mezzetino to Lalage, someone in there is attached to the Narrhalla President's rump, Brenthrop joyously himself, elephantine, plunging among fellow marine sponges, his hands at large on the broad-hipped wife of the Master of Revels, who in turn is hanging on to the panniers of the girl in eighteenth-century costume in front, and Lucas Sliep between the twins is aware of Francesca's touch at his waist as his own fingers on Giovanna's shoulders drum a tatoo *ka dud duh dá*—

13

On the ballroom floor they all sing the chorus:

Ka   duh   duh da boo   pé   ka   duh duh   da!

14

Tail lengthens by natural accretion, wiggle, waggle, magnetic sexual attraction – *phut! phut! phut!* – people seated in all seriousness are suddenly sucked in like metal filings and stick fast to that weird bent blue magnetism, wonky bruised electric-blueish heavy metal attraction, sticking fast, fast, faster the dragon's tail drags in thrashing coils across the ballroom floor – *phut!* – bystander sucked off the wall, table overturned—

15

Seen from the far end of the foyer, where Piero Zancopé
with a big lip stung by a queen bee receives the consolation
of her tongue with mixed feelings inside his mouth (why
should the dark lady first bite and then kiss him?), the
dragon dance shows up as a jigsaw silhouette against a backdrop of sky in pale theatre paints before bursting out of the
ballroom door. The scenery collapses and is scattered under
the onslaught of a fire-breathing swarm that engulfs everything in its path, leaving a scorched paper city in ruins in its
wake. Piero looks on in horror as the danse macabre
approaches, the cloaked figure in the white mask, the horde
of people who jig and dance behind him. 'This way,' Piero
says, takes his companion by the arm and escapes through a
fire exit that leads backstage. The human tide floods past,
swills carnival welter down the stairs, bursts through the
foyer doors and washes out into the street among cars,
horns, the reflections of green and amber lights splashing on
tarmac moistened by a light night rain.

16

At half past three in the morning the cloakroom is the
bazaar of desires. Here they come, here they come! The
walls nudge and lean in to listen. The floor squints up with
a leer. Single girls in black stockings yawn at the mirror as
they check out their coats. Unattached males scavenge with
bold stares. Who's left? What's available? Is there a fuck in
the evening somewhere? The masks are coming off in the
cloakroom. How about a nightcap? A coffee? Wouldn't
mind a coffee somewhere. Suggesting directions, soliciting
reactions, casually a hand at her elbow, just getting a general feeling. The iris of all the senses dilated, all-night-long
arousal, booze, dance, her body still sheds heat, his body
too, come on, what, come and spend the night with me. I
love you. I hate you. You're fantastically sexy, you know.
Take your hands off me. Do that again, please. Fingers

squeeze and pry, lips touch. The cloakroom is the bazaar of
desires, they all show up here, here is the trade-off, the
pay-off, the come-on, the fuck-off, the volte-face, the end-
of-the-night unmasking, the dark lady takes off her dancing
shoes and Piero helps her into her coat.

17

'How about a night-cap?'
'I wouldn't mind a coffee somewhere.'
'There's my hotel.'
'Is there?'
'We could take a cab.'
'I'd prefer to walk.'
'In the rain?'
'It's only ten minutes. It's not far.'

18

Carnival duty commissionaire in a coat of silver-braided
Aegean blue comes out onto the pavement as three buses
pull up and disgorge their passengers simultaneously at the
hotel entrance. More noise and congestion at what – frowns,
tipping his watch out of street-lamp reflections – ten past
four in the morning. He consults his night schedule. Ball of
Municipal Savings Banks. Happy Birthday, Son of Dracula.
Carnival in Venice. Homecoming wreckage litters the
entrance outside as house guests at the Magnolia Ball of
the German–American Women's Club inside are just on
their way out. Hotel residents, ball guests, they all seem to
depart or return at the same time. Hatted, draped, weighed
down by dead animals, German–American women plunge
across the foyer on shock-absorbent hips, the spin-door
scoops them in and bats them out like tennis balls from an
automat, municipal banks are batted in, one for one, a rapid
turnover at exorbitant hotel exchange rates. Dracula are
dead on their feet, Venice alive and singing , capering as they
sniff a scent of home in the shiny rain-wet street.

'Donata! Dona-a-ah-ta!'

She hears her name as she walks away, crossing the tram-lines and the traffic island, echoes of her name accompany her, mocking, all the way down Pacelli Street.

19

Piero admires her figure as she leans out of the window. She's been leaning out of that window more or less since they came into his room. Window seems to hold special attractions. Vaguely Piero is beginning to resent it. He wonders if she's one of those people who can feel gravity pulling them down. Wonders if she's contemplating a jump. 'What is it,' he asks, 'is there anything the matter?' 'Not exactly the *matter*,' she says, 'just rather odd.' She turns back into the room. 'I can hear someone down there singing my sister's name,' she says. There is spray on her face. Her cheeks are flushed. She looks as if she's just been for a walk in the country.

20

Polaroids lie strewn on the bedroom floor. Formal portraits of girls in historic costumes, background of historic curtains. Other pictures show Giovanna pulling funny faces; Francesca dialling room service; both girls laughing, champagne glasses toasting the camera; wrapping towels round their heads; two odalisques, reclining on the bed in a sultry pose. Wide-hipped white dresses on strut frames are hanging from the cupboard like stranded kites. Slips, shoes and stockings lie where they were dropped. A picture of each girl naked is propped against the leg of a chair. Hollow voices, tiled surfaces of laughter and splash accompany the image of Lucas Sliep behind the tripod, releasing the self-timer before plunging into a group portrait in the bath.

21

Cesare d'Arbes wipes make-up off his face, drops crumpled tissues on the dressing-table. In the mirror he can see the boy's reflection on the bed. The boy smokes and watches a video. Cesare feels greyness in his face. He draws a finger under one eye and pulls the skin tight. He can still see dirt in the pores. He rubs in more cream.

22

Warm snuck at half past five, warm-walled murmur, thock of gold-warm glasses on counter, gold-warm dreams drawn dram by golden dram from barrel and drum, light-flecked foam on gold brew, good fellows all of them, excellent in fact, excellent Piontek, Nellie sagacious and round, cream-white bosom light-splashed, that student Hemsing with miraculous connections in Buenos Aires, retirement plans already made, plane tickets virtually in their pockets, only snag is the punctuation, Johnny wants to pay for this round but all he can find in his wallet are small brown commas, there's been a drain on gold, Sartorius, the swine, has snitched the lot, pulled out all the stops, shit, where does that leave Ploog's column now, a thousand words on Carnival in Venice by ten o'clock this morning and no more change than a handful of commas, Johnny pockets wallet, misses, holding it he stands, time Johnny go home, leans across Nellie and traces the veins on her cream-white ledger with a felt-tip pen, she's got Johnny's name down there all right, a thousand words of him in black and white, his byline please or initials at least, he gropes through air thick with the brew of beer and tobacco smells, 6 a.m. and the place still chock, warm aisles walled with buzz, basics, so long as the verbs and nouns are in place, good place, Donisl, much improved by glasnost roof shedding light on its forty-thieves past, food, drink and the companionship of friends or at least their illusion, Donisl supplied basics in empty nights, Mrs Ploog admittedly beyond salvage but otherwise things could be worse and in the spring they definitely would be, redundancies expected on the paper, redundancies on view right here, near the exit, come to that, the standing only section on the way out of Donisl, the small change, thinning hair, shiny trousers and small beers and those other minor reductions, careful, Johnny, a marginal balance, Sartorius said, cases of lateness much increased in the last six months, slipshod work, stinking breath, Johnny feels Donisl and gold-warm hive abruptly recede and he sobers up fast as the door stands open in one cold gasp—

23

She turns over and floats on her back. 'What are *calza*?' she asks.

'Garters.'

'Garters?'

'No, as you were. I mean tights. What they called hose. Hose in different colours. You could tell families apart and the parts of town where they lived by the colour of their hose.'

'So you are a member of the Company of Hose and Antiques.'

She laughs helplessly and goes under. In the water she feels weightlessness, the lightness of laughter throughout her body, and comes up with a splutter.

Piero swims alongside. He grins.

'I guess it does sound ridiculous.'

Still relishing lightness, she paddles herself round in circles.

'Are you fairly antique then?'

'Fairly antique. Fifty.'

'Not you. Your hose, I mean. The Zancopé family.

'The records go back five hundred years or so. Zancopés belonged to the *calza* then. We are listed in the eighteenth century, when it came to the split between the *ridotto* and the *casini*.'

'The what?'

'The issue was whether to hold parties in the ballrooms or the taverns.'

'Interesting. And now?'

'Now we do what we like.'

'Do you? Wasn't the carnival revived in Venice just to attract the tourists there in winter? Putting on a show for tourists – don't you feel demeaned?'

'Not just for the tourists. Also for ourselves. We may be in decline but we're still vain. We still enjoy celebrating ourselves.'

Piero swims round her as she floats on her back. Her breasts swim on the surface. Naturally he's reminded of water lilies.

'But you're always hiding behind questions.'

'Am I?'

He chuckles. Swimming round her in circles, Piero watches the illuminated city skyline come up again beyond the pool terrace.

'You're keeping yourself mysterious. You come up to my hotel room so that I can have the pleasure of phoning down to room service for a cup of coffee, which of course I'm delighted to do. You suggest a dip in the pool upstairs, take off your clothes and allow me to admire your body, but you won't tell me your name. You arrange intimate situations in which you continue to be formal. It's as if your interest in temptations is to see how well you can resist them.'

'Oh? Did you have anything particular in mind?'

She rights herself and treads water.

'Sex, for example?'

'Sex is always there.'

'Men like to think it is.'

'Women like to deny it is. That's part of the game. We like ambiguities. We need disagreements. Did you ever watch fish making love?'

'Tell me about it. How do they?'

'The male is dressed to kill.'

'What does she wear?'

'Because to kill is his intention, only he changes his mind and they copulate instead. It's a close-run thing. Split second timing.'

Piero swims out, drawing a wider circle.

'Sex is there but it can wait. I realise I am a minor character. I help along a plot involving another man. Isn't that so? The only temptation at issue is your loyalty to him, and loyalty may be just one of many other words for your stubbornness. You are competitive, I guess. You see things in terms of win or lose, and you hate to lose. Maybe you would hate losing more than you would losing him.'

He climbs up the steps and goes into the changing-room, leaving her standing in the pool. She is speechless with astonishment.

Behind her she hears early morning sounds, voices and clatter, as staff arrive in the adjoining breakfast-room to begin the day's preparations. She wades towards the steps. Piero has disappeared.

How dare he sneak off like that. She is speechless with anger. How dare he tell her who she is!

She is aware of a lull in the breakfast-room. The waiters fall silent. She can feel their eyes on her back. She doesn't care. Furious, she walks up the steps.

She feels water, dregs of the night, rush off her body as she comes out. Dripping with water, cold and naked, she stands on the pool-side in the broken morning light.

24

Johnny Ploog sprawls over a white sheet, now at his desk, now at his bed, pairing off nouns and adjectives for the opening polonaise in his room in Lederer Street. The nouns are recalcitrant, bald and disgruntled, bearing a tiresome resemblance to his Editor. Who wants to dance with Sartorius? Johnny goes over to the fridge in search of a verb, a lubricant, why not a beer. Verb is operational base. Foam rises promisingly in the glass, white suds twinkle and dance. Now then: the leading lady. Adjective from Murano, whatsit, narrow-waisted on a frail stem, with pale connections in antique glass. He considers this. Weighing her fragility against heavily nounish partner,with his broad male smells, sweat stains and drinking habits, he considers narrow-waisted again from the point of view of incompatibility, the brittleness of children and the shattering effects of divorce. He adds a few loops to narrow-waisted, wreaths of molten glass uncoiling as drops of condensation form on the outside of the bottle. Figuratively speaking, he needs to body fragility out. Blow her up. Top her up with beer. The word is tankardy.

TANKARDY

With a moist finger Ploog writes this in the dust lines on the table top. Here is the first word of his article. He looks at it for a while from a variety of angles. From under the table it looks terrific. What next? There's already an impressive degree of self-sufficiency about tankardy. Tankardy can go it alone, a portmanteau word, a figure of speech, standing in for two thousand invited guests who now needn't bother to come.

Cheers! The monk on the bottle label raises his mug and says cheers. Haven't I seen your byline somewhere before? I wouldn't rule it out, says the celebrated columnist

J. TANKARDY PLOOG

signs himself off and falls asleep with a pillow in his arms.

Wakers

The snow dreams had gone and instead of white hills Stefanie saw herself walking beside a stream. Through the clear water she could see pebbles on the bed of the stream. Bending down to pick them out, her hand broke the surface of the icy water and she woke up after only an hour's sleep. She went yawning through the apartment. Conny and her last night's man were up and gone. Through the door she glimpsed a bedroom still warmly tousled, as if they'd just left in a hurry.

In the living-room, on a trapeze of sunlight by the balcony door, a ginger fluff of tomcat floated. She prodded him with her foot, and the cat rolled over with sparring paws. 'Silly old nit,' she said, 'did you nearly drown in the loo?' *Keep Closed Because of Cat* read the sign now taped to the toilet seat. Stefanie went into the kitchen and ate an apple.

From the kitchen window she looked down into a grey well of courtyard surrounded by apartment blocks, and out across the roofs of Schwabing in the morning haze. This was one of the best hours of the day, washed up out of her dreams and still disentangling herself, with sleep-heavy eyes still looking over the things they'd left behind. Sea-horses emerged from the foam and plunged in white harness through a storm, ploughing the ocean in mile-long furrows that had turned into Ludwig Street, full of carriages and strewn with dung. How'll they get rid of all that horse shit, she wondered, squatting and making pies with her hands, climbed over the orchard wall and found herself on the bank of the clearwater stream.

'The stream is back again,' she said, coming out of the bathroom, 'stream is an old friend.' Never again would she need to be dependent on anyone but herself. She went to her room to get dressed.

Never again, she said to herself, stepping into the lift, and as she came out of the house: *Damn that man!*

'You see things in terms of win or lose, and you hate to lose. Maybe you would hate losing more than you would losing him.'

Piero's words fell like a shadow across her mind.

What the hell – but why had she lied?

She turned the corner and went on quickly into the bright morning of Leopold Street.

Rollers

'How was Paris? I hate Paris,' the American says, 'broke my fucking back in Paris. Did I ever tell—'

'Yes,' says Zelda, 'you already told us three times.'

'Oh.'

For a moment he looks crestfallen, only for a moment, turns the corner and catching sight of the Assistant Picture Editor walking down the corridor yells at her triumphantly.

'Hey, sweetarse!'

Sweetarse may have a vague idea who's meant, but she's certainly not doing *him* any favours. She says primly over her shoulder: 'I beg your pardon, Mr Ziegler?'

Ziegler drops to his knees. Right there in the middle of the corridor, drops to his knees and implores the Assistant Picture Editor to get off her perch, be nice to him just for once and call him by his first name. Hal. *Please.* Not Mr Ziegler, just Hal. What has he done to offend her? Isn't he nice?

Heads slide out of doors. People are gathering in the corridor. Ridiculous spectacle, Editor on knees with outstretched arms, and no one is more aware of that than Asst

Pic. Ed. The heat is on. She transfers the folder from her right hand to her left, nudges her glasses up on her nose, and blushes.

'Good morning, Roswitha,' says the Editor formally.

'Good morning, Hal,' says the Assistant Picture Editor.

Chuckling, he gets to his feet. 'You know, we must get together some time,' he says, 'you and I,' slipping an arm round her waist as they walk on down the corridor, 'unless I'm mistaken there are pictures of the haughty culture show in Paris to discuss for the next issue, Roswitha.' 'Yes,' she says in confusion, brushing her hair out of her eyes. With a parting squeeze Hal turns away and is already walking into his office.

Zelda closes the door and Ziegler now turns to Stefanie.

'What the fuck's wrong with this country?'

'You are, Hal.'

'Shut up, Zelda. I wasn't talking to you. That Roswitha girl. I mean, she's been here from the start. For three fucking months. I can't work with people like that.'

'And people like that can't work with you,' says Stefanie, 'they don't know how to handle you and they probably find your charm resistible.'

'They do?'

Ziegler spreads his hands, wide-eyed, and Zelda and Stefanie have to laugh. He thrusts his hands in his pockets, saunters along the window, looking out into Leopold Street. The morning parade, back view: the comeback of the aristocratic classic, brushed silk and Shetland, baby corduroy and velvet. Ladies, how do I look? So far in a different suit every morning Stefanie has seen him, small-man dapper, among other things attractive on account of his small feet, undeniably with a sort of cosmetic-tan handsomeness. Hal turns back, displaying front-view a limp, rather dowdy Armani tie, and this time he says in earnest:

'I hate this town.'

'You should try a few other places,' says Zelda as she

lights a cigarette, 'maybe you'll hate them even more.'

'I hate the folksiness,' Ziegler goes on, 'I hate that green Loden stuff and those hats with goat's beard or whatever it is stuck into them. I hate the food and the dogs and the language and the early closing times of the stores, and I *really* hate all those depressing churches. But New York needs me here.'

New York is Zieglerspeak for the Publisher, the only two syllables in any language received with something like approval in Ziegler's mouth.

'I am their man here. This is my post. I *am* the fucking magazine here for Christ's sake.'

This may be going a bit over the top. Even Ziegler sees that. He backs off with a grin.

'Let's not start getting bitchy about this. I'll say that much for Munich. It's not half as bad as Paris. How was Paris, by the way?'

'Interesting you should bring that up,' Zelda says sarcastically, 'Steffi and I just got back from the fashion shows there. You may have forgotten. We thought we'd have a chat with you about it. You know, when you have time. Less important things on your mind, and that.'

Ziegler eases himself down onto the sofa. He winces.

'Spare me Zelda, spare me . . . What've I done to deserve—'

'Lots,' says Zelda.

'Oh my God!'

His voice breaks. He sounds in real pain. Stefanie gets up.

'Are you all—'

'He's fine,' Zelda cuts in, 'just give him that.'

She hands Stefanie a folder. Stefanie takes it and hovers by the sofa on which Ziegler is lying with closed eyes.

The phone rings. Zelda takes it.

'Mr Ziegler is in a conference . . . No . . . What? You're who? OK, I'll put you through to the Design Director. Yes. One moment.'

Ziegler has used the interruption to make an unobserved recovery. He is holding up the folder, crowing.

'Look at the hat. Look at that fucking hat. Christian Lacroix? My God, he's slipped. Rural images, my arse. Little Red Riding Hood with her basket. Check the grin under the hat. Look at that hungry-idiot grin. Damn big teeth for RRH, I'd say. Who's that facing?'

'Hanae Mori,' says Stefanie.

'Oh no. Tulips. Walking tulips.'

'They're supposed to be,' says Zelda, 'this year flower-printed cloths are—'

'Give me a break. Where are hemlines?'

'Above the knee, was the last thing I heard.'

'You're kidding. How much?'

'A hand's breadth.'

'A *hand's breadth*. Wow.' Ziegler cackles. 'Whose hand is that? Hanae Mori's or mine?'

'Hal, you never cease to surprise me. When I think I've heard it all you still manage to surprise me with your unbelievable crudeness.'

'Thank you, Zelda. I know how to appreciate that, coming from an old cynic like you. Hey. Now this one is *nice*.'

'Madame Torrente,' says Zelda. 'A strapless ensemble.'

'I like what's underneath. Strapless torrent. Strapless . . .'

Ziegler strokes his waistcoat and reads aloud: '*The main surprise at the first shows Monday was the open-heartedness of cleavages. Rounded shoulders and slim waists, flounces, quilts, and bold accessories such as waggon-wheel hats, lace trimmings and strings of pearls to enhance subdued qualities of seductive feminine grace, emerged as the outstanding spring and summer trend* . . . Who translates this stuff?'

'That's the original PR soundtrack. Bodo will work it over.'

'I bet he will. Those open-hearted cleavages must be taken in hand. Can I have my pill?'

'Just a minute. I'll get you a glass of water.'

Zelda goes out. The phone by the sofa rings. Ziegler ignores it. He lies with crossed legs, drumming his fingers on his chest and watching Stefanie in silence. Stefanie watches back.

'When Zelda left the room,' Ziegler says after a while, 'there was a long silence between them. She saw him staring at her from the sofa. And she didn't like what she saw.'

'Not much,' admits Stefanie. 'Although you're not as bad as you want to seem.'

'True.'

Ziegler strokes his chin, approving his morning shave.

'I'm even worse. I deteriorate on acquaintance. I'm a highly sophisticated thug. I'm an animal in Armani. They let me out of the jungle on parole. I'm flash, trash, sex-mad and money-mad, and even then I tend to understate the case. I'm pretty much most things Europeans like to despise.'

'Are you proud of it?'

'Who cares? I've been running trash magazines for twenty years and I know it all, and it's no different over here, only it's hidden better, whose vanity is biggest and who wants power most, who's fucking whom and who's paying, who can be broken and at what price.'

Stefanie gets up.

'Is that all?'

'That's all.'

'I feel sorry for you, Hal. You don't care about anything.'

Ziegler laughs.

'Oh, come on. I care about the bottom line. Can I take you out to lunch?'

Breakers

Ziegler had broken his back on an escalator in a hotel lobby in Paris. He was on his way up, so busy watching a woman passing him on her way down that he failed to get off and fell down the escalator. He could now stand OK and lying was fine, but since the accident he hadn't sat much. During lunch with Stefanie he roamed between courses, haranguing the Italian waiters, so Ziegler's back story, which in fact she'd not heard, came in instalments between the melon with prosciutto and the capuccino with ice cream.

Ziegler liked the story. It was the story of his life. The hero found women so irresistible that he risked life and limb in pursuit of them and was finally carried off on a stretcher. Steffi, too, found it quite an entertaining story. The point she stopped liking it was when the hero got bored of one woman and moved on to the next. This was the untold side at either end of Ziegler's story. Women's stories were mainly about this untold side at either end. Men's stories were mainly about the bits in between, seams glossed over or censored out, from Bocaccio and Don Giovanni to

Truffaut's *L'Homme Qui Aimait les Femmes,* which she saw on TV that night. All the women whom *l'homme* had loved showed up for his funeral, and if Ziegler died tomorrow all the girls in the office, including Zelda and especially Roswitha, would show up for Ziegler's too. They knew where they stood with Ziegler. For a time they'd have fun with no commitments. Boredom and betrayal would be the downside of the deal. Ziegler's candour about that was part of his technique. He issued challenges. For his part he made things explicit, touching with his hands and daubing with his words, suggesting a compliance in intimacy where there was none. In this way he made accomplices of women. They would be left with the options of assent tinged with submission or the hollow conclusion of a refusal. They could stop the ball rolling, and with Ziegler they had to. Wanting to go to bed with a woman probably mattered more to a man than not wanting mattered to the woman. She could stop the ball rolling, but why? Both alternatives appealed to Stefanie less and less. It would be nice for a change to be told a story in which all the men turned up for the funeral of a woman who was neither a man-eater nor a whore.

Steffi had left Max and moved into a room in Conny's apartment in Schwabing. She and Max had lived fast, and after four months they seemed to have burned out. The entirely sensual relationship with Max had captivated her, exhilarated her, begun to pall, and finally liberated her: she became free of the need to feel dependent on Brum. 'Don't let me keep you,' said Max, cynically offering her money, but she got a job with Ziegler instead. Never again would she need to feel dependent on anyone but herself.

At the office she wore blazers and ties, and something of a carnival spirit brushed off on the Borsalinos and slouch gangster hats favoured by Conny when the two of them set out at night. They raided Schumann's a few times to pick up strangers at the bar, but by the third night there were no strangers left at Schumann's and they found it easier just to move on. Conny knew her way around the disco scene. She took Stefanie to places like Why Not and Open Gate and Bab-ba-lu and Park Café, most of which Stefanie had never even heard of before. But night for night it was always the same crowd on this circuit as well. She felt them tying her down. She wanted a different audience every time to make her feel different herself. She gravitated to the mass carnival balls she had always despised. She danced with Greek waiters at the Pontos Ball in the Schwabinger Bräu, with producers who offered her jobs at the Film Ball in the Mathäser cellar, deserting them half-way through in favour of a transvestite party at Jet Dancing. At the Carnival in Venice she went as a page, at the Hungarian Ball as a gypsy, wore a green wig and a moustache at the party held by Radio Xanadu, a white satin dress to the Ball Paré and *dessous* in the Löwenbräu cellar, and whatever she wore it was always a disguise. She spent her nights becoming someone else.

A dress and two tickets to a costume ball were sent anonymously to the address in Wilhelm Street. The costume was one of those quaint old-fashioned dresses with balloon sleeves and a bustle, and to her surprise it fitted her perfectly. Stefanie gave the tickets away and hung the dress in a cupboard.

The weekend after the Carnival in Venice there was a party at Ziegler's house. Ziegler was different at home, less static crackling around him in the shade of his serene wife. Steffi felt herself drifting along airy orbits in slow-motion through the rooms. Guests arrived in bursts. As they came through the door they seemed to hit something and start slowing down too. There was no one there she knew. She drank more cocktails than she could remember, greedily sucking cigarettes for a scorching sensation when they flared. Wearing the strapless ensemble she had borrowed from Conny, she sat on the stairs and talked to Ziegler.

She wanted to know what had been so special about the woman in the hotel lobby. 'Nothing special,' said Ziegler. 'Just the anxiety of passing up the opportunity of spending time with a beautiful woman.' 'What anxiety?' she wondered. Ziegler said there were moments in his life that were like prisms, in which everything seemed to be collected that otherwise escaped him. He grinned and told her she looked pretty collected herself in that torrential dress, and he wondered who for. 'Just for myself,' she said, 'but you're allowed to look.' 'You're very competitive,' Ziegler said, 'you always want to win. Nobody does anything just for themselves.' He bent over and blew on her shoulders. Steffi was reminded of what Piero had said. She left the party early and went home.

She spent the weekend at home. For two days she felt her life interrupted.

With reluctance she conceded her life lacked a purpose. She had complete freedom and nothing to do. This had been one of the troubles with Brum. She had been jealous of Brum's work. She resented something that could preoccupy him to the exclusion of herself. Years had been spent hanging around in Brum's life. But a part, at least, of what she had been inclined to see as Brum's responsibility for the lack of purpose in her life had of course been hers.

Thinking about herself as perhaps different from the self she had hitherto taken for granted began with the lie she told Piero. She lied about having met him in Venice because she felt it as an unwanted intrusion from the past. She didn't want the claim of intimacy those memories had clearly implied for Piero. She didn't want any claims on her at all. A sea voyage of several thousand miles had left Brum on the other side of the world. She had taken photographs of dolphins and shoals of flying fish in silver bursts as the ship ploughed mile-long furrows through the ocean, and now those pictures were surfacing in her dreams, the sea-lanes turned back into Ludwig Street and ran on as a stream she had reached into for pebbles. She made drawings of the pebbles to keep them in place. The pebbles seemed to be weighing down something at the core of herself. She drew pebbles arranged on the seat of a chair or lying in a half-open drawer. She tried to express a sense of their forlornness, isolated in their surroundings. She tried to listen through the half-open drawer to what they might be saying.

At night she stood aside and watched herself turn into another person. At night the city sucked her in like a drain. She picked up strangers in bars and told them lies. She invented other lives for herself. She had suffered a recent loss. Someone close to her had died. Scrutinising faces for signs of sympathy, and finding embarrassment or awkwardness, she felt a gleam of lust inside herself. It was not in her nature to be doing such things. It exhilarated her she was able to do them nonetheless.

She came home late to find a man waiting for her at the entrance to the house. He was a thin, dark-haired man whose face under the street-lamp looked extraordinarily pale. At first she took him for a vagrant. He stood there in old clothes that didn't seem as if they belonged to him. Without any preliminaries the man told her that a week ago he'd sent her a costume and two tickets for a ball. He was a friend of Brum's. He wanted to speak to her. Visualising him waiting there for hours to say these words, shrunk into his coat on a cold night, Stefanie felt a spark of pity. They went into a bar down the road.

He was a church painter, the man said, making notes on a pad on his knee, he painted frescoes, angels and things, the trouble was that he couldn't dance. He sat in the bar, taking silent dictation, in the same unbelonging way he had stood in the street. Stefanie blew on her coffee and asked him where dancing came into it. The man said he thought the problem was that he couldn't dance because he was incapable of feelings of joy. He stopped writing for a moment and looked up. That was a terrible emptiness, he said. So he had just sent her the dress with the two tickets after all. Had she gone to the ball? She thanked him for the dress. The tickets she'd given away. But why had he sent her a dress? I wanted to see you wear it, the man said. That particular dress? That particular dress. It was the one he'd painted her wearing on Brum's mural in Brewers Hall. It was the one in which he'd imagined her ever since. Hurriedly the man got up, handed her a piece of paper and said:

'You know, if I could see you wear that dress – that's the upshot, I mean.'

Stefanie looked at the piece of paper on which he'd written Jonas Heidenreich and the name of a hotel in Hohenzollern Street.

She passed the hotel on her way to work every morning. In the March issue they were doing stories on Joop and Escada and summer beachwear shot in Belize. Images lived to perfection on magazine pages that didn't exist anywhere else. The publisher poured money in to make them live. Belize was shot three times over to keep improving on the reality, until Ziegler was able to see with approval his own reflection in the glossy pictures that lay shimmering on his desk. Stefanie watched staff and buildings full of machines churn feverishly in support of that shimmer. Like them she made a living from the triviality of illusions whose commercial reality was incontestable. She was herself a member of the suntanned audience that listened to bell'arte concerts in Blutenburg, prepared an image of herself for a drink at Schumann's or Harry's Bar and wore designer label clothes to dine with Max and Candice at Byblos while they watched a belly-dancer perform – a certain lifestyle expected certain things. Sometimes she found it difficult to align this lifestyle with the turmoil that surfaced despite herself, the aimless nocturnal wanderings, drawings of pebbles, her involvement with a church painter in trouble with his angels because he was unable to feel joy. She had difficulty recognising what seemed to be a declaration of love so narrowly bound by an image of herself in a particular dress. Despite herself she felt sympathy with the unbelonging church painter who waited for her in the hotel in Hohenzollern Street. When she sat at her desk opposite Zelda, drinking coffee and checking proofs of the March issue with the feature on Belize, she continued to brood over the narrow bounds that seemed inescapable in any image. Imagining those tiny, fortuitous windows desires seemed to need to look out at the world, she thought of the cleaner's tag hanging at the back of Brum's trousers and its inexplicable fascination. Later she'd noticed the things about Brum that reminded her of her father. She wondered what ghostly predecessors the church painter Jonas was meeting in her when she walked up and down his room in the uncomfortable dress with the balloon sleeves, and why it was in her power to bring to life the feelings in him he had told her were dead.

She told him she was going away on business for a few days. That was all right, said Jonas. The cold weather would soon be over; he had to get back to work in any case. He sat on a chair by the bed, writing pad poised as usual on his knee. She had changed back out of the costume and stood at the window, watching a glimmer of moon behind the clouds. A shoe-box stood on the window-sill. It contained miniature items of furniture Jonas had carved out of balsa wood and fitted inside nutshells: 'A present for when you move house,' he told her when he handed her the box.

'You must come and visit us,' she said. She couldn't think of anything better to say.

But a feeling stayed on that lit her up inside. An inscrutably chaste little man she'd done a favour just by wearing a dress had somehow put her back in touch with herself. The nutshell furniture belonged in the same place as the drawings of pebbles. When she came home and opened the chest of drawers she could feel how something at the core had spread.

The full moon was rising and riddled the apartment with bolts of light. Conny's software programme had fallen behind schedule. Restless and hungry, gnawing her fingernails, she got up every ten minutes to put things in her mouth. Stefanie sat cross-legged on the floor in a splash of moonlight and listened to her rattle away in unconnected bursts, her thoughts always running ahead of what she was saying as she trekked to and fro between sofa and fridge. There was a crackle and zesty pop from the kitchen whenever Conny ripped open another yoghurt. In the morning there would be a trail of things marking these greedy night excursions, spoons, cigarette ash, screwed-up tissues behind cushions. Conny paid someone to come in and clean up. She was twenty-three. She made a lot of money. She had a good time. There was a trail of litter that Conny had shed in the course of her carnival life.

She ran a sideline in DJs. After Stevie at Why Not, Charley and LX at Lipstick, she currently fancied Lupo, who did weekends at P1. Some time she would have them all in her collection. She thrived on the competition. She liked the challenge of crowds of girls dripping round the DJ and begging him to play their record. The DJ alone didn't interest her. It was the three-sided relationship between the DJ, the girl and the record that interested Conny. Sex only came into it when the record began to spin. She looked after her DJs. She didn't flirt, disdained to plead. She bribed Lupo. She bought him clothes. Lupo appreciated that. He appreciated Conny. She wasn't anything sensational to look at but she knew she was a terrific dancer. Lupo put on Conny's record, a smile at the corners of his mouth as he watched her kick into action.

A millionaire industrialist hired P1 for a private fancy-dress party. Lupo brought in a few of his special girls. Conny

came with Steffi. The theme of the party was Down and
Out. Costumes were provided on site. The guests took off
tuxedos and gowns and exchanged them for old clothes,
genuine cast-offs that had been organised from charities or
the municpal depot in Haidhausen. The stuff from the
depot was factory surplus, too good to be seen down and
out in. There was a scramble for the charity garments with
the authentic old-clothes shine.

At some point in the evening, somewhere between the
second and third bottle of champagne with the friendly
banker who thought her face was familiar, Stefanie caught
sight of herself in a mirror as she was on her way to the toilet. She saw herself in baggy trousers held up with braces, an
old leather waistcoat and a bowler hat, and the blur of figures cavorting in the background as Lupo blasted them with
Techno House and Rave. On the spot she decided she
would never again allow herself to take part in anything so
degrading, got her coat and left.

Rain pricked her face as she made her way back across the
park. Walking up Ohm Street, she had an extraordinarily
vivid memory of standing in the garden of a house there,
talking to Brum who was leaning out of an upper window
with a parrot on his shoulder. Perhaps they should try again.
Perhaps she could keep her room in Conny's apartment and
spend weekends with Brum at the Copper Lodge. With a
pang she thought of her mother at home with Gottfried.
Bapa no longer recognised anyone, not even Constanze. A
gust of wind met her as she turned the corner into
Hohenzollern Street. Passing the hotel, she wondered if
Jonas was still there and pressed the buzzer for the night
porter.

She climbed the stairs to the top floor. Jonas always left
the door unlocked so that she could let herself in whatever
time she came. She opened the door and called. No one
answered. All the lights were on. She went into the room
and looked round. His things were still there. She knocked

on the bathroom door. There was no reply. She opened the door and looked in. She couldn't understand what Jonas was doing lying on the floor. He had a white T-shirt on and no pants and the T-shirt was soaked in blood. He was lying on his side with his eyes closed. His arms were splashed with blood. He had something in his hand. His groin and thighs were covered with blood. She tried to say something, but her voice seemed to have dried up in her throat. Blood was still dripping from his genitals and splashed onto the tiles. She couldn't believe what she saw. She told herself it must be some crazy carnival stunt. She couldn't understand what Jonas had done.

Later an ambulance arrived. The night porter said the guest in 523 had already paid his bill. He was due to check out the next morning. Still dazed with shock, still unbelieving, Stefanie put his things together and followed in a taxi to the hospital in Schwabing where Jonas had been taken. She sat in the hospital corridor and read words she must have watched him writing down. She tried to find an explanation, some connection between the words, something she might have overlooked.

Coffee! Arms, sleeves! Elbows! Collar buttons! Joy!

Just columns of words, arrested by exclamation marks.

After a time a doctor came and told her Jonas had been operated on. He had attempted to emasculate himself and had lost a lot of blood. He was still in a critical condition. The doctor gave her a phone number and told her to call the next day.

Stefanie took a cab back into town. Sitting in the cab in somebody's old clothes she watched the windscreen wiper go back and forth and she began to feel cold. The cab stopped at traffic lights. A crowd of party-goers at the corner, drunk and shouting, crossed the road. Someone banged on the cab window. A masked face looked in with a grin. The light changed. She told the driver she had changed her mind and would like to go to Nymphenburg instead. She started to shiver. They drove against the early morning traffic, a stream of oncoming headlights blurred in the rain. It was six o'clock when she paid off the cab and rang the bell of her mother's apartment in Monten Street.

Candlemas

How was it one remembered past and not future?

Why could one remember Martha eating cream cakes at Kreuzkamm this afternoon, but not her having eaten them there tomorrow?

Koepenick said it was because of the second law of thermodynamics. Within a closed system, disorder, or entropy, would increase with time. Things could only be remembered in the order in which entropy increased. One had no choice but to feel the passage of time in the direction of this cumulative disorder. This was the same direction in which the universe expanded and disorder increased, until it collapsed into another state of infinite density, the big crunch, at the end of time.

But how did Koepenick know the universe was a closed system?

And what of the present, edges blurred and overlapping before and after: what of the indeterminable instant already gone when the lagging perception of it arrived?

Incredibly, when he and Martha lay in bed, they were

hurrying entropy along. Between them they must still be converting at least a thousand calories of ordered energy ingested by way of their supper at Franziskaner into disordered energy, heat lost by sweat and convection to the surrounding bedroom air. Particles of converted venison pie whizzed invisibly around them in the dark. Consider particle emission from the total surface area of Martha's body alone – still an immense figure, if less than it had been a while ago. Martha was not expanding with the universe. On the contrary. She had already contracted appreciably.

He heard her creak beside him in bed.

With the arrival of Katryn and Liselotte there had also come the loss of an expectation, so long desired she had been unable to grasp its fulfilment, unable to emerge from the shell of her desire in the moment it broke.

There was a puncture now in that self-sufficiency which had become her solitude in the last six months. Sometimes tears ran down her face when she sat on the sofa and her babies sucked at her. Forfeiting the privacy of the rest of her body, Martha's breasts had changed and turned into a semi-public institution. Martha was now on the menu and organised food and she had to remain open day and night. At last Hieronymus found himself able to look at his wife's body with a tenderness that wasn't compromised by desire.

Husband had undergone contraction, too. In the mornings, leaning over to kiss her before he left, he breathed in the scent of soap at her neck while eavesdropping on the snuffle and plop of the twins as they badgered Martha's fat moist nipples, and he would be overcome by nothing more lurid than a sensation of warm glee.

He whistled on the stairs and arrived humming in the store. Stray glimpses of Astrid in black stockings on her ladder had mysteriously been defused. Days would pass without the intrusion of Astrid's once potent rustles.

He felt as if he'd emerged from a tunnel. During her

pregnancy Martha had withdrawn from him altogether; groping for other women in his fantasies, he'd watched with unease how the appetite formed in the privacy of his thoughts was increasingly warped by an element of deceit. When at last her bubble burst and her self-isolation ended, Hieronymus was surprised to find Martha accessible again in needs that sprang up around vulnerable edges, her whims and anxieties and sudden tearfulness. Within the closed system of their apartment (according to the second law of Martha's absentmindedness) his wife's natural entropy-proneness had increased by a factor of three. A mother-and-two-child software programme took over, self-multiplying until it had obliterated that surgically methodical arrangement of things which Hieronymus had insisted on all his life. Comforters roosted on his barometers. Plastic bottles crept in and littered his father's sacred Meissen. New sounds, smells and ineradicable stains proliferated in all the rooms. He found himself neglecting his tide tables and almanacs, forgot to wind up clocks. He had no time for his old habits. Changing rhythm, he adjusted to requirements other than his own. Hieronymus looked back into the tunnel and saw in its enclosing walls the fixedness of his previous life.

Darker days became lighter. Since the winter solstice the sun climbed an hour longer above the horizon now, peeling strips of light again through morning blinds. Anticipating them from memory as he lay in the dark was like remembering tomorrow and the day after in the shape of the same sunlight stains that year by year he watched spreading from the same spot on the bedroom floor. Force of habit ingrained patterns onto a database similar to a genetic code. By old convent habits Martha still arranged her year churchwise. She didn't need to look in her calendar. 'It's Candlemas,' she said, when she woke up that morning.

Constanze arrived with jams and knittings to look after the children while they were out. He walked with Martha down Ludwig Street through the soft light of the late winter afternoon. Winter sales were closing. Martha wanted to stop and look in the windows of all the stores. 'Just for once,' she said. 'Don't be impatient. And why can't we look at things together?' He followed the tug of her arm, looking at things without his own interest but not minding, interested in hers, astonished they could give her so much pleasure.

At Kreuzkamm, predictably, she surrendered and went in. Martha lived with cream cakes in an unhappy if unavoidable symbiosis. They attracted her, they repelled her. For long periods she denied their existence altogether. Between the greed before and the guilt after she spooned an interval of perfect bliss – the same pattern that Martha had followed in almost all her pleasures ever since he had known her. At Kreuzkamm the connotations were supplied at the surrounding tables by widows in hairnets and woollen hats, spooning dead husbands between sips of coffee. Hieronymus wondered if there was any comparable loss, a lack of sweetness or self-indulgence, which Martha might also be compensating for. He watched his wife fondly, in her state of milkiness, as she shut her eyes and recycled a variety of dairy products with inward relish. 'Won't you have some,' she asked him again. Sweetness required a partner, sometimes an accomplice, and as he opened his mouth for the gobbet still poised questioningly in mid-air, Hieronymus observed two flecks of cream that had been marking time move swiftly outwards at the corners of her smile.

Koepenick had said in passing as he left the bookshop that morning that if the sun went out they would not be affected for a while because the Earth would be in the elsewhere of the event when the sun stopped shining. Hieronymus asked him on his way out where the elsewhere was, and Koepenick said over his shoulder that the elsewhere was the region of space-time outside the future or past light-cones of an event. Hieronymus wondered if the present didn't always belong in the elsewhere; he was having problems getting the present to fit into this arrangement of cones on account of light needing time to travel to the place where the present could only happen when the light arrived. In fact he was wondering how the present could be fitted in at all, but by the time this notion had filtered through Koepenick was already in the elsewhere of Schelling Street and well on his way to lunch.

Quantifiable, if infinitesimal, that space-time region for example in Kreuzkamm between the event of Martha's cream-capped smile and the perception of it in his eye. Nothing stood still. Receding light sources in the night sky had their spectra red-shifted, while approaching objects appeared blue-shifted. Measurable the sound-waves as Martha shifted (in which direction in her night sky?), travelling in fractions of space-time and thus arriving fractionally later on his side of a king-size bed. Nothing stood still, and according to the uncertainty principle one could say for sure either where something was at any one moment or how fast it was, but not both, for mutually exclusive reasons that Koepenick had hurled at Hieronymus and Hieronymus was not able to grasp. He was left with an indigestible view of his lunch-hour, during which he watched himself and Astrid eating their sandwiches in fractionally exclusive states of present time.

In the spiral arms of the galaxy the stars rotated round its centre once every few hundred million years. The stars moved, the sun and the moon and the planets. Among all this motion it seemed extraordinary that earthlings had only recently cottoned on to the truth that they inhabited a growing universe.

'There's a mass at St Michael's,' Martha said for the third time, 'I'll go alone if you don't want to come.'

Walking with her down Kaufinger Street, Hieronymus found himself arriving at the uncomfortable notion that

any two persons' present times could never be perfectly
flush. Martha would go into St Michael's with her own
measure of time inside her bell-jar, Hieronymus in his.
Hundreds, thousands of candles had been lit inside the
church. They were there to be blessed, Martha whispered;
the candles, she added, and bought two herself, which she
balanced on paper coasters on the ledge of the pew in front
of them. It made her indescribably happy, Martha said, to
have him sitting there beside her, and why had it taken him
such a long time to do a simple thing when he knew how
much it meant to her. Hieronymus was taken aback.
Martha's refrain throughout the years had always been how
she would prefer to be left to herself to pursue her devotions if Hieronymus dismissed them as mummeries. But in
sentimental moments – he looked at her broad flushed face
in the cone of candlelight – perhaps susceptibility in church
to unchurchy thoughts? 'I think I'd like to join you in there,'
he said, 'inside your light-cone,' and he slipped his hand
inside her coat. 'Ssh,' she nudged, 'they're coming,' but
she let his hand stay where it was. Two lines of children carrying candles came abreast of their pew, two lines of
light-cones flickered past. 'The candles are brought for a
blessing,' Martha whispered again, explaining everything
twice, 'the priest is consecrating light, which is the light of
the world, so it's really Our Saviour the priest is blessing.'
For Hieronymus, the ritual he watched was nothing other
than sun worship. The priest intoned inaudible words,
raised his arms to bless a dark place full of candles. The
deity had taken himself off into the elsewhere in a huff.
His congregation invoked him to come back inside the cone
of light as Hieronymus slid his hands between his wife's
legs. Nothing stood still. He remembered that receding
light sources had their spectra red-shifted in the night sky,
but on their way home on a damp Candlemas night he
could feel his wife turning back to him for the first time in
many months, and the waves were blue-shifted that reached

him on the far side of the king-size bed when Hieronymus turned out the bedside lamp. The elsewhere evaporated. In the darkness her beam focused as a glare in which he felt her coming in his arms, heat spreading, smithereens of exploded dark still hurtling out behind his eyelids as Hieronymus entered Martha's cone of light.

Grand Cellar on St Blasius Day

Three sporting gentlemen, representing the fencing association Allotria in the pro-patria suite scheduled for that
evening, arrived with their seconds and supporters at the
Black Lodge in Ungerer Street punctually at half past five.
Groups of men wearing the caps and colours of the two
fencing associations stood chatting in the corridors. The
clubbish atmosphere of an all-male gathering spread up
from the beer lounge via passages and stairs to the huge
attic room, where the guests invited to the sporting preliminaries of the Grand Cellar on Founder's Day began to
assemble at six. Beneath the chatter and the beer-moist
horseplay, a keen edge of anticipation never blunted. The
ceremonial duels that were about to be fought with sabres
did not require a bloody outcome, but it was in the hope of
seeing blood that so many spectators had come. By half past
six satisfaction had been given. In three brief skirmishes
three combatants were cut open, emerging from the attic
room with bloodied heads to be stitched by the doctor on
the landing. Celebrations got off to a cracking start.

A hundred and fifty men took their places on benches at

wooden tables in the candlelit cellar of the lodge house. The senior welcomed the lodge members and guests and formally opened the Grand Cellar in celebration of their one hundred and eighty-eighth anniversary. He thanked the sporting gentlemen from the Allotria fencing association for accepting the drubbing they had been given upstairs in a spirit of fair play. Drubbed but sporting Allotrians rose to declare there were no hard feelings. On the contrary, they felt honoured to have been invited by such hospitable opponents to contribute to the proceedings of their Grand Cellar. Beer mugs rumbled on tables signalled the lodge members' approval of this. More chivalrous speeches followed, punctuated by quaint flourishes in Latin, and the audience rumbled its approval more thunderously each time. Caps were impaled on swords, florid oaths of loyalty pledged. The lodge song rose at last in chorus. Pigs' knuckles were served with beans. Grand Cellar grunted and hiccoughed and then settled down to the serious business of drinking. This continued for a number of hours.

Shortly before midnight the senior rose to move that Cellar should now proceed in the private matter of Hollmann *versus* Brum.

The terms of the engagement were no doubt irregular, but since they complied with the proviso *according to means* whose choice had expressly been left to Brum, it was the considered opinion of the Lodge Council that the member Hollmann was obliged as a gentleman to honour those terms. The senior proposed this offensive business should be dealt with outside, at a suitable spot in the lodge garden.

There were no dissensions.

The two contestants now sat down to second and third helpings of pigs' knuckles and sauerkraut. Prunes were served as a side dish. Egged on by his supporters, Hollmann completed a fourth bowl of beans. Brum capped it, promptly calling for a fifth. Sweat broke out on his brow. His features gave the impression of beginning to crowd his face, as if they would have been grateful for additional space.

Cellar meanwhile rose to lounge. Bitters were served upstairs with coffee. The senior conferred with the two contestants on what exactly was to be understood by the description *a bigger turd*. Should the issue be decided by length or weight? They agreed on weight. The senior sent one of the lodge probationers to ask the housekeeper for cling film and a set of scales.

The contestants took a digestive stroll in the garden, accompanied by their seconds. It was a dark, gusty night. Hollmann, in a black dinner-jacket, was recognisable at the end of the garden by his luminous shirt-front whenever he turned and walked back to the terrace where the spectators were beginning to gather. The doors of the lounge stood open. Lodge probationers in uniform passed in and out, serving the spectators drinks. A set of kitchen scales stood in readiness on a table. Stewards in white gauntlets would referee the proceedings from the parapet. The senior called the contestants and told them to be ready. They would have a time limit of half an hour in which to complete their evacuations. He handed each of them a tray. A steward struck a gong and the parties retreated to the shrubbery at the far end of the garden.

Hollmann shat first. After twelve minutes and six seconds by the senior's stop-watch his second emerged from the shrubbery and came forward with a tray. The senior weighed Hollmann's presentation in at 1165 grams. A round of applause greeted this announcement. Hollmann went into the lounge with a glass of champagne to await his rival's challenge.

But Brum was taking his time. He hunkered down in the shrubbery, brooding on the great wrongs he had suffered and the great turd that would vindicate him. Dwelling on the many shameful memories, he relived them in his imagination and sweated them out all over again, the undertaker on horseback who had purloined his wife and laid her out, his humiliation as a horned goat-fish, the ignominious dredgings he had endured. Above him he heard the branches rustle, and invoking the name of Blasius, guardian of the winds and patron saint of stricken souls, Brum opened his bowels with a groan and shat, emerging from the shrubbery with minutes to spare.

Brum's stupendous presentation tipped the two kilogram mark on the steward's scales, trouncing his opponent.

Declaring him the winner, the senior reminded him of the terms of the contract drawn up with Hollmann. Brum wrote out a cheque for the sum that Hollmann had paid for portraits of Brum's wife and Brum had stolen from Hollmann's house earlier that year. Hollmann, for his part, undertook to refrain from further legal action, and the paintings reverted thereby to Brum's lawful possession.

The Metamorphosis
of Harald Hemsing

Sitting down to breakfast with me in Bodo's Backstube on
the windy aftermath of St Blasius Day, Brum banged his
knee against the suitcase containing everything I owned.
Putting it under the table was stupid, OK. But that all my
possessions could fit inside a $20 \times 60 \times 100$-centimetre fibre-
glass suitcase and still represent the sum of me on what I
calculated to be the ten thousand one hundred and twenty-
eighth Haraldian day since my inception – this struck me as
a far more painful reflection regarding the suitcase than any
hurt it had done Brum's knee. I was a scarecrow in transit,
I gibbered, and when Brum, still on a post-excremental high
of a catharsis long overdue, replied sententiously that in a
sense we all of us were I said, no, listen, in the literal meaning of the case: since my eviction from my cousin's house in
December I'd been leading the life of an evacuee. Brum finished peeling the skins off a pair of white sausages and
reached for the mustard. Come and stay with me, he
offered. I said that wouldn't be necessary, and slipped him a
news-in-brief item. After a haggard week on Topher's living-
room sofa, where the train of thought of my diploma thesis

(now nervously into the home straight) had been derailed by
the nightly interruptions of Topher's sporting room-mates
and the pungent all-day smells that lived with them, I was
now on my way to pick up the keys to a seven-room pent-
house off Maximilian Street. I'd been appointed its caretaker
for the next month.

My caretaker duties would be minimal, a fruitcake voice
informed me when, to my astonishment, the famous actor P
called about the Accommodation in Exchange for Services
ad I'd put in the *Evening Herald*. The only condition was
that as long as my whereabouts overlapped with P's premises
I agreed to keep them secret. P is as famous for his screen
exposure as for his private life as a pathological recluse. I
agreed without hesitation, stressing the overriding demands
of my academic work. What would my caretaker duties
entail? There was Mack, said P, Mack could fend pretty
much for himself but now and then I should top up his
feed. Mack was P's parrot. There was also a poodle, by the
name of Pip. P asked me if I was an animal lover. I enthused
about the animals in my life for several minutes. Good, said
P. Pip responded extraordinarily to just a little affection. I
think we all do, I said. Pip's curriculum was attached to the
fridge, P continued, the times of her walks and the days on
which she was to be brought to the stage-door punctually at
half past four for her walk-on part in Dieter Dorn's production of *Faust*, currently in repertory at the Kammerspiele.
That would be no problem, I said. Asked for references, I
gave him the names of Professors Eckstein and Schlindwein
at the Faculty of Social Sciences. P said he would be in
touch.

So there I was, my life miraculously back on the rails –
two sets of rails, academic pistons booming by day in P's
apartment, the bacon-bringing run for *Foolscap* by night. At
intervals I took the air with Pip, walking down Maximilian
Street and returning invigoratingly nitrogen-dioxidised to
my studies. The parrot lived, or pretended to live, in a semi-

fossilised state in P's dressing-room. Beakily with one glass eye, feathers frostily disarranged in huff, the old bird watched me enter his domain with no other interest than my leaving it. The three of us made our living arrangements and settled in. A god had descended in a machine. I could feel his presence everywhere, benevolent, slippered, turning with a smile between one room and the next, always urging me to come on in and help myself. The evacuee woke up from a long winter dream to the illusion of the reality he had been lent, squirming deliciously in P's silk pyjamas between the lavender sheets of P's bed. With Dotty inside it this image of paradise would be complete, and within twenty-four hours it was.

Her scent was vanilla and her dress was white. All other adjectives were filtered out, weighing ten pence each, and tipped into the account of the evening I would write for *Foolscap*. Verbs partnered nouns, hand in hand the consorts shuffled across the floor of the ballroom in the Bayerischer Hof, always in the direction of a question mark. Vanilla and white, not so much scent and colour as a cloud of softening, offsetting the knobbliness of Dotty's nouns, elbows, chin, collar-bone, the abrasions that were in her nature. In P's black tie and borrowed eau de cologne, an apartment with seven rooms broadening out behind him, Hemsing successfully impersonated a sophistication she mistook for the confidence she thought I otherwise lacked. At any other time her surprise would have hurt me. But all those rich girls coming out in white at the Chrysanthemum Ball impersonated an innocence they'd never had; the press, the businessmen, the politicians and their wives buying raffle tickets for charities – everyone was doing an impersonation. 'I can't wait to see,' Dotty said. The buttons at the back of her dress nudged my fingertips as I told her about P's apartment. We left the ball early, following the question mark into the hotel cloakroom, where I could see it quivering in the air as Dotty put on her coat. – Which way? – Bits of the day's debris, cartons, newspapers, perhaps an issue containing Hemsing's column, cartwheeled in gusts down Theatiner Street. Oh look, she exclaimed in her exclaiming way as we came out opposite the Opera House, the aqueduct! The lake! They've taken it all down! Boards and scaffolding stacked in the square was all the Venetians had left. The doors of the Opera House opened and people came streaming down the steps. – Where've they gone? – Who? – The Venetians? – To Pasing. – *Pasing*? – They've moved into the whatsit, that old factory by the station, turned it into Trausnitz Castle. – Oh! – Lights came rushing up the street. Dotty jumped, a streetcar clanged, horns blared as cars braked. Granted, Dotty's absentmindedness, her complete inability to handle traffic: but indiscreet? Stepping into the alley on the other side of Maximilian Street, I fingered the key in my pocket. The matter of my whereabouts and P's premises to be kept secret. P's wraith receded icily up the hallway stairs. Darkness connived here. At the top of the stairs the lights went out. I groped. Handle the matter and kiss the visitor. One didn't talk about these things beforehand. Instead I detonated a time switch and the stairway sprang alight. The atmosphere of celibacy tinged with staleness in P's apartment cracked the moment Dotty came in. Suddenly I could see not just the fadedness and old-maidishness of the rooms in which he lived, but the dinginess of the solitude behind them. Clocks whispered to themselves on the walls. Carpets lay dead on the floor. Windows opened with reluctance, leaving the rooms to hoard their smells. Dotty dropped her coat where she was standing and kicked off her shoes. – Well, Hoo, what are we waiting for? Aren't you going to show me around? – Her scent was vanilla and her dress was white, a question mark standing out starkly against that threadbareness I suddenly saw. Dawdling at the entrance, explaining I must feed the parrot first, I had a vision of myself as P, ageing into a same emptiness of rooms because of a same opportunity lost. The impression of P's apartment recoiling from the prospect of twosomeness was a shrinking of instincts inside myself. – You open the door but for some reason I never feel invited in. D'you want to feed the parrot, Hoo? Shall I put my coat back on and go? – Please don't go. – You're ridiculous. You know? *Ridiculous.* – Dotty squatted on the floor, groped in her coat pocket for cigarettes and struck a match viciously. I leaned against the door and held my head in my hands. Dotty sat smoking in silence. This wasn't the scene I'd imagined. – And I don't want to be in that column, OK? I want you to stop talking *about* me. I'm not material. OK? I'm not someone else at the ball tonight. I want you to talk to *me* for Christ's sake. – At this moment, as if on cue, Pip came trotting out of the kitchen, and without thinking that under the circumstances this might not be the response Dotty was waiting for, the line came straight out of my head. – 'D'you know, Dotty, that poodle has a walk-on part in Faust.' – Only when I'd said it did I see it was a mistake. Dotty began to cry. At once, cried and cried, as if I'd turned a tap on. I must have tapped something, tears of something that had been collecting inside her for months and now came pouring out. I knelt down beside her and took her shoulders in my hands. Talking a lot and talking fast to retrieve the opportunity of my life I'd maybe already lost, I told Dotty how she'd got off her bicycle by the fountain last summer and had been getting off it ever since in the photo I had in my wallet, reminding her en route that I'd fallen out of a pear tree on her behalf, risked life and limb, risked my heart, staying at Little Monten Castle to change Bapa's nappies and make cocoa for herself and her other lover because closeness to her at any cost was the only love I'd felt able to offer. – But why didn't you *fight* for someone you loved? – I'm not much of a fighter, Dotty. The way not to lose is not to fight. – Then why didn't you tell me? – I did, but you didn't hear. – What did you tell me that I didn't hear? – In as many words.

A rose, you may remember, which you asked me to bring and I brought – *delivered by hand* – for you to wear in your hair when you went out that evening with your other lover. – But that's just it. Because you never showed you cared. You didn't seem to care. – You didn't seem to hear. *Lo cors mi dol.* Remember? – The tears were ending and Dotty sniffed. Handing her P's handkerchief, I became aware of Pip sitting there on her haunches, watching us with all the compassion for our human-ness her poodle eyes could muster. Tacitly agreeing that we had reached a stage where Dotty might appreciate a gesture of reconciliation, I put my arms around her and kissed what was available, the tip of an ear. Dotty's face rose blindly, turning to me for more.

We lay on P's bed fully clothed. We had reached an end of words. Then we were lying inside the bed and had reached an end of clothes. I lay inside her body's form, naked she lay in mine. We lay inside each other's arms and fell inside each other's sleep.

Woke to whiteness in the morning. Snow had come overnight, powdering a smatter on roofs, transposing the shadows, keying to brilliance the light reflected from the ceiling of the room.

I asked her if she was asleep and she said yes. She rolled over on her back, vanilla overlaying lavender, and murmured sleepily that she would not in principle object if I molested her a little. So while she snoozed I began to browse, from the collar-bone down, through her proper nouns, and when I felt I was deep enough into the corn I mentioned fairly off-hand that I'd never actually slept with a woman. I half expected she'd be surprised, and she was. I could feel her body sort of stiffen. She told me to come up from under the covers. I said I'd rather she came down. Above the covers there was pause for thought. I could feel her thinking about that one, too. Then her body suppled and Dotty came sliding down. Her face loomed over me, flushed, with a frown. –

Are you playing a trick on me? – Of course I'm not. – Honest? – Honest. – Hmm. Will you be truthful? Whatever I ask? – All right. But you too, OK? Dotty ditto. – OK. – She slid down further, until her face was level with mine. Suffusion of blush still on her cheeks, or just getting darker down there, I couldn't say which. Her face was brimming. I thought she looked miraculously beautiful. – So what did you do if you didn't actually, you know, with girls. – I touched them. – That was all? Did they touch you? – Sometimes. – Did you like it? – Yes. As far as it went. – What went? – I mean, it never went far enough. The whole hog. – Hog? – She eased down a little further. I could feel her body all around me, entwining, in fluid slow-motion. I had a sensation of floating. My cock lay small inside her hand. She squeezed. I could see her eyes widen. – D'you play with yourself? – On and off. Do you? – When I'm feeling lonely I sometimes award myself a consolation prize. – Ah. – I know my mother does. I expect the cardinal does. What d'you think of when you do? – Sometimes it's Nellie at the newsroom desk. Sometimes Marianne on the sofa. It's a two-camera shot. From the side I can see her breasts swinging while I service her from behind. Sometimes I see you with Alexander. That's a thr— – Don't. Please. – What do you think of? – Rain. – *Rain?* – Lying naked on the grass and being rained on. – That sounds nice. What's Alexander's cock like? – What d'you expect it to be like? – Well, for example, is it bigger than mine? – Yes. – How much? – D'you want me to go and fetch a ruler? – Dotty laughed, and with relief I joined in. We swam around a bit. We romped. I felt a nipple graze my cheek, my thigh brushed between her legs. Dotty drew back her head and looked at me. – I don't really know what you're like. – You'd only know if we lived together. Think how much time you spend around yourself and still don't know who you are. – *I* do. – Knowing what someone else is like means you can predict what they're going to do. I can't even predict that about myself. And then of course there's the question of FTTs. – The what? – Familiarity Tolerance Thresholds. How much of someone else can you put up with. – How d'you know? You've never lived with someone else. Are you making this up? – One can imagine what it's like. – Have you been living with that woman on the sofa? – No. – What are those FTT things? Give an example. – Well, for example. Answer yes or no only, OK? – K. – Would you mind me using your tooth-brush? – Oh come on! – Or finishing the leftovers – the meal is eggs and mashed potatoes – on my plate? – No. – Or feel awkward if I fart, or you fart, when we're sitting next to each other? – Maybe the first time. But this is silly. None of these things *matter*. – You'd be surprised. There's a whole list of stuff like that. Little things that don't seem to matter at first, but later you find them getting on your nerves. Sociologists at MIT have compiled a ten-volume index. – You're making this up. – Man has wife whose reading habit is never to spread the book open in case she damages its spine. Doesn't read books. Peers into them. After years of watching her peer into books like that man divorces wife. – You are, aren't you. – The case histories fill archives. – Piffle. Will you be good? Will you? – Ouch! – Gotcha. Shall I squeeze a bit more? – Dotty for Christ's sake! – Do you love me? – Yes! I do! I do I do! – Dotty let go of my balls and before I had time to think about what we'd do next she was on top of me, splashing me with kisses and breasts and already she'd put me inside her, her body arched under the covers, spanned over me like a tent, her face in the tent light brimming, brimming, until I ran over and rained on her, miraculously, upwards.

Das also war des Pudels Kern—!
Whispering with Dietz under the stage floor of the Kammerspiele, waiting for Pip to come down, I was numb-struck by Faust's exclamation. I knew exactly what he was talking about. I could see how my life's hectic search had

been impaled on one instant of forgetfulness. Blissfully
beside myself, moved out of my mind. On stage the poodle
had just turned into Mephistopheles in a thunderclap and a
puff of smoke, but for me the little black bitch now gingerly
sniffing the ladder, lured down by the cinnamon-flavoured
biscuits P instructed me to have ready, had come into my
life as a marvellous joy-bringer. 'It's Pip,' I said to Dietz. 'Of
course it is,' said Dietz. But I had something else in mind, an
illumination I felt I ought to share with the stage manager
with the sallow face and thinning hair which would set his
life in a different light. 'I'm in love,' I whispered to Dietz.
'That's always good,' said Dietz, 'but we must get the dog
off the ladder first.' Pip had stopped on the second rung and
was now looking back-up. She could hear Faust droning on
above, and she knew him a lot better than Dietz and me.
'Will she won't she,' Dietz cursed under his breath, 'little
bitch on a ladder, eh?' Standing on tiptoe (I'm not very
tall), biscuit in hand, I whispered in Pip's defence, confident
she would come down. It was Pip's appearance on the landing that night which had been my salvation, no less.
Otherwise I'd never have made the remark that so upset
Dotty. Otherwise there'd have been no tears. Otherwise I'd
never have taken my heart in my mouth and found the heal-
ing words she mysteriously needed to be wounded first in
order to be able to hear. Otherwise she'd have gone out of
the door and pretty much out of my life. Pip took the biscuit
and came trotting down. 'Congratulations,' said Dietz, shaking my hand, and in the auditorium I could hear the
applause.

Shrove Tuesday at Trausnitz Castle

Dear Diary,

The Venetians are holding Routs & Masques in the Rococo style to end the carnival season. The whole Town has been invited. Persons wishing to take part must present themselves in suitably Historical mode, and so, dear Diary, must you. I parted reluctantly from Hoo and returned to mother's yesterday to ask her help with my costumes.

Have decided on the following wardrobe. Item. For the masques a three-cornered hat worn over one side, a thick silk gown and over it all a zendaletto of black or white lace, which is monstrously becoming to the face and form. For the wedding at Trausnitz Castle a White Moire gown, ruffled with pink Lilac Satin, and a Striped Peau de Soie. If I go to the Commedia Dell'Arte Ball as Colombine I shall have to make do with the sky-blue costume with Bouquets of Flowers & thick Ruching I already wore once to the Carnival in Venice. Mother niggardly and Peevish on account of the Expense.

Bapa wasting away in bed. He's been lying like a ghost for all these months. I have gained four pounds. Inspected myself in the mirror, not altogether to my Dissatisfaction.

Regarding my Form. My breasts are rounder and my hips undoubtedly fuller. Shall have to ask mother to take out the sky-blue costume at the bosom and waist. Must have the gown lower in the Bodice. If one is blessed with a white bosom, why conceal it?

I suppose I must attribute these inches not to Guzzling Cake, as mother says, but as a Toll exacted on young females in our family when they reach the Maturity of a Woman. Imagining dear Hoo, I passed my hands over my body and confess I experienced a lively sensation of Pleasure; but then I thought of poor Bapa lying in the next room and felt Ashamed.

A propos H. Stefanie and me had a Serious Talk together. She thinks a union based on Mutual Esteem often proves more happy than a Passionate one, and a woman married to a man she Esteems is always more amiable. In this description I could recognise my sister's own portrait. Esteem might rise in one's appreciation, I said, perhaps a little archly, in proportion as passion ebbed. Had she paused to consider her opinion of Insufficient Esteem from the insatiable perspective of her own Wounded Pride? I told her to come down from her high horse and allow herself to be convinced by the evidence of Brum's good intentions she would find ensconced in the Copper Lodge.

Reflected afterwards that I had been too harsh. Fresh and easy in love, I had been carelessly severe in my judgement of her affairs. Far from being that Mature Person I supposed, I had shown all the sensibility of a bouncing girl eager to show off her new Toy.

Very downcast, I reprimanded myself in this fashion while I went in to change Bapa's linen. For sheer Frustration I must have exclaimed out loud how very trying this Business of Life was. I swear I saw Bapa smile and move his lips for the first time in weeks. So for an hour I sat there to keep him company, reading troubadour love songs in the Provençal language; poorly enough, I suppose.

Ravenous for the moon, as if the thirst in my body could only be slaked by its light, I went to the window & opened it, but no moon was out. I strained my eyes into the night, imagining there the Expectations of my Life, already buoying out of the dark, whose forms I could not yet discern, however. I was seized by a peculiar restlessness to know my future state *at once and in its Entirety*.

Rebecca and Melissa arrived after breakfast and closeted themselves in my room for a rehearsal of costumes. Melissa very becoming in a Sack dress of red brocade made low and tight in the bodice, completed by frills and fichu of lace. Rebecca in some sort of Undress, sumptuous as a Turkish slave in a costume of silver cloth that sets off her dark complexion handsomely. She said she had worn it at the Ball of the Lonely Hearts and inadvertently come Unbutton'd, with what effects one can imagine.

People continued to arrive at the house all day, and by six o'clock Bustelli's company was complete, excepting Harald, who has business in town and will follow later as Scaramuz. The four couples are borrowed from Bustelli's commedia dell'arte figurines, *viz*. Leda and the Capitano, impersonated by Rebecca and Melissa; Annette as Lalage and her handsome Hungarian as Mezzetino; Alexander in the part of the tedious Anselmo, escorting Dolly, very decorative as Corine; & myself as Colombine. Alex as Versatile in his Appearance as he is in his Affections, which he has shown himself capable of transferring seamlessly to another Subject in less than four weeks. I see now how Vain he is, and all women no more than his Mirrors.

Former warehouse or whatever it had been, we were Amaz'd to see that ill-favoured place in Pasing which resembles nothing so much as an enormous Kennel now transformed beyond recognition by the Venetians' art. A curved awning, or Dome, was spanned over the grounds outside, whose walls, hung with damask & cut velvet, rose and sank as they exhaled the night air. In an artificial garden complete with lawn, thickets & flowering shrubs, our hosts held a *fête champêtre* to welcome their guests.

A Magnificent affair. The Dome heated with burning braziers & illuminated with torches & lamps. Many-coloured fruits hung luminous in the night. A great crush of Cleopatras, Courtesans, Nymphs etc. showing quantities of white flesh and contributing a Luxuriance of scents that settled on the garden like the illusion of its own perfumed haze.

The Doge in a Cambric hat and golden robes opened the ball with the Queen of Courtesans, escorted by trumpets & other Pomp. My dear Scaramuz arrived at last, wearing high shoes to improve his height, and finely shaped calves on display in silk stockings. Lent him to Corine, whose eyes had fastened on that masculine Feature for which she has a Known weakness. I encountered a pair of insistent moustaches in reluctant embrace with Mezzetino. Attempted to make love to me in Swarthy Fashion while standing on his feet. The dancing went on until daybreak.

The entertainments continued throughout the following day, which was St Valentine's. All went separately and in Masks. Self in hat and zendaletto, in which I own I looked so becoming that I wished I might have been among the Admirers who slipped their notes into the bosom of my gown. Throngs crowded the entrance to the building, today open to the Publick for the celebrations commemorating the wedding at Trausnitz Castle.

Here was one Astonished by the illusions painted on cloths that covered the walls. They showed scenes from the Festival of the Betrothal of the Adriatic, with the Doge performing the Ceremony on a gilded vessel, the Bucentaur, surrounded by gondolas, feluccas, galleys & skiffs in such brilliant swarms that one might have walked to the Lido over the water without wetting a shoe buckle. The Piazza in the foreground was filled with booths & stalls & high poles with banners, the crowds emerging so vividly from the perspective of the scenes in which they had been painted, and converging so naturally with the mass of spectators in the hall, that one was hard put to find where the Illusion ended and the Reality began.

Thus an Exquisite young man in a suit of lemon coloured Melodino stepped suddenly out of the doorway where I had fancied him Stationary in paint, and took advantage of my confusion to enjoy Liberties with my person. I asked him to desist, which by and by he did, remarking with a sigh and a parting Squeeze that it was 'easier to watch a Sack of Fleas than a woman.' I could have found occasion for a dozen such Amorous Adventures and had no misgivings, for the Mask does away with the need to blush.

This was not merely a Convenience but a blessing when I reached a suite of rooms depicting the interior of Trausnitz Castle, where actors from the Medebac company showed a satire of those nuptials we had come to celebrate which reduced all intercourse between the sexes to mere collusion of their Grosser parts. These were represented by organs of a Ridiculous size, attached to the actors and near Engulfing them when inflated or elevated by means of mechanical bladders. The audience laughed at these antics less with good humour, I thought, than out of a Strained amazement, made the more Disconcerting by the sight of the surrounding masks looking out on these scenes of grossness with entirely Dispassionate stares.

A banquet was held at midnight, followed by the masked ball known as Il Travestito in the piazza. Anything, however droll, served as a disguise – a Pig's head or a pillow case thrown over the head. Some of the females wore moustaches, while the men attired themselves as courtesans, old women and Apes. Danced with a Devil, an Archangel and a Bear on a Wooden Horse one after another in succession, while a Turk in Petticoats performed a tightrope dance over the piazza.

Lemon coloured Melodino attached himself to me with Ardour and made Sheep's eyes all night long. A handsome, witty Wretch, and of course quite worthless. I was therefore dismayed to feel Palpitations in my heart when we danced, and a flushing of the skin, a sensation throughout my body that was not entirely disagreeable, as if I had acquired an undergarment of liquid silk. I attributed this to the Heat & Crush, for the dancing continued without respite until noon the following day. Worn to a Shred and went to bed in tatters.

Early on the morning of Shrove Tuesday I was woken by a Tracasserie below my window. Brum and fellow painters dressed as Bearded Nuns stood in the garden making a din with bells and buckets for drums. Brum said he had come to collect his wife for the masking in town, and asked if they had serenaded the wrong window. Leaning out in nothing but my chemise, I told him the window was right but the sister was wrong, for Stefanie was not in her room. One of the bearded nuns who had been ogling my shoulders said that either he must come up or I must come down, as they would make do with the Wrong Sister very well.

So I went to my room and woke Rebecca & Melissa, who were fast asleep in my bed. Throwing on an assortment of Bapa's old gardening clothes to appear suitably Ridiculous, we hurried down to the street. This unexpected Enlargement of the wrong sister by two charming additions was greeted by the gentlemen with Exuberance.

The traditional breakfast of beer and white sausages at Donisl, where a hungover company, among them Hoo, costumed as a Donkey and rummaging in a corner with a Bleeding finger and colleagues from the *Herald* who were all in a Bad Condition. It seems they had all gone to P's apartment to settle an argument as to whether a parrot could be taught Greek. The bird had not survived instruction, and Expired with fright in a heap of feathers. Returning unexpectedly to town after a long absence, P had unfortunately chosen this moment to arrive at his residence and find the Corpus Delicti of his Ancient Pet with beak prised open while a posse of journalists attempted resuscitation by the introduction of brandy. P flew into a terrible rage, threatening reprisal with a whole book of litigations, & kicked them out; leaving Hoo's possessions, and, even worse, the manuscript of his thesis Irrecoverably inside. The account of this escapade provoked considerable hilarity at Hoo's expense, while the fate of poor Poll received no sympathy at all. Hoo's ingenuity will be taxed to extricate himself from this Scrape.

Beginning at the Viktualienmarkt, a Snake Dance wound in a serpentine across Marienplatz, where it attracted a few thousand people more, growing a tail of masked revellers down Kaufinger Street, until by the time it had reached Karlstor it must have been a mile long. The whole place gone mad. Even the dogs were masked. Lost Hoo again in the crowd and hung on to a Pirate in front while one of the bearded nuns was very Jolly behind. We jigged past St Michael's church and crossed a border from shadow into sunlight, where a band suddenly struck up and a flock of pigeons roosting on top of the fountain took off in the same instant, as if they embodied the sounds flying out of the band's instruments. The band played and the flock of pigeons wheeled on all these Eddies of sound that had been unleash'd at the winter's end, and surprised by a surge of inexplicable Joy I watched them fly up into the sun.

Went home and changed into the White Moire gown for the last carnival ball at Trausnitz Castle. All festivities end at midnight before Ash Wednesday, so the ball already begun in the afternoon.

The opening polonaise was danced by two actors from the Medebac Company in the roles of the guests of honour, William, son of the Duke of Bavaria, and his bride, whose Betrothal the ball commemorated. Applause for the bride's costume, white satin embroidered in silver, flowers, Pomegranate in her hair. I felt a little Envious. Hoo very sweet when I told him this, saying I was much Lovelier etc. The Doge and the Queen of Courtesans attired as the hierophant and the high priestess, with other dignitaries from the Compagnia de Calza i Antichi representing figures from the Tarot cards, performed a dance & mime in which The Lovers in jeopardy were shown to emerge Victorious.

Under this Good Omen the ball continued without interruptions until shortly before midnight. Suddenly the music broke off. We heard a tracasserie behind the hangings and a hoary figure rushed out, dressed as a Shroud and carrying a Coffin. The Mobbing of Winter went on up and down the stairs and around the piazza, with Hissing & Shouting and the whole place in uproar until the Spectre had been chased through the building and driven out.

Thus Carnival came to an end with the commedia dell'arte plays & the entertainments at Trausnitz Castle, the departure of the Venetians, the mysterious return of the stolen figurines to their glass cabinet in Nymphenburg, exhaustion followed by a great quiet, a new moon in Áquarius and my sister's dream on the morning of Ash Wednesday, emerging at last from a long winter night.

Stefanie's
Ash Wednesday Dream

She dreamed she walked along a riverbank and arrived at a walled garden. A gate in the wall stood open. She went in. Bird-song pierced the shadows in an enclosed space not clearly seen. A white walk floated up out of the dark, lined with cedars slowly emerging, topiary of shrubs trimmed in the shapes of heraldic beasts. The light rose and she came to a lawn on which griffins sat and peacocks with spreading tails. She crossed the lawn to a rose garden and a hedge surrounding a summer house where a lion with an eagle's head and wings lay asleep on the steps. The lady wearing an antique costume strolled in the garden, accompanied by a man carrying a mandoline. 'For the burial of the Queen of Hearts,' the man said, strummed a chord and she began to recite:

> *The knave of hearts (the lady said)*
> *was brutish and snored in bed.*
> *I've been as many different things*
> *as desires that I've lain under,*

a covered queen whose eyes
grew everything but wise.
Burial by water I wish to be
my last and only exequy.
All hours, pleasures, pains, the bloody tides
on which the plumed shoals suck and swim
disgorge from my body's caves and I become
coral for the ocean to comb and spin
and scatter as grains of sand.

The lady put her hands in her sleeves and froze at once.
Behind her the garden stood up vertically in the same
instant. The roses at the four corners and the winged lion at
her feet formed a frieze on a playing card from which the
Queen of Hearts stared out. The man receded, until there
was nothing left but a disembodied voice, singing.

The lady leaves behind a card
with her portrait as the Queen of Hearts.
Relinquishing my body, I shall be
like a wandering blind memory,
a disembodied soul imagining
faded incarnations of itself,
as whiteness recalls magnolia bloom
or greenness remembers summer grass.
Embracing her, it used to seem
I already embraced her memory,
and now, remembering, I dream
again the thoughts that she
warmed when her hand was touching me.

She stood on a bridge on a hot afternoon. The garden with
the heraldic beasts turned into a design on the playing cards
she was holding in her hand. She looked down and saw
shimmer of brightness on the water. 'Just a dream,' she said.
She watched the river flow and listened to the insects whine.

From the far side of the river came the sound of traffic. She dropped the cards from the bridge and watched them flutter down. Crossing over to the English Garden, she saw two fishes leap downstream, flashing in the sunlight on the river.

THE TWO
FISHES

The Spring Thaw and the Excited Insects

STEFANIE

'When Pa died Bapa said he'd turned into a tree, I don't know why, maybe because Bapa knew I sort of believed in trees. As a child I used to put my arms round trees. I wanted to become trees. To cross the borders between myself and the things living around me in a solitude I felt I was never able to reach inside.

'There was the summer in Florence the year I left school. Drawing bridges and churches and stuff and watching them trying to come out of the tip of my pencil. But the other kids on the course could do that so much better than me. They were all miles better. They wanted a live model, so I would sit for them and watch it happen the other way round, the mysterious way I could go through a dozen different pencils and come out different every time. People looking at me and breaking me down inside their minds and putting me together on paper again. It was even more satisfying that way round. Borders seemed to be dissolving. Satisfying. I had a crush on the teacher of the course, remember. People blurred in the sun at pavement cafés, and I blurred with them. Looking at the colours on some of those old stone walls when he was showing us around town I couldn't tell where one colour ended and another began.

'I admired him. Someone who could draw like that seemed to have a key to open the solitude of things. He could make them pass in and out of his brush. It was a wand. It touched landscapes and moved them around. Moved me around. I flowed. The colours ran. A blur of hormones, looking back, but at the time it was just happiness.

'Don't. Please don't move. It's nice with your arm like that. I want you to stay as you are and listen till I'm through.

'Remember Bellucci?

'I think you met him once. By the end of the summer I'd run out of my money, and it was Bellucci who gave me the introductions so that I could get a job at the show in Milan. I couldn't believe the money. So easy it just wasn't true – at seventeen I was making more money in two days than Constanze made with her dressmaking in a month. That was it. From Milan to Paris and on to London and back again to Munich for the fashion show in the autumn. My life seemed to script itself. I stood aside and watched it happen. I never made a choice. I was too young. I didn't know who I was. Other people told me – the commercial interests that had already bought me up before I knew what was happening, and by then it was too late. I felt trapped. After several years of being photographed all the time I wanted to hide. I didn't want to be me. I still wanted to be the way colours are that run into each other you can't exactly say where on some of those old stone walls. I told you how I wanted to be, but even as I was telling you I realised it was no longer true, because more or less the moment I met you I knew I'd arrived. Surprisingly you got interested in the idea, in the idea, not me, and I went along with it as a way of holding your interest until it noticed me. So we traipsed around and found those weird locations at the old fish market and the scrapyard and the disused iron works, where you painted all that junk onto my body, you know, the rusty iron bolts and the light switch and strips of flex and stuff, and stood me up against the wall to duplicate the bit of background I was covering up; except all those ruins of things that had run down and died were on my body instead, and it was only afterwards, when I saw the pictures you took, that I realised how we had somehow brought them back to life. In those photos I had the feeling of going through matter, into those walls and out the other side. I was merging and dissolving with the things around me, until I could hardly make myself out, and we finally wound up doing that series on the beach where you camouflaged my body with paint and took photographs of me lying half-buried in the sand with the sea in the distance and photographs without me in the picture at all, and in the end I couldn't tell which was which, if I was there or if I'd gone.'

That was what you wanted, Steffi.

'That was what I wanted. I guess I wanted to reach Pa, joining him in the mysterious vanishing act when Dotty was two and I was still only nine, remember, and couldn't quite figure out how it had been done, but I didn't reach Pa, Pa was no longer the issue, in the meantime I'd arrived at you.

'It helps me to see it that way, arriving at you via Pa, because now I know that what you were to me was always so much more than what what you were in yourself. I was so full of the feeling I'd arrived at you that I didn't notice you weren't there. The fault was in the high expectations I had of you. We have to talk this through, because deep inside yourself you don't really understand. I didn't stop you in your tracks like you did me, you went coasting by and never arrived at me. You can't know what it means to have the feeling you never need or even want to look round a room again on the chance of finding that elusive someone who

extraordinarily matters because you already carry that someone inside you, you float at anchor, you just don't have those
longings that otherwise hurried you on; and if you don't
know that feeling you won't understand what it means when
it dies, and you wait for it to come back, until you realise
that dead feelings never come back. You're adrift again, not
on a waiting emptiness any more but just emptiness, a
numbness in the space where someone used to be. Brum as
he used to light me up had already gone out for me when I
went away in the autumn. There's still a numbness where he
was, but that will pass like the pain before and finally the
memory will have gone too.

'I want you to understand why I left you, am still leaving
you and won't come back. I have to get you behind me. I
don't want these things pulling me back into the past. I
don't want to live in the past.

'There are things that may be different in men's nature,
some men's at least, not only yours, I could live with them
then and I could live with them again if I felt that I could be
there for you, OK, from time to time another woman, your
becoming too accustomed to the person who loves you
most, putting me second best to the other interests you
expect to hold the same fascination for me, because the
adjustments have always been on my side, yes Brum, on my
side, the availability of meals, money, sympathy or sex or
whatever pretty much on your terms and at your times,
needing you in the end because needed by you, being there
for you even inside my dreams, half-buried in sand and in
the end not knowing if I was there or had gone – that pattern
held for seven years, until you stopped being able to see
me, and then it broke, and I knew I'd gone. I'm there for
myself now, Brum. You're no longer what's closest to my
heart. You were wrong. That's not the answer. I am. That's
the pity. All of us are closest to our own hearts.'

That's not the answer you had in mind at the time.

'It was a different question I had in mind at the time.'

BRUM

'Those were the sounds at sunrise this morning, around 7 a.m., February the twenty-ninth.

'The lead singer comes over very clearly. I just played back the tape, and you can hear him very clearly. He sits in that tree you can see through the skylight upstairs. He breaks the silence, and you hear him solo for the first couple of minutes. Hear him? He'll draw the others. They pitch in and brawl. The dawn chorus starts up, although to me it sounds more like a free-for-all. They all want to make themselves heard and stake their claims, the beautiful, barbarous tangle of their love calls. The females sit tight, I guess, a bit sceptical about all this, listening in the dark with folded wings.

'Yesterday the temperature rose to fifteen degrees, and a warm wind blew all night. I sat at the open window in the corner to your left as you come into the living-room, and held the microphone over the rainwater butt outside. You can hear drops of water, one at a time, and then flurries as they start coming faster. It sounds like rain, but it's not. It's the ice melting in the gutter above and dripping into the water butt. It's the spring thaw. I don't remember hearing sounds like that in Zenetti Street. I guess we didn't have them there. So I'm recording them on tape for you to listen to. That was the overture, and now my voice follows. This is where I come in. It's a biggish part, around one hundred and fifty square yards. I'm geared up to play the part of the house. I'm having to spread myself a bit thin to handle this – skimp on things like curtains, bathroom appliances, sink still missing in the kitchen – but the basics are plotted and I have a grip on the part.

'You'd be surprised at the changes, you really would. A terrific improvement on previous performances in Zenetti Street. I think we agree that was pretty much a one-man show and had to close. It was collapsing under its own

density. The new part has been expanded to accommodate a little more variety. It may interest you to hear that
the one-man show has moved into the patio. You should be
especially pleased that Hößli's styrofoam nude, the sacks of
clay and what you affectionately call the ironmongery, my
Senefelder lithograph press, to all of which I'm profession-
ally attached but were sometimes in the way when you
wanted to go to bed – well, all that's now in the patio and
not allowed in. In fact they can be excluded from even visibly interfering with what goes on in the living-room by
pressing a button that operates an electric blind.

'Oh, and bed. Bed has acquired four legs and gone up in
the world by ten inches – it was time we got that mattress off
the floor, but the mattress itself was still in good shape and
there are reasons why I'm attached to that too, so for a couple of hundred I got Oscar to knock out a cast-iron frame,
and for a hundred more he threw in a pair of trestles to
screw that slab of oak onto which we had to squeeze past in
the hall in Zenetti Street, remember, whenever we went to
the loo. It stood in the hall for I don't know how many
years, but I expect you do. At any rate we now have this
monumental dining-table which can seat anything from sixteen to two at either end with a dozen candelabras between
them and needing to raise their voices only slightly, but the
size of the thing shouldn't suggest any kind of imposition,
none at all. I mean, I can sit out there and eat quite intimately by myself, although there's still no other furniture in
the room and there are days when having meals can feel a bit
like picnicking on Ayer's Rock. There's scope for some taste-
ful furnishing in there, lots of scope. There's no hurry. One
has to hang around and get the feel of a house. I mean,
should one plunge in at this early stage and buy sixteen
chairs right off, and what do the chairs do the rest of the
time? Actually, I did buy six chairs. A terrific bargain at that
store round the corner which Lolly runs, and very like the
ones I remember you admiring at Mimi's party last summer.

Collapsible, that's the thing, so when you don't have people around you fold them up and put them in storage. They're in the neighbour's garage at present. Clutter has been a sore point in the past, and believe me, that's changed. This place is as bare as a board. I shed a lot of excess in transit. A whole lot of stuff went out.

'My moustache is also off, but you didn't comment on that when I came round to see you at Conny's, and I didn't comment on your hair either. Did you notice that? There was a sense of strangeness which put the old familiarity sharply in focus. We were polite in the way that strangers are. Treading carefully to avoid stepping on broken glass. But if we hadn't fought we wouldn't be making up.

'Have you thought of it like that?

'You can count the dead and pull out, Steffi, and if you feel that's what you want, then that's what you should do.

'The things I did to hurt you I wouldn't do now if I were in the same situation again. I'm sorry I hurt you. I hadn't realised how much. I'm not saying I've changed, because I don't believe people change so much as move on.

'There are things you say I haven't understood, and maybe there are some you haven't either. I didn't hurt you wilfully so much as in the course of resisting you. There's a point on that line we've travelled along when I came late for our wedding because I was in two minds about wanting to arrive at a wedding at all. From the very beginning your feelings were much clearer than mine, and for as long as I've known you that difference, and that difference in your nature, have led you to claim a moral edge over me. Intellectual, but also emotional certainties, Steffi, both can overlap with bigotry. A whiff of overkill has hung around. I have to live with your bossiness, the firepower of your convictions. You have to live with the lack of mine. That's why we've had fairly serious arguments about things like your laying the table at night for breakfast the next morning.

Buying Christmas presents six months in advance versus
buying them the day before. Planning what you'll wear
before getting up in the morning versus only finding out
when you've got it on.

'Imagine you had to live down to my standards. Day by
day, for years. Imagine you had to resist turning the toaster
upside down to knock out the crumbs before putting it away.
Imagine not making the bed, not putting everything in boxes
before allowing it inside a cupboard, not turning on the calendar at the end of the day. The sum of little things, given
enough time, scale up as biggish erosions. Not trivial at all.
We've covered this ground before, many times. We've had
rows about these things one at a time. Consider them as a
whole. It adds up to a tremendous row potential. Put yourself in my position and see the effort I have to make to live
up to your standards. Imagine a Fiji islander trying to run a
Japanese car factory. From a cautious distance on my sunny
island I admire your efficiency. I've seen it work. You get the
boring stuff that has to be done out of the way very quickly.
You get it out of the way to have time for things that matter
to you more. There's never a rut, the common things in life
have never seemed to be commonplace with you. Me, I feel
subject to occasional forces of human gravity. Sometimes I
feel the weight of ordinariness pulling me down and I let
things slide. I can kick my socks off and leave them lying
under the bed for a week without feeling a qualm. I can sit
happily in front of the TV with a pound of peanuts and a
crate of beer. I can get by just going through the motions,
anaesthetized by substitutes, while I watch you busy with
your private and much more imaginative world. Sometimes
your always caring so much about everything has left me
worn out and indifferent. I miss the middle range.
Sometimes I've felt you love me more for your sake than
mine. Sometimes I've felt the enclosures of your affection as
a prison. But sometimes all these oppositions of you and me
and yours and mine dissolve and come seamlessly together

as we. Let's not forget that when we change the rest of the
pattern.

'How much do we want it? Because I believe the sum of
little things can be handled another way to scale the erosion
back down. We have a terrific start. We move out of the
Zenetti Street apartment to the Copper Lodge in Nymphenburg. I mean, almost in the country, which you've always
wanted. A lot of the old stuff we leave behind. We bring in
new things. I expand my repertoire beyond eggs on toast
one evening a month. We bring in new things and switch old
ones around. We leave in town a lot of those things you said
mattered more to me than yours did, but also some of the
complaints casting morally superior shadows, OK, we leave
that stuff behind, too.

'When you come into this house you'll see on the door
facing a brass plate inscribed STEFFI'S DEN. You have yours
at one end of the house and I have mine at the other, and
the space in the middle is ours, with the refurbished bed
upstairs on legs and sleeping arrangements now off the floor
and refined generally, I hope, in an effort to give you pleasure. I hope you'll find this house has more common ground
altogether. You're not a quitter and neither am I. Energy is
converted but never lost. Laws of thermodynamics predict
in our favour. Maybe the fault has been more on my side,
and so is the effort now to make up for that. I'm asking you
to give us a chance.

'Incidentally, I've been looking through that cookery
encyclopaedia Gisela gave us for our wedding, trying a dish
or two in alphabetical order. Brazilian vegetable dish.
Broccoli with boiled ham. Eggs in cream and cheese sauce
Parma style. I had that in the oven last week. Not quite
Parma style, as I couldn't find the cheese grater and had to
slice the cheese instead. Is green-grained pepper a substitute for white? I have the book open right here, as it
happens. I'm almost through the Ks now. *Kiymali börek.*
That's a Turkish meat pie, for your information, black

pepper this time. Another Turkish dish I did last night, neighbour came round with his wife, fellow whose garage I've got my chairs in. Yoghurt kebab. Here we are. Fried slices of pork with cream yoghurt sauce dip, spiced with garlic, dill, alternatively mint. Two hundred and eighty-five calories. Next time you're round I'll do us that. How about that? I cook. We change our cuisine. Six thousand dishes are listed here. New perspectives open up. There are twelve, fifteen pages here just on ways of eating cherries. Unbelievable desserts. Apple with walnuts, dates, baked in wine . . . Danish pastry with four-fruit jam, sugar, two yolks of egg, and yes, four thousand calories. I could do you the yoghurt kebab with an olive and tomato salad, banana Copacabana to follow. Hot chocolate, ice-cream, rum, amazing value at only two hundred and ninety-one calories

'How about next Friday? That's March the fourth.

'Or Saturday, if you prefer.

'I expect I could manage Sunday, too, if neither of the others works.

'The phone's installed at last, by the way. The new number's one-seven-four, zero-two-zero.

'Perhaps you could give me a call some time this week.'

STEFANIE

'Brum, it's me. Your tape arrived. Thanks.

'It's Wednesday, ten p.m.

'I've been trying to reach you the last two days, but you were never in. So I'm leaving a message on the machine. Dinner's fine, but I'm afraid the weekend's no good for me, as I'm driving with Ziegler to Verona. Tomorrow I'll be in Frankfurt, but the plane gets in around seven, so I could be in Nymphenburg around eight. Either tomorrow or the weekend after next, because I'm in Rome and Florence most of next week. There's always this rush in the spring. On top of that Zelda's decided to leave and Ziegler's asked me to take over as his personal assistant. I'm not sure. We'll have to talk about that. Can you leave a message with Zelda about tomorrow? You can reach her at Condé Nast at three-eight-one, zero-four-zero. Talk to you soon.'

'Brum?'

'Steffi? Where are you?'

'In Frankfurt. Didn't Zelda call you?'

'I only just got in.'

'Didn't she leave a message on the machine?'

'I haven't checked. I've just been checking the mail. My tape arrived back. Thanks very much. Didn't you listen to it?'

'Yes, I did. I've sent it back for you to listen to it yourself. Look, I'm sorry, but I won't be able to make dinner this evening. I have to see a photographer. I'll be staying overnight.'

'With the photographer?'

'Would you mind?'

'Yes, dammit, I would. I'd mind a lot. Steffi? Are you there? What? I what? For Christ's sake you're crying. What's the matter for fuck's sake. Listen, I'm the one who—'

'That's the first thing you've said in a very long time that shows you care just a tiny bit. You you you you you! Always you! You never think of anyone but yourself.'

'OK. Did I say something on the tape that hurt you?'

'You bet you did. I want you to listen to that tape. Listen to your own voice saying those incredibly hurtful things. So cold, so complacent. So goddamn condescending the way you talk!'

'What things?'

'You're a sadist. D'you hear that? You're doing this delib-erately. You keep on doing it. You do it to hurt me and make me cry so that I put you down and you feel sorry, because that's the only feeling you're capable of. That one tiny pattern. You're despicable. D'you hear? I despise you.'

'So who left whom? Who's been screwing around for the last six months while I've been moving the leftovers of the house? Who's been hurting whom for the past six months?'

'What do you know about hurt? Listen to your own tape! Not a single word about being hurt. Not a single word to say you missed me.'

'I don't think we can be talking about the same tape. The one you've been listening to isn't the one I recorded.'

'That's why you're a lousy artist. You don't get things across. You don't care about anything.'

'The old tactics. You keep on shifting ground. If you want to be bitchy, then be specific. What were those incredibly hurtful things I said?'

'I wish you could hear your own voice when you say that. I wish you could hear how the frost gets into it, the deep, deep cold that creeps up from the bottom of your heart. It's frightening, Brum. What sort of a person are you? Who the hell are you?'

'What were those incredibly hurtful things I said? Either you tell me and we try to talk about it or else I'm hanging up.'

'Who are you?'

'A shit. A monster. A lousy artist. Anything you care to name so long as it serves your purpose.'

'Because it's true, Brum. Listen. I wrote them down. I have the piece of paper right here in my hand and I'll read to you the things you said. I quote. *You'd be surprised at the changes, you really would. A terrific improvement on previous performances in Zenetti Street. I think we agree that was pretty much a one-man show and had to close. It was collapsing under its own density.* How does that strike you when I read it back?'

'It strikes me as someone attempting to swallow their pride, say they're sorry and will try to do better.'

'Does it? A terrific improvement on previous performances. Pretty much a one-man show. Had to close. Collapsing under its own density. Just for the record, that's seven years of our life you're talking about.'

'OK, not a very good attempt. The way attempts often are.'

'Where am I?'

'You're taking this out of context, Stefanie.'

'Exactly. The context is me and I'm not there. *A one-man show*. Are you listening?'

'I'm listening.'

'Do you at least see what I'm saying?'

'I can see the point you're wanting to make.'

'No, you are. The point you're making, Brum. It gets worse and worse as you hammer it home. Listen. *There's a point on that line we've travelled along* – point. Line. What's this line we've been travelling along, Brum? What's this vocabulary? Is this a geometry lesson? Is this the way artists talk?'

'At some point in our life together.'

'Well that sounds a bit different. But that's not what you say. Instead you say, *there's a point on that line we've travelled along when I arrived late for our wedding because I was in two minds about wanting to arrive at a wedding at all. You say a threat of emotional overkill has been hanging around. It adds up to a tremendous row potential. Put yourself in my position and see the effort I have to make to live up to your standards. Sometimes I've felt you love me more for your sake than mine. Sometimes I've felt the enclosures of your affection as a prison.*'

'The trouble with you is that you can't take criticism.'

'You disgust me.'

'You can't bear the thought of having to live with flaws. You offload everything on me. When have you been ready to see a fault on your side? Have you ever considered that what I do is not just what I am but also how I respond to you? You've been involved with other men and I've been involved with other women, and maybe for similar reasons, only you're less honest about it than I am.'

'For example?'

'Max, for example. It's true for Christ's sake that I've taken you for granted. It's true I've been a selfish prick. But Max? What the fuck has he got to do with it? You went to live with Max of your own free will. There were alternatives, weren't there? You could have stayed with your mother. Or Martha. You could have skipped the intermezzo with Max and moved straight in with Conny. Is that true or isn't it?'

'You've always sounded more convincing on the attack. It must suit you better.'

'Is it true or not?'

'OK! I wanted to get my own back. I wanted to hurt you.'

'Well, you did. You did a great job. Look at the feeling way you used Max. Look at the way you humiliated me. You threw in a few extras free of charge.'

'Would you be asking me to come back if I hadn't?'

'I'd be asking you whatever happened.'

'How do you expect me to believe that?'

'Because you want to believe it.'

'Is that really all you have to offer?'

'Needing me as much as I need you.'

'I have to go now, Brum.'

'Being the elusive someone who extraordinarily matters.'

'I have an appointment. I've got to go.'

'And my love.'

'Thanks.'

'Did I wake you?'

'I was just on my way up to bed.'

'If you'd been asleep I'd have hung up.'

'I'm not asleep. Don't hang up.'

'If you'd been out again like you were the other night, that would have been it. What were you doing for the whole of Tuesday night?'

'I was in Passau. I picked Jonas up at the hospital and drove him home and stayed the night.'

'I tried calling you all night. I felt so mean, checking on you like that. I'd lost all my trust. I didn't believe you any more.'

'Where are you now?'

'In my hotel room.'

'How was the photographer?'

'Pretty good. How was the kebab?'

'Procyon ate it while we were on the phone.'

'Have you got him there?'

'He won't come up. He has his mat in Steffi's den. He can read the sign on the door.'

'Did you listen to the tape?'

'It was painful.'

'I couldn't sleep. I wanted to hear your voice. Not just because of that. I've been sitting here in the dark in my room on the fifteenth floor, looking at all those skyscrapers standing out there in the night. Then I went for a walk. From the car park I looked up and saw the same tall buildings and they didn't look pretty any more. There was a man rummaging in the rubbish bins behind the hotel. I went for a walk and saw bits of people's lives in the night. In doorways, coming out of bars, wandering around with their plastic bags, nowhere in particular to go. I came back into the hotel foyer and was handed my key and felt angry with us. The selfishness of our lives. The tiny focus of our interest, and still getting it wrong, still unsatisfied. We've lost all sense of proportion. Say something, Brum.'

'We'll keep on trying. We'll try to do better.'

'I bought you a present this afternoon.'

'What did you buy?'

'A cheese-grater.'

'Cheese-grater?'

'Is green-grained pepper a substitute for white?'

'What?'

'As I watched the guy going through the rubbish bins that was the refrain, the little ditty I kept hearing in my head. You asked me on your tape, the cheese sauce Parma style. Only you couldn't find the cheese-grater, so you sliced it instead. That's what you said. So I bought you a cheese-grater. I couldn't think of anything better.'

STEFANIE

Crossing the Alps, we left the winter behind us at the top of the pass and came down into the spring on the other side. The sky over the plains seems it's having to stretch itself to make room for the more new light, taut with such blue-white brilliance that it almost hurts. Perhaps it's an impression of sky I'm talking about, perhaps it's just something inside myself. The sense of being alive sometimes comes in flashes so sharp that it actually hurts. Ziegler and I spent the weekend in Verona seeing people who run the opera there about a shoot he wants to do this summer. He drove back on Sunday and I went on to Rome to go location hunting with the photographer I met in Frankfurt that evening I called last week. From Rome we drove back up to Florence. First time I'd been back in ten years. I poked around the places where I used to hang out, trying to pin down memories of how they had seemed to me then. The name of the man who taught that art course was no longer in the phone book. Belluci died somewhere in Africa a couple of years back. The family who owned the pension where I'd stayed had sold up and moved on. I came out of the pension and walked down a long flight of steps, and when I reached the road and looked back up it seemed no different whether I'd come out of that house a minute or ten years ago. The images of one's disappearance are the same. Perhaps you can imagine painting a picture like that, identifying traces of someone having been there in an image of their disappearance. Think of one of those pavement cafés with a fast turnover on a busy day, clientele changing in its entirety every hour or so, and me asking you where I am, and you saying I'm taking this out of context, and me saying that I'm the context only I'm not there. I'd like you to visualise that picture, and if you should come to paint it, to convey the feeling of someone in the foreground who's no longer there. I saw an image like this in a dream I had the night I arrived in Prato. We drove on there from Florence, along a road bordered with cypress trees, coming into a small town with a cathedral and a view of hills. The photographer knew someone there with a warehouse he wanted me to see. The warehouse was full of old clothes, millions, literally millions of people's cast-off clothes. There were men squatting in front of vast piles, sorting them by hand according to the colour and the feel of the cloth, and forklift trucks kept on coming with more piles, scooping up the sorted heaps and scurrying away like ants to store them in the warehouse. The clothes were stored by colour in tiers twenty feet high. One could walk maybe for miles along narrow aisles that were like ravines of colour, reds, blues, greens, through bright yellow and ochre to dark brown, and feel and imagine not clothes but people lying stacked to the roof in tiers. The warehouse was like a mortuary of dead souls. And in the afternoon the photographer took me round the tumbledown factory with cracked girders and peeling, bloated walls in the dingy interiors where machinery stood, spikes and rollers and stone basins where the clothes were shredded and ground to pulp. We were told they spin new yarns out of the old, but I didn't see that. I saw a dark mass of waste fibre clotted in a sieve, and in my dream that night the people at the café had turned into their clothes, in piles on chairs, depleting and vanishing and being replaced again— Surely I wrote and told Brum about this, I thought, sitting on the hotel terrace overlooking Prato, because I could smell the pines and feel the sun on my arms and then not on my arms as it went behind a dark row of cypress trees standing like sentinels on the slope above. I heard you walking up the gravel path behind, the scrunching sounds as the gravel scattered, and I thought why am I writing this to him if he's there, but when I looked round you'd disappeared and this was part of the dream too. On the way back there was that same blue-white brilliance of sky until Bolzano, where we suddenly drove into a curtain of sleet. It was snowing at the top of the pass and on the other side the winter had come down again into the valley. Arriving here in a cold drizzle, I felt completely out of rhythm. I checked the car in at the rental and stood outside the main station, watching the snow melt and slide down the roofs. I had the feeling I was sliding with it, clinging to the edge and afraid to fall but unable to move back either, because there was nowhere to go back to. It had melted away behind me, second by second, right up to the brink I was standing on. Moment by moment whatever was there had been and gone and left nothing behind but an image of its disappearance. Perhaps you can see it in your mind, the running line whose sense of movement is its self-obliteration as it shrinks across the page. Bear it in mind when you come to paint that picture. The snow came down from the roof with a spatter and I got into a cab, and this cab driver, a Greek I think, asked me where I wanted to go. I didn't know where I wanted to go, so I asked him to just drive around. We drove around for a couple of hours. Munich felt like a story I'd been out of for too long a time. It was like being a stranger in my own town. We drove down Oettingen Street past the house where Gisela lives and I tried to get a sense of the difference between having come out of it on that September afternoon months or only minutes ago, but I couldn't feel any. I was

looking for a way to come back into the present from which
I'd disappeared, and driving down Prinzregenten Street on
the way back into town I saw the P1 sign outside the Haus
der Kunst and I thought here, the point was here, that disco
party where the guests dressed up as tramps, only I hadn't
seen it then, I mean I was there, I'd stayed and drunk champagne with the rest of them. That was the night Jonas
emasculated himself and I sat in the hospital corridor trying
to make sense of scraps of paper, and then I thought of all
the others I'd been passing by, become so immune to them
they'd frozen in banality, the old guys routing in the hotel
rubbish bins, the refugees in transit at Frankfurt station and
an armless man playing an accordion with his toes in the
shopping mall, desperate people, obliterated by the background noise of a carnival that seems to get louder and
louder the less we want to hear what it's drowning out. We
should hang that up in the house somewhere, you know, the
way Constanze does, whatever you think of those famine
pictures she has pasted up inside the doors to remind her
whenever she opens her kitchen cupboards. There has to be
something else around, to balance the sixteen chairs and
the four thousand calorie desserts. There has to be another
way for us to live. I lay awake the first night I came, curled
up on one side, with a warm shadow that was you spreading
across my back and your hand still resting on my breast the
way it was when you fell asleep, thinking about all these
things as I listened to the rain. Listening to the rain as my
thoughts ran, losing in the warmth our bodies shared any
particular sense of where you ended and I began, I could
feel myself slowly unfreeze and become just a drop of myself
on the brim of our sleep. Later the rain had stopped, the sun
was up, then it was midday and the house was bright, we lay
awake completely still, the same surface of a single pool, did
not move, said nothing, all thoughts suspended and no sensation beyond the sound of that one drop, all that was left,
just the one drop splashing at intervals on the rainwater butt

outside. You want to hear the last drop and you wait. The intervals grow longer and longer, and during the broad warm days around the middle of March the winter dries up and disappears. You want to hear the last drop and you wait, but you never can.

The Equinox

Sitting on her balcony that first spring day Constanze must have slipped through the net of consciousness and dozed off for a few minutes. Soon she will go upstairs to resume her chores, take in the washing, see to Gottfried, polish the silver trophies and wind up his clocks as she does every Sunday. The children's voices come up from the garden, voices she still hears or perhaps already remembers, following her across the threshold of sleep. 'The last time we were all together was at Harvest Thanksgiving,' Martha says. 'Present company excepted,' interrupts Stefanie, and Hieronymus goes on telling Brum that the earth has travelled two hundred million miles through space to come round to the first point of Aries again, only it's not there, because the procession of the equinoxes has moved it back to Aquarius, and in that sense nor are we. As Dotty is saying she'll pinch Hieronymus to prove he is, Constanze lets go and feels herself dropping off, falling in retrospect through millions of miles of space. 'Why, after all, did Bapa take to his bed?' There's a tone of accusation in Dotty's voice when she asks her mother this question. 'Bapa's never been ill in

his life.' 'He caught a cold, dear,' Constanze begins, goes
back a bit further and begins again. 'Bapa was always missing things in recent years, you know, things he said he'd lost
or which had been stolen but actually things he never had. I
think he just went to bed because that was where he felt
warm'. 'We still have an hour in hand,' Hieronymus says,
reminding Constanze she'll need it when she puts the clocks
forward next week. Uneasily she begins to search the house,
doubtful she'll recognise it even if she finds what she's looking for. What has she done with the hour? Once in a while
she would like to think of herself, and feels guilty at the
other thought which this implies. Where's that hour? What's
happened to that cup with the elongated spout? And the
portrait of the Kaiser – did you burn it? Constanze hears
Gottfried's voice and the drawn-out chiv-chivvying call of
the bird in the tree, and knows that presently she must go
upstairs. She must go much further back. The last years
he's been missing things he never had, resents these sub-
tractions from himself and turns crafty, malicious, obsessed
with thieves in the house. For ten years before the accusations began she had to learn to live with the confabulations
of his senility, arranged around the virile, rumbustious figures of his father and grandfather, whose escapades he is
always capping in the havoc of his imagination. He makes
his father a Field Marshal in the Great War because of his
kindness to horses, proposes a scheme to raise the streets of
Trieste to prevent flooding, rechannels the course of rivers
in Russia and journeys to the moon, where his grandfather
has been before him on horseback with saddle-bags full of
conifer seed, reporting that pine groves have sprung up since
and herds of horses are running wild through the forests of
the moon. Constanze remembers the family reunion in
Cividale del Friuli the previous summer when Gottfried
talked the company into silence with an account of a weekend trip to the Himalayas, where he climbed Mount Everest
without oxygen and lost his fountain pen on the summit.

Isolated by the family, the old man came home embittered, and not long after that he took to his bed. Subdued but stubborn, because at almost ninety all the people who mattered in his life were long since dead and TV programmes had persuaded him the rest of the world would shortly follow, he pressed ahead with his plans for a philoprogenitive mission to found a colony at the North Pole. Who are you, he would ask Constanze when she came into his room, are you the dentist? The nurse? And told her to come back later because he was busy in the mountains. Sometimes the bed in the tower room was empty, and she found him peeing over the balcony onto the terrace, or a neighbour spotted him wandering naked in the street and brought him back, or someone called from somewhere and asked her to fetch him home. Nobody outside the family came to see him, but there were many visitors in his imagination. He claimed to have inherited from his father a unique blood group he felt it was his duty to contribute to the dwindling gene pool of the species. A succession of ghostly figures, ageing and childless heirs of European houses threatened with extinction, came to Little Monten Castle to moot arrangements for wives still able and willing and in need of Gottfried's help. Some of these women were impregnated on board the belly-windowed Zeppelin during the flight to the North Pole. A garrulous ancient mariner in bizarre bed-wear, the old man would sometimes come down from the tower room to where Constanze was busy dressmaking, scandalising her customers with his bulletins from the North Pole. Unaware how his listeners shrank, he reported cheerfully on the institute in the middle of the frozen wastes where daughters from the very best families underwent their training as the wives of priests; at the hospital a Polish countess had given birth to a son of Gottfried's who later became Pope. The distaste, the disbelief and at last the lack of interest of an audience that got smaller and smaller as the years went by left the old man alone in the wilderness of his mind, to

which no one but Constanze had access. No one listened to
the yarns of a former travelling salesman in ladies underwear, supported for the last two decades of his life by the
charity of the last customer on whom he had happened to
call, the Cadillac with the antique trailer left to rust and
finally rot away at the kerb outside Constanze's house. But
Constanze knew the stories from a time when Bapa's memory had been more reliable. The taller and taller stories she
heard grow out of these retained for her a truth in the perspective of the events that preceded them; before the castle
he had inhabited with one of his nephews had burned to the
ground, and for the last time he hooked up the trailer containing the photographer's studio that between the wars
stood parked in the courtyards of decaying palaces while
Gottfried was taking pictures of the families inside. The less
he was believed, the taller the stories he told in self-vindica-
tion. By the time people began to ignore him the habit had
become an obsession. Constanze knows all these things. She
knows of the real succession to which the spooks in Bapa's
imagination are heir, the grandfather with fifteen children
and the father who had twelve, of whom Gottfried is the
only and childless son. She can recall, for anyone interested,
the trail of royal houses from the Atlantic to the Red Sea,
popes, pashas, archdukes and grand duchesses, titles or
estates or both since vanished, their portraits preserved in a
collection of photographs the itinerant court photographer
had taken between the wars – photos for the most part vanished too when the castle in Friaul burned down. Bapa has
ceased to be sure of all these things himself, and the images
that can still surface so luminously in his memory undermine rather than reinforce his sureness of their reality.
Vividly he sees again a design on the tiles of some oriental
court, fifty, sixty years back, bleached by sunlight, the wedding group posing on the steps outside the consulate in
Cairo where he married and half an hour later divorced a
Hungarian woman whose name he has forgotten and for

reasons he can no longer remember, blurred suddenly by muffled figures skating across miles of frozen fields somewhere on the Baltic coast. Watching him disintegrate, Constanze becomes the curator of his relics, stateless memories shoved back and forth across borders, assigned an always temporary belonging in changing orders of reality. Gradually the airship begins to take shape as a device to circumvent these borders, the harrassment of officials and the questions to which he has no answers or does not understand. He flies the cargo of his memories on whatever course he chooses, unimpeded through the free air. The co-ordinates of time and space are changed at random, ballast is jettisoned, passengers co-opted en route. The Zeppelin turns into an airborne ark, the journey a survival mission. The family of women on board are the women who surrounded him at either end of his life; eleven elder sisters in the real castle in Cividale and four younger women, his nephew's widow and her three daughters in the house in a Munich suburb that is a castle only in name. Presently Constanze will go upstairs to find out where they are. He is careless with nomenclatures and their restraints, his exact age or nationality, perhaps because it has changed so many times already. His attitude to his female relatives is ambiguous. He sees and appreciates their nature as women, regardless of conventions of family status or age. For twenty years after her husband's death Constanze has lived together with his surviving uncle in a relationship of many-layered affection for which she could never find a name. Perhaps he has not forgotten but chooses not to use her name because she has been to him so many kinds of woman, for which there are as many nicknames; these in turn regressing, the older he becomes, to nameless endearments adorned with gratitude – thanks, sweetheart, those were the last words she heard him say more than three months ago. Even in his seventies, when Dotty was still small but Stefanie already entering puberty, Bapa continued to bathe the children and put them to bed, the name the children gave him was a grandfather's, he was there for them in place of a father, and the eyes with which he watched them as he posed them for his camera were not the eyes of either. By the time Bapa has ceased to be sure of the reality of events in a past as long as the unbelievable century that has coincided with the span of his life, the same uncertainty has begun to undermine his grasp of the present; and when in the wake of the burning forests and the fish-barren seas he reports pine forests springing up on the surface of the moon where his grandfather scattered the seed, it takes place by the same redressing act of will that claims responsibility for Martha's child and gives his favourite daughter-wife away at her wedding not to her designated husband, but to himself. After Steffi's desertion of Brum his imagination founders. The airship is abandoned. There is a rash of missing objects, people mislaid. Then things begin to burn. The archive goes up in flames, he shuts his eyes and mutters names as behind his eyelids he sees them burn, the Grand Duchess of Toscana, the Countess of Toledo-Loe and Martini-Borghese, all the portraits burn, the Cadillac with the mobile studio in the trailer, long since scrapped, come back to burn, forests burn and leave islands scorched, the sparks spring across the Mediterranean and wall mainland cities with fire, foxes with burning tails run into the corn and set it in flames, gutting fields and leaving them deserts, the castle in Cividale burns, the airship burns, the bed burns in which he lies. The carnival of fire burns out in the year of the dragon, coming astride a dolphin and spewing the old man out at the foot of a mountain. He sits up and sees a greening tree. A woman bends over him, dressing his sores with an ointment that cools his inflamed skin. He speaks to her in Italian, but she answers in a language he doesn't understand. Are you the nurse? She smiles and goes away. He goes back through the fire and arrives at a castle that is still unscathed. The castle has not yet burned, stands whole on the ridge of the valley just as he remembers it every spring. He waits under the tree at the foot of the mountain. He is waiting for his mother and sisters to arrive in Cividale with the baggage so that they can go up the castle where the family spends the summers. Every day the woman comes. He sits up to be washed and made ready for the journey up the mountain. She tells him in the language he doesn't understand that it's March and the spring is here. The days go peacefully by, surrounding him with more light, the spring scents and the chiv-chivvying call of a bird in the greening tree. His mother and sisters arrive from Klagenfurt with twenty-six suitcases, the household silver and the rubber bath with which his mother always travels. He wonders how they will get all these things up the mountain. Women come from the village in long skirts, with panniers to carry the children in, and stand around knitting, waiting for the warmer spring weather. His mother says they can wait no longer – the party sets off, children in panniers, the women knitting, the dogs running on ahead. They enter the forest and he smells the resin of pines as he admires the pouring waterfalls frozen in mid-air. It begins to grow cold. The bright bars he sees lying across the path are not strips of sunlight but snow, and when they come out of the forest the mountain has turned white. Only the tips of poles sticking up out of the snow mark the route for them to follow. The light begins to fade. They continue on up the slopes in a blizzard and the surroundings whiten out. The whiteness seems to grow more dense, solidifies, takes on shape as wall of a white building with frost-caked shutters drawn over windows resembling blindfold eyes. The steps leading up to the entrance to the building have disappeared in a snowdrift. He goes inside and looks around a flagstoned hall with inscribed tablets set into the walls. Already his grandfather is walking towards him across the hall, only it's not his grandfather, it's one of the fathers from the Jesuit school he sees approaching. 'You're cold,' the father says, touching his sleeve. They walk across the hall and up a flight of steps. 'I'll show you across to the annexe,' the father says, taking out a key, 'are you warm enough, it's cold where we're going, the annexe is unheated,' and he opens the door into a gallery. Mysteriously snow hangs on the walls inside. Drops of moisture on the floor have frozen and formed welts of ice. Crossing the gallery he feels the cold lean into him with a sharp intake of breath. He emerges from the gallery and walks towards a diffuse light at the end of a passage. Snowdrifts lie piled up outside open doors and in the space between the frames hang slabs of ice where snow has frozen to the doors. He moves down a passage of increasing brightness, the snow reflecting from the passage walls, the passage dissolving into walls of standing light that spills over and opens out endlessly into whiteness all around.

Calendar of
The Feast Of Fools

(PERSEPHONE)

Sept 23 Autumn equinox, calendar beginning of autumn
The sun reaches the first degree of zodiacal Libra
Stefanie marries Brum and leaves him on the same
day
New moon

Sept 27 Clocks are put back one hour
Liselotte Pfaffel, the flower-seller, dies
The Munich beer festival (Oktoberfest) begins its
second week

Sept 29 Michaelmas
Harald Hemsing celebrates his 10,000th day
Martha Kornrumpf attends Liselotte's funeral mass
and the flower seller's obituary appears in the
Evening Herald

Sept 31 Opening of Brum's exhibition of twenty-three portraits of Stefanie

Oct 3 On his 10,004th day Harald falls in love with Dotty

Oct 4 Harvest Thanksgiving and last day of the Oktoberfest

Oct 5 Anniversary of the calendar reform on October 5,
1582, when the switch from the Julian to the
Gregorian calendar resulted in the 'loss' of ten
days, a loss that preoccupies Harald in a dream

Oct 7 Harvest moon, the moon which is full within a fortnight of the autumn equinox

Oct 23 The sun enters zodiacal Scorpio, the sign which in
astrology is associated with the genitals

(THE KING OF THE RAIN COUNTRY)

Stefanie eats a pomegranate and has her hair cut

Oct 29 Max Hollmann seduces Stefanie during a 200th

anniversary performance of *Don Giovanni* at the Gärtnerplatz Opera House

Max buys up all Brum's portraits of his wife, and the exhibition closes

Nov 1   All Saints

The beginning of the far more ancient pagan celebration of the time when the dead were believed to return to the earth coincides, in a dream of Johnny Ploog's, with the arrival of an impenetrable fog that incapacitates the city

Nov 2   All Souls

Nov 11 St Martin's Day, traditionally the opening of the carnival season, locally known as Fasching

Nov 20 Brewers Hall, the former liquor factory on an island in the Isar river, is inaugurated in the quincentenary year of the Pure Beer Edict (1487)

(Advent)

Nov 22 The sun enters zodiacal Sagittarius

Nov 28 *Götterdämmerung*, the fourth and final opera in Wagner's 'The Ring of the Nebelungen', is performed at the Munich State Opera House

Brum dreams Stefanie comes back to him, and solves the riddle she had set him

Opening of Christmas markets all over town

Nov 29 First Advent Sunday

Nov 30 Quincentenary of Duke Albrecht IV's Pure Beer Edict

Brum is taken in hand by Candice, who arrives to help him with the move from Zenetti Street to Nymphenburg, and with a few other things besides

Dec 5   Full moon

Dec 6   St Nikolaus' Day (Santa Klaus), patron of children

Harald gets a job with Rentasanta, a firm that

employs students to attend functions dressed up as Santa Klaus

Harald devises a strategy for wooing Dotty away from Alexander

Dec 20   New moon in Sagittarius

Dec 22   Tropic of Capricorn, the shortest day of the year and the calendar beginning of winter

Entering zodiacal Capricorn (the horned goat-fish), the sun at the winter solstice is at the farthest point from the equator and appears to stand still before starting its journey back

Martha's labour pains begin

(THE HORNED GOAT-FISH)

Dec 25   On Christmas morning Brum makes his way on skis through a city stricken by a record snowfall

The Twelve Nights begin with the star over Haidhausen, a laser light show put on by the Arthouse, with a hermaphrodite as a special attraction

Dec 31   Johnny Ploog reports on New Year's Eve as celebrated at the Arthouse

Jan 1   A. Koepenick, a leading Munich astrologer, draws up the horoscopes for Martha's Christmas twins

Jan 6   Epiphany (also known as the feast of the three holy kings, Caspar, Melchior and Balthasar)

Brum and accomplices steal the twenty-three portraits of Stefanie from Max Hollman's house in Bogenhausen

Official opening of carnival (Fasching)

Harald gets a part-time job with the carnival broadsheet, *Foolscap*

Jan 9   At the Fencing Associations' Ball Dotty sees her sister Stefanie for the first time since she disappeared

Jan 15   Onset of unprecedentedly cold weather, which
         Brum sits out at the Mayr'sche Hofkunst, a
         mosaic and glass workshop where Brum is assem-
         bling a stained-glass window, waiting for the
         weather to thaw

(THE FEAST OF FOOLS)

Jan 20   The sun enters zodiacal Aquarius
– Feb 1 The 'Carnival in Venice' Ball opens with the arrival
         of the Venetians on a custom-built canal through
         the inner city
         Stefanie has broken with Max, taken a job and is
         now living with her friend Conny in Schwabing
         During carnival she has brief relationships with
         various men, including Jonas Heidenreich, one
         of Brum's assistants on the mural for Brewers
         Hall, who has fallen in love with a portrait of
         Stefanie that Brum had incorporated in his mural
         Jonas attempts to emasculate himself
         Stefanie returns to her mother's house
Feb 2   Candlemas
         Hieronymus re-enters the light cone of Martha,
         from whom he has remained estranged through-
         out her pregnancy
Feb 3   St Blasius Day, patron of winds
         Brum emerges as the victor in a duel with Max at
         the Black Lodge
Feb 4   Harald has another part-time job as caretaker
         At the Chrysanthemum Ball he partners Dotty, and
         in all senses is united with her at last
Feb 16   Shrove Tuesday
         Dotty presents herself in a suitably historical mode
         for the last carnival ball, hosted by the Venetians
         at Trausnitz Castle
Feb 17   Ash Wednesday
         New moon in Aquarius

Stefanie dreams of two fishes she sees as she is crossing the river from Bogenhausen back to the English Garden

(THE TWO FISHES)

Feb 19 The sun enters zodiacal Pisces during the last days of winter, which in the ancient Chinese calendar used to be known as The Spring Thaw and the Excited Insects

Brum and Stefanie are working towards a reconciliation

On a warm day in early March she hears the sound of the spring thaw when she comes to the new house in Nymphenburg for the first time

Mar 20 Spring equinox, calendar beginning of spring

While Gottfried lies dying the family is gathered once more at Constanze's house, exactly six months and two hundred million miles further on in space since they were last together at Stefanie's wedding, but no one can follow Bapa when the old man finally arrives at the top of his mountain

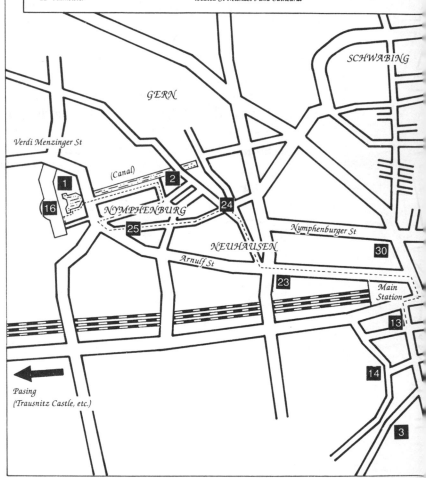

SCHWABING

GERN

Verdi Menzinger St

(Canal)

1

16

2

NYMPHENBURG

24

25

Nymphenburger St

NEUHAUSEN

30

Arnulf St

23

Main Station

13

Pasing
(Trausnitz Castle, etc.)

14

3